ALSO BY MELISSA GOOD

Dar and Kerry Series
Tropical Storm
Hurricane Watch
Eye of the Storm
Red Sky At Morning
Thicker Than Water
Terrors of the High Seas
Tropical Convergence
Stormy Waters
Storm Surge: Book One
Storm Surge: Book Two

Other Titles
Partners: Book One
Partners: Book Two

Winds of Change

Melissa Good

Yellow Rose Books
by Regal Crest

Texas

ISBN 978-1-61929-194-2

First Printing 2015

9 8 7 6 5 4 3 2 1

Cover design by Acorn Graphics

Published by:

Regal Crest Enterprises, LLC
229 Sheridan Loop
Belton, TX 76513

Find us on the World Wide Web at
http://www.regalcrest.biz

Printed in the United States of America

Chapter One

A STEADY FALLING of snow dusted the yard and gates outside the window of the broad, three story mansion tucked near the crest of a hillside in Saugatuck, Michigan. Thick clouds clustered overhead, and two men were steadily shoveling the snow from the circular driveway, while two more were brushing off the tops of the multitude of cars parked along the curb.

On the second floor, the lights were on along the series of bedrooms, and in the corner one on the end the occupants inside busied themselves in dressing amidst the scents of apricot body wash, silk, and lightly spicy perfume.

"They're going to regret asking the wedding party to go strapless." Kerry regarded her reflection in the mirror with a sense of slightly wicked bemusement. "I think Mom forgot about the tattoo." She studied the snake pattern on her chest, fully revealed on the tan skin over the neckline of her pale blue, floor length, snugly fit gown. "Besides, is this the weather for this kind of thing?"

"Could be worse." Dar eased into position behind her, putting her arms around Kerry and giving her a hug. "Besides, who cares? You look gorgeous."

"Thank you." Kerry bumped her gently. "I'm glad I picked this one out myself. The one the bridesmaids are wearing reminds me of my prom."

"Mm. You have exquisite taste." Dar kissed the top of her head.

"Well, sure. I picked you, didn't I?" Kerry chuckled as she was squeezed again and released. "I can't believe it's snowing. My sister said it's been in the sixties all month."

"Knew I was coming and had to drive," Dar said. "Anyway, isn't snow at your wedding supposed to be lucky?"

Kerry eyed her with a tolerant smile. "No." She lifted a pair of sapphire earrings and fastened them to her ears as she watched Dar get into her burgundy, knee length dress and settle the mid arm length sleeves. "Are those supposed to be that short?"

"No." Dar turned the cuff of the sleeve up one turn. "But I didn't have time to get something custom done." She looked up and met Kerry's eyes in the mirror. "Look awful?" She smiled at Kerry's rolled eyes. "We could discuss a sleeveless option. I'm sure your mother has a pair of scissors around this place somewhere."

Kerry merely chuckled. "Now that we're doing this, I kinda wish I'd turned my sister down on being in her wedding party." She sighed. "It would be more fun sitting with you and Mom and Dad in church." She finished fastening her other earring, then adjusted the crystal necklace that settled right above her breastbone.

"Won't be long." Dar put her hands on Kerry's neck and massaged her gently. "My mother's loaded her purse with paint gun balls, by the way."

"What?" Kerry paused, turning and looking up at her.

"Mm." She's got a slingshot in there too. She hears anyone making remarks about either of us, she's gonna let go with it. Hope your mother doesn't mind green paint stains."

Kerry blinked, unsure of whether to take her seriously or not. Dar's expression was mild and had a hint of gentle questioning, but after a moment, she saw the twinkle appear in her very blue eyes and relaxed. "Hon, you nearly got me there. I wouldn't put that past your mom."

"Me either," Dar said, cheerfully. "C'mon, Ker, you've got the service, then a party, then tomorrow night we'll be home in time to share a glass of champagne in our hot tub for New Year's." She picked up the brush on the dresser and moved it through Kerry's pale blonde locks. "Chill out."

Kerry felt the tickle of the brush tines on her scalp, and considered the words. Was she unchilled, really? She let her eyes flick around the green tinted walls of the suite in her mother's home and had to admit that yes, in fact, she was a little uptight, even though their visit so far was benign.

There were just too many bad memories here. Even though her father was gone, and her mother had stopped trying to reorder her life, still, she was hyper aware of the eyes on her, and the constant judging that seemed to permeate the place no matter how many changes it had recently seen.

"Hey, at least your uncles won't be here." Dar leaned over and blew gently in her ear.

"Yeah, that's true." Kerry turned and put her arms around her partner. "Thanks, Dardar."

Dar returned the hug, giving Kerry's back a little scratch. "Anyway, it's nice to have a little break, even if it's here. Too much going on otherwise."

True. Kerry released her, then went over to sit down and put on her shoes. They were mid height heels and matched her dress. "You wearing hose?"

Dar shook her head. "Nope. They'll never tell with this tan, or yours either."

Also true. She regarded her companion's long legs. "You have sexy knees," she commented, after a moment of silence.

Dar rolled a droll look in her direction. "What's sexier, this scar or this one?" She pointed at both, jagged white lines that bisected the front of her joints.

Kerry chuckled. "They just give you character." She got up and looked out the window. "The limos are here," she said. "Must be time to go."

A soft knock came at the door. "C'mon in." Kerry picked up her full length leather jacket and shrugged it on, looking over as the door opened and Ceci Roberts stuck her head in. "Hey, Mom."

"Ah." Ceci entered and sauntered over. "You ready? I heard that major-domo of your mother's inserting another baseball bat up his ass downstairs. I think the cars are here." She came over to stand next to Kerry, both of them about the same height, and with Ceci's silvered blonde hair, appeared more related than Ceci did to her tall, dark haired daughter.

Dar snickered and stood up, going over and removing her own jacket from the closet. "Glad I'm driving the rest of us. We're gonna stop at BK before the pâté parade, want me to get you a fish sandwich?"

Kerry sighed. "Wish I was going with you," she said. "I have to ride with my mother and three of Angie's sorority sisters." She fastened her jacket and put a dark green pashmina scarf around her neck. "When's our flight tomorrow?"

Ceci patted her on the back. "Try to have fun," she said. "Say mean things with big words they won't understand."

Kerry pondered that. "Hm." She grunted thoughtfully, as she followed Dar and Ceci from the room, pausing to join Dar's father, who was loitering in the hall. "Hey, Dad."

"Kumquat." Andrew was in his naval dress uniform, with an all weather parka over it. "Dardar, you want me to drive in this here stuff?"

"No," Ceci answered for her, taking his arm and leading him to the stairs. "She has to learn to drive in snow, Andrew. She's going to be spending a lot of time in it if the government keeps pecking at her."

Dar and Kerry strolled after them. "That remains to be seen," Dar said. "Far as I'm concerned, I'm still retiring in three months."

"Me too," Kerry said. "We've got travel plans." She reached out and took Dar's hand, interlacing their fingers. "They're pretty persistent though."

"Gov'mint," Andy groused. "Always wanting you to do something."

Dar and Kerry exchanged glances. "They still calling you, Dad?" Dar asked.

"Jackass," he said. "Told them ah do not want to be no consultant for nothing for 'em."

They walked down the staircase as a group of other people came in from the hall, a gust of cold air blowing in from the now open door. The entry's marble floor reflected the sconces and chandelier, and the buzz of voices started to echo.

Kerry paused as they waited near the bottom of the steps for the crowd to clear, spotting her mother standing near the grand entrance, talking to her staff, while the rest of the wedding party assembled. "Dar?"

"Hm?" Dar removed a pair of gloves from her jacket pocket. "Here, these are yours."

Kerry took them. "Next time I volunteer for something like this, spank me."

"Hang in there, hon." Dar draped an arm over her shoulders. "It'll be over before you know it."

She knew that. Kerry put her gloves on and sighed, content to stay in her little huddle of Roberts before she had to join the wedding party assembling at the door.

"Ah, Kerrison." Her mother spotted her and headed over. "All ready?" She turned to the others. "I am so sorry we don't have room in the limos for you to join us. Would you like my driver to take you over to the church?"

"We're fine," Ceci answered graciously. "But if there's not much room, maybe Kerry should ride with us. After all, she knows how to get there. I'd hate for Dar to get lost and end up at Dairy Queen."

"Ah, wouldn't." Andrew muttered, under his breath.

"Oh." Cynthia Stuart seemed taken aback. "Well..." She half turned. "Kerrison, would you mind terribly? Then Aunt Mildred can ride with us. She's quite upset."

"No, Mother. I'd be glad to," Kerry answered in the warmest, most sincere tone possible. "I know Aunt Mildred really wanted to be with you. Please, let her take my place. We'll meet you over there."

Cynthia smiled. "Thank you," she said. "Let me go let her know. See you at the church shortly." She hurried away, leaving them to edge down the stairs and thread their way through the crowd.

"That was slick," Dar commented, as they ducked out the front door and she blinked at the snow hitting her face. "Nice job, Mom."

Ceci chuckled as they walked past the waiting limos. Each one had at least one doorman standing by. They picked their way carefully past the clouds of exhaust obscuring the snow slick driveway to the bottom of the entrance, where a dark blue SUV was parked.

Kerry glanced behind her as they got to the car, watching the swirl of activity around the limos as the rest of the wedding party got situated. She imagined herself getting into the car with them, the women and her relatives so far nothing more than a collection of disapproving eyeballs she'd had to deal with over breakfast.

Why had she thought it would be different this time? Because her mother had visited her in Miami and liked her cabin? She got in the car and repeated the question aloud. "Thanks, Mom. I have no clue why I thought things would be that much better this trip."

"Well." Ceci got in behind Dar, while Andy folded his long legs in behind Kerry's seat. "Just think of being here for your sister, kiddo. The hell with everyone else."

Dar put the car into drive and eased forward, leaving the brightly lit mansion behind.

THE CHURCH WAS already filling when they got there. Dar parker as close to the building as they could in deference to the worsening weather. Kerry spotted the press, and as they climbed up the steps to the front door of the stately brick church, the press spotted them.

Andy got between them and the photographers, and they made it to the door and inside before the cameras could catch them. "Jackass." He shook the snow off his shoulders as they cleared the door, almost crashing into a tall, spare man with a priest's collar. "Sorry 'bout that."

The man's face twitched as he recognized Kerry. "Miss Stuart," he said. "Your sister is in the second dressing room. She was asking for you."

Kerry took a breath and released it. "Thanks." She touched Dar's arm. "Go on in and sit down. I'll meet up with you after the service."

Dar patted her on the side. "Say hi to Angie for me."

"I will." Kerry ducked past the pastor and slipped into the inner hallway that led to the schoolrooms and side chambers she remembered roaming through as a child. The smell was still the same, a mixture of wax and old paper, the wooden floorboards creaking a little under her steps.

Happy memories, the earliest of them. A time when Sunday school was just a time to gather with her friends, and listen to Pastor Robert, then himself just out of seminary, teach them basic, simple lessons that held no charge and didn't weigh them down morally.

She remembered being at Sunday service, with her family sitting in the first pew, not understanding why everyone paid so close attention to them, or why her father was always the center of attention.

The place rubbed her raw now. She found the second dressing room and knocked lightly on it, loosening the belt on her coat as the door opened and swung back. She spotted her sister inside. "Hey, Ang."

"There you are!" Angie looked up from fiddling with her bouquet and waved her inside. "I thought you'd never get here."

Kerry smiled and entered, removing her scarf and hanging it on the coat rack just inside the door. "I skipped the limo," she said, "or I'd still probably be on Mother's doorstep."

"Ugh." Angie got the ribbons sorted and put the bouquet down. "I should have stuck to my idea of having it be just Mom, you, Mike, us, and the justice of the peace." She turned as Kerry stripped off her coat and hung it up. "Dar outside?"

"I left her and her folks with Pastor Durham." Kerry turned to face her. "I figure if he survives he'll just shut up and marry you without any commentary."

Angie grinned. "I love that dress. You look gorgeous."

Kerry felt her shoulders relax and she grinned back. "You too. I really like that lace top." She joined Angie, who was wearing a cream colored dress, simple and elegant, strapless as her own was and flattering to her somewhat angular figure. "Was the strapless bit your idea of rebellion?"

Angie chuckled. "Hey, it's my second time," she said. "They say you're supposed to know what you're doing after the first, and none of this princess neckline stuff or veils. Besides," she studied Kerry's chest, "I wanted everyone to see my sister's gorgeous tattoo."

Kerry glanced down at the mark, the snake's intricate scale pattern glistening slightly, its sinuous body wrapping in and out of Dar's name inked clearly and distinctly on her skin. "Everyone's going to freak."

"Yeah, I know," Angie admitted. "But I may break dance with Brian at the banquet so at least they'll all be loosened up for it." She gently touched the tattoo. "Are you mad?"

"No. Everyone's going to be pissed off at me on general principles. Might as well give them a solid reason." She sighed. "Too bad you and Brian couldn't have gotten married down at our place last week."

"I wish." Angie patted her shoulder. "But remember Mike stayed those extra two days?"

"Yeah?"

"He got his nose pierced."

Kerry covered her eyes with one hand. "Jesus."

Angie chuckled. "So don't worry, sis. You really are going to turn out to be the Republican in the family."

PASTOR DURHAM CLEARED his throat. "You are friends of Kerrison, I believe?" he said, in a chilly voice.

Dar regarded him, then extended her hand. "We met in the hospital," she said. "I'm Dar Roberts, Kerry's partner." She waited for him to very reluctantly shake her hand. "These are my parents, Andrew and Cecilia Roberts."

He released her. "Yes, I recall seeing you there," he said. "I'm Charles Durham, the family pastor." He gave them a brief nod. "Excuse me. I need to prepare for the ceremony. It will be held in there." He pointed at the entrance to the nave. "Someone will seat you." He turned and went through a side doorway, shutting it behind him with a distinct bang.

"Nice feller," Andrew said, rocking up and down on his heels.

Ceci sighed. "What a wasted opportunity, really." She started for the door to the chapel. "I had a perfectly good set of Samhain robes I could have worn to this thing."

Dar followed them in, using the time as they stood in line to be seated to look around the place. She noticed they were noticed, people looking at them from their seats, or behind them in line, and she returned the stares until they all looked elsewhere.

It was overt. Dar's face twitched as she acknowledged the sense of discomfort. The last time she'd had to interact with Kerry's family and their friends it was at Kerry's father's funeral service, and the circumstances themselves had diverted attention from them.

But here, as invited guests, she could sense an undercurrent of outrage in this conservative community, not willing to accept the acceptance determinedly shown by Cynthia Stuart to them. She had to give Kerry's mother credit, the senator had stuck to her guns and welcomed them as family with open arms, ignoring the distaste of her social circle and displaying a surprisingly solid backbone when her political and private councilors tried to derail her.

A young page guided them down the aisle to the second pew on the right hand side, where Angie and Kerry's brother Mike was already ensconced, along with a young lady in purple leather with one half of her head shaved.

"Nice." Ceci nodded at her in satisfaction. "Hello there," she greeted Mike.

"Hey." Mike grinned at them, the ring in his nose catching the light. "Welcome to the dark side." He indicated his companion. "This is my girlfriend, Tracy," he said. "Trace, this is my sister-in-law, Dar, and her parents."

Dar felt her sense of the absurd stir. "When do the juggler and the two headed dog show up?" she asked, as she took her seat next to him. "Kerry was worried her tat would raise eyebrows."

Mike chuckled and sat down. "Yeah. I figure the rate we're going, we'll talk Mom into a leather biker vest pretty soon."

He leaned back as Tracy put her hand on his knee and leaned toward Dar. "Hey, you're the computer genius, aren't you?" she asked. "I saw you in the paper a couple months back."

"More or less," Dar admitted. "We did some work on the terrorist recovery."

The woman nodded. "I'm one of the senior copywriters at the marketing firm we work for." She indicated Mike. "My brother got sent to New York last month as part of the rebuilding team. He sent pictures back. Puts it in perspective, you know? We're writing copy to sell Jaegermeister shots and he's there."

"It was pretty horrific," Dar said quietly. "Something I will never forget."

"Dar and my sister were there too," Mike said. "I told you what was going on at the house when it was all happening, right?"

"You told me." Tracey gave him a tolerant look.

The chapel was filling up, and the pew they were in gathered a few more people, older women and men who were, Dar figured, aunts and uncles of some kind. None of them seemed eager to talk, and after about ten minutes, they saw the pastor move to the front and the crowd quieted down.

Brian and his best man, a red haired and freckled specimen Dar didn't know, moved to the front of the altar and stood there quietly, dressed in sharply creased morning suits and bow ties.

Then an usher came down the aisle escorting a woman, who was seated in the first pew on the other side.

"Brian's mom," Mike whispered to Dar. "Freak show in a bowl."

Dar nodded slightly. The woman was sitting bolt upright, a hat firmly perched on her head.

An organ started to play. It had a mellow, sweet tone and Dar folded her hands in her lap, cocking her head to listen. After a few minutes, her peripheral vision caught motion, and she turned her head to watch the procession coming down the center aisle.

The sorority sisters and three men in morning suits marched down, taking up their place near the altar, then Angie's young daughter, Sally, came trotting down, carrying a pillow with a small box on it, focusing on keeping the surface even as she ended up almost bumping into Brian's knees.

Dar glanced around to see if, by freakish chance, Angie's ex-husband, Richard, was around, but a quick scan didn't turn him up. Then she forgot about looking further as she spotted Kerry walking quietly up the aisle, eyes forward, ignoring the stares of the crowd.

Dar felt a smile stretch her lips as she watched Kerry make the journey up to the altar, her sculptured, muscular shoulders shifting a little as she walked up and took her place across from Brian, regarding the crowd with a wary expression.

Then her eyes met Dar's and she smiled, folding her hands in front of her as she waited for Angie to arrive. The bridesmaids next to her were dressed in similar style, but in Dar's admittedly biased eyes Kerry's poised confidence easily outshone them and her understated beauty would likely do the same to her sister once the bride was in place.

Kerry glanced back over at her. Whatever she saw in Dar's expression made her blush slightly and she looked away as Angie came up to the altar, escorted by their mother.

Cynthia gave Brian a little nod, then seated herself in the first pew, her solitary presence lending an unexpected dignity to the moment.

Pastor Durham cleared his throat and stepped forward, his eyes sweeping over the party, his face twitching as he faced the bride and groom and put his back to the crowd. As he lifted his hands, a crackling pop sounded, and then all the lights went off.

Ceci sighed. "Somewhere, PT Barnum is laughing."

KERRY SAT ON one of the dressing room benches, old pews repurposed in the small room. "Shoulda done this last week down by us, Ang," she said. "You could have had it out on the little island Dar and I had our commitment ceremony on."

Angie sat on another bench across from Kerry with Brian next to her, and Sally sitting on Brian's lap. "You think they found enough candles yet?" she asked, looking wryly amused. "I know I should be upset about this, but really it's sort of funny."

Her three bridesmaids were occupying the temporary chairs they'd brought in to do makeup from, and one of them was fluffing up the corsages with a mild, bored expression on her face.

"Very," Brian agreed. "Especially since power's out all over town. I was listening to the local news on the radio and everyone's freaking out."

"Well." Kerry folded her hands on her knee and wished she could go change into her jeans, mourning the fact they were back in her mother's house. "At least the house has a fireplace."

"You volunteering to go chop firewood?" Angie said. "She hasn't used it in probably ten years."

Kerry exhaled, glancing up as the door opened and Mike slipped in. "Hey. They ready?"

"The church is ready. The pastor is arguing with Mom." Mike came in and dropped down onto the bench Kerry was sitting on. "Saying all kinds of crap about how this was a sign God's pissed off with her."

"What?" Kerry barked.

"What?" Angie echoed her.

"Jerk." Mike shook his head. "He was telling her she's been living an immoral life and we all turned out to be scum buckets because of it."

Both Angie and Kerry stood up at the same time. "Fuck that," Kerry enunciated crisply. "Let me go kick him in the ass. I don't care if he's a priest."

"Don't worry." Mike waved them back. "Dar and her mom and dad got into it. It was really entertaining there for a minute, but then they went into his office."

"He's been on that kick," one of the bridesmaids said. "You know it, Ang. He was preaching last Sunday that all the bad things happening, like 9/11, are because we're not living right."

"Missed it," Angie said. "My Andy wasn't feeling well so we stayed home. Now I'm glad. Does he really think God sent terrorists to fly planes into New York because we aren't being pious enough?"

Kerry reseated herself. "Well, who knows," she muttered. "After all, I'm gay, you're an adulterer, and he's got a tattoo on his ass and a pierced nose." She turned her head and regarded Angie. "Maybe you all should move to Miami."

Angie started chuckling. The bridesmaids looked a little shocked, and Brian just laughed and shook his head. "Yeah," he said. "People are weird."

"So," one of the other bridesmaids spoke up. "Kerry."

"Mm?" Kerry eyed her.

"What's it like being gay?" the woman asked in a mild tone that had no edge to it.

Kerry pondered that then shrugged. "I don't know. What's it like being straight?" she returned the question. "I guess it was hard for me when I figured it out because of how I was raised. But now? It's just... it's normal. I don't feel any different just because Dar's a woman not a guy. It's kind of cool, you know? Not having to explain things like my period, or worry about that Mars versus Venus thing."

Angie chuckled. "You've got a point there."

The other woman nodded. "My brother's gay," she said, surprising everyone else in the room apparently. "He just came out to my parents. Really bad scene," she added. "They flipped. I thought they were going to throw him out, but they didn't."

"Scott's gay?" Angie asked, with a fascinated expression. "Really, Chris?"

Chris nodded. "Yeah. He's going to college next year, so I guess he figured he'd better get the word out before he came back with a boyfriend." She stifled a yawn. "God I hope you have coffee at the reception, Ang."

"Hope they can figure out how to heat it up," Angie responded. "I can just imagine all that quiche gone cold."

Kerry felt a sudden shift in perception at the offhand discussion. She'd known Chris and the other two women as friends of Angie's from years back, but this studied acceptance, honest or not of her relationship, was an unexpected pleasure. She relaxed, extending her legs out and crossing them at the ankles.

The door opened again and one of the ushers poked his head in. "We're ready to start," he said. "Could you take your places again, please?"

The wedding party filed out obediently and re-entered the chapel. The altar area was lit up with candles of many sizes and shapes, and though it provided an irregular light, Kerry decided it was actually pretty charming. There was a dim glow from the narrow stained glass windows on the back wall and the illumination lent a beauty and mystery to the altar she hadn't felt before.

The pastor hadn't returned yet, but as she watched the guests file back in, she spotted Dar and her folks coming down the far aisle and sliding into place in their pew. Dar's temper was visibly bristling and as she met Kerry's eyes, she shook her head a little, sitting down and folding her arms over her chest.

Kerry folded her hands and flexed her fingers as the pastor came back in, his long face twitching in annoyance as he came to face Angie and Brian again.

For a moment, his eyes slipped past them and fell on Kerry, and the stark dislike in them chilled her. She wondered if he was going to start ranting at her, but after that brief pause, he straightened his robe and cleared his throat.

She saw her mother enter, but instead of going to the first pew, she went to the second, and seated herself next to Ceci, leaning close to whisper something to her.

Ceci patted her knee and then, looking pointedly at the priest's back, raised her hand and extended her middle finger at him, nearly making Dar's pale blue eyes come out of her head.

Kerry suspected there were lots of things she was going to regret finding out just as soon as the service was over. She spotted reporters now in the back, and she straightened a little as flashbulbs started to pop, and found herself wishing very hard it was just done.

She heard the pastor going through the motions and tried to focus on the service, willing to give respect to Angie's wish for a new life for herself, and for her kids. She also acknowledged a twinge of sadness that no matter how her own life contrasted to Angie's, she could never stand in that spot and have a pastor of her own church read those words he was saying to her sister.

No matter her commitment ceremony was held in a far more beautiful space, with lots of her friends around her, and celebrated by an ordained pastor of her faith — it was not a marriage. It didn't give her and Dar the legal rights this simple ceremony would give them, even held in the clerk of courts office.

Did that matter? Kerry listened to Angie's quiet "I do." Did it matter that her own, internal, until death do us part was far more binding in her heart than her sister's now second set of them was?

Did it matter it had taken months of laboriously drawn legal papers to give her and Dar the basic rights to each other's person and property that this five minute exchange of words would for Angie and Brian?

"You may kiss the bride."

And then the words tickled her sense of the absurd, because who in the hell was this old jerk to be giving permission for two people to kiss each other? Kerry regarded the candles, and stifled a smile, as the recessional started playing, and she watched Angie and Brian as they retreated up the aisle toward the doors, with people standing and tossing rice balls in gauze at them.

So it was over. Kerry relaxed a little, as Dar got up and headed her way, evading the milling guests as she dodged past the pastor. "Excuse me," Dar said, just missing crashing into him as he stepped back without looking.

The man turned and stiffened, recognizing her.

"Problem?" Dar straightened up to her full height, matching his.

He stared at her for a moment. "God has a problem with you. I would just prefer you out of his house," he said, then turned and retreated toward the small door just to the left of the altar.

Kerry regarded Dar. "Sorry," she said, with a sigh.

"Nice." Dar shook her head. "How could God have a problem with me if he gave me you?" She turned to Kerry, putting a hand on her hip. "What a jackass."

Kerry handed Dar her corsage, ignoring the chatter of conversation as she only just resisted the urge to lean over and kiss her. "I really am sorry, hon. Wish we were home."

"Peh." Dar half shrugged. "I don't know if it's just what we went through, but it's hard for me to let morons like that bother me, Ker." She sniffed the flowers, and leaned a little against Kerry. "He's just pissed because my mother ripped him a new one."

Kerry let her hand rest on Dar's shoulder, glancing past her at the crowd, waiting for it to clear a little so they could escape.

Cameras were still popping, and she figured given their position she was probably going to be at least page two of the daily tomorrow. "So." She watched Dar nibble on one of the roses, the warm candlelight gilding her skin. "What happened in there? Mike said you were going at it with him."

"Asshole," Dar muttered back, aware of the press now moving forward to get a shot of them. "Tried to pull a guilt trip on your mother."

Kerry sighed.

"Not over you." Dar gave one of the nearest reporters a smile. "Matter of fact, it didn't get that far. Started on Angie having an affair and then my mother lit into him."

"Ah."

"Said she was an immoral whore."

Kerry straightened. "Your mother?"

"Yours." Dar bumped her. "My mother started chanting some sort of pagan curse at him."

"Fucking asshole," Kerry said audible enough for the front rows to hear her. "Let me get out of this dress and I'm going to go kickbox him into February." She got down off the raised platform and headed off, but had to pull up short as two reporters blocked her way.

Dar caught up with her as she stopped. "Hon."

"Ms. Stuart." The older of the two reporters said. "Would you mind speaking to us for a moment?"

Cynthia arrived at her elbow. "Kerrison, we've sent the staff back to the house to prepare for the reception, with all the difficulties." She glanced at the press. "Excuse us please, gentlemen. This is a private social affair."

Dar was surprised when the press nodded and backed off. "Sorry about that, Senator," The older one said. "We were just looking for a few minutes with your daughter."

"Some other time," Cynthia said, firmly.

They retreated. "I hear the pastor caused some problems," Kerry said in a quiet tone, as her mother turned back to her.

"He was unkind," Cynthia admitted. "But we mustn't dwell on it. This is a happy occasion and I'm determined it will stay that way. Now, shall we go? I've been told this power outage is quite extensive. I'm sure someone will want to talk to me about it." She gestured them forward. "As though I could actually do something."

"I'm surprised someone hasn't called me to see if I could do something about it," Kerry said. "They must have forgotten I'm here."

Cynthia regarded her. "Could you?" she asked, hesitantly. "Do something?"

"Depends on what the problem is," Dar said. "If a tanker truck ran into the power station, probably not. If it's a computer glitch..." She lifted her hands, then let them drop.

"I see," Cynthia mused. "Well, never mind. You're a guest here. Let someone else who's probably being paid a lot of our budget dollars fix it." She took the lead and the crowd parted as her aides cleared a path. "Excuse us please!"

"Hm." Kerry tucked her hand inside Dar's elbow and suffered the resulting flash bulbs. "My mother's growing on me." She felt the faint chuckle rippled through Dar's body. "She's getting a lot more...uh..."

"Ballsy," Dar said, glad enough to follow her down the aisle and out of the church, as Ceci and Andrew joined them. "We're heading out."

"Good," Ceci said. "The overbearing stench of orthodoxy is making me want to light a passion fruit firecracker in this place."

"Lord." Andrew handed them their coats. "Had me more fun at Navy training."

Kerry covered her mouth hastily, muffling a laugh as they were hustled outside by Cynthia's aides, who kept the crowd back as they walked down the steps and headed past the waiting limos, escaping the line of press who had stopped the Senator at the door to hers and were questioning her.

"Hon." Kerry put her hand on Dar's back. "Better let me drive back. The lights are all out and I know this place better than you do."

Dar handed her the keys and they got inside, waiting for the doors to thump closed before being subjected to Ceci's bursting into speech. "What a son of a bitch that man is," she said. "Kerry, if that's the church you grew up in, my hats off to you not turning out to be a wing nut."

"Who says I'm not?" Kerry felt her guts relax as she adjusted the seat and started the car up. "But yeah, he's always been very conservative." She got the defroster on, and flexed her hands. "I have no idea how they're going to do the reception without any power. This is a little crazy."

"Yeap." Andrew folded his arms over his chest. "Just a little bit."

Ceci made a snorting sound.

The snow was coming down harder, and there were no lights working. Kerry was grateful that she knew where she was going as she carefully navigated through the storm. "Not all the people in that church were like that," she said. "I remember when I was graduating from high school, there was a big thing about him, because his wife was caught embezzling money from the church and then she ran away, ended up crashing into a tree and killing herself."

Ceci cleared her throat. "I'll try to refrain from commenting about judgments from God."

Kerry turned up the street her childhood home was on and accelerated cautiously. "He certainly doesn't like me. Never did, matter of fact. Said I was impertinent and that my father should punish me more." She turned in at the gate and paused, as the security guard came over, shielding his face from the snow as she opened the window. "Hey, John, just us."

"Ms. Kerry." The man waved them through. "What a day, huh?"

"What a day."

IT WAS COLD inside. Dar pondered the possibility of having to wear thermal underwear to the reception as she waited for Kerry to get off her cell phone. They'd left them in the house, and she had two voice mails on hers, but she'd felt no inclination to listen to them.

It had become hard to remain engaged with work. Dar folded her arms and regarded the window, watching the snow fall in thick, drifting waves. She'd gotten to a place where she wanted to move on, and as hard as she was trying to tie things up, it was even harder to get people to realize she was serious, and wanted out.

They kept trying to drag her back in.

"Dar?"

"Hm?" She turned as Kerry came over, folding her phone shut "What's up?"

"Lansing's on generator. Just wanted to let me know they're mostly online and just monitoring stuff. Said it was pretty quiet. Some people called but they know the blackout is what it is."

"Good." Dar leaned her arm on Kerry's shoulder. "What's the protocol for wearing a bearskin rug to your sister's shindig?"

Kerry chuckled. "If this keeps up, we're going to have to find a way to keep warm tonight. There's no fireplace in this room."

"I'm sure," Dar tilted her head and gently blew in Kerry's ear, "we'll think of something."

"Maybe we should start working on ideas right now." Kerry turned her head and their lips met. "At least this gives me an excuse to change out of my scandalous dress and into something more comfortable." She rested her head against Dar's. "Wonder if they figured out what the power problem is yet?"

"Change." Dar gave her another kiss. "I'll call around and see if I can find that out for ya." She angled around behind her and unzipped the strapless gown, running a finger across the back of Kerry's neck.

"Didn't need more goose-bumps, hon." Kerry smiled, getting out of her gown while Dar picked up her phone, and opened it, Dar already dressed in a pair of casual pants and a blue knitted sweater. The chill hit her and she hurriedly changed, reluctantly bypassing her jeans for a pair of wool slacks and adding a sweater of her own to them.

Dar waited for the phone to answer. "Wonder how long the cell sites will be up," she mused. "Batteries can't last that long." She listened. "Yeah, this is Dar Roberts," she said. "Yeah, happy new year to you too. Listen. There's a power outage up here in Michigan. Do a search and tell me what the deal is, will ya?"

"You should put a t-shirt on, Dar."

Dar looked down at herself, then at Kerry, one brow lifting. "What?" She covered the phone with one hand. "It's cold!"

"Under the sweater." Kerry fished a cotton shirt from Dar's bag and handed it to her. "Layers, right?"

"Oh." Dar juggled the phone and the shirt, pulling off her sweater and laying it on the dresser as she donned the shirt, then put the heavier garment on over it. "Yeah, I'm here." She listened to the phone. "Ah. Okay. Thanks. Bye." She closed the phone. "Iced over high tension power lines snapped."

"Ah," Kerry brushed her hair. "Well, that's fixable at least."

"Not before we have to make heat I hope." Dar put her arms around Kerry from behind and leaned against her, watching their dual reflections in the mirror. "Maybe everyone'll decide to go to bed early."

"Mm...maybe we'll inaugurate the green room." Kerry snickered. "We can put our initials on the wall."

Dar looked at her in puzzlement. "Didn't you say this is where they put the married people in your family?" She watched Kerry nod, eyes twinkling. "And married people don't have sex in the Stuart clan?"

Kerry regarded her. "We've had this whole parents and sex conversation, Dar."

"Ah...that's right. Kerry Cabbage Patch Stuart. I forgot."

They both chuckled. "Let's go downstairs," Kerry said. "See if they have any crackers and cheese at least. I'm starving." She patted her companion on the side and they sat down to put their shoes on. With the dim gray light outside, it was almost twilight in the room, and without any electricity they heard the pops and creaks of the house around them.

"Hope Mom has candles around." Kerry stood up. "If this lasts all night it could end up getting creepy."

They left the room and walked along the hallway toward the stairs, coming face-to-face with Aunt Mildred. "Hi, there." Kerry mustered up a smile. "Crazy weather, huh?"

The older woman merely stared at her, then turned and started down the steps, leaving them behind.

Dar and Kerry sighed in unison, then followed her. "At least Mom didn't invite my uncles," Kerry said under her breath. "Next time, please tie me up."

The main entry of the Stuart family house was filling with guests, but even with all the people the chill was evident. Someone had put candles in glass jars around the space, and there were two servants putting more out between taking heavy overcoats from their owners.

There was no press around this time. Dar saw a line of them outside, but they weren't getting much for their efforts and she put her hand on Kerry's back as they reached the bottom of the stairs and paused. "There's your brother." She indicated the far corner of the space. "Should all the black sheep gather together?"

"Baa." Kerry led the way through the crowd, ignoring the veiled and not so veiled stares as they were recognized. Then she had to stop as a woman got directly in her path. "Excuse me."

"Don't you have any shame?" the woman asked her.

Kerry stared thoughtfully at her, one hand going back to put a halt on Dar's forward motion, as she sensed her beloved partner about to take severe offense. "No, actually I don't," she answered in a mild tone. "Please get out of my way, Aunt April. This isn't the place to make a scene. My mother wouldn't appreciate it."

The woman shook her head. "Your father would be so ashamed."

Kerry squeezed Dar's hand. "He had a lot of reasons to be ashamed. Now please excuse us." She pushed past the woman, keeping tight hold of her growling spouse. "It's going to be one of those days isn't it?"

"I vote we go back to bed."

"Soon, hon, soon."

Chapter Two

"IT WAS A complete screw up," the stocky man told Dar, as they both held drinks and watched the candle lit crowd in the grand hall. "They knew those towers needed repair, but all that warm weather we had made them push it off."

"A mess," Dar commiserated. "They know how long it'll take to fix it?"

The Governor shook his head mournfully. "I was hoping it was some systemic mistake because I knew I'd be seeing you today and maybe I could ask you to fix it." He winked at her. "But no, they've got to take the grid offline, repair the cables, and power it all back up. Maybe late tonight. Probably tomorrow. I'm getting lambasted in the news."

"As if you could do something about it."

"Not only that, instead of sitting in my office being a martyr to public opinion I'm here, having a glass of the late Roger's good scotch and wondering how Cynthia's going to pull off hot canapés." The Governor chuckled wryly. "Ah, the life of a public servant."

"You can have it." Dar was happy enough to be holding up her bit of wall, the presence of the state's magnate keeping off any of Kerry's bolder relatives. "I'm looking forward to retiring."

The Governor eyed her alertly. "Do tell?" he said. "Aren't you a little young for that?"

Dar smiled, lifting her glass of white wine in acknowledgment. "Been fifteen years. I want to see the world a little without worrying about my cell phone ringing because someone's mainframe crashed." She spotted Kerry returning, carrying a plate. "I gave them six months notice. They're working a package for me."

"Wow," he said. "After everything that just happened? I heard you were neck deep in the recovery effort. Someone told me they were looking to suck you into the public sector."

"After everything that just happened," Dar restated the words, "Life's too short."

"Going to go out on your own?" he asked, with a shrewd glance at her. "Be your own boss?"

"Eventually. I'll have to stay out of the business for a while. Then probably get back in, do some consulting," Dar replied. "Or who knows? Maybe I'll open a dive shop down in the Keys where our cabin is. Leave tech alone."

"More power to you, lady." He tipped his glass back at her. "Don't tell my wife, she'll be jealous."

Kerry arrived, offering up her small china platter. "Jealous of what?"

"Are those sliders?" Dar started laughing.

"My sister picked the menu," Kerry said with a smile. "They're brisket sliders, matter of fact. With horseradish sauce."

"Nice." The Governor took one. "I was just telling Dar here my wife would be jealous of her retiring."

"Ah." Kerry waited for Dar to serve herself, then took a sandwich and put the platter down on a nearby table. "I'm looking forward to that myself. I've got such a bucket list to get through." She took a bite of the slider. "Mm."

"You too?" The Governor exclaimed.

"Oh, yeah." Dar licked a bit of the horseradish sauce off her fingertips. "I think we're going to start with a visit to the Grand Canyon, then a cruise somewhere."

"White water rafting," Kerry clarified, with a grin. "I figure I should get the camping stuff out of the way first because I know Dar doesn't like it much." She wiped her lips with a small napkin. "I think we're going to fly into Vegas, then rent an RV and do the tour."

He chuckled. "Well, I can't say I don't envy you ladies." He munched on his own sandwich. "Wish I could look forward to the same, but I've got four kids, and three of them are in college at the moment. I'm lucky I can manage Pizza Hut on Fridays."

"One of the bright points of only having a dog." Kerry leaned against the wall next to Dar. "Besides, after all the world saving Dar's done, she's due."

"You haven't done bad for a newbie." Dar's eyes twinkled a little.

One of Cynthia's aides approached them, catching Kerry's eye. "Excuse me?"

"Yes?" Kerry responded. "Did you need something?"

"The Senator asked me to come find you. She'd like to speak to you for a moment," the man said. "Could you come with me?"

Dar and Kerry exchanged looks. "Excuse us," Dar said, putting her glass down. "Probably needs some help with logistics." She put her hand on Kerry's back. "Lead on." She met the aide's eyes, daring him to exclude her.

He looked like he wanted to. But Kerry motioned him on and he ducked his head, turning to lead the way across the room toward a cluster of people on the far side from where they'd been. The room was lit barely from the gray light of outside and the candles around the edges. As they approached where Kerry's mother was, several servants appeared with more candles in their hands.

Cynthia had a cluster of family around her, and Dar saw from where she was the dour faces and glaring eyes as they were spotted heading their way.

What the hell was wrong with those people anyway? Couldn't they take a damn day out to enjoy a wedding and leave off all the moralistic bull crap? Dar sighed, and felt an itch between her shoulder blades.

Cynthia saw them and turned. "Ah, Kerry. Thank you for coming over. Your Aunt Mildred had a question and I thought perhaps you could answer it."

"Sure, if I can," Kerry replied with internal reluctance, regarding the short, dumpy looking woman watching her with a sour look. "What is it, Aunt Mildred?" She was aware of Dar behind her, and as she took a breath waiting for whatever it was, she felt the casual warmth as Dar's forearm came to rest on her shoulder.

Backing her up. Kerry had to smile. Just like when she was at work, when present or not, Dar cast a very long shadow everyone was very aware of. She didn't even have to drop her name anymore, it was just assumed by everyone that Kerry had her in her pocket.

Aunt Mildred was Uncle Edgar's wife. Uncle Edgar was explicitly told not to show up for the wedding, and Kerry knew that was for her benefit since their last interaction hadn't been pleasant. She suspected Aunt Mildred was about to unload her resentment over that, though she was a little surprised her mother had bought into it and called her over.

"I would like you to explain all this about log cabin Republicans," Aunt Mildred said, in a firm tone. "Are you a part of them? You must be."

Kerry blinked a few times, her eyes flicking back and forth as she prodded her memory. Then she turned and looked at Dar. "Do you know what that is?"

"I think," Dar said, after a pause to consider, "it's people who are gay, who are also Republican."

"Yes," Mildred said. "They've been petitioning our firm about something. So you are a part of that?"

"What does being gay have to do with log cabins?" Kerry wondered.

"Tell you later," Dar said, with a wry smile. "Let's not get into that debate here."

"Huh?" Kerry gave her a searching look, then shrugged when Dar merely winked at her. "And no, Aunt Mildred, I may be both gay and a Republican but I don't belong to any groups of either type, so I'm not sure if I can help you with whatever it is they want from you," she said. "I stay clear of politics unless it concerns high technology."

"They want us to offer benefits to our employees, benefits like we offer to married people. To people like you," Mildred said. "It's ridiculous."

"Mildred," Cynthia said, sharply.

She turned on Kerry's mother. "Don't Mildred me. It's terrible, how you promote this. We all remember how you and Roger felt about her lifestyle. Now you pretend you don't? At least I'm honest about it."

There was, Dar recognized, a bit of truth in that. "I'd like to think there's no dishonesty, just a learning process," she said in a mild tone. "As in, she learned we don't have horns and tails and walk around seducing children. There's nothing immoral about health benefits. You attract a better employee base if you treat them well."

"Of course you'd say that," Mildred snapped.

"Of course I'm the CIO of an international Fortune 500 company. So, yes, I have an opinion about that regardless of my sexual orientation," Dar said, her voice taking on a sharper note. "But Mrs. Stuart also has the right to form her own opinions as well as have them change over time."

Cynthia gave her a brief, acknowledging smile. "There is more truth to that then you perhaps believe," she said. "Mildred, this is not the place for your bias. Kerry has answered your question, now let's all go sit down for some lunch."

"Disgusting," Mildred said, unrepentant. "I don't know how she had the gall to enter that church, or you had the temerity to allow it."

"Mildred, that's enough," Cynthia said. "Either go in to lunch, or leave. I will not have you here speaking this way to my daughter." She gestured to the aide. "John, please escort my sister-in-law."

"Ma'am." The tall security aide moved closer to Aunt Mildred, who ignored him and moved off in another direction, taking the elbow of another older woman and guiding her aside.

"Sorry about that, Kerrison." Cynthia sighed. "I really don't know what's gotten into people these days. Goodness knows there have always been feelings like this, but in public you were expected to act polite about it."

"Has been getting more blatant," Dar noted. "Whole country's gotten more conservative leadership, so they think it's all right to say stuff like that. We're the socially acceptable to bash minority people of this age."

Cynthia's face twisted into an expression of distaste. "Surely not."

"Surely yes," Dar replied. "Seen the Westboro jackasses on television?"

"Tch." Cynthia made a sound of irritation. "Those people are insane."

"Insane, yes. But they get air time."

"Yeah, Dar's right," Kerry murmured. "But you just reminded me that we've got to go out and get health insurance before we cut loose from ILS, Dar." She motioned toward the grand hall. "Should we go sit down?"

"Yes."

Cynthia joined them as they walked. "Does your company take care of that now?" She asked, diffidently. "I mean, do you have the same issue as Mildred's firm?"

Dar shook her head. "Nah. We offer domestic partner benefits. Even if Kerry didn't work for us, I could put her on my health insurance. But she's right, we have to go get private policies now, and it won't work that way. We'll need to get individual ones." She paused.

"Fortunately we already had the legal work done to give us both medical authority over each other."

"I see." Cynthia frowned. "Hm."

"We're lucky. We can afford it," Dar said. "A lot of people can't."

They entered the hall and paused, drawing to one side to find their way in the dim light.

In the rear, the fireplace held a brightly burning wood fire. The room was liberally lit with candles, at least four on each table, providing a warm and almost medieval air.

"Come sit at my table." Cynthia pointed to the one closest to the fireplace. "They're using the gas stoves and warmers to keep everything. I hope it turns out all right."

"I'm sure it'll be fine, Mother," Kerry said. "The sliders were great."

Cynthia grimaced a bit. "They were quite a surprise for some, but your sister insisted."

Ceci and Andrew were already seated at the table, and Mike and his girlfriend joined them as they arrived. "Hey, guys." Kerry was about to sit down, when her chair was pulled back for her, and she paused, giving Dar a brief grin before she dropped into it. "Thanks."

"Anytime." Dar sat down next to her and surveyed the room. Despite the lack of electricity, everyone appeared to be determined to make the best of it, and she leaned back and folded her hands, hoping they wouldn't encounter any more of Aunt Mildred.

Or Aunt Alice. Or any of the rest of Kerry's relatives, all of whom seemed to have color coordinated baseball bats up their collective asses.

"Hey, Dar?"

She looked across at her mother. "Yes?" she said, drawing out the word.

"You going back into the office when you get back?"

"No." Dar felt a sense of satisfaction in saying that. "Kerry and I are going to go down to the cabin the rest of the week and go back in next Monday." She leaned back in her chair. "We have the time coming to us."

"Such a lovely cabin," Cynthia said. "Really, just charming. And the view from the porch, amazing." She smiled at both Dar and Kerry. "I completely see why you like to spend time there. So peaceful, really."

"It is nice there," Ceci agreed. "I'm doing a set of paintings from that point, in different weather," she said. "The colors are wonderful. The water changes every minute."

"It does," Kerry said. "We spent a few weeks out there after we got back from New York. You can really unwind there."

Cynthia smiled. "I can imagine that." She looked up as Angie and Brian arrived, and plopped down in seats next to her. "Oh! There you are."

"Here we are," Angie said. "Hey, guys." She gave her brother and sister a grin. "Sorry we're late, Mom. We ended up dropping Brian's mom off at home. She got lost and we passed her heading here."

Cynthia frowned. "Oh my. She didn't want to come to lunch? I'm sure she was invited."

"Um...no," Brian said. "She's kind of...she doesn't like parties. She's really just into church."

"Ah." Ceci nodded. "She didn't want to hang out with the infidels. Gotcha." She inspected the basket of rolls on the table. "Raisins. Mm. Lunch is looking up."

Brian had the grace to look embarrassed. "Really, she's more embarrassed and disgusted by me than by anyone here," he said, in quiet voice. "It was just hard on her. She's worked in the church for a really long time, and it was hard for her to face all those people."

"Why does she think she's responsible for what you did?" Angie asked.

He shrugged.

"People who are very traditional are not comfortable with what they view as—ah." Cynthia paused. "Well, things that are non-traditional," she finished somewhat lamely. "Just as the pastor felt that I perhaps should have tried to regulate the morals of my family as Roger tried to, many others feel that this lack of holding to traditions has put us all at a disadvantage with God."

"Really?" Kerry felt her back stiffening.

"I did not say I agreed with that," Cynthia said, somewhat more forcefully. "But I cannot ignore the fact that many do, in fact, believe this."

"Like them people at the church last week," Andrew said. "Figured to close down that place to keep their kids from walking next to it." He handed over a plate of butter and knife to Ceci. "Just a lot of hating for no reason."

Angie nodded. "Yeah, I got some advice warning me not to let my kids near my sister," she said. "I don't think the person expected me to slap them."

"Near me?" Kerry blinked. "Aside from making them want Labrador puppies, what am I supposed to do to them?"

"Give them ideas," Angie said, straightforwardly. "What I told them was, given how bright you are, the best thing that could happen to them is for you to give them ideas."

"Right on," Brian said, giving Kerry a thumbs up.

"Terrible," Cynthia muttered. "I must look into finding another place of worship."

"Want to try mine?" Ceci suggested. "Bet I could find a c...I mean chapter up here."

The waiters swirled around them putting plates down on the table. Kerry stared at hers, then she turned her head and looked at Dar, who was leaning forward with her forearms braced on the tablecloth. She saw the flare of her nostrils and as Dar's eyes met hers they were in total emotional sync.

Outrage. Horror. A little revulsion with a tinge of anger. Kerry saw from the set of Dar's jaw and the tension of her hands that she was on the verge of blowing up about it, and knew they both had the same ball of tension in their guts for the same reason.

And that, curiously, made everything all right again. Kerry reached over and tweaked Dar's nose, coaxing a smile out of her as she dismissed the bullshit swirling around her like a cloud of gnats.

Screw it. Just wasn't worth it. "Well, I sure can't change what people think if they want to think stuff like that," she said. "So the hell with it. Let them suffocate in their own close mindedness."

Cynthia still looked disturbed. She shook her head and pushed her plate forward a little. "Terrible." She glanced at Ceci. "Perhaps we can talk later about your faith?"

"Sure." Ceci observed her plate. "Ah, asparagus."

"Sorry about the bacon wrapping it." Angie leaned toward her. "I forgot you were a vegetarian."

"No problem." Ceci unwrapped the bacon and handed it over to Andrew, who swapped it for his own asparagus. "Andy and I have this all worked out."

Everyone chuckled, as the servants brought a round of mimosas to the table, setting them down as a hum of voices started to fill the room, while the snow kept falling thickly outside.

"OH MY GOD." Kerry crawled under the covers, free at last of her clothing, her relatives, and the room full of intently watching eyes. She snuggled up next to Dar and put her arm around her, taking her reward for having to stand in the downdraft of a shitstorm most of the day. "That was so bogus."

"Mm." Dar curled her arms around her and exhaled in satisfaction. "But it's over."

"It's over," Kerry agreed. "Now we've just got breakfast to get through, then it's off to the airport. You think the lights will be back on tomorrow?"

Dar shrugged. "Airport's on a generator."

"Thank goodness. I keep saying I'll never come back here. Wonder when that's going to actually be true? How much abuse do I have to take to stay a part of this family, Dar?"

Dar thought about that for a bit, her fingertips making a slow, gentle pattern on Kerry's back. Then she finally sighed. "Maybe we should just have them visit us. That wasn't so bad."

No, it hadn't been.

"Ker?"

"Yeah?" Kerry breathed in the scent of Dar's skin, which still held a hint of the perfume she'd put on that morning. It was dark out now, and dark in the room, chilly, and a little damp from the weather outside. There was a small battery powered lamp on the bedside table, giving them just enough light to see by.

"Sorry about all the crap today."

"Not your fault." Kerry heard Dar's heartbeat under her ear, with that tiny little echo thump from her oddly structured heart. "People are jerks. My family is full of them, apparently. But at least my mother's gotten better. Right?"

"Yup."

"And your mom offering to induct her into paganism was worth the whole day."

Dar chuckled. "I got lucky in the parent dice roll," she said.

"Oh baby did you ever." Kerry exhaled. "And by extension me too." She blinked a few times, thinking in silence. "You know something?" she finally said. "I think I do want to change my last name, Dar. I know I messed with that when we were in the Caribbean, but now? I want to do it."

She tipped her head up to see Dar studying her in the dim light. "Would you mind that?"

"Would I mind that?" Dar mused. "No, I wouldn't mind that, if you want to do it. You sure?"

"There's nothing here for me anymore, Dar. I love Angie and Mike, and Mom's gotten better, but the rest of them? Why would I want to say I'm related to people who think I'm a godless whore?"

Dar considered that. "Your sibs are okay," she said. "And I like your Aunt Penny. But I'd love you to share my name if you want to." She smiled. "That was kind of a kick when you did it in the islands."

Kerry looked pleased. "Rocking." She kissed a spot just above Dar's prominent collarbone, and then, as Dar reached over and shut the battery lamp off, she slid a little higher and found Dar's lips as she settled back on the pillow, glad to swap the chill of the room and the coldness of the crowd for the heat of passion.

Dar's hands touched her and brought a welcome warmth, and in a moment she was being gently rolled onto her back and Dar's thigh was sliding between hers.

It felt wonderful.

It was fantastic to let that familiar burn start in her guts, and savor the teasing touch against sensitive skin that washed away the taint of the long day. She'd joked about inaugurating the room, but as Dar coaxed a low, guttural sound from her she focused on doing that in earnest.

If they were going to think she was an immoral whore, well then — Kerry released a low growl. Then she'd show them how that would roll. She felt Dar's lips nibble down the centerline of her body and the pressure built, her body craving release as she let it chase the gloomiest of her thoughts right away.

She was looking forward to smirking over her morning coffee, even savoring the looks she knew she'd get.

Hell with all of them.

KERRY CUPPED HER hand over her free ear and pressed her other against her cell phone. "Yes, I'm here." She listened intently to the voice on the other end. She looked up as Dar entered the dining room, her heavy jacket already on. "So, Jake, you think it's okay to take off at eleven?"

Dar came over and stood next to her, hands in pockets, rocking back and forth on her heels. "Was worth booking the jet," she said. "News said the regular airport is slammed."

"Okay, so we'll head over," Kerry said. "See you in a few." She hung up the phone and tucked it into her pocket. "We all ready?"

"Yup. Car's waiting outside."

Kerry felt a distinct sense of relief as she followed Dar through the grand hall toward the entrance. The lights came on halfway through breakfast, bringing on a blare of lighting to distract the stilted conversation.

No one was rude, but it was also obvious that this was more because of Cynthia's wishes than anything else.

She saw the door open, and outside the snow falling. Andy and Ceci were already out in it and the only thing between her and them was a few members of her family.

"Thanks for coming up and being my bestie, Sis." Angie held her arms out and embraced Kerry. "Hope you have a good trip home."

"No problem." Kerry returned the hug. "You guys have to come visit us again soon, though, huh?" She turned to her mother as Dar stepped forward to give Angie a somewhat awkward embrace. "Mom, you too."

Cynthia smiled. "Certainly, we should plan for it. Please let us know you get home safe."

Then they were outside and stomping toward the SUV through a thick coating of snow. Kerry already had a firm grip on the keys and she slid behind the driver's seat and slammed the door shut. "Brr."

"No offense, Kerry, but I've never been so happy to see a place in the rear view window." Ceci settled herself behind Dar. "I swear to the Goddess your family is a bowl of pits with no cherries."

Kerry sighed. "Yeah, I know. Thanks for coming up here with me and keeping me company in my insanity." She got the car into gear and started off down the hill. "I was glad to see Angie married."

"That boy shoulda stepped up before," Andrew grumbled. "Not be so candy assed."

"Oh, c'mon, Andy. He's not that bad." Ceci poked him. "He's a nice kid."

"Actually," Kerry said. "I agree with him. When I went up the last time to help Ang move, I was all set to kick him in the nuts for not taking responsibility for his son."

"Damn straight," Andy said. "Ah would not expect any child of mine to be acting like that."

There was a little silence. Dar glanced at herself, then at Kerry, then half turned to regard her father. "Dad? I'm a girl. I don't think it's going to come up."

Kerry chuckled. "It wouldn't anyway." She reached over and patted Dar's leg. "I have total faith in your honor, sweetheart."

Ceci snickered. "Actually, when Dar first told us she was gay, I think the one thing that relieved Andy was that he wasn't going to be spending long summer nights sitting in the driveway with a shotgun waiting for her to come back from dates."

Kerry spoke up. "I actually thought he was doing a good job of checking me out when we met to make sure I wasn't going to take advantage of his little girl."

Andrew blushed. "Ah did not think any such thing of you, Kerry."

"I was never worried." Dar circled one knee with her hands and rested her shoulder against the car door.

"Considering you started our relationship out by saving me from carjackers, I'm not surprised." Kerry navigated down the back road, passing very few other cars on this quiet Tuesday morning.

"Mm." Dar smiled, but remained silent.

"Kerry, why is it all those people are so nasty to you?" Ceci asked. "Is it because of you and Dar? Or what?"

Kerry sighed. "It's always been tough around those people," she admitted. "It was always very judgmental. About everything. You're supposed to conform, but I think even if I'd married Brian and taken a job as a clerk somewhere, that judging would have still been there."

Ceci shifted a little in her seat. "Had that in my family too, but it had nothing to do with religion."

"So, in this case, it's everything." Kerry slowed down to turn into the small regional airport. "My leaving home, my getting a job in high tech, my living in Miami, my being gay, my turning over my father's records to the papers, there's nothing there they can approve of."

"Probably causes them more heartache seeing you than it gives you," Andrew commented.

"Absolutely true," Kerry said. "Especially with you all here." She turned and faced them, having turned the engine off. "Thank you for teaching me what family can be." She studied her in-laws, watching them smile and feeling Dar's touch on her leg, warm and real. "So now let's go home."

The lights were bright around the Lear jet crouching on the tarmac, a boarding ladder tucked up against the side of it. The pilot was waiting for them inside the small terminal, and they surrendered their overnight bags to him as they waited to board.

"I really like that plane," Ceci commented. "My brother Charles flies around in one of those, and so do most of his friends. Didn't think it was in my plans."

"No, me either," Dar said. "We always had the option. But the first time I flew in a private jet was coming back after the attacks. I liked it. That's why I didn't say no when Alastair and the board offered this one." She saw the pilot motion and she led the rest of them across the snow dusted ground, glad to mount the steps and enter the sleek interior. "We are paying for this ride though. I told Alastair I wasn't going to get into any arguments about me using company resources for personal use."

"It's worth it." Kerry took off her jacket and took it and Dar's to the small closet where Andrew was already putting Ceci's. "I can just imagine traveling today."

They sat down and buckled in, and a moment later the flight steward came in as the door was sealed shut and the pilot retreated into the cockpit. "Hello there."

"Hey, Jaele," Kerry greeted the woman. "Ready to get out of this snow?"

"You know it, Ms. Stuart." The steward brought over a tray and served them all coffee. "Jake's just doing the checklist and filing our flight plan. We should be rolling in about ten minutes."

The inside of the plane was warm, and it wasn't too different from the private plane Kerry remembered her mother using. It had eight seats, two groups of four facing each other with tables to work on between them. The chairs were thick and comfortable, soft leather that warmed to her body as she sat in it.

Jake and Jaele were the A crew and there was a B crew that took over for them sometimes. They were on call around the clock for Dar, and the attention had outlined a new sense of understanding from the board over just how important Dar was to the company.

Funny, after all the time she'd worked for them and all the things she'd done, for them to now decide that. Kerry watched Dar swinging around in her chair in an almost childlike motion. All the attention from the government and the new requests for service had caught their attention like nothing else before had.

Funny. Crazy. Strange. Kerry leaned back in her chair and crossed her ankles. So much change in their lives in such a relatively short time.

"Okay folks." The pilot stuck his head out of the cockpit. "We're de-iced and ready to go. Buckle up."

"Thanks, Jake." Dar lifted a hand and waved at him.

Kerry relaxed as she heard the engines spin up and felt the gentle jolt as the plane started to back away from the terminal. She stifled a yawn. "Hope Angie has a nice honeymoon."

"Where's she going?" Ceci asked.

"She's doing a western Mexico cruise." Kerry smiled faintly. "You know, Acapulco, and all that? She's really excited. She's never been on one."

"Mm." Dar made a skeptical sound.

"Yeap," Andrew said. "Won't catch me on one of them, not after that whole hoo hah you done got into."

"She got a good deal on a suite," Kerry said. "They got a whole honeymoon package and it sounded like fun."

"Mm," Dar repeated the low, growly noise.

"Well, honey, we have our own boat." Kerry reached over and patted her knee. "She doesn't."

"Oh I don't know." Ceci leaned her elbow on the chair arm and rested her chin on her hand. "I always thought an Atlantic crossing cruise might be fun."

"It ain't," Andrew said.

"Not on the ones you sailed on, no," she conceded. "But on those nice fancy ones it might be."

"Mm." Andrew made the same noise his daughter had, only an octave lower.

Kerry chuckled as the plane swung out and headed for the top of the runway. She folded her hands on her stomach as Jaele took her seat, and they felt the increase in power as the jet turned onto the runway.

It paused, then with a solid surge of power headed off, and after a far shorter time than a larger jet, it bounded up into the air and arched up into the sky.

"Ah." Ceci fished into her coat pocket. "You get to see the papers, Kerry?"

"Oh no." Kerry winced. "Let me guess, I got a picture in one."

Dar chuckled. "One?"

"What are you laughing at, kid?" Ceci tossed the folded newsprint over. "Just be glad *USA Today* wasn't there."

"HEY, CHEEBLES!" Kerry sat down on the love seat to properly appreciate the greeting of their pet Labrador. "You ready to go down to the cabin with us?"

"Growf!"

"Car or boat?" Dar dropped down next to her, then thumped against the back of the couch as Chino leaped up onto her lap. "Oh...hey! Chino!" She got her arms around the big dog, who proceeded to lick her face with earnest thoroughness. "Hey!"

Kerry chuckled. "I just imagined my sister getting slobbered on like that. She's going to have a cow."

Dar got Chino turned around and watched as the dog regarded them with a look of doggy delight. "Boat? We can break out the three mils and dive a few reefs on the way down?"

"Sure." Kerry played with the end of Chino's otter tail. "Let's stop at Pennekamp on the way down. That's a nice shallow dive."

"Sounds like a plan," Dar said. "We'll leave early. Let me go check the marine forecast." She deposited Chino on the couch and stood up, angling around the couch and heading into her office.

It felt good to be home. Kerry smiled as Chino curled up on the leather surface and rested her head on her thigh. She stroked the animal's soft, silky ears and watched the tiny eyebrows over her gentle brown eyes twitch. "Did you miss us, Cheebles?" she asked. "Did I tell you my sister's getting one of your baby sisters?"

Chino peered up at her. "Growf."

"We're going to have to have her come down here so you can visit with her. Although, y'know, it would be pretty hilarious to have you visit there, and see the two of you turn that house upside down."

Chino wagged her tail.

Kerry chuckled, flexing her bare toes in the throw rug surface as she leaned back, very glad to have the quiet peace of their home around her. She could still smell the faint scent of new paint, the walls now a soft misty blue color, and just past the sliding glass doors she saw the colorful all weather hammock they'd added to the swing chair already installed.

"Hm." She got up and went to the door, sliding it open and taking a breath of the cool, salt tinged air. Seagulls were coasting over the surf and she sat down on the hammock, then swung herself into it, watching Chino go over to the wall and stand up to look over it.

With a contented sigh, she extended her legs and crossed them at the ankles, then folded her hands over her stomach and studied the vivid blue, cloudless sky.

So different from the cloudy, snowy skies of Michigan. She heard the gentle rush of the waves against the rocks that lined the edge of the island and caught a blurp of music carried on the wind from nearby South Beach.

Damn it was good to be home.

The door slid open behind her and she heard the rasp of bare feet against the tile. "Weather good?"

"Be a little choppy, but yeah." Dar went to the railing and looked over, putting her arm around Chino as the dog stood up again to see what she was looking at. "Picked up my voice mail. We're going to have an unexpected visitor tonight."

"Yeah?"

"Alastair." Dar turned and leaned against the low wall. "Just said he wants to have dinner with us, but I get the feeling something's behind it."

"Oh boy."

Dar half shrugged, a mildly bemused look on her face. "Guess we'll find out," she said. "He'll be here around six. You want to make noodles for him or take him somewhere?"

Kerry put her hands behind her head and pondered the question. "I don't feel like cooking but I also don't feel like getting dressed up. Not after that wedding. Want to just go to the beach club? Or...no, we had him over to the Italian place that last time."

"Let's have something from the main place delivered here," Dar said. "Good compromise?"

Kerry smiled at her.

"Thought so." Dar yawned. "I'll go make some coffee."

"I'll go check the menu online." Kerry rolled up out of the hammock and joined her at the door. "C'mon, Chino. We'll get you a little steak too."

"Growf!"

Chapter Three

KERRY POURED ALASTAIR a glass of wine, handling the bottle with casual expertise as she handed the glass over to him. "So what's the board's problem, Alastair?"

Alastair McLean, their stocky, gray haired boss, the CEO of ILS, swirled the glass and took a sip before he answered. "Well, now we come down to it," he said. "Glad we left it 'til after that nice meal to talk about, ladies." He rested his elbow on the table and regarded the two of them.

"Uh oh." Dar leaned back and folded her hands over her stomach. "That sounds like trouble."

"Well." Alastair waggled his free hand. "It's like this. Y'know we've been on a talent search the past few months looking for replacements."

"For us." Kerry seated herself and put her napkin back on her lap.

Alastair gave her a wry grin. "Let's put the cards down. I can be replaced. You can be replaced." He looked over at Dar. "You, on the other hand, are a big problem."

Dar blinked mildly at him. "I've been a big problem since birth if you ask my mother," she said. "C'mon, Alastair. Don't tell me they can't find another CIO. Give me a break."

"Board's been interviewing potential candidates since fall," Alastair said. "Not that there's a lack of people out there, but frankly, Dar, you're a tough act to follow."

Dar rolled her eyes. "Oh please."

"No, please." Alastair drummed his fingers on the wooden table surface. "The last six all told the board the same thing. It would be career suicide to have to follow you in that position. They don't want it, not at any price."

Kerry chuckled softly under her breath. "I only had to fill in for her for what...one day? I totally believe that."

"So what are they going to do?" Dar lifted a hand, a puzzled expression on her face. "Alastair, I'm not an indentured servant. I am allowed to leave, right?"

Alastair sighed. "The problem is, the logical person to move into that position is someone in your direct chain."

Kerry cleared her throat.

"Exactly." He tilted his head in her direction. "So my moment of turning a blind eye to your relationship is now biting us very hard in the ass."

"The board knew," Dar said. "We've made no attempt to hide our lives the last few years. Anyone with a brain would have figured if I left, Kerry would too." She frowned. "What the hell would you have done if something had happened to us? We've had a few close shaves."

Alastair agreed. "That's why they dedicated a jet to you, Dar." His voice went serious. "You are, like it or not, an extremely valuable corporate asset." He took another sip of wine. "Of course you're not an indentured servant. None of us are, but we've put ourselves into a sticky situation that I'm not sure I know how to get us out of."

Kerry watched Dar's face, as the words sunk in. She had, privately, been wondering if they could find someone, or someones, to replace them, since she was more aware than most of just how integral they were in the operations of the company.

So to hear Alastair say what he was saying didn't surprise her nearly as much as it seemed to surprise her other half. Dar had a weird, somewhat self blinded view of herself sometimes, and this was one of the times it showed. "So, the problem isn't that you can't get a replacement, the problem is, any replacement you want doesn't want the job, and people who want the job, you don't want."

Alastair nodded.

"Well, crap." Dar lifted her hands and let them fall, an exasperated expression on her face.

Kerry got up and went over to her, putting her hands on her shoulders and squeezing. "Honey, I've always told you that you're one of a kind." She gave her a kiss on the top of her head. "Let me get the ice cream." She went into the kitchen and got a small tray out, removing the ice cream sundaes the restaurant had sent over that she'd stored in the freezer.

Chino followed her in, and sat down next to her, tail sweeping the floor with anticipation.

"Oh, you think you get ice cream too, madame?"

"Growf."

"SO, WHAT ARE we going to do?" Dar asked. "Alastair, not being able to hire a replacement...what the hell?"

Alastair smiled. "You surprised?"

"I am," Dar said. "It's just a CIO position. There are at least 499 other companies in the Fortune 500 and I'm willing to bet most of them have someone like me."

"Do you really believe that?"

"Yes," Dar answered honestly. "I'm not unique. What I do isn't unique. It's just infrastructure operations. Are you telling me the donks they interviewed were so scared of stuff I've done they don't have the balls to come in and better me?"

"Yes," he said. "That's exactly what I'm saying."

"Alastair."

"Dar, it's just bad timing," he said. "If we hadn't been so visible during the attacks, hadn't been on TV every other day, and then the follow ups, and those interviews you did for CNN. The spotlight's pretty bright on us, and now, the government's calling, asking for more."

"I don't want to do anything for that government," Dar answered, flatly. "And you shouldn't either."

Alastair lifted his hand and let it fall. "I've got a pretty thick skin. I know where they were coming from trying to nail me, and while I don't like it, Dar, I do understand it."

"I don't like it, and I don't want to understand it," she responded. "I've had enough. I want to spend some time just living my life. The board's going to have to get over itself and just hire someone who can keep the pie plates spinning."

"And they will, Dar." Alastair held up a pacifying hand. "No one's saying you can't leave if you want to. What I'm saying is, it might take a little longer than we planned."

Dar made a low growling sound deep in her throat.

"C'mon. You gave the company a good part of your life. What's a month or so more?" Alastair said. "Besides, if you cooperate with the board, they'll hand you everything you want. You can even get out of the exclusion clause if you want to. If you put them in a corner."

"If we put them in a corner, what?" Kerry came out with the tray and deposited the sundaes in front of them. "What would they do, Alastair? Take away Dar's stock and pension or something?"

"They might," Alastair answered, with quiet honesty. "But the thing I don't want is for them take advantage of the two of you and decide to get ratty. You've served the company with a lot of honor, Dar. I want you to go out that way."

Dar eyed him over the sundae. "Well." She picked up her spoon and glanced at Kerry. "We'll work something out. I don't want to get them all in an uproar, now anyway."

Kerry looked back at her. "Now?"

"The other voice mail was that adviser of the President," Dar said, selecting her cherry and biting into it. "He wants to talk."

"Oh." Alastair frowned.

"Yeah."

KERRY TOOK OFF her sunglasses and tucked them into her jacket pocket as she passed through the front doors to ILS's commercial headquarters. It was still very early, and the office was very quiet, only the security guards and a few junior secretaries around to see her enter.

"Good morning, Ms. Stuart," the guard greeted her quietly. "Did you have a good holiday?"

"I did." Kerry dutifully swiped her badge into the reader. "Did you, John?"

"We went to Disney World," he said. "Me and Sarah and the kids. It was nice."

Disney World. Dar had promised her a holiday visit there. Kerry tucked that thought away for later and made her way across the lobby to the elevators, hopping inside one to find Mariana, their VP of Human Resources, already inside. "Hey, Mari."

"Good morning," Mariana cordially replied. "You look suntanned. Down by the cabin?"

"All week," Kerry said. "Dar's about ten minutes behind me. She's dropping her truck off for service." She watched the floors pass. "How'd your holiday go?"

"Nice," Mari said. "I was glad we decided not to do a company party this year. We ended up on a catamaran in the Bahamas."

"Nice," Kerry said. "Yeah, I was glad too, except that while I was at my sister's wedding, I was kinda wishing I wasn't." She smiled briefly. "Would have rather been here having those paella canapés."

Mari chuckled, as the elevator stopped and the doors opened. "Yeah, I forgot you were going to be up there with your family." She walked alongside Kerry as they entered the big, gray carpeted and maroon walled hallway. "Family's tough. I know mine's always leery of Louis. They think atheists are equal to Satanists."

"How do you think my family felt about me and Dar showing up with Dar's Southern Baptist dad and pagan mom?" Kerry asked. "At least now, it gives them a bigger heartburn than they give me."

Mari chuckled again.

"Not to mention my sister decided to have her whole wedding party wear strapless gowns," Kerry continued. "Well, the women anyway. So I'm pretty sure my chest was front page in the local paper the whole next week."

Mari laughed louder.

Kerry sighed. "Jesus. It actually feels good to get back here and just have some usual IT stuff to deal with." She paused to turn into her office. "Later, Mari."

"Later."

The other woman walked on, and Kerry continued into her outer antechamber, where she was surprised to find her assistant already there working away. "Hey, Mayte."

Mayte had looked up when the door opened and smiled. "Good morning, Kerry," she said. "And a happy holidays to you. Did you have a good time off?"

"I did. How about you? Nice to have the extra time, huh?" Kerry said. "I think it was a good idea to give everyone last week off."

"Oh yes." Mayte stood up. "May I get you some cafecita? Mama and Papa had a big party at the house, and all of our family came over for it. It was very nice, and I got to see some of my cousins for the first time in a while."

"I'd love some." Kerry continued on to her office. "And I'm glad to see someone enjoys their family." She winked at Mayte, then opened her door and went inside.

It was quiet, as her office usually was. She crossed over and put her laptop case down, circling her desk and going to the big floor to ceiling windows at the rear. They looked out over the ocean and she put her hands against the glass, watching a speedboat turn out of the cut and roar into life.

With a smile, she turned and sat down in her chair, reaching down to start up her desktop and then leaning back to enjoy the peace and quiet that would last just long enough for the machine to boot up and present her email to her.

The week at the cabin was fun. They'd gone to a little island party their neighbors had thrown, and spent a lot of time in the sea, even though the waters were colder than she really liked. Dar had set herself the challenge of finding a meal for them a day, and she'd gotten to taste all sorts of things Dar dredged back out of the ocean for her.

Yum.

The machine finished coming up and Kerry logged in, folding her hands and waiting for her desktop to assemble itself. For better or worse, the holidays were quiet in the disaster arena, and now she sat there, thinking about what short term goals she had to put in place.

Short term, because they were leaving.

Kerry considered that, finding the thought of them actually walking out of the building and not coming back still surreal to her, and even more so to the staff they managed.

Her phone buzzed. She glanced up and hit the button. "Yes?"

"Kerry, Mark is here to see you."

"Send him in, by all means." Kerry watched her screen fill with emails, sparing a glance toward the door as it opened and admitted their MIS manager, Mark Polenti. "Hey Mark."

"Hey, *poquito* boss." He dropped into one of her visitors chairs. "Big D in?"

"Probably by now. She was dropping her ride off to be serviced," Kerry responded. "How was your break?"

"Sweet. Rode the bike down to Key West." Mark grinned. "Nice to have the extra time off. You guys down by Largo?"

Kerry nodded. "Yeah, after I got back from my sister's wedding." She rested her elbows on her desk. "So what's going on? Anything besides my entire inbox I have to worry about?"

Mark shrugged. "Been quiet. I think everyone's waiting for the other shoe to fall."

"What does that mean?"

"See who they're gonna hire to try and take yours and big D's place," he said. "No one's looking forward to it."

Kerry sighed, lacing her fingers together. "I'm sure there are people in this company looking forward to it, Mark. Dar has enemies here. I met most of them, remember?"

He shook his head. "Not really. Not anymore. Big diff between when you came here and now, Kerry. You know it."

She did.

"Dar was always tough. She still is," he said. "But one thing you could take to the bank was, you could trust her."

Kerry thought about that in silence for a moment. "You know, you're right about that," she said. "I felt that, even from the start with her. If she said something, she meant it." She looked at Mark. "I get it," she said. "But she's entitled to have a little life with her life, you know?"

Mark nodded. "I know. I feel great for her and for you. Just not for me, or the rest of us." He glanced around. "So anyway, everything's sort of in a holding pattern. No one wants to start anything new, cause we don't know what the deal is going to be. You know?"

"I know," Kerry said. "Just between you and me, it might not be as soon as we planned. They're having a problem replacing her."

Mark started chuckling softly. "I bet they are."

"Well, I mean how'd you like to follow that act?" Kerry smiled wryly. "I sure as hell am glad I'm not going to try it."

"Oh, yeah," Mark said. "Hey, who knows? Maybe they'll take a year to find someone." He perked up visibly. "Anyway, the one thing cooking is the new network center coming online downtown. I got five guys over there running cabling and it should be ready to go in about a week."

"Oh. Good." Kerry had almost forgotten the new center, its need established way back when she and Dar had gone to North Carolina, and its commissioning overshadowed by recent events. "It'll be good to be able to double home services into that thing. Dar was looking for someplace to land those international circuits from South America."

Mark nodded. "Okay got that on the agenda. See ya at the ops meeting?"

"See ya." Kerry watched him get up and walk out, going over his words in her head as she delayed having to deal with her mail. A moment later, she put even that on hold as she heard footsteps approaching down the back hallway to her office and looked over as the inner door opened and Dar poked her head in. "Hey."

"Hey." Dar entered and parked her tall frame on the edge of Kerry's desk. "Car won't be ready for a few days. They have to replace some gaskets."

Kerry leaned on her chair arm. "Isn't it time we went and picked you out a new car?" she asked. "The last time my car had to have major work that's what you made me do."

Dar opened her mouth to protest, then paused with a thoughtful expression. "Hm." She wrinkled her nose. "Maybe that's an idea. Let me think about it." She cocked her head. "Speaking of thinking about it, I told the government if they want to talk to me they have to come here."

"Ah." Kerry, who had more exposure to the government, winced. "Y'know, hon."

Dar shrugged. "They want me. I don't want them," she said, with a truculent note in her voice. "Screw it, Kerry. I don't owe them anything. I delivered above and beyond a few months ago. Maybe if they think I'm going to be an asshole to deal with they'll go elsewhere."

"That didn't stop them the first time," Kerry said. "Is it really smart to get someone that high up in the government mad at you?" She put a hand on Dar's thigh. "I don't want that kind of trouble."

Dar sighed. "Too late." She managed a wry grin. "His office is going to call me back." She glanced out the windows. "Ah, who knows? Maybe it's a short little something that'll keep me occupied until they find someone to replace me."

"Dar." Kerry patted her leg to get her attention. "They'll never do that." She watched the pale blue eyes focus on her, and a small smile appear. "The best they're going to be able to do is find someone who's got guts, who'll get in there and weather the tornadoes until they can start putting their own ideas in."

"You could do that," Dar said

"I don't want to do that," Kerry replied in a mild tone.

Dar smiled again.

"That thing we did? In New York? That did something to me." Kerry leaned back in her chair. "I don't want to spend any more time just clearing the next problem off my desk."

"Me either." Dar reached over and tweaked her nose. "So let me get back to my handover plan, and see what the government says about my badass self." She pushed off the desk and sauntered back to the hallway. "See ya for lunch."

"Speaking of cleaning problems." Kerry turned her attention, finally, to her inbox as she heard Mayte come back with the coffee. "Let's get the party started."

DAR TWIRLED A pen in her fingers as she listened to the voice coming from the phone. "Listen, Gerry, that sounds like ten times the scope you talked to me about a few months ago."

"War'll do that to ya," Gerald Easton replied. "Got them throwing money at me right, left, and up my keister. Don't want to hear about resources, just get it done. So here I am on the phone with you, finding out how we're going to get it done."

Dar rubbed her temples. "Gerry—"

"Dar, I know what you're going to say. This all is not your cup of tea. I know it. But they know, and I know, and you know, that you can get this done."

"Yeah, yeah." Dar took a breath, and released it. "Okay," she finally said. "Let me see what I can work up on it and I'll get back to you."

"Fantastic," General Easton said. "My people want to have a meeting over it. Can we get you up here? Got some folks who want to wring your hand anyhow."

Dar recalled Kerry's words. "Not a bad idea, Gerry." She resigned herself to the trip. "I've got to go talk to some brass up there. Might as well knock both of you out on one trip."

"Brass?"

"Same guy who wanted to talk to me last time."

"Ah." The general grunted. "That one."

"Mm."

"Well, looking forward to hearing from you then, Dar," he said. "Just let my gal here know when you're on the way."

"Sure. Talk to you later." Dar hung up the line and leaned back in her chair, folding her arms over her chest and studying the phone somberly.

This seemed like trouble to her. Gerry's project was an overhaul of the government's intelligence systems, and while Dar knew that individually all that was well within their scope, navigating the political nightmare that would ensue was not.

She'd had enough of that on one small base with one small system.

The end goal was a logical one—so that all the systems the various agencies used could talk together and share intelligence and data, and yet she suspected none of the agencies would go easily into this new world of collective knowledge.

So logic and egos would clash. Dar didn't really want to have to deal with that, but she was aware of the fact that despite her steadfast desire to separate herself from all this, it wasn't going to happen fast enough for her to avoid getting involved.

Damn it.

And then there was whatever the president's advisor wanted. That might prove to be tougher and more serious. Dar turned to her desktop as her mail dinged and studied the screen.

Clients. Alastair. Mari. She bypassed them all and clicked on the one from Stuart, Kerry

        Hey.
        So I checked online about changing my name.

"Huh?" Dar stared at the screen in puzzlement, then it came to her. "Oh."

        It's a weird mixture of civil legal stuff and
        stuff that comes from when everyone lived in a tiny
        town and all went to the same post office. You have

```
to post the paperwork on a bulletin board for a
month. But anyway, I'm going to stop during lunch
and pick the forms up. I'll bring you back some
Thai.
```

Dar regarded the mail in bemusement

```
You were serious.
```

She rested her weight on her elbows and thought about it.

```
I'm jazzed. I think the hardest part of it will
be getting my Social Security card changed.
```

Dar wondered what it would feel like to think about family the way Kerry did, and make the change she was contemplating making.

What would she have done if she hadn't been gay, and had gotten married and been faced with changing her name. Would she have? Dar regarded the pen in her fingers as she thought hard about that. "Damned if I know if I'd have done that," she finally said. "I think I'm proud of that name."

"What?"

Dar turned to find Kerry crossing the carpeted floor. "Hey, thought you were going to the post office."

"I am. But Mark said something earlier and I wanted to talk to you about it."

Dar leaned back in her chair. "All ears."

"All legs, actually." Kerry tickled her knee. "Dar, what does this whole hiring thing do for our time line? Mark was saying people are just sort of holding their breaths and waiting to see what happens. How long can we operate like that?"

"We can't," Dar said. "What would you say if I said I think I want to retract my resignation for now?"

Kerry blinked, caught by surprise. "What?" she paused, watching Dar's face. "Are you serious?"

Dar nodded. "I was just thinking about it. We gave them too much warning. There's no way we'll get out of here in one piece if we keep the date."

Kerry walked slowly around the front of Dar's desk and sat down in the seat across from her. "Wow. I don't know what to say to that, Dar. I thought we had this worked out and decided."

"I know." Dar leaned forward and put her head down on her crossed wrists.

"Do I get a say in this?"

Dar felt like she should be mad at the question, and she could see Kerry's temper prickling. "That's why I asked you what you'd say. It was something I was just thinking about. Gerry just called. They want to quadruple the scope of that systems refresh."

"And?"

"And, if I'm fully involved in that government clusterfuck, chances are I can't get sucked into whatever the President has in mind."

Kerry watched her quietly. "Can't you say no to both of them?"

"I could," Dar said. "But my gut instinct is, if I walk out now, everyone we know here is going to pay the price. Do I want that on my conscience? I should have just handed in my creds in NY."

"Mm."

"I'm not going to say anything," Dar said. "You chew it over and see what you think." She smiled. "While you're on your way to go change your name to mine." Her eyes twinkled a little. "Ker, I want to do what's best for us. That means long term as well as short term."

Kerry sighed. "I wanted to go travel with you. It really makes me feel crappy to know that's not going to happen, Dar. I'm tired of doing this. I don't want to spend more time listening to people yell at me, or want me to pull cats out of my butt for them."

Dar got up and circled her desk, holding out her hands to Kerry and pulling her upright when she grasped them. "'Nuff said." She leaned over and kissed Kerry on the lips. "Then we go."

All the roiling tension that had built up in the last few minutes evaporated. Kerry leaned against her and rested her head against Dar's collarbone. "Now that I've had my mini tantrum and you've indulged my brattiness, let me mull it over," she said. "Talking to Mark was making me think about it too. There's a lot of people here who are invested in the leadership we give them."

Unseen, Dar smiled.

"Especially Mayte and Maria," Kerry said quietly. "There's a lot of trust there."

"A lot of your hard work salvaging my reputation there," Dar said, then she looked down as Kerry pulled back and looked up at her. "Damn good job."

Kerry stretched up and gave her a kiss, then patted her on the side. "Be back in a little while." She headed for the door, a faint smile on her face as she shook her head.

Dar sat on the edge of her desk and folded her arms. Then she got up and went back to her chair, whistling softly under her breath.

KERRY STOOD PATIENTLY in line, her sunglasses perched firmly on her nose as she ignored the din around her in the county courthouse. There were a lot of people inside, doing a lot of things she really had no interest in or knowledge of. The line she was in at the moment promised to end up with her obtaining the forms she needed, and the notary public she would need to sign off on the papers was available as well.

It felt a little strange to be here. Kerry folded her arms over her chest, keeping her eyes mostly on the ground and not meeting anyone's gaze.

"Thanks for nothin!" The man in front of her slammed his hand against the window and left, leaving the clerk behind it shaking her head.

She paused a moment, then glanced at Kerry. "Next."

Kerry walked up to the window. "Could I please have the forms I need to change my name?"

The clerk gave her a bored look, then got up and went to a file cabinet, opening a drawer and shuffling through some folders. She withdrew a set of forms and came back, sliding them under the bulletproof glass window into Kerry's hands. "There ya go."

"Thanks." Kerry took her papers and went to a nearby stand up desk, removing a pen from her pocket and studying the questions. "Okay, well, let's get this over with." She started filling it out, resting her arm on the table and scribbling through the questions.

Some she got. "Full current legal name." She printed hers in neatly spaced letters. "Second question. What is my complete present name. What?" She peered at it. "Isn't that the same thing?" With a shake of her head she obediently filled it in. Then — "I request that my name be changed to?"

Kerry paused, and studied the line. She took a breath and flexed her fingers, then filled the line in. "Kerrison Roberts."

It was a very strange feeling, a mixture of relief and apprehension, a mental awareness of a vivid crossroad visible only to her.

Did Dar get why she was doing this? She had seemed okay with it, pleased, in fact, but how could Dar really understand when she herself had never faced the question?

Ah well. Kerry took another breath and carried on filling out the rest of the form, all four pages of it, racing through the rest of it not pausing to wonder why they needed to know what college she went to, or what her profession was.

When she finished, she took it over to the notary desk, and paid the fee to have it stamped, signing it in front of a sleepy looking man with a bad toupée and a tattoo of a smiley face on the back of his hand.

He didn't actually look at the papers. He just signed his name and applied his stamp, and pushed the papers back at her without even looking up.

"Thanks," Kerry said, taking her forms and going back to stand in line again. She checked her watch, then opened her palm pilot and tapped in a quick note. After about fifteen minutes she was at the front of the line again, and stepped forward to hand the woman her forms.

The clerk sniffed and shuffled through them, reading quickly through it. "Two hundred and five dollars please." She looked up at Kerry expectantly. "Cash or check."

Kerry removed her checkbook from the inside pocket of her jacket and filled out a check, glancing at the chipped plastic sign to determine who to make it out to. She signed it, then removed it from the book and handed it over. "So I have to post this somewhere now?"

The clerk looked at her like she was crazy. "Say what?" she asked. "No. You gotta get a court date. You go over there, and fill out that form and put it in the box. They'll call you." She stapled the check to Kerry's form, put it into a plastic folder, and handed her a slip of paper. "Your case number. Next?"

A little startled, Kerry backed off from the window and got out of the way as a man and woman pushed into her place. She hesitated, then went to the form on the wall, examining it. "Request a hearing?" She pulled a copy down and filled it out, putting the case number on it before she dropped it into the slot.

Then she looked around, the din suddenly harsh and metallic, irritating her senses. She put her pen away and went for the door, fastening her jacket as she cleared the doors to the courthouse and emerged into the bright, cool, sunny weather outside.

Her cell phone rang. She pulled it out and stepped to one side to avoid the crowd on the stairs. "Kerry Stuart," she answered, covering her free ear.

"Hey," Dar's voice echoed softly. "Where are you?"

"Just leaving the courthouse." Kerry glanced around. "Why?"

"Meet you for lunch? My noon conference call just got canceled," Dar said. "Big storm over in Europe, everyone's going home."

"Sure," Kerry said. "Thai place, ten minutes."

"See ya."

Kerry hung up the phone and leaned against the stone wall, collecting her wits and composure. The process hadn't gone at all how she'd expected it to, and now she was really glad that Dar was coming out to join her for lunch. She wanted to talk. About the court, and about Dar's sudden revelation.

All of a sudden the world seemed to be moving too fast.

"SO IT'S DONE?" Dar looked almost comically astonished. She slid into the back booth in their favorite little lunch place and rested her hands on the table. "Holy crap."

"Yeah I..." Kerry glanced at the waitress. "Usual for me."

"Me too." Dar leaned forward as the waitress left. "It was that fast?"

Kerry took a breath and released it. "It's not all the way over. They have to call me for a hearing, but...I mean, I thought I had to post it up in public and all that but I guess not anymore. Serves me right for trusting the Internet." She looked across the table as Dar removed her sunglasses, and found herself captivated by her pale eyes. "So I guess now I wait to hear from them, then they sign it and it's done."

Dar grinned. "I sent an email to my parents telling them. My mom said my dad wants to formally adopt you."

Kerry blinked. "Can he do that?"

Dar shrugged. "We could check the Internet. But you know he really loves you. They both do."

Kerry felt unexpected tears sting her eyes.

"And of course, I do," Dar added gently. "You look freaked out."

"I am."

The waitress came back and delivered two ice teas and two bowls of soup. She put them down and retreated in silence.

"Why?"

Kerry took a sip of her tea. "You know, I'm not really sure. Could be because I'm due for my period tomorrow."

"Ah." Dar reached over and chafed her hand. "We got supplies?"

The talk of something so prosaic and mundane snapped Kerry right out of her funk. She chuckled softly and felt her body relax. "Yeah, I'm good." She released Dar's hand and picked up her soup spoon. "Dar, would that make me your sister? Because that would be really, really weird."

Dar started laughing, almost spilling her tea. "I think he just wanted to express the intent, hon." She picked up her soup bowl, drinking directly from it. "He already considers you one of his kids."

Kerry watched her fondly. "So." She dipped her spoon into her soup and consumed it in a more conventional manner. "So what made you decide to pull back your resignation? Was it something someone said, or..."

Dar paused to think about it, setting her bowl down. "Yeah," she said. "Something Alastair said stuck in my monkey brain. I was thinking about it while we were down at the cabin, about how walking out right now just didn't feel good to me."

"Mm."

"Or it could just be my ego doesn't want to let go of this position," Dar said, in a wry tone. "Sometimes I like being me."

Kerry smiled. "I think you do enjoy it. I enjoy you being you. Why shouldn't you have fun with it too?" She finished her soup and pushed the bowl aside. "But, Dar, you'll be successful at whatever you end up doing. Don't you want to be your own boss?"

The waitress came back with their lunch and set it down. Dar had her hands folded on the table, and she waited for the woman to leave again. "Do I?" She applied herself to mixing her curry with its attendant rice. "Yeah, I do. I'd like to be rid of that damn board, and not have to answer to anyone."

Kerry felt a sense of relief. "That's what I thought. I know I would."

"It's just hard for me to turn my back on the responsibility." Dar rested her head on one hand. "And... will I like being a consultant? Just suggesting things without having the ability to make those things happen?"

Oh. Kerry paused in her motion, as the words penetrated. "I didn't really think about that."

"Mm." Dar sighed. "Occurred to me when Alastair was at our place for dinner. He's sort of in that place, you know? He has to take crap from everyone, but he depends on people like me to make things happen in the right way."

"Well. We don't have to be consultants. We can make our own super high speed network and sell it to people," Kerry said. "You know you're really good at that."

Dar tapped her fork against her lips. "You mean, build out infrastructure in direct competition with my own design here? That'd take a lot of money to bootstrap."

Kerry watched the little twitches shift on Dar's face. "It would," she agreed. "But we could start just in Florida, and build out as we get customers. Sort of like what you did, with provisioning only where we had clients."

"Hm." Dar's eyebrows arched up. "We had a hell of a time finding an alternate datacenter, maybe we can offer that service too. I know we could find someplace on the west side of Dade or Broward to put one in." She reached over and tweaked Kerry's nose. "I like that idea, partner."

Kerry munched her peanut chicken in contented silence. It was hard for her to really put her finger on why she was so intent on a life change, but she knew she was, and she really wanted Dar to buy into that. It wasn't that she didn't appreciate the sentiments about responsibility, and their staff trusting and needing them. She did. She understood at a gut level the ties that held Dar in place, and why it was hard to break them.

But she was determined to. "You know what I think it is, Dar?"

"Bet I'm about to." Dar grinned at her.

"You were right. We waited too long. We should have done it in October. Wrapped up everything while everyone was still in a tailspin and gotten out. We gave them a chance to suck us back in." She glanced up to see Dar nodding at her. "So we've got to turn that around."

Dar's pale eyes twinkled a little. "You really want out."

"I do."

"I do too. I just feel bad about it. I've been there a long time, and even though I fought with a lot of those people like cats and dogs it's still..." She paused. "I don't know."

"They were your family when you didn't have one," Kerry said, quietly.

Dar stopped eating and lowered her fork, gazing at Kerry in silence for a long moment.

"Weren't they?" Kerry asked, into all that quiet. "I mean, not Jose or Eleanor, but Maria, and Mark, and Duks and Mari?" She stopped eating as well, and waited. Wincing a little as she reviewed her words and wondered if she'd insulted Dar without meaning to.

"As much as I'd let them, yeah," Dar finally said. "Boy that hit a spot."

"Sorry." Kerry reached over and touched her arm. "I didn't mean to bum you out, sweetheart. Maybe I should have just brought you back something."

Dar smiled, after a brief pause. "No, you didn't. I was just thinking about the year before you came into my life. I remember going to the office over Christmas for some stupid broken thing and walking in and finding a bunch of little presents on my desk."

"Mm?"

"Just little stuff. Candies and whatever," Dar said. "With no name on them. Just a random kindness and when you said that I remembered it. I still don't know who put them there."

"Could have been the cleaning staff." Kerry felt the tension in her guts relax. "Could have been ops."

"Could have."

"Could have been the security guards."

"That's true too, so maybe you've got a point," Dar said. "I've been there a lot longer than you have."

"Yeah." Kerry sighed. "I'm just being a jerk today. Maybe I should go home."

"Let's both go home," Dar suggested readily. "Screw it. You got anything on your schedule for this afternoon?"

"Nope." Kerry felt a grin forming again. "Too much beginning of the year to be stuffed with crap yet."

Dar took out her phone and dialed. "Maria? It's Dar. Listen, Kerry's not feeling well. I'm going to take her home. Just clear my outbox and I'll pick up again tomorrow." She smiled. "I will, thanks. I know she'll appreciate the thought. Thanks, Maria."

She closed the phone and picked up her fork. "I'm going to see if I can get her an early retirement package."

"I'm going to see if Mayte wants to watch our place while we're traveling and start the process of setting up our new company," Kerry said. "Do you mind if I hire her as our first employee?"

"Nope." Dar smoothly handed her credit card to the waitress. "Tell you what. Let's go out to South Beach for dinner. Have some stone crabs."

"Walk out on the beach?" Kerry leaned back and spread her arms out on the seat back. "How about we go out to Crandon and relive our first kiss?"

Dar's grin morphed from just amused to criminally adolescent. "Let's do that."

Kerry grinned back. "At this rate, I could get to like Mondays."

"WE NEED TO stop by this place on the beach on the way." Dar relaxed in Kerry's passenger seat, extending her long legs out. "They've got this new phone thing they want me to look at."

Kerry had unzipped her leather jacket, and paused to let traffic go by as she waited to turn onto the causeway. "What kind of phone thing?"

"Company called Handspring." Dar stretched her body out contentedly. "Some new phone and mail gizmo. I said I'd give it a try. Their distributor's got a small place down on Washington."

"Can I get one too?" Kerry turned right and proceeded down the road. "You get all the cool toys."

Dar chuckled. "Absolutely." She folded her hands over her sweatshirt covered stomach. "Nice to use the gym while everyone else is at work."

"It was." Kerry felt a little sore, her legs had that slightly heavy feeling of hard use and she suspected her night might end in the hot tub. "I think I overdid the presses a little though...where on Washington?"

"Second Ave." Dar flexed her hands and then laid them down on her denim-covered knees. She had leather boots on, and her sweatshirt had a hood on it, and she was looking out the window with a contented expression.

Kerry's cell phone rang, and before she could get it out of her pocket, Dar had. "Thanks, hon."

Dar glanced at the caller ID. "Ops." She opened the phone. "Yes?"

Dead silence. Then a male voice. "Uh...ah, sorry...ah, is that Ms. Roberts?"

"Yes," Dar said. "You got it in one try. Congratulations."

"Um...sorry, ma'am, I meant to call Ms. Stuart. I must have dialed the wrong number...uh, let me try again."

"Relax." Dar watched the palm trees flash by. "You got the right number, I just happen to be answering her phone because she's driving and I love her too much to have her risk her life answering a phone."

Kerry's nostrils flared. "Dar, for cripes sake!"

"Uh." The ops tech stuttered.

"So what is it you need?" Dar continued without missing a beat. "I assume you called her for a reason?"

"Ah, yes, ma'am," he recovered bravely. "Sorry about the call but we're seeing some latency in the network here and we've gotten some calls from people still working."

Dar considered the phone. The urge to stop, pull out her laptop, and find the issue tickled her. Then she recalled that she hadn't put the laptop in the car and stifled a smile. "Okay," she said. "Let's have a little troubleshooting lesson. If there's latency in the office network there are only a couple things that can cause it. Know what they are?"

There was a period of silence, then the tech cleared his throat. "I asked the guys who called what was slow. They said everything."

"Uh huh."

"But...usually that's not really true so I tried some stuff myself," he said. "It's files, ma'am, and my mail store. I checked the DNS with Nslookup, and it's answering snappy, so I know it's not that."

"Good man," Dar said. "So what does that mean?"

"Well, usually that would be the file servers, ma'am, but we asked the MIS guys to check and they said they didn't see a problem."

"Good." Dar nodded approvingly. "Who did you talk to in the MIS team?"

"Johan."

"Call Johan, and tell him I said there's a problem with the file servers, and he'd better find it."

Kerry turned down Alton Road and glanced at the street signs looking for 2nd Ave. "You're such a maestro."

The ops tech sounded much happier. "Thank you, ma'am, I'll do that. Is it okay if I send Ms. Stuart a text when it's fixed?"

"That's fine," Dar said. "Goodnight." She closed the phone and dropped it back in Kerry's pocket. "You know what else occurred to me?"

"That you do most of the thinking for a company of two hundred and fifty thousand employees?"

Dar chuckled. "Something like that. It's easier to call someone than think for yourself, but we don't get that option."

Kerry remembered having to face that when Dar was in New York and she'd been faced with solving a complex technical issue. "It is easier. I had to teach myself not to just call you and ask." She pulled into a parking lot of a small strip mall and parked. "Not easy."

Dar turned her head and regarded Kerry with a bemused expression. "I should have forced everyone to do that."

Kerry opened her door. "Let's go get your toy, maestro. At least they call me first now." She hopped out of the car and closed the door, zipping up her leather jacket as the wind off the water chilled her skin. It wasn't the cold of Michigan, but she had a short-sleeved shirt on under her coat.

She followed Dar to the sidewalk and then around the side of the building to a small shop in the front of it, with a window full of screens and gadgets, and a radio controlled dog outside patiently barking at all passersby.

The sun was going down, and as they entered the shop its outside lights flickered on, and a gust of air puffed into their faces full of the smell of electrons and plastic. Dar went to the counter and put her hands on it. "I'm looking for Douglas."

The man behind the counter nodded and turned, sticking his head inside a back room. "Doug? Some women here to see ya."

Kerry wandered around the store as Dar waited for the owner, peering into the counters and finding her attention caught by the myriads of cell phones and accessories, and the cameras.

Hm. She was due a new camera. She leaned on the counter and studied the offerings, debating in her head if she wanted to move from film to digital this time.

"Hey, Ms. Roberts," a low, gravelly voice boomed out. "Thanks for coming over. I thought you'd really like this thing here, maybe you want to try it out."

"Ker?"

Kerry left the counter and returned to Dar's side. "Hm?" She inspected the device in Dar's hands. It wasn't unlike her palm pilot, but it had a keyboard, and the screen was color. "Oh. Hey." She took it and touched the keys. "You type with your thumbs?"

"Yeah," Doug said. "Not my thumbs, yeah? That's why I was looking for a lady to try it. I can't type on them tiny keys."

Kerry tried a few. "Hm." She took out the stylus and touched the screen, watching the applications appear. "Cool."

Dar grinned. "She's sold. Got two of them? I don't know if I can type on it with these mitts, but I'll give it a try."

Beaming, Doug disappeared again, popping back out a moment later with another box. "There ya go. These are like, beat units? Won't be commercial for a couple months. They run on Tmo."

"Beta units." Dar took hers. "We'll give them a workout and let you know, Doug."

"Great. Thanks!" He gave them a wave as they made their way back out into the crisp air. "Nice ladies."

His assistant looked up at him, and shook his head. "Give up them phones? You're crazy."

Doug gave him a clout on the back as he went back into the storeroom. "Crazy like a fox, bro. That tall lady likes that thing, we can sell a truckload to her. Big shot in that high tech stuff."

"Yeah?"

"Yeah."

Chapter Four

KERRY WAS GLAD of the cool air, and the cloudless dark night sky that presented a perfect, full moon as they strolled out onto the boardwalk.

Dar paused after a few minutes and leaned on the railing, eying Kerry with a slight grin. "Here we are."

"You remember?" Kerry chuckled, leaning next to her. "I can tell you I was far too slathered with my own hormones to figure out where on this walk we ended up at."

"Mm." Dar looked out over the silver lit sands. "I do remember, because I was figuring out how far it was to that lifeguard station so I'd know how long to run before I could dive into the water and soak my embarrassment if you ended up that kiss with a — yuk!"

"Oh, Dar." Kerry chuckled. "You knew I wasn't going to do that," she said. "I knew we were probably going to end up kissing each other when we left that restaurant."

"Did you?"

Kerry nodded. "Uh huh. At least, I knew I was going to end up kissing you. I wasn't entirely sure what you were going to end up doing."

"Oh, Kerry, please," Dar drawled in response. "You're lucky I didn't start licking that butter sauce off you at that restaurant." She bumped Kerry with her shoulder. "Give me a break."

"You would have scandalized my friends."

"Didn't you want me to?" One of Dar's brows lifted.

Kerry chuckled.

"We've come a long way." Dar straightened up and turned, much as she had that night and gazed at Kerry. "Thanks for deciding to share my life, even though it's been a roller coaster the last few years."

Kerry gently put her hand on Dar's cheek, then leaned closer and kissed her. "Pleasure's been all mine." She took a breath of the cool, salt tinged air and let her hand drop to grasp Dar's. "Can I ask you a question?"

"You found one you haven't yet?" Dar's eyes twinkled gently.

"I'm serious. I thought about it when we were driving out here," Kerry said. "Are you letting me push you into doing something you don't really want to do, Dar?"

Dar looked puzzled.

"Do you really want to quit?"

"Ah." Dar leaned on her elbows, the breeze ruffling her hair. "You know what I think?" She turned her head and regarded Kerry, seeing the lines of tension along her jaw as she clenched it. That made her pause, especially when Kerry's eyes drifted off and didn't meet hers. "Ker?"

"Yeah."

"Hey." Dar moved closer and reached over to give her a tickle on the tip of her nose, waiting until Kerry looked up at her. "Yes," she said. "I think you're forcing me into this. Ah ah ah!" She put her finger on Kerry's lips, reading in her body language an emotional explosion she didn't want to trigger.

Kerry went still, watching her intently.

"It's a good thing," Dar said. "Left to my own devices, I'd stay in the same program until someone pushed my off button." She smiled wryly. "You started changing me the minute we met. I don't regret that, Ker. Honestly." She draped her arm over Kerry's shoulders and bumped her. "Let's walk and talk."

She felt the tension in Kerry's body relax a little, as they strolled along the wooden walkway, empty at this time of night except for themselves. The silence went on for a while, only the rustle of the palm trees and the rush of the surf echoing softly.

"I just feel so adrift," Kerry said, suddenly. "I can't even focus on stuff at work, Dar. It all feels so...I don't know."

"Mm."

"Maybe I need to just step down," Kerry said. "Just go do something else."

They walked along for a little while, as Dar chewed that over. It was hard for her to determine exactly how she felt about it. On one hand, she wanted Kerry to be happy. On the other hand, she didn't want to have to replace her, and have to deal with someone else in her position.

On a third hand, it occurred to her that she'd walked away from work without a thought today and maybe all her arguing with her ego really had no point. "I'd like us to go out together," she finally said. "Can you hang in there for me a little while so we can get things tied up?"

Kerry studied her profile. "Do you really want to leave? Level with me, Dar."

"I do," Dar responded easily. "Or...let me be more specific." She smiled with wry self knowledge. "I want to try something else, do something else, be part of something else," she said. "I just don't walk away from things easily."

"You're loyal."

"Call it that."

"It is that," Kerry said, in a mild tone. "You are a very loyal person. I don't think that's a bad thing, Dar." She paused and regarded the horizon. "I trust you. I don't want to make you unhappy doing something just to make me happy, you know?"

Dar turned and studied her. "I don't know. I'd go through endless amounts of unhappiness in order to make you happy."

Kerry fell silent for a moment. "That's what I'm afraid of."

Dar shrugged lightly and grinned. "I'm not," she said. "It won't make me unhappy to go do something else, or travel with you for a year for that matter, and we both know that. I just have to get over my upbringing and realize I don't run the world and I'm not going to get the satisfaction of saving everyone's ass every ten minutes."

Now it was Kerry's turn to ponder. "You're really self aware sometimes," she remarked.

"Yeah. Thinking about how I think gives me a headache though. I'd rather we started kissing again. Or go down the beach and get some ice cream. Seriously, Ker, I'm fine with it."

Kerry regarded her pensively.

Dar put her arms around her and gave her a hug, lightly scratching her back as she felt Kerry respond and exhale. "Change is a pain in the ass. But we'll muddle through it."

"I know." Kerry finally let it go. "I'll see what I can do about some networking to find some people brave enough to come do what we do. Maybe that tech seminar next week will stir up some interest."

"At's my girl." Dar patted her on the back. "You do that while I fly to Washington. Get them off my back."

They started walking back up the boardwalk to the parking lot.

KERRY CAME BACK into the living room with her hot tea to find Dar sprawled on the couch, hands folded on her stomach as she patiently waited for Chino to return with her toy to throw. "Whatcha thinking?" she said.

"What am I thinking?" Dar tossed the soggy green frog across the condo. "What do you think about Roberts Automation as a name for our new company?"

Caught by surprise, Kerry set her tea down and dropped onto the love seat. "Oh. Wow. Hm." She leaned on the love seat arm. "Yeah. I like that. So you hooked on to that idea?"

Dar nodded. "That took my brain somewhere. Like a dozen things popped into my head about it...what services we can offer, that kind of thing. Hosted services. Why pay for a datacenter, that kind of thing."

Kerry blinked. "You going to keep a running list for a year?" she asked. "Or can you talk the board into not putting a non compete on you?"

"Me?" Dar eyed her. "That clause doesn't say anything about you." Her eyes twinkled. "You can be my front. After all, if they want to split hairs, we're not legally married."

"Ah." Kerry started laughing. "No that's true." She sighed. "I could do the startup work. But you know what, Dar? The non compete is not going to be their problem."

"No?"

"Half the company wanting to come work for us is going to be their problem."

Chino trotted back over and tossed the soggy frog onto Dar's chest. "That's not illegal unless we solicit them." Dar tossed the frog again, this time onto the love seat. Chino obligingly hopped up next to Kerry and burrowed for it. "Get it, girl."

"Chino! Ow!" Kerry grabbed her digging paws. "You have claws."

The dog looked at her in astonishment.

"Here." Kerry tossed the frog onto her laughing partner's chest. "Is that ethical, Dar?"

"Is what ethical? It's a right to work state, Kerry. People have the right to apply and be hired by whatever company they want. So as long as we don't solicit them, or initiate contact, why couldn't they come work for us? Besides, don't you think whoever takes our jobs is going to bring in their own people?"

Kerry picked up her tea and sipped it. "Well," she said. "I think there are a lot of people who are actually loyal to us, not the company."

Dar nodded, tossing the frog at the sliding glass doors, watching it bounce off. "Listen, the benefits ILS pays are good. We won't be able to match that for a long time, so in the end, people will balance what they need, with wanting to come with us. Don't worry about it."

A knock on the door surprised them both, and sent Chino gallumping toward it, almost bowling Kerry over as she inadvertently got in the way.

Dar got up from the couch and skirted the table, getting to the door before Kerry could recover from her impact with Chino. She opened it to find her parents there. "Hey."

"Hey." Ceci had her hands in the pockets of a patchwork leather jacket of many colors. "Can we come in?"

"Sure." Dar stepped back to let them enter. "What's up?"

"We all are going to haul up out of here, wanted to give you a heads up," Andrew said. "Them people at the Navy will not stop bothering with me."

"What?" Kerry evaded the circling Chino. "What do they want from you, Dad? You're retired."

Andrew and Ceci took a seat on the couch. "Ah do know that, kumquat. But them folks are working hard to get ever'body to sign back up to go mess around ovah there."

"That makes no sense," Dar said.

"As if the government ever does make sense?" Ceci said. "Anyway, we're going to take the boat and go cruise around the islands for a couple of months. Let them go bug someone else."

"Good idea," Dar said. "I might have to join you if I can't shake off the feds when I fly out there on Thursday." She crossed her arms. "When you get back, want to come work for me?"

"I thought you weren't supposed to solicit existing ILS employees, Dar." Kerry head-butted her in the back.

"My father and you don't count."

"You two going to finally set up your own shingle?" Ceci said. "Hey. I could be your receptionist."

Andrew started laughing.

"Hey!" Ceci elbowed him.

"Can they make you go back in the Navy, Dad?" Kerry perched on the arm of the love seat.

Andrew stopped laughing and frowned. "Jackass," he said. "Ain't got sense to go pull some farm boys in do a better job than me now."

Ceci also looked serious. "Actually, Kerry, they can. Now, technically because of his record they shouldn't, but that hasn't stopped them from calling, and we'd rather just avoid the question. If they can't find him, they can't twist his arm either."

"That kinda sucks. I'm going to miss you guys," Kerry said. "But if the government tries to draft Dar, maybe we'll join you."

Both sets of parental eyes swung from her to Dar. "They really bothering you, Dardar?" Andrew asked, mildly.

Dar shrugged. "Same guy wants to talk to me, has something he wants to ask. I said I'd go up there and talk to him, and swing by Gerry Easton's."

"That does not sound good." Andrew frowned. "That was some big old mess they got into."

"Doesn't much matter. I can take notes to pass on to my successor," Dar said. "Because I'm going to make it clear to both of them that they'll need to deal with them if they want something done. Kerry and I will be busy relaxing and planning the startup of our new gig."

"Roberts Automation," Kerry said, a moment later. "We were just talking about it before you got here. Got a nice ring, doesn't it?" She got up. "Can I get you guys some tea? Or a soda?"

"Sure." Ceci also got up. "Let's both go." They headed off into the kitchen, leaving Dar and Andy behind.

"Yeah," Ceci said, as she removed a couple of cups from the cabinet. "The last straw was Andy's old commander leaving a message on the boat voice mail. He was filing a float plan before I stopped sputtering." She leaned against the counter. "We're parked in your backyard there. We're going to stay overnight then leave in the morning. Didn't even want to overnight at South Pointe."

"Wow." Kerry pushed her hair behind her ear as she waited for the water to boil. "I can't believe they'd do that to him."

"Oh, I can," Ceci responded. "I don't have any illusions about the service. I never begrudged Andy his love for it, but I never shared it. Bottom line, you're a number."

Kerry measured some tea leaves into a strainer and set it into a pot. "Am I really going to be giving tea to Dad, or would he rather have chocolate milk?"

Ceci chuckled. "He actually likes iced green tea as long as I dump enough honey in it. But yeah, he'd probably do better with milk. This whole thing's got him ticked off." She went to the refrigerator and opened it, studying the interior. "That milk dispenser cracks me up every time."

Kerry smiled. "The first time I saw it, I was like, what the heck is this?" She poured the water over the leaves. "Now I can't understand why everyone doesn't have one."

Ceci came back with the milk, stirring some chocolate syrup into it. "So I hear you're considering a name change?" She eyed Kerry.

"I filed my papers today," Kerry said, with a smile. "I really didn't think it would be as easy as it was, but apparently as long as you're not doing it to avoid the law, it's pretty simple."

"Well, I never regretted it," Ceci said, firmly. "I don't think this is something you had to do, but y'know, kid, I'm glad you are."

Kerry's smile broadened. "Me too. It's change time, you know? I can just feel it. I'm glad Dar's jazzed about starting up the new company. I know she feels a lot of responsibility for ILS."

"I'll tell her the same thing I told Andy. Don't waste time being loyal to corporations or government. They'll never return it," Ceci said. "The only thing that's due loyalty is people."

Kerry handed her a cup. "Two peas in a pod." She indicated the living room. "And to be honest, if I wasn't leaving, I'd be on my knees begging her to stay, so I can't say I blame the board."

"I bet," Ceci said. "But she'd be an idiot to. She's done all she can there. Can't go higher, if what I read about corporate structure is true."

"Well..."

"Kerry, it's true," Ceci insisted. "Andy's the same way, and Dar's come from a very long line on both sides of stubborn traditionalists."

Kerry eyed her skeptically.

"They skipped a generation with me." Ceci grinned a little. "But I remember banging my head against the wall with the two of them wanting to find people who dropped pennies in the street to return them."

"Yeah, I know. I just don't want to egg her into doing something just because I want to," Kerry said. "I know she doesn't care, but I spent my whole life before meeting her being egged into doing things and I feel kinda skunky doing that to her."

"Don't." Ceci's expression went serious. "I mean it, kiddo. She'd stay because she thought it was the responsible thing to do. Sometimes it ain't."

Kerry toasted her with Dar's cup of milk, and they proceeded back into the living room where they found Dar and Andrew poring over a map of the Caribbean. "What are you two up to?"

Dar stood up and accepted the milk. "I told him to go hang out at that place we went to." She pointed at the map. "That place on St. John?"

"Oh yeah!" Kerry circled around her and leaned on the table. "That was a pretty cool place. Once the hurricane left."

"And we stopped chasing pirates," Dar said.

"And you all stopped getting into hellacious trouble," Ceci added.

"Hm." Kerry regarded the map. "Maybe you should go to Bermuda instead."

IT FELT GOOD to climb into their waterbed, and settle under the cool cotton sheets, as the warmth of the heated water cradled her body. Kerry exhaled, and consciously tried to relax as she waited for a handful of Advil to take effect. "What a pain in the butt."

"You have cramps in your butt?" Dar ambled into the bedroom, turning off the lights and crawling into the other side of the bed. Want me to see if I can fix that?"

Kerry chuckled. "You're such a goof sometimes." She felt the bed shift as Dar came closer, then a gentle touch against her skin as she was enfolded in a hug.

No words. Dar wasn't much for them. But Kerry felt the affection soak into her skin as she relaxed against Dar and finally felt a moment of peace after the long and somewhat stressful day. "We didn't play with our new gizmos," she said, feeling Dar's body move in a faint laugh. "I've got meetings all day tomorrow, let's text each other the whole time."

Dar laughed harder

"Keep my mind off my cramps," Kerry added mournfully.

"Take the day off," Dar said. "You're going to have to hold the fort down when I leave for Washington." She started a gentle massage down Kerry's back.

Kerry had opened her mouth to protest, then paused. Then she sighed. "I committed to hanging in there until we're out of here, Dar. I can't really just not show up for work, especially since we both flaked out this afternoon."

"You could hang out here and start looking up how to set up our new company." Dar said, undeterred by the demurral. "And...hey, how about finding out if we could rent an RV for our drive around the Grand Canyon."

"An RV, what kind of RV? Like a trailer?" She felt Dar's powerful hands working at a knot in her lower back. "You just want to skip out on sleeping in a tent."

"And you don't?"

"I'd like to try one night in a tent," Kerry said. "I've never slept in a tent. The closest I ever came was sleeping in the Dixie during that power outage."

"We can sleep in a tent when we do that white water rafting trip," Dar continued, working her way around Kerry's body, ending up easing her thumbs in circles just below her navel. "And we'd better time that right cause I was reading that folder they sent us and you've got to pack everything in and out with you."

Kerry studied her shadowed face, the light from the digital clock just bringing out faint highlights. "Huh?" Her face scrunched. "Oh. Ah. Yeah," she said. "Let's time that right, and speaking of timing..."

Dar sighed. "Yeah. I'll be bleeding all over Washington."

"Well." Kerry, finally, relaxed. "At least my PMS is over, so maybe I'll be less of a nut case. Maybe I should come with you to Washington. You can go bleed on the Pentagon, and I'll tell my mother I'm changing my name. Think that'll get them to leave us alone?"

"Hehehe," Dar snickered, almost into her ear.

"Then we can go kiss on the steps of the Lincoln Memorial. Did I tell you I found out about all that log cabin stuff?" She felt Dar's body shaking with laughter. "Holy pooters, Dar, I should have joined that years ago! Where the hell was I? I should go visit their offices in DC and apologize for my father."

Dar's forehead pressed against hers and she looked up, staring right into those ice pale eyes. They were both momentarily silent, then Kerry exhaled. "Take me with you," she whispered.

"Always," Dar responded. "I'll have Maria book your flight with mine. Now," she kissed Kerry on the lips, "bedtime for nerds."

They snuggled up together and relaxed into peaceful silence.

"Can we get one of those RVs that do all that transformer sliding out stuff?" Kerry asked, after a moment. "And a barbecue grill?"

Dar started laughing again. "Sure."

"And a satellite dish."

KERRY APPRECIATED A moment of peace in her busy morning, leaning back in her chair and sipping on some tea as she gazed out the window.

She was, she acknowledged, going to miss her view. Her fourteenth floor office overlooked the water and Biscayne Bay, and she adored it. She remembered fondly the first time she'd seen it, walked down the back corridor by Dar on her first day working at ILS.

She remembered dressing for work that morning, stressing over the position of every hair, and twitching her new jacket endless times to adjust the drape of it.

Now? Kerry smiled as she hiked one ankle up on her knee, smoothing the cotton fabric of her loose fitting cargo pants down. She'd been glad enough to compromise with her solicitously hovering significant other, insisting on coming into the office but grateful her boss relaxed the dress code so she hadn't had to deal with a business suit and heels.

So now she was perched in her comfortable leather chair, drinking a cup of honey laced blackberry tea, taking a break from completing her personnel reviews that were due for imminent raises.

With a contented sigh, she turned her chair back around and put her cup down, pulling over her note pad and picking up her pen. She checked her list of names and continued making notes, the sound of her writing echoing only slightly as she rested her head on her left fist.

After a few minutes, a soft buzzing interrupted her, and she glanced at the gizmo resting on her desk. "Ah." She nudged it over and regarded the screen, seeing a new note blinking for her attention. She tapped the screen, and it opened.

    Hey. Blue or purple? DD

Blue or purple. Boy that could be almost anything. Kerry picked up the device and using the thumb keyboard, she typed an answer.

    Green.

She paused, then grinned and tapped again.

    KD.

Then she put the device down and picked up her pen, checking off the next to last name on the list, and turning over the last review in her pile.

Mayte's. She reviewed her printed comments, then she added a long hand written postscript, smiling a little as she praised her admin, and indicated she thought she was ready for a more responsible position when one opened up.

She'd gotten her first technical certification just before Christmas, and while Kerry appreciated her dependability and eye for detail, she knew there were bigger and better things in the company for her to do.

A soft knock at the door made Kerry look up. "Yes?"

The door opened and Mayte poked her head inside. "Kerry, may I ask a question?"

"Of course." Kerry turned over the page and leaned her elbows on her desk, folding her hands together as Mayte came in and sat down in one of her visitor's chairs. "What's up?" she asked. "I like that scarf. The color rocks."

Mayte grinned, reaching up to touch the red Pashmina scarf around her neck. "We went to the international shops last weekend and my mama got me this. We don't get to wear them so often, but it's nice and so soft."

"Yeah, I have hats and scarves and gloves somewhere in a box in the back of one of our closets." Kerry said. "Dar has a sweater that color that I love on her."

"Yes." Mayte said. "Kerry, what is it you're going to do when you go from the company?"

Ah. "What are we going to do? Well, we have some travel planned, going to do some stuff in the Grand Canyon, a visit to Machu Picchu, and some skiing and that kind of thing. Maybe go up to Alaska, or visit the Far East," Kerry said.

"And after that?" Mayte nodded when she finished. "Will you come back to Florida?"

Kerry smiled. "Yes, we will."

Mayte took a deep breath. "If you make another company could I come to work for you?" She got the words out quickly. "I would not like to be here if you are not."

Kerry was actually a little surprised it had taken so long for someone to ask. "Well, you know, Mayte, there are rules and things we have to go by that are part of our leaving here. We wouldn't want anyone to think we were trying to take people away from ILS."

"Of course not, no," Mayte said softly.

"But." Kerry's eyes twinkled. "If we were to start our own company, sometime, I would love for you to come be a part of that with us."

Mayte's face lit up. "Oh!"

"Shh." Kerry put a finger to her lips.

"I know. We must be quiet about it," Mayte said, in an almost whisper. "Do you think my mama can come too?"

Kerry rested her chin on her fist. "I think Dar's going to take care of your mama, Mayte. I think she's going to make it so she doesn't have to work unless she wants to."

Mayte blinked at her in silence, then lifted one hand up to cover her mouth.

"But if she wants to come and hang out with us, you know she'll be welcome," Kerry concluded. "It will be a little while before things start happening, but you'll be one of the first to know about them, okay?"

Mayte nodded, wiping her eyes a little with one finger. "Yes, it is very okay. Mama will be so happy. She was so upset about you leaving."

"Yeah, Dar and I were talking about that yesterday," Kerry said. "There are people here who are like family to her. It's hard."

Mayte nodded again. "But if we can come with you, it's not so hard." She smiled shyly. "Correct?"

"Correct." Kerry grinned back. "I want Dar to be happy," she said. "And I know that will make her happy, to have people around us that she knows and trusts. But we found out, when we were working with the government during the emergency, that a lot of what we were doing, and why we were doing it, wasn't in our control."

"Yes, Mama was telling Papa about that," Mayte said at once. "About how the big jefe was going to be in so much trouble, but that you fixed it, at the very last moment."

"We did," Kerry said. "Dar and I, we personally did, risking ourselves to make it all right for Alastair and for the company, and we don't regret doing that, but we don't want to have that kind of pressure on us, you know?" It felt comforting, somehow, laying it out for Mayte like that. "Because no one really appreciates it."

"That is just what my papa said."

"Yeah, Dar's papa said that too." Kerry chuckled. "So anyway, that's the deal."

Mayte got up. "Thank you, Kerry. I will not say anything to anyone, I promise."

"I know you won't." Kerry watched her leave with a sense of mild satisfaction. Then she sighed and turned the paper on her desk back over, taking a sip of her cooling tea. "Absolutely no one appreciates what we did." She shook her head and paused then put the cup down and picked up the gizmo, tapping a message into it and sending it on its way.

She was still trying to decide if she liked the little keyboard. It did seem easier to type out a message, her old standby palm pilot using the stylus and having it recognizing her handwriting did end up with her re-writing it's interpretations a lot. Dar's more regular scribbling seemed to be more to its tastes.

Her phone buzzed. "Kerry, I have Personnel on line uno."

Kerry reached over. "Thanks, I got it." She hit the button on the phone. "Mari?"

"Good morning," Mari responded. "I was going to schedule an interview with you for some candidates on Friday, but I understand you'll be out of town?"

Ah. "Yes, I'll be going with Dar to Washington to talk to the Joint Chief's office, and the Executive Branch." Kerry said, managing to stifle a wry grin. "So maybe it's better we wait until after that so at least I'll be able to warn my replacement."

"Oh, boy." Mari sighed. "I don't know if I like us being so Washington Post front page."

"Us either," Kerry agreed promptly. "Consequence of success, according to Alastair. But hey, that might coax a few people into taking a chance on coming over here. Power's an aphrodisiac I hear."

"Might, at that," Mari said. "Somewhere, somehow we should be able to find a sucker to take over for the two of you. I'm guessing it'll be a guy."

"Yeah?"

"Kerry, c'mon."

"Yeah." Kerry chuckled. "I know. I've got a call with two of our biggest network vendors this afternoon. Maybe I can see if there's any interest there."

She hung up and went back to her scribing, finishing up Mayte's appraisal with only the slightest tinge of impending hypocrisy for recommending her for advancement. "Hey, it's true." She regarded the paper. "Just because I have other plans for her, doesn't make it any less true, and besides, it'll be a while before Dar and I set up shop."

She sorted her forms with a sense of satisfaction, and inserted them into a sealed envelope for delivery to Mari's attentive hands. It was good to have that task done, and a little bittersweet to know it was for the last time. The next time that staff was evaluated it would be by someone else, and Kerry found herself determined to make sure that whoever that was had a proper appreciation for good people.

Because she had some really good people.

DAR SETTLED INTO the chair in the presentation room, pulling her sleeves straight and running her fingers through her hair before she touched the button on the video conferencing system.

She was alone in the room, the door locked and the do not disturb sign set. The late morning sun poured in the windows, and she saw parasailers from the corner of her eye as she waited for the system to come up and start to sync to the video gateway.

The weekly executive board meeting was never one of her favorites, and now that the board was aware she was going to leave, it made it all the more unpleasant.

They were pissed. Dar, viewing it dispassionately, could not blame them. It was one thing for a CEO to be resigning, quite another for them to be losing at the same time the senior structure of her operations group.

The screen flickered, then resolved, and one after the other, the board members appeared in their separate squares. Dar kept her hands folded and her mouth shut, having little to report at this the first meeting of the new year. The Houston video center appeared last, with Alastair just dropping into a seat that was the mirror of the one she was in, giving her a wry wink as he rested his elbows on the conference table there.

"Good morning, or good afternoon, all." Alastair said, after a moment of silence. "Everyone on?"

The group muttered assent, from their sedate squares. They had only recently started using the upgraded video conferencing system, put in place after the 9/11 crisis. Dar wasn't at all sure she liked it, really preferring the ability to sprawl at her desk on voice only, free to roll her eyes or make rude gestures without giving offense.

"Okay," Alastair said, shuffling some papers. "This'll be a short meeting, since we're just back from holidays. The accounting group has advised me that year end closing is well underway, and preliminary numbers look all right. We haven't seen the impact of contract alterations from September, which will probably not really hit until end of first or second quarter."

"You'll be gone. Why even care?" One of the board members asked, shortly.

Alastair looked mildly at him. "Because until I do walk out the door for the last time, I'm the CEO of the company. I care because that's my job," he said. "I'm sorry it's all twisting your shorts that I've decided to retire after almost being railroaded on your behalf, but there ya go."

"Alastair, that's not true," the man protested.

"John, it is," Alastair corrected him gently. "All the after the fact revisionist history doesn't make that different. I'm not mad about it. I just want to enjoy my life for a while. That so hard to understand? None of you were there. No one was standing next to me when all those Secret Service men were hovering, ready to grab my elbow, and you all agreed it was right and appropriate for me to take the fall. No harm, fellas. I'm a big boy, and it was my call."

Dar cleared her throat.

"All right, I got to stand there and it was really Dar's call." Alastair smiled at her. "But anyway, this'll be a short meeting. So let me finish with my comments and we can do a round table."

Dar laced her fingers together and simply waited for her turn, having already been to the December board meeting and dealt with the outrage in person. They could, and would, continue griping, but now, hearing the muttering, her half formed idea of retracting her resignation seemed craven and candy-assed.

What in the hell had she been thinking?

What was really behind that impulsive urge to turn around and stay?

"Operations."

Dar looked up. "Kerry and I will be in Washington end of the week. I have meetings scheduled with both the Joint Chief's office, and the president's advisory board." She paused briefly. "In terms of the Pentagon, General Easton has advised me that the job scope we were engaged in prior to the attacks has been expanded. It remains to be seen exactly how expanded, but it appears at this time to be a four or five fold increase."

More mutters, but less negative. "That'll end up being a huge contract," John Baker said, distracted from his annoyance at Alastair.

"It will," Alastair agreed. "I've had the personnel group here keeping in close touch with Dar. I think we're looking at establishing a major hub in Maryland to support the effort, we can't run it out of the existing one. Too small."

"In terms of the advisory board..." Dar paused again. "At this point, I don't know exactly what that request is going to be. I do intend on presenting them with a bill for the last thing they asked us to do."

Small, crabbed smiles appeared. But Baker cleared his throat. "Dar, did they ask for us, or for you?" he inquired bluntly. "Seemed to me the last time it had very little to do with us."

"Ah, yes," Jacques Despin said. "But of course, the resources they demanded were ours, not our esteemed colleague's."

Dar nodded. "He asked for me because someone told him my name, but what I committed were company resources and efforts. Same as for the City of New York."

"So what's going to happen when you tell him you're leaving?" Baker asked. "And that you can't even tell him who he'll be talking to when you're gone?"

There was a more significant silence. Dar unfolded her hands and lifted them, then let them drop to the table. "I guess we'll find out," she said. "It could matter to him, and it could matter to Gerry Easton. Or maybe it won't, and they just want to get things done."

More mutters.

"Look," Dar said. "I'm not going to apologize, just like Alastair isn't, for wanting to take possession of my own life. You can all go kiss my ass. The only thing I ever got from this board is bullshit and a lot of happiness in having us, meaning me and him," Dar pointed at Alastair, "take the fall for everyone else. Screw off."

Alastair smiled fondly at her. "Ahh...now that's my Dar."

"You've been adequately compensated," Baker said, stiffly. "You get paid well for what you do, Roberts."

"Do I?" Dar said. "We walked into both New York and Washington with the possibility of dying. What's that worth? How many people working there are going to end up paying for that in years to come? What's that worth? What's Kerry's broken ribs worth? You think anything in my bank account can cover that?"

The board looked uneasily at her.

"It's never been about money for me," Dar said, after a long pause. "I just want to take myself, and my family, and do something else. If that causes you inconvenience, too fucking bad."

"Look." Baker held up a conciliatory hand. "Dar, we all know what you've meant to this company, and our bottom line. So the frustration is not at you, it's just we have to figure out how we're going to rearrange things and not get hung out to dry by our shareholders. You know?"

"I know." Dar simmered down, feeling her virtual hackles settle. "We want to make this a successful handover. I have a lot of people in this organization I feel responsible for. No one wants to screw anyone."

Alastair took control of the meeting again. "We done with that subject? Dar, thanks for going to Washington on our behalf. Just get what information you can, and try not to project the future to them, if you get me."

Dar considered that. "For the advisory board, sure. But Gerry's a family friend. I'm not going to lie to him," she said. "I think he's worked with us — meaning ILS — enough to have confidence that we'll deliver what we promise regardless of who sits in my chair."

The look of doubt was, in a way, a backhanded compliment and Dar acknowledged that. Despite her contentious relationship with the governing board, she knew they knew that when it came to delivering on promises, she was rock solid reliable and always had been.

So she got that they were upset and angry at having to trade that for an unknown. "Hey," she said. "Maybe whoever takes my place will play golf and smoke cigars with you all. And not tell you to kiss their ass. Could end up being a good thing. You never know."

Alastair chuckled dryly. "You never know. Now. Pier? I heard we have some new leads in Africa. Wanna fill us in?"

The meeting stumbled on. Dar exhaled, picking up her new gizmo and glancing at it, then tapping the screen to display the message she saw waiting there.

A smile appeared on her face, and she put the device back down, returning her attention to the screen. "Houseboat," she muttered softly. "That's an idea."

Alastair had been watching her. "Dar, did you say something?"

"No, just taking notes," Dar replied dutifully. "We'll need to hike the back haul to the continent if that all comes through. Bring it up through the new Euro hub maybe, or invest in an equatorial tie line."

Everyone nodded as if they knew what she was talking about, and the round table continued on.

"SO WHAT WOULD be the difference between this and a houseboat?" Dar asked, as she set the anchor and they drifted against the current, coming taut against the line and rocking gently.

"Well." Kerry finished setting the table, looking up and appreciating the clear, winter cooled sky above them, the horizon just painted with the last bit of sun. "A house boat is bigger, for one thing."

Dar paused and looked around at the deck of their boat, her brows lifting a little in puzzlement. "This isn't exactly a dinghy."

"No, I know." Kerry chuckled. "Be right back." She went back inside the cabin of the boat, rolling a little with the motion as she went to the small galley, retrieving a platter of fajitas fixings and a round container of tortillas. She brought them both outside with her and set them down on the table. "But it's more like a house."

"The houseboat?" Dar was pouring sangria into wide based glasses. "That would make sense, what with the house in the name and all that."

"Dar."

"Hehe. I'm being an asshole. Sorry." Dar took her seat and relaxed, extending her sweatpants covered legs out and crossing them at the ankles. "I remember seeing houseboats off the west coast, and they were like trailers on pontoons. I'm assuming that's not what you're after."

"No." Kerry sat down and took a sip of the sangria as she took a tortilla and selected some contents for it. "I just think of stuff like, taking one of them up some of those canals, like in Holland, and seeing something new every day."

"Hm." Dar copied her. "That might be fun. I'll have to look at some of those river cruises they have. That could be a hoot, going through locks and stuff like that."

"Ah." Kerry leaned back and regarded the horizon. She was in a thick hoodie, and had sheepskin lined boots on, a radical change from their usual t-shirts and shorts. The weather had gotten colder as the day went on, and now it was in the upper 40s, crisp and chilly out on the water.

But with a pretty sky, and hot chocolate to look forward to, it didn't matter. "There's just so much I want to see and do," Kerry said. "Like, where do you start?"

"Yeah," Dar agreed. "Well, we know we're going to start at the Grand Canyon, March fifteenth." She pulled a packet from her jacket pocket and put it on the table. "We pick up our RV March twelfth in Vegas."

Kerry paused in mid bite, surprise obvious on her face. "Buh." She put her tortilla down and picked up the paperwork. "Wow. Didn't know you..." She studied the contents. "Oh, wow. And the parks too?" She looked up at Dar, seeing the grin working its way around a mouthful of steak. "I thought you were still thinking about the timing."

Dar shook her head as she chewed. She swallowed, then chased the mouthful down with some sangria. "Me wanting to stay is bullcrap. I still think we should have gotten out in October, but drawing it out now doesn't do service to anything but my ego. Meeting with the board showed that today."

"Ah huh." Kerry nodded slowly, taking a bite. "Bottom line," she said, after a swallow.

"Victim of my own success." Dar settled her shoulders a little more comfortably. "You were right." She lifted her glass and toasted her. "Besides, making plans always makes me feel better."

Kerry chuckled.

"Plans okay with you?" Dar inquired, after a moment.

The packet was a complete set of reservations, including the plane flight to Vegas, a rental of what looked like a pretty snazzy RV, overnights in cabins, the whitewater trip...Kerry sorted through it all with growing delight. "When did you do all this?"

"Me?" Dar eyed her. "I just told the island travel agent what we wanted. She did the heavy lifting."

"It's awesome. I'll go talk to her this weekend and get all the loose ends tied up." Kerry smiled, putting the papers away. "Thanks, hon. You've made me a very happy woman."

Dar responded with a contented smile, as she retrieved another tortilla. "She even made reservations for Chino at a pet resort while we're on the river. They have hot stone massages."

Kerry stopped in mid chew. "The pet resort?"

"Uh huh."

"Do they take people reservations too? I think we're gonna need it after a week on the river."

"UGH." DAR SWALLOWED several Advil, washing them down with a swig from a chocolate milk chug. "Mind if we order room service instead of going out?" she asked, as she heard Kerry return from the bathroom after storing their overnight sundry kits.

"Of course not." Kerry went over to the luggage stand and removed Dar's pajamas from it, retreating back to drape them over Dar's shoulder. "Get undressed, and I'll see what they have to offer. Do you really think I'd rather go out to eat in downtown Washington and risk running into people who think they know me?"

Dar was glad enough to exchange her jeans and sweater for her long, threadbare t-shirt, folding the clothes and packing them neatly before she picked up a magazine and retreated to the couch in their sedate hotel suite. She curled up in one corner, willing the drugs to quickly settle her cramping.

Pain in the ass. Dar exhaled, and opened the magazine, full of the ocher and sand colors of the Southwest. She'd started feeling it as the plane took off, and resigned herself to dealing with the monthly annoyance. "Should be a pill for this."

"You mean to prevent it?" Kerry sat down next to her with the menu. "I've been saying that for years. At least it was a short flight."

Short and private. "Mm." Dar flipped the pages. "I really am gonna miss that jet," she said. "Spoiled my ass."

"We just have to get rolling fast enough to get our own, hon." Kerry studied their choices. "Twice grilled par boiled snails or hamburgers?"

Dar looked at her, one brow arched.

"Yeah, I know. But those conch you brought into the cabin were sort of snail like. I thought maybe you'd gotten fond of them." Kerry smiled as she picked up the phone. "Hello, yes. I'd like something delivered."

Dar went back to studying her magazine, looking at the pictures of the rafting trip they'd planned. It looked fun and exciting, and she could almost feel the twisting and turning of the boat going through the rapids.

It made her smile. Even the thought of having to sleep in a tent didn't really bum her out. "I bet when we're out there at night, we can see a lot of stars. Like out on the water."

Kerry leaned on the back of the couch and looked at the page. "You're really jazzed about this, aren't you?"

Dar nodded. "I am. I really want to make up for not taking a vacation for fifteen years. It's going to be pretty cool, out there with that small a group." She flipped a page. "We reserved for the first trip of the season."

"April." Kerry nodded. "So we can take the RV around to all the parks first, and then end up there for the rafting trip." She exhaled in contentment. "This is going to be so much fun."

It was. Dar wished they were already on the other side of the remaining two months of work. The thought of going through the stressful separation was starting to annoy her. "Just you and me and Chino, seeing cool stuff. I even got them to send me a brochure for hot air balloons."

"Oh. Hot air balloons." Kerry rested her head against Dar's shoulder. "I saw those on TV taking off at dawn once, is that what you mean?"

"Yup."

Kerry closed her eyes and imagined it, the silence of the pre-dawn and the soft hiss of the wind. "Awesome." She sighed and got up, replacing the room service menu on the desk in the room and retrieving her own pajamas. It was after dark, the flight had landed just after sunset and they had a full day planned for tomorrow, with meetings at the White House in the morning, and the Pentagon after lunch.

Then they had a late night flight home, at their own schedule, with a weekend to look forward to. Kerry slipped into her shirt and put away her traveling clothes. "You think they're going to mind me being at those meetings, Dar? I could just hang out here if you do."

"Don't care." Dar had her head resting against her hand as she studied the pictures. "They tell you to leave I'll be right behind you."

Kerry regarded her with a smile. "At least we don't have a Louisiana lawyer with us this time." She closed the top on the suitcase and went over to the window, looking out at the familiar landmarks. They'd decided to stay in the center of town this time, and if she were on the roof of the hotel she could hit a few of them with a rock.

It felt strange, to look out at that landscape, and yet feel so disconnected from it. She no longer even felt her father's shadow there, and she was debating whether or not to call her mother, who she knew was here in town in her Senate offices.

After all, she'd just seen her. Right?

"So what if they throw us out?" Kerry mused. "We could go to a museum."

"We could go have lunch with your mother," Dar counter suggested. "Or go swimming in the Potomac."

Kerry chuckled. "I forgot you're not fond of museums," she said. "Oh, hey...how about the Air and Space Museum?" She turned to find a much more interested pair of blue eyes watching her. "Ah, better?"

"Air and Space? Absolutely." Dar put the magazine down.

"Though, I have to admit the first time I wandered into a museum of modern art and saw something of my mother's it was hoot." She leaned her head on her hand. "It was some stupid new client meet and greet, and I remember the jackass regional salesman turning to me and saying something snarky like, I'm sure there's no relationship to you, right?"

Kerry chuckled. "Did you say there was?"

"Sure." Dar grinned. "Stopped all conversation within hearing. Pretty funny actually. Remind me to tell Mom about that when they get back."

"Okay." Kerry squirmed around and put her head down on Dar's thigh, regarding the swirled plaster ceiling. "So what do you think they're going to ask you? Hey, maybe they want to make you the US's chief nerd."

"Ugh."

"Nerdmeister-in-chief. I like that. It's got a nice ring."

"Last thing I want is to be a federal employee." Dar draped her arm over Kerry's body. "Though that would get around the non-compete injunction."

A knock sounded on the door at the same time as Dar's phone rang and Kerry unwound herself to get up and walk over. She opened the door and gestured the room service waiter in. She followed him over to the desk and waited, signing the room charge and giving him a brief, polite smile.

He left without commenting.

"Nice guy," Kerry said to the closed door, before she returned her attention to the tray. She sorted out the silverware, half listening to Dar's end of the conversation. "Problems, hon?"

Dar rolled her eyes. "Trying to bring the new datacenter live. Having routing problems." She mouthed. "Give me some ice cream."

"I was going to suggest we eat that first anyway." Kerry brought the bowls over. "It'll melt otherwise, and it looks a lot better than the burgers anyway."

Dar set her bowl on the sofa arm and maneuvered a spoonful of the chocolate into her mouth, as she listened to the phone. "Well." She managed to swallow in time. "You know what? I'm not going to drag my damn laptop out, Mark. Get in there and figure it out."

She got another few spoons down before she had to talk again. "Then we need to hire, in addition to a CIO, a damned senior network engineer." She listened. "Fine, I'll talk to Mari in the morning. In the meantime get in there or get someone in there and waste some brain cells on it."

"CIO and VP ops, and senior network engineer, and network architect, and writer of adorable gopher programming." Kerry was ticking off on her fingers. "Y'know what, hon? It's going to be freaking expensive to replace us."

Dar gave her a look. Then she looked back at her phone in surprise.

"He hung up on me," she said. "I wasn't even that rude, was I?"

Kerry ran her mind over the words. "No, you really weren't. I think Mark's really pissed off we're leaving."

Dar put the phone down and recaptured her bowl. "Is that any reason to hang up on me? I didn't call him, he called me for help."

"Mm." Kerry pressed her shoulder against Dar's.

"I don't want them to call me for help, Kerry. I want them to start thinking for themselves. If I have to piss people off to get them to do that, then fine."

"Mm."

Dar rested her head against Kerry's and sighed.

Kerry offered her some butter pecan, and they munched in silence for a few minutes. Then Kerry wiped her lips with her napkin and picked up her own cell phone. "I'll call him," she said. "Let him vent at me for a while. Maybe an idea will bounce out of that and he'll have a brain wave."

"I love you."

Kerry smiled, as she hit one of her speed dials. "Back at ya, and hold that thought, because I think this ice cream's about enough dinner for me so we can head off to that big bed after this."

Dar wrapped her arms around Kerry and nuzzled the side of her neck. "Sounds good to me."

"Hey, Mark, it's Kerry." Kerry wrapped one hand around Dar's arm. "Yeah, I know, but you know, it's gonna happen. What can I do to help?" She felt Dar's breath warming her ear. "No, honest, I can't. She's not feeling well."

Dar's brow lifted.

"Yeah, that time of the month. So can I get the vendor on the phone for you? No? Oh, okay, you did? Good. Call me if you need me." Kerry folded the phone shut and held a hand out. "C'mon. He's fine."

"Mm."

"They'll get through it."

"Mm."

Chapter Five

KERRY TWITCHED HER jacket straight as she followed Dar through the gate toward the security entrance of the blocky office structure ahead of them. She remembered their last visit, and she was hoping this time it would be both shorter and more pleasant.

Dar was presenting her identification to the guard, and she motioned Kerry forward as the man studied them with a frown. "Are we dangerous again?" Kerry handed over her company credentials. "Dar, don't you have an invitation?"

"No." Dar waited, rocking back and forth a little as the guard went to go make a phone call. "I have, I think, an email from that guy's admin telling me what time to be here. Not worth booting the laptop."

The guard came back. "Okay, Ms. Roberts, I've got you on the list, but not this lady." He indicated Kerry.

"Please call whoever made the list and have her added. I'm not coming in without her," Dar said in a mild tone. "I was asked to come here, not the other way around."

The guard looked grumpy and frustrated, but he just shrugged and went back to the little booth guarding the entrance and got on the phone.

Dar hummed under her breath. "Glad I took all those Advil before we left," she said. "Otherwise I might have seen jail time in my near future."

Kerry chuckled. "Yeah, glad I took some too. My cramps lasted way longer than usual this time." She leaned against the fence post and pulled out her new gizmo, tapping the screen and regarding the results. "You can actually surf the Internet on this thing, Dar."

"At one bit per twenty seconds?"

"And it has ringtones. You can make your phone ring songs," Kerry said. "How about if I had jingle bells as my phone ring?"

"How about if you record me singing "Jingle Bells" for your phone ring?" Dar countered. "At least that would be unique."

"Oh, honey, in a freaking heartbeat."

Dar grinned, then turned as the guard came back. "Well?"

"It's okay," the guard said. "Please come with me."

They followed him past the booth and in a side door, which he carefully closed behind them before leading them on. The halls were all polished linoleum, and despite the fact it was a civilian office building, there was a touch of the military about it. Kerry kept her eyes slightly down as she walked, just keeping aware in her peripheral vision of the fast moving bodies going in either direction around her.

Then they were going down a hallway and into an antechamber

that she last remembered filled with nervous, rushing people dealing with an unimagined disaster.

Now there were four or five people present, quiet, calm, giving her and Dar brief glances and then returning to their work as they passed them by and went into the conference room.

"Please wait here," the guard said, then left them.

Dar went to one of the comfortable seats and took it, resting her forearms on the table and folding her hands. "Sit."

Kerry took the chair next to her and settled into it. Her heart was thumping a little, and she was aware of being nervous but she wasn't entirely sure of why.

Time ran out to think about it, as the door opened and Michael Bridges came in. "Ah." He regarded the two of them. "You two Siamese twins or something? I only asked for one of you." He was a tall man, with a craggy face and a spare frame wrapped in expensive silk trousers and a white shirt with the sleeves rolled up.

"Yes," Dar responded in a mild tone. "Next question?"

"We were separated at birth," Kerry added. "But in reality, Mr. Bridges, if this is a professional request, I have a piece of it because I'm the Operations Vice President of ILS. If it's a personal request, I have a piece of it because Dar's my spouse. It's just how it is."

"Uh huh." Bridges closed the door, then went to his seat and sat down. "Well as it happens you all did me a very big favor so I suppose you can bring anyone you like in here." He paused. "Glad you skipped that lawyer though. God damn he was a pain in the ass."

"I'll pass along that compliment," Dar said. "So." She pushed the envelope she'd brought with her over to him. "That's the bill for your last favor."

He took the envelope and tossed it into a bin behind him. "All right, so let's get down to brass tacks." He paused. "What the hell does that mean? Who uses brass tacks anymore, anyway?" He didn't wait for an answer. "Here's the situation. What we found out a couple months ago is there's too much we don't know."

Kerry cleared her throat and waited for him to look over at her. "Didn't know, or didn't recognize?"

His lips twitched faintly. "Good point. Maybe both. Maybe that plus we didn't know our ass from a hole in the wall. Maybe that plus no one had the sense to share anything with anyone across the hallway. Could be," he said. "Point is, that has to change."

Dar nodded. "That's a point."

Bridges looked at Dar. "I know we gave Easton a budget to revise all his dinosaur systems. He's talked to you about that?"

"He's our next stop," Dar said.

Bridges nodded. "Okay, that's his problem. My problem is, I need someone to take charge of how we deal with technology and information and all that horse crap at the federal level. I want to bring you on board as what we're calling the..." He glanced at a paper he was holding. "Half ass horsecrap. Anyway, they want to call it the techno czar." He looked at Dar. "When can you start?"

Dar blinked. Then she turned and looked at Kerry. Then she looked back at Bridges. "Are you saying you want me to come work for you?"

"Good catch," Bridges said, dryly. "Yes."

"Me personally?" Dar clarified. "As in, not the company I work for?"

Bridges laced his fingers together and gave her a faintly exasperated look. "Yes, you." He glanced at Kerry. "No offense, Stuart, but you were not in our plans."

"I'm not offended," Kerry said. "So don't worry about it."

Dar inhaled and exhaled. "What exactly does this position do?" she asked. "Aside from talk to the press in incomprehensible terms about things they don't and won't understand?"

The presidential advisor chuckled dryly. "Don't worry, Roberts. It's not a talking head job. I don't think you really fit the administration's image ideal in any case." He cleared his throat. "The job is to find a way to get this government the ability to see into everything and anything, and find out what's really going on. Needs...what do you call it? Software. Whatever."

"What do you mean by everything and anything?" Dar asked.

"Everything. The Internet, the phones, we need to see everything people are doing so we can find these bastards and get them out of here," Bridges said. "So you agree? When can you start?"

"You want me to figure out how to spy on everyone," Dar clarified.

Bridges shrugged. "You could call it that, I suppose. But if a terrorist is sending an email to another terrorist about planting a bomb, I want to know that."

Kerry watched Dar's profile, which was as still and cold as she'd ever seen her.

"Well." Dar folded her hands carefully and precisely on the table. "That's not something I want to do. So you'll need to look elsewhere for your candidate." She stared Bridges right in the eye. "I'm sure there are a lot of them out there."

Bridges cocked his head to one side. "You understand what kind of offer this is, right?" He looked at Kerry. "I know you understand, so why not explain it to her?"

"I do understand," Kerry said. "And I really don't have to explain anything to Dar. She gets it." She leaned forward a little. "Wouldn't this really be something better just outsourced, or maybe you could create a group in the Joint Chief's office to handle this?"

"No." Bridges shook his head. "Every existing division in this government wants to be put in charge of this and the infighting isn't worth it. I need an outsider."

Kerry nodded. "I see."

He looked back at Dar. "Want to think about it for a couple days? Look, Roberts, I know you probably want to work for us about as much as I want to have to pay you, but I'm a realist, and despite how hoary and old fashioned it is to say it, I'm a patriot. We need to be able to do this so that no one can do what they did on 9/11. You agree with that, yes?"

"Actually no I don't," Dar said. "I don't think you can ever stop someone from doing that at the sharp end. You have to stop them wanting to."

Kerry felt a sense of pleasurable surprise hearing the words, but had no time to appreciate them as she sensed Dar starting to move and she got her feet under her to stand up.

"I'll spend the weekend thinking about what you asked," Dar said, crisply. "Talk to you on Monday."

Bridges looked relieved. He stood up and held his hand out. "Monday it is. Have a good weekend ladies." He ushered them out, holding the door open for them and gestured to the guard. "Please walk these folks out, Dustan. They're friendlies."

The guard smiled at them, and opened the outer door. "Yes, sir, I will take good care of them." He held the door for them and followed them out, as the sound of the halls started to echo around them.

Dar and Kerry exchanged glances. Then Kerry reached up and pinched the bridge of her nose, giving her head a tiny shake. "Dar, I need a drink."

"Me too."

"Well, hey." Dustan's ears pricked."I know a good sports bar round the corner, wanna go there?"

"No thanks," Dar said. "We've got to go to the Pentagon." She put her hand on Kerry's back as they maneuvered through the crowd. "But with any luck, Gerry'll have scotch in his desk drawer."

THEY DIDN'T GET far after leaving the White House. Dar found the first little grill and pulled into the parking lot, turning off the rental car's engine and leaning her hands on the wheel. "My brain hurts."

Kerry had her arms folded across her chest, and she regarded the windy and overcast weather outside with a pensive expression. "Are you really going to think about this?"

Dar's eyebrows twitched and hiked. "Hell, no," she said. "What I'm going to think about is how to say kiss my ass in some politically acceptable way that won't mean I get the last twenty years of my tax returns audited by members of the Westboro Baptist Church."

"That guy really wants you. I was joking before, but sheesh." Kerry exhaled. "What do you think about his idea?"

"His idea to spy on everyone?" Dar said. "I think I'm going to find another country."

"Really?"

Dar half turned. "Kerry, if he'd asked me to coordinate the intelligence services, or evaluate new technology, or find a way to integrate the multitude of data systems...maybe I would have thought about it for a few minutes. The country needs that."

Kerry nodded.

"But figure out a way to snoop on my neighbors? Not my gig. Let's get a cup of coffee or something."

Kerry got out and zipped her jacket closed as they walked across the parking lot toward the grill. She paused in mid step when Dar did, and stopped when Dar turned to face her. "What?"

"Listen." Dar's face was unusually somber. "I'm really sorry that guy was such a jackass to you."

Kerry smiled. "Thank you, sweetheart, but I felt nothing but happiness that he didn't want any part of me. Honest." She patted Dar on the chest. "C'mon. It's cold out here."

"Really?"

"Really." Kerry towed her toward the door. "If I'd wanted a political career, don't you think I could have managed one from my family?"

"No, I know." Dar opened the door and followed her inside. It was early for lunch and there were only a few patrons inside, mostly at the bar. They were given the once over as they walked by, and settled gratefully out of sight in a small booth against the wall.

They looked at each other, then started laughing. "How in the hell do we get into crap like this, Dar?" Kerry asked, after a moment of chuckling. "That's crazy, you know?"

"I know." Dar glanced at the waitress as she arrived. "Coffee for me." She eyed Kerry. "Want to share some sliders?"

"Sure," Kerry said. "Ice tea for me and one of the six slider plates."

The waitress studied her briefly, then nodded and took the menus back, disappearing behind the service counter without any comment. "I think we were just pegged as not being from around here, Dar," Kerry said. "We should have ordered a salad to share."

"Yuck." Dar was busy with her little gizmo. "I'm going to text the pilot, and see if Gerry's available now. Maybe we can get out of here early."

"Music to my ears." Kerry leaned against the seat back, folding her hands over her stomach. "How about some handball at the gym tonight?"

"You feeling brave?" Dar laughed, as she finished texting, then pressed one of the dialing buttons. "You know, I sorta like this thing." She put it to her ear. "Yes, this is Dar Roberts. Is General Easton there? I'd like to talk to him for a minute."

Kerry smiled, considering the sense of relief she felt. Part of her had been a little afraid the government was going to ask Dar to do what Dar had mentioned, a logical, and needed request she knew would have tugged hard at Dar's innate sense of honor and likely result in some real soul searching on her part.

This? Write a program to spy on citizens? Aside from outraging Dar, it shunted aside any other consideration of the request and selfishly, she was glad.

Glad. Absolutely happy that it took one piece of complication out of her life, and left only Gerald Easton and his systems refresh.

"Okay, Gerry, we'll be there in about forty five minutes." Dar was speaking into the phone. "See ya." She closed the phone and put it on the table. "I think I'm going to end up being a jackass to him," she said. "After that last meeting, the less I have to do with the people in this town the happier I'll be."

Kerry picked up her tea and sipped it. "You don't expect me to disagree, do you?" She'd been prepared to. She'd had all her arguments marshaled and her objections ready, absolutely intent that nothing was going to get their hooks into her beloved without her having a chance to stop it.

Kind of skanky, in an overly possessive, really, honestly selfish kind of way, but Kerry was in a place where she cared more about their future together than that.

"No." Dar mixed as much sugar and cream into her coffee as was possible given the level in the cup. "I know you're here to keep me from doing something stupid." She glanced up, her eyes twinkling a little. "I don't think you have anything to worry about though," she added, as a blush became evident on Kerry's face.

"Sorry I'm that transparent," Kerry muttered.

"Shouldn't you be, to me?"

Kerry took a breath to protest, then paused, regarding the look of mild affection on Dar's face.

"Remember you once made me promise I'd think of both of us before I made decisions, even about myself?" Dar asked. "When I quit that time?"

Kerry nodded.

"Trust me."

Kerry blushed again, this time more intensely, as she moved her cup to let the waitress put the sliders she now had no interest in eating in front of them. "Wow," she said, as the woman left. "Now I feel like a complete creep."

"C'mon, Ker." Dar picked up a mini burger and took a bite of it. "Ease up. We've got a twenty minute scope inspection and then we're outta here. I want to go back to planning our trip."

Kerry studied the angular face across from her. "Why the hell am I being such a jerk?" She sighed, shaking her head a little and picking up a burger. "Maybe I need to go get my head examined."

Dar munched in silence, regarding her.

"You think Doctor Steve knows someone I can talk to?" Kerry nibbled at the bacon sticking out of the slider.

"Probably." Dar swallowed and took a sip of coffee. "Yeah, I think he does. He suggested someone he knew for me to talk to after they told us about Dad."

"Did you?"

Dar's lips twitched "What do you think?"

Kerry felt the angst ease a little. "Let me guess, that would be no."

"Correct. But doesn't mean you shouldn't if it would make you feel better," Dar said. "There's a lot of people who were part of that whole situation who say they've been socked with PTSD."

"You think that's what this is?"

"I have no idea, hon." Dar selected another burger. "I don't know if there's anything for it to be, but if it'll make you feel better to talk to someone, hell, do it."

Kerry chewed thoughtfully for a few moments. She watched Dar's body language, the relaxed and easy motion matching the casual speech. Things usually didn't chew at Dar. She tended to dismiss things that were in the past, the one exception to that, her relationships, but even now that seemed to have faded and left her living pretty much in the moment most of the time.

There was value in that. Kerry wished her mind worked the same way. "I guess I'll talk to him next week," She said. "So...this government offer."

"Mm?"

"Why you?" Kerry asked. "I mean, don't get me wrong, sweetheart, you know I think you're the greatest gift to IT the world has ever seen."

Dar started laughing.

"But why would this guy want you to come work for him? I love you, but you'd be a political nightmare and we both know that." Kerry wiped her lips. "I don't really get it."

Dar sat back and took a sip of her coffee, clearing her throat a little. "Those are pretty good." She indicated the plate. "I think this guy is someone who mostly cares about results. I'm sure he knows my background and my rep, and he's made the decision that he's willing to deal with that to get what he wants."

"Hm."

"Victim of my own success," Dar reiterated her earlier statement. "He asked for the impossible, and I made it possible. I can see why he wants someone like me to make this impossible dream of his reality."

"Is it impossible?"

Dar motioned the waitress over. "It's impossible for me." She handed the woman her credit card. "It's not right. I won't do it. I'm sure they'll find someone who will."

Kerry rested her hands on the table. "Dar?"

"Mm?"

"I actually suggested that to them."

"What?" Dar's head cocked slightly. "That they find someone else?"

"That they go to the Tier 1 providers and put their sniffer in there to find bad guys," Kerry said, quietly. "I didn't even think about it from a personal angle. I just wanted them out of our datacenter."

Dar blinked a few times, much as she had in the White House office. "That when they wanted in to the Herndon office?" she asked. "When I locked everything down?"

Kerry nodded.

The waitress came back and handed the check to Dar, with a pen and a slip. "Here you go."

"Thanks." Dar signed it and took back her card. She folded the receipt up and stuck it in her pocket, then leaned her elbows on the table. "Given where we were right then, you told them the right thing," she said. "It's the same thing we told the yahoos in that guy's office the last time. Follow the money." She held up her card, then put it back in her wallet. "Besides I'm sure that idea occurred to more than one person."

"True." Kerry slid out of the booth and followed her toward the door. "But, Dar, that's what we told them to do, wasn't it? To find those people, they would have to do that."

"Mm." She opened the door back out into the cold windy weather. "In an abstract sense yeah," she admitted. "So I guess I'm sounding pretty hypocritical, but all the same, I'm not doing it. Besides, by the time you designed a metric and parser, the real bad guys would find out how to hide from it, and it ends up becoming a way to embarrass political rivals."

Kerry sighed. "That's probably true."

"Probably?" Dar opened her door for her, and watched her slide inside. "Think your father would have used it to get dirt on people?"

"Huh."

Dar closed the door and walked around to the driver's side, pausing to glance around the parking lot before she opened the door and got in. Just a scattering of cars were around them, but one had a guy behind the wheel, reading a newspaper and she spent a moment indulging in a moment of spy fantasy.

Then she shut the door and started the car, wanting nothing more than to get past the Pentagon and go home. "Today is kinda sucking."

Kerry reached across the center console and put her hand on Dar's thigh, rubbing gently with her thumb against the cotton fabric covering it. "Yeah," she agreed. "Let's hope it turns around."

Dar paused as they reached the exit, and waited for traffic to slow before she pulled out. She glanced in her rear view mirror out of long habit, and felt a faint shock as she saw the guy with the paper behind her, waiting to turn as well.

Coincidence? "Yeah, let's hope so," she said, turning right out of the lot and proceeding along the street, keeping an eye on her mirror until she saw the guy pull out also, but to the left, heading away from them. She exhaled "Let's hope so."

GERALD EASTON'S OFFICE was quiet, and there were comfortable leather chairs to sit in near an open space off to one side of his desk. Kerry took a seat as the general arranged for some coffee, leaning back and crossing her legs at the ankles. Off in the distance she heard the sounds of construction, or more to the point, reconstruction as the area damaged by the attack was rebuilt.

"Now then, Dar." Easton crossed over to them and took a seat. "What's this all about you leaving?"

Dar cleared her throat gently. "We're resigning," she said. "Kerry and I. We gave ILS six months notice." She exchanged looks with Kerry. "We're going to form our own company."

The general looked thoughtful. "Well now, that's a bit of good news."

About to continue speaking, Dar halted, and looked at him in mild puzzlement.

"It is?" Kerry asked, equally surprised.

The general's admin came in with a tray, bringing it over and putting it down. She poured out cups for them and handed them over, then smiled, and withdrew.

Easton took a sip of his and wriggled his nose a little. "Sounds a bit funny," he admitted. "Fact is, there's been a bother about your whole lot there, being in so many areas, y'know?"

"No, I don't know," Dar said.

"You mean, because we're international?" Kerry asked. "Is that it?"

Easton nodded. "Too big an exposure, people say. Some of the spooks were talking to us about it the other day. Said it was dangerous having all those technical things in the hands of people who talked to so many non-Americans."

Dar reached up and rubbed the bridge of her nose. "You're kidding me, right? Most of the Fortune 500 are international."

"Sure," Easton said. "But they don't handle all our private stuff, don'tcha know?" He reached over and patted her knee. "That's what I wanted to talk to you about in person. We want to do that project, but I'm getting a lot of push back on using all those fellers of yours who aren't from around here."

"Wow," Kerry said. "General, most of the staff that handles our government accounts are from the US. Only a few of the follow-the-sun monitoring services aren't, so we can give twenty-four hour support."

Easton shrugged. "Got those spook fellers who think differently. Told the President we should change it. So here you are, and I'm thinking I'm going to have bad news for you, and then you tell me this. Wonderful. So we'll just hire you to do it. Problem solved." He looked extremely pleased. "Nicely done!"

Dar set her coffee down. "Gerry, we can't do that," she said. "I'll be under a non-compete clause, and it'll take us at least a year to get our company set up and going to where we'll be able to take on something as major as this is. Especially since we'll in effect be taking this business away from ILS."

"Pah," Easton said. "That's just legal mumbo jumbo. We'll pay off that other thing. Why now, it's chicken feed to the dollars they're pushing at me. Best news I could get, you saying you're cutting out of there, Dar. I was feeling bad about taking the work away. Would have anyway, but still, this is better."

Kerry rubbed her temples. "Dar, you want me to have boxes of Scotch sent to the board for your next meeting with them?"

Dar sighed. "Gerry, of the two offers I got today, believe me, yours is the one I'd jump at. But I can't just..." She paused. "I've got a pension and out package coming to me."

"Ah." Easton nodded. "Understand that, Dar. I really do. Got mine in my back pocket too, don'tcha know? But the fact is, the boys upstairs don't want us to put our fannies where someone might take a shot at them. I know, how about we just draft the two of you? That'd get around your lawyers, eh?"

"Whoa." Kerry held a hand up.

Dar sighed.

"C'mon now, Dar. I know you filled out a draft card." Easton chuckled. "But we'll find a way around it. Long as I know you're bound to get off their payroll, we'll think of something."

Dar propped her head up on her hand. "Got any whiskey? It's been that kind of day."

"Now, Dar, relax." Gerry patted her knee again. "What did the Executive Branch want from ya?"

"Don't ask." Dar slid down in her chair and put her arm over her eyes.

"They want Dar to be the technology czar for the government," Kerry supplied helpfully. "She doesn't want to."

"Hell no!" General Easton straightened up. "That's a scapegoat looking for a place to be shot in. Heard them talking about that. Let 'em find some politico to fill that slot."

Dar sighed. "I just want to go to the Grand Canyon," she said in a mournful tone. "Play with my dog, watch Kerry take shots of the sunset, and park my RV downwind from the barbecue grill. Is that too much to ask?" She looked over at Gerry. "After we leave ILS in March, we're going on a tour."

Easton studied her.

"The agreement that Dar is going to sign requires her to stay out of our industry for a period of time," Kerry said. "So we're going to take time off and go travel."

Easton sighed. "Soldiers don't get vacations, ladies. Not when we're at war."

Dar slid upright. "We're not soldiers. I had the chance to do that, and I turned it down." She met his eyes. "If we can work out a way to work together, that's great. If not, Gerry, I'm sorry if you don't want to continue with ILS. They're a good company, and they have a lot of good people who have done a very good job for you this last year."

"It's politics, Dar," Easton said. "Nothing personal, you know? I'm sure we can work something out. I've got no quarrel with your people, in fact I like that McLean fella a lot. Got a good head on his shoulders. But I trust you."

Dar sighed again.

"Victim of your own success, sweetheart." Kerry had, at this point, to find it almost funny. "You said it."

"I said it," Dar agreed. "Now I wish I'd stayed a technical manager running saturation reports on the tenth floor."

"I'm glad you didn't," Kerry said. "We would never have met. General, I'm sure we can work something out. Even if Dar can't participate officially, there's no reason I can't sign a deal with you."

Easton beamed at her. "That's the ticket!"

"Kerry." Dar eyed her.

"You were the one telling me to get moving on setting up the company," Kerry reminded her. "Fish or cut bait, Roberts." She watched Dar's hands, waiting for any sign of the fidgets she knew meant she'd pissed her off. But they remained relaxed and open on her knees, until one lifted to prop her head up. "Dar, someone has to do this. You know they need it. If not us, who?"

General Easton sat back in his chair, sipping his coffee, his eyebrows wiggling around as he listened.

Dar remained silent for a minute, then she half shrugged. "We'll work something out. I'd feel a lot better about bringing the military into the twenty-first century than dealing with politics."

Kerry patted her knee.

"Great," Easton said, after a bit of silence. "Well, Dar, how are your folks? I tried to give them a call the other day, but no one was home."

Dar took a sip of coffee. "That reminds me. Can you get them to leave my dad alone?"

"Eh?"

"They're trying to drag him back into active service," Dar said. "He and Mom took off for a while to get away from it."

Easton frowned. "Hmph." He considered. "I suppose he's inactive retired...I know they're doing some stuff with retention, but surely he'd not be in line for a call back?" he said. "I'll sort it out, Dar. Should only die once for your country, eh? He's put in his time."

"That's what I thought too," Dar said in a quiet voice. "Gerry, I don't want to lose my father again like that. Tell them to lay off, please?"

There was an awkward little silence, then Easton leaned forward and put a hand on her arm. "I'll take care of it, Dar, I promise."

"Thanks," Dar said. "And I'll do my best to sort out this contract."

"Deal." Easton stood up. "Tell you want, c'mon to dinner, the two of you over at our place. We've got a pile of puppies there, don'tcha know? Alabaster's. I think one's going to your family." He looked over at Kerry. "Jack's carrier's out in the Med, but the wife'll be glad for company."

"Sure," Dar said. "That'd be great."

"Never say no to puppies." Kerry smiled. "We'd love to."

THE PUPPIES WERE as adorable as she'd imagined them to be. Kerry sat with her legs sprawled out in the utility room of the Easton's house, as the litter of eight puppies climbed all over her, snuffling and squeaking and bringing back memories of Chino when they'd first gotten her. "Oh my gosh."

Dar was in the living room with Alabaster and the Eastons, and Kerry had tactfully elected to spend some time with Alabaster's litter to give them some privacy. The puppies were eight weeks old, and in a week or so one of the little girls would be leaving for Michigan.

"Sweetie, you'll love it," she told the chosen one, who had a little red collar on and a perfect black button nose. "There are two little kids to run around and play with and a big, big yard for you."

The puppy sat back and stuck her tongue out at her, small silky ears flopping around as she rocked her head back and forth, squeaking with delight when Kerry picked her up and cuddled her. "You're such a cutie."

Curled up next to her was a large black Labrador, who, she'd been told, was Buford, the puppies father. He seemed very relaxed and dignified, his muzzle resting on her thigh as he watched his puppies gamboling around.

Kerry chuckled softly, as she felt a tug on her shoelaces and a nibble on her ear at the same time. The puppy smelled clean and dusky, its breath holding that indefinable scent of new life and she had a sensation of being surrounded by that steadfastly trusting adoration she'd come to associate with Chino.

It soothed her soul.

"You know what, you little baby you, I want you to be good friends with my niece and nephew. I know Sally's going to love you, so try not to eat all her toys before you grow up, okay?"

The puppy made a squeaking, growling noise as she snuffled down the back of Kerry's collar, making Kerry bite her lip to keep from giggling. She looked down to find another puppy, a chocolate brown little boy climbing up on her leg to sniff at her kneecap. "Hey, I'm not your bed!"

The puppies were a range of colors to her surprise. Of the eight, five were a creamy whitish gold like Chino, two were chocolate brown, and one was inky black.

"Adorable."

Kerry looked up to find Dar in the doorway, watching her with an affectionate smile. "Oh, Dar, they're so darn cute." She indicated the puppies, two of whom had rambled off to investigate this new intruder. "I'm remembering all over again the day we got Cappuccino."

Dar sat down on the step and scooped up a puppy. "That was a beautiful day."

"It was." Kerry watched the girl puppy chew her finger. "That was the day I knew we were us." She watched the smile on Dar's face broaden. "So I hope this little girl makes Sally as happy as Chino made me."

"Aw." Dar leaned against the door jamb, giving the brown puppy in her arms a scratch behind his ears. "I remember just thinking about you and your little spaniel and how angry that made me," she said. "Just so pissed. I wanted you to know I was committed to our relationship and that wasn't ever going to happen to you again."

Kerry nodded, savoring the moment. "So what's going on out there?" she asked. "We okay with them?"

"Yeah." Dar gazed fondly at the little boy puppy. "They've had time to come to terms with the fact I'm gay," she said. "Did I ever tell you they were hoping Jack and I would get married?"

Kerry made a little face.

"I told Jack if it came down to it, I'd have a kid with him to give Gerry a grandkid," Dar said. "Glad I didn't have to make good on that. He's hooked up with a supply lieutenant and it looks serious."

"Guy or girl?"

"Girl."

"Ah huh." Kerry pursed her lips and nodded. "Well, I think my eyes would turn lime green if I had to deal with that, but you know, Dar, I did tell you your genes should stay in the pool."

"We have a dog," Dar said. "Matter of fact..." She eyed the puppy. "Think Chino wants a little brother?"

"Do we want to deal with Chino's little brother?" Kerry demurred. "You're the one who lost half her shoes."

They reluctantly extricated themselves from the furry pile and rejoined the Eastons in the living room. "Those puppies are so cute." Kerry dusted her hands off. "Thanks for letting me snuggle with them."

"Oh, that's all fine, honey." The General's wife smiled at her. "Now tell me, you're that nice young lady who talked to us about Thanksgiving dinner, a few years back aren't you?"

Kerry chuckled. "Matter of fact I am. I think I saved Dar from Brussels sprouts."

"You did," Mary Easton agreed. "I told Dar then I thought you were fond of her, and I was right. Wasn't I?"

"No doubt at all," Dar said. "Thanks for not freaking completely out about us, by the way. My parents were really proud of you all."

Easton chuckled with a touch of embarrassment. "Different times," he said, briefly. "But after all, we've known you since you were knee high."

They walked into the dining room where a meal of meatloaf and sides was waiting. Kerry excused herself to wash her hands, and pondered her reflection in the mirror as she did. "Do I even remember what it was like to be on the other end of that phone call?"

She remembered getting it. Mari's admin had called her, apologizing for interrupting her but saying someone was calling asking about Dar, and Maria was out. Could she talk to them?

Of course she could. She recalled the little, nervous start she'd gotten about it, almost a sense of guilt as she spoke to this unknown, friendly sounding woman taking possession of her new lover, while wishing wistfully she was going to join her for the now sprout free meal.

She'd forgotten completely about it, in her own holiday misery.

Drying her hands she returned to the dining room, taking her seat at Dar's side and putting her napkin in her lap in time to hear Dar relating a story about her and Jack in a tree that she thought she'd heard at a party sometime. "I can picture you doing that," she said. "I remember coming into that wiring closet on our first floor and finding you hanging upside down like a bat."

"Why were you doing that, Dar?" Mary asked.

"Why was I doing that?" Dar mused. "Damned if I remember. Was I stretching my back out?" she asked Kerry. "Yeah, I think I was. After sitting on that concrete floor all that time. I'm not a kid anymore."

"Oh you poor thing," Mrs. Easton mock clucked her tongue at her. "Wait 'til you get to be my age, young lady. Then we can talk about aches and pains."

"Well, Dar's retiring, matter of fact," General Easton said. "From that company, that is."

"Really?" Mary said. "My goodness."

Dar nodded. "We both are." She indicated herself and Kerry. "But we're going to open our own company after we take a break to go do some traveling."

"That's wonderful," Mary said. "Could you hire Gerry? He needs a better job." She eyed her husband. "And Jack also. His air group is being assigned to active duty in the Arabian Sea and I don't mind telling you, it makes me nervous."

The general frowned. "Least he's not on the ground, Mary."

"Anytime," Dar said. "I told Jack the last time we hung out I'd be glad to hire him at ILS, matter of fact." She looked at her plate of meatloaf with satisfaction. "Hell, I hired my father."

"He's a great research analyst," Kerry said.

"See?" Mary said.

"Now look here." The General shook his fork at them. "I'll retire soon enough! Service has been my whole life. Done us well so far, hasn't it?"

"Yes, but you're here," Mary said. "Jack isn't." She turned and regarded Kerry. "He's my only child."

"Mary, enough."

Mary subsided, but her expression was still stormy, and Kerry sorted through possible changes of subject. "So, aside from my sister, do you have homes for the rest of those adorable little kids?"

Gerald Easton gave her an approving look. "Well now, most of them do, in fact," he said. "Only one we have left to place is one of the brown boys."

Dar and Kerry exchanged looks.

"Really," Kerry said. "So tell me, do Labradors like company? We worry about Chino home alone all the time," she said. "Do you think we can maybe give that little boy a home?"

Easton's eyes lit up. "Why sure! That's a grand idea, isn't it Mary?"

"Absolutely," she said. "You know, they're really social dogs. Alabaster is such good stock, we only breed her every couple of years, and quite a few of her pups have gone on to do all kinds of things. But she's always a little disconsolate when all the puppies leave. I'm so glad she has Buford to keep her company."

"They are very social," Kerry said. "They're almost human, you know? Their expressions and everything. I really think Chino understands what I'm telling her when I talk to her."

"Got the smarts of three, four year old kids." Gerry relaxed, happy to be discussing one of his favorite subjects. "Very smart animals." He glanced to the side as Alabaster arrived, as though she knew she was being spoken of. "Isn't that right, madam?"

"Growf." Alabaster sat down next to him with her tail sweeping back and forth.

"So of course it would be great company for her to get her little brother," Mary said. "Have you thought of breeding Chino?"

"No," Kerry said. "Dar and I have such a busy life, it would be hard to do that, but I think we can handle another puppy, now that we'll have more time for a while."

"Not for too long." General Easton winked at her. "Got customers lining up. Don't forget that."

Dar and Kerry exchanged another glance, with a completely different set of emotions reflected in it. "Right," Dar said. "So tell me about Jack's new squadron. New planes?"

They launched into a military hardware conversation that left Kerry and Mary Easton regarding each other in bemused silence. "Do you like Washington, Kerry?"

"No, not so much." Kerry had finished her meatloaf, and was now sipping on the blackberry ice tea Mary had served with it. "I spent more than enough time here while I was growing up. Never really liked it."

"No, I guess not. Gerry told me a little about you having some family issues." Mary looked at her sympathetically. "My father was a state representative. I did my share of cheese and pâté parties."

"Yeah." Kerry smiled. "It can be tough for a kid growing up in that world. That was one of the reasons I wanted my sister to get a dog like our Chino for her little girl. I think she feels it, and they've had some family problems so..."

Mary smiled back. "Nothing like a little unreserved love, is there?"

"No. Nothing like it."

"I was so glad when Jack said Dar was going to take one of the last litter. When she was here, she seemed a little sad." Mary lowered her voice. "I always felt she missed out not being in the service, no matter what I said before about Jack being out there. It's a family, you know?"

Kerry nodded. "I know. I'm glad there's a family now around her." she said. "I love her parents."

"The Lord certainly looked after them," Mary said. "No doubt."

"I'm sure something was," Kerry said. "Good people have a way of winning out that way."

Chapter Six

KERRY STRETCHED OUT in the passenger seat, watching the dark streets go by as they headed for the airport. "They're a nice couple."

"They are," Dar agreed. "I'm glad we stayed and had dinner with them."

"And got a puppy." Kerry said. "Was that hasty?"

"I like hasty," Dar said. "Besides, it's true. He'll be company for Chino, and he can go in our RV with us."

Kerry thought that was going to be more chaos than the casual words indicated, but that was all right. "Let's make sure the RV has a washable floor."

"Mm." Dar turned into the small private airfield, already spotting their plane waiting to one side of a fenced wall. "That'll be a pleasure to deal with after all the crap we're going to have to get through with all this." She shut the car off and got out, handing over the keys to a uniformed valet.

"Thought about what you're going to tell them?" Kerry zipped her jacket up and followed her into the airfield building, lifting a hand in greeting at their pilot.

"I already know what I'm going to tell them. No." Dar handed over their overnight bag. "Sorry to keep you so late, Kent."

"No problem. Friend of mine came over and took me for dinner," he assured them. "And I took a four hour nap. It's all good."

They followed him out to the plane and boarded, trading the cold wind for the smell of leather and a hint of aviation kerosene. Dar dropped into a seat, then grimaced as her phone rang. She removed it from her pocket and glanced at the caller ID. "Uh oh."

"Uh oh?"

"Alastair." Dar hit the answer button. "Dar Roberts."

"Hey there, Dar," Alastair's voice echoed softly. "Just wanted to find out how everything went today. Board's a little anxious."

Dar sighed. "With good reason, Alastair. I don't have news you want to hear."

"Ah."

Kerry removed her jacket and hung it up in the little closet, as the flight attendant came out with some cappuccino, and a plate of warm cookies.

"You know, Ms. Stuart, I have to say I really wish you two weren't leaving the company." The woman said, with a sigh. "I'm sure going to miss you." She offered the cookies. "The last exec plane I worked the only thing I got to service was vodka and caviar."

"So you like cookies and hot mocha better?" Kerry laughed, taking a cup and a cookie. "I'll tell you it's nice to come back to after a day like today." She saw Dar's grimace. "Better get her some milk."

"Look, Alastair, what do you want me to tell you? Want me to lie? I didn't ask for this." Dar leaned back in her chair and gave Kerry a pathetic look. "It was about as welcome as a hemorrhoid."

"Gotcha." The flight attendant went back to the small galley as Kerry brought her cookie over and broke off a small piece, offering it to her beleaguered partner.

Dar accepted it, chewing and swallowing it as she listened. "Just don't say anything about the government position. The board half figured that was something directed at me personally anyway. I'm going to say no."

Kerry fed her another piece.

"Well, honestly, Alastair, it was me that got them Gerry's contract," Dar said after another long moment of listening. "I get their point, we are international."

The flight attendant came back and offered a glass of milk, which Dar took after giving her a bemused glance, which she then turned on Kerry, who smiled and took the seat next to her.

"Then I suggest you tell the board we're going to have to form a US only subsidiary if they want to pursue that. Maybe I can convince Gerry to go that route," Dar said. "I gotta go, they want to take off." She paused to listen. "Yeah, I know, Alastair. For what it's worth, I'm sorry."

She hung up as they started to taxi and let the device rest on her thigh, turning her head to regard Kerry. "He thinks they're going to want me to come to Houston again," she said. "Maybe I'll get lucky and they'll decide to let me get out of there early."

"Us," Kerry replied instantly.

"Us." Dar took a sip of her milk. "I hope to hell they find someone to take this damn job soon."

"LOOK AT HER." Kerry was sitting on their couch as Chino subjected her to a complete and very thorough sniffing. "She knows I was messing with those puppies."

"Of course she does." Dar stood looking out of the sliding glass doors, watching the lights of the channel blink in their red and green pattern. "You smell like puppy. You think she's dumb?"

Kerry studied Chino, whose tail was wagging wildly. "I think she likes it." She stroked Chino's thick fur, and the dog settled down and put her head on Kerry's lap, tail still thumping against the couch surface. "What do you think, Chi? You want to play with your little brother? He's really cute."

She glanced at Dar's back, seeing the tension in her shoulders. "You still freaking out?"

Dar's hands lifted and then fell again. She turned and came over to the couch, sitting down on the other side of Chino and draping her arm across the back. "I feel bad," she admitted. "I wasn't counting on Gerry's deal."

"Yeah." Kerry slid her arm outside Dar's and stroked the skin of her shoulder through her shirt. "But what you told Alastair was right, Dar. You did get that account for ILS. I remember when it happened."

"I remember using it to make your numbers work and save your buddies' jobs," Dar mused. "But it was legit. That second one, when I coerced him into giving me all those extra contracts to keep my mouth shut on the Navy base, that wasn't so legit."

"ILS won, either way."

"They did." Dar let her head rest against the couch back. "You know what, maybe I don't feel bad. Maybe I'm just frustrated at being in such a weird spot with everyone," she said. "Anything you particularly want to do this weekend?"

Kerry accepted the subject change gracefully. "I don't know. We'll figure something out tomorrow." She held her hand out palm up. "It's midnight. Want to join me in our water bed?"

"Yes."

They got up and went into the first floor bedroom, where they undressed in companionable silence, and then eased into the water bed.

The phone rang.

Dar sighed and reached over, picking up the receiver. "Hello?" she said, then paused. "This is Dar Roberts."

"Ugh." Kerry eased over and snuggled up next to her, listening to the voice issuing from the telephone. "That doesn't sound good."

Dar moved the phone closer to her. "Go on."

"Okay, Ms. Roberts? Look, I know it's late, and I'm sorry, but they cut all this stuff over to the new place yesterday and we're having all kinds of problems with it. I'm getting chewed alive."

The man's voice sounded aggravated and upset. "It's not fair, you know? They just told me to deal with it."

"Who told you that?" Dar asked, gently.

"Night supervisor in ops, in Miami," the man responded. "I'm sorry, I'm Jack Bueno. I'm kinda new. I forgot to introduce myself. I know the chain of command and all that but I'm running out of things to tell these customers so I figured I'd put my cojones on the line and see if I could get some help."

"So you want me to help you?" Dar asked, as Kerry rolled off in the other direction and got out of bed, a mild, bemused expression on her face. "For technical problems?"

"Ma'am," Bueno said. "I don't mean to be rude or anything, but your name's all over the base configs of everything in this center. I hope that's not because someone has your login."

Dar chuckled. "No, it's not." She rolled out of the bed herself. "All right, hang on and let me get some lights on here and go into my office. See what I can do to get things sorted out for you."

"Thank you." Bueno's voice sounded utterly relieved. "I'm real sorry to get you out of bed. I just didn't know what else to do."

"You get points for doing it." Dar pulled a shirt over her head and trudged from the bedroom into her office, finding the lights already on, and smelling coffee on a gust of air coming across the living room. "Matter of fact, I'm sorry you had to call me. Disappoints me like you would not believe."

"Yes, ma'am, I get that."

"Call me Dar. It's after midnight." Dar sat down and flicked on her monitor. "By the way, welcome to ILS."

KERRY RESTED HER head on her hand as she scribbled notes on a light purple notepad with a dark purple pen. It was four a.m. and she'd been recording changes Dar was making in the new datacenter's networking. "Want more coffee, hon?"

"I want a shotgun and a concrete block construction wall," Dar growled, making Kerry smile in pure reaction. "I'm so pissed."

"I know." Kerry reached over and patted her arm. "How about a chocolate milkshake instead of coffee?" She watched Dar's profile, as its tension eased and one brow rose, reading the positive reaction with no trouble at all. "Be right back."

She put the pen down and got up, walking around behind Dar and giving her a brief hug and a kiss on the top of her head before she retreated to the kitchen with a sleepy Chino ambling after her.

Dar had every right to be pissed. Kerry considered that, as she got out the required ingredients for a milkshake. In reality, she herself should be in the trenches getting this sorted out, but she knew getting in Dar's way and trying to get between her and the staff would just end up counterproductive for both of them.

She'd learned that the hard way. Four a.m. was no time to be getting into an argument with Dar about their respective areas of responsibility, seeing that her boss had spent the last four hours untangling the configuration Kerry's staff had implemented.

Just wasn't any point in it. Dar wasn't mad at her and she didn't want that to change.

She'd assigned the commissioning of the center out to her infrastructure teams. Apparently, there was a screw up, or to be fair, a design choice made that hadn't worked out. Dar was in the middle of doing multiple alterations of the systems to fix that, but the changes were extensive, and they impacted already upset customers and she was reserving herself to handle those phone calls to keep them off both the operations and Dar's back.

Of course they could have called in the groups in question and forced them to make the systems right. From a business and learning perspective that might have been a better choice. But at midnight, faced with a call from a customer facing director in trouble, Dar was in no mood for a coaching moment.

It was what it was. She scooped out some chocolate malt and scattered it over the balls of chocolate ice cream, then added milk to the blender before she started it mixing. "Want a cookie, Chi?" She fished a treat from the doggy jar for the patiently waiting dog, and offered it to her. "It's weird, huh? All dark outside and us up and doing stuff."

Chino crunched the treat, scattering tiny crumbs on the tile floor. She sniffed after them, and licked them up, as Kerry poured out two thick milkshakes and debated adding whipped cream.

Sometimes Dar liked whipped cream, sometimes she didn't, saying it blocked access to the ice cream.

"What the hell." She added the cream and headed back to Dar's office, coming in to find her studying her screen, pecking away at her keyboard in absorbed attention.

She set the shakes down and resumed her seat, picking up her pen again. "Okay, so now what did you do to that second core, Dar?"

"Made it virtual across the two chassis," Dar muttered. "Why in the hell wouldn't they do that, Kerry? Not only is it our standard, it's industry standard."

"Don't know, hon. I will ask at the staff meeting I called first thing Monday." Kerry scribbled down a note. "Is it getting any better?"

"Meh."

Kerry tapped her pen on the pad. "Would it help for us to go there?"

"Peh."

"Okay." Kerry ticked off the items she had to do and wrote a few more notes. "Do you need to add equipment in there? So I can get that prepped?"

Dar scowled. "Let me get back to you on that." She made another change and reviewed the results. "Holy shit, what a hairball."

"Ms. Roberts?" Jack came back on the conference bridge. "Whatever you did about five minutes ago really helped Interbank. They're running normal metrics now."

"Oh, good." Kerry drew a small line, and made a note on one of the checklist items. "Good to hear, Jack."

"Thanks, Ms. Stuart. Sorry you had to get into this too. Getting Ms. Roberts up was bad enough."

Kerry studied the phone, then looked at Dar. "Does he not know?" She mouthed, inclining the pen toward her own chest, then at Dar.

Dar pressed the mute button. "He's new," she said, apparently reading Kerry's mind. "I don't think they go over our relationship in new employee orientation. Yet."

Kerry chuckled, and shook her head. She reached over to release the mute. "No problem, Jack. Let's just get this squared away so our customers are happy," she said. "We can worry about who and when and why later."

"Yes, ma'am," Jack agreed instantly. "That's what my big problem was. I don't mind having arguments about doing it this way, or doing it that way, but when it starts to impact the people who depend on us, we can't be sitting here arguing with each other."

"Yup." Dar was busy typing. "That's the whole point all right."

"I was surprised," Jack said, after a brief pause. "I had heard ILS wasn't like that. One reason I took the datacenter director job here."

Dar stopped typing and she and Kerry exchanged glances again.

"No offense," Jack said, after an awkward pause.

"None taken," Dar said. "Okay, I just made another change, and reconverged everything. See what that does."

"Okay." Jack walked away from the phone and they heard a door open, and the airplane engine sound of a datacenter that was cut off as the door closed.

"What he just said bothers me," Kerry said. "Because I believed that too, Dar. So what's going on? Are people that pissed off that we're leaving that they're doing this stuff on purpose?"

"Or is it just that we've told them to think for themselves and this is the result?" Dar responded. "Not sure which I'd hate more."

"Mm." Kerry shook her head back and forth. "Boy that's a tossup."

"Ker I wrote our design standards," Dar said in a serious tone. "It's not like I just kept it all in my head. It's on the process server."

"Going to be a long Monday." Kerry sighed and made a few more notes, listening to Dar slurp her milkshake as they waited for Jack to come back. "As if it wasn't going to be long enough already."

"No kidding," Dar groused.

Kerry sipped her own drink for a few minutes, then jerked slightly as her own phone rang. "Kerry Stuart." She answered it without bothering to check the caller ID.

"Hey, Kerry."

"Hey, Mark. What's up?"

"I guess I need to ask you that." Mark sounded glum. "Night ops finally called me and told me the new datacenter's having problems."

"Wow," Kerry said. "Dar's been working on it for about four hours or so. I think she's almost done." She looked up to see Dar watching her over the rim of her glass, a thick white whipped cream mustache on her upper lip. "I scheduled an all hands meeting on Monday to talk about it."

"They said they were having some issues, but it didn't sound serious yesterday," Mark said. "I figured it could wait for us to come in next week."

"Well." Kerry exhaled. "By my count Dar's made about forty changes to the configuration in there. So apparently it was more serious than that." She took a swallow of her milkshake. "It's been getting better though."

"Shit."

"Yeah."

"She pissed?"

"Yeah," Kerry said. "I am too, actually. I wasn't looking to stay up all night fixing someone else's mistakes tonight."

Mark was silent for a long moment. "Shit," he finally said. "Okay, let me start the research. See how we can make sure it doesn't happen again."

Kerry felt a sense of relief on hearing that. "It can wait for the morning, Mark. I think Dar's got it now. We can pick up the details afterward so long as they're good until after the weekend." She paused, as she heard the sound of the datacenter pick up on the call and then cease with the bang of the door. "Hang on."

"Okay." Jack got back on the bridge. "That looks a lot better. The graphs have settled down, and my phone's stopped ringing." He sounded tired, but elated. "The ops center said the metrics are coming back into normal range."

"Good." Dar licked her lips. "So let's hold it here for now, and we can do a complete review in a couple days to see if anything else needs adjusting. Call me if anything else wiggles loose."

"Ma'am...ah, I mean, Dar, thanks a billion," Jack said. "I really, really appreciate the help."

"Any time." Dar smiled. "Good night." She released the speaker phone button and regarded Kerry, shaking her head when Kerry pointed at her phone.

"Okay, looks like we're all right for now, Mark," Kerry said.

"Sure. Big D touched it." Mark sighed. "I have no fucking idea what we're going to do without her."

Dar's ears twitched, hearing the words in soft echo. She sat back in her chair with her glass cradled between both hands, and sucked at the contents in silence.

"Hopefully we can make it a learning moment," Kerry said. "You know, Dar had to learn it some way, right?"

"No," Mark said. "She was born knowing that stuff. It's organic. We were talking about that in the shop the other day. But we'll have to come up with something. Maybe we'll get her to code a virtual Dar in the ops console."

Kerry watched Dar's eyebrows shoot right up to her hairline. "Hm...that's an idea," she said. "Talk to you later, Mark. Have a good night." She closed the phone and returned Dar's somber gaze. "Yuck."

"Yuck," Dar repeated. "Let's go to bed." She got up and stretched, grimacing as her shoulders popped. "Did we have plans tomorrow?"

"Nope." Kerry drained her glass and stood up to join her. "I vote we sleep in."

"Unless someone else calls for help." Dar took both glasses and headed for the kitchen with them. "The one bright spot of the whole night was that guy Jack. They found a good one there."

"Let's hope we don't lose him," Kerry muttered. "We've got to get this under control, Dar. All those times your folks and my family would ask why the hell the two of us were involved in every damn thing is coming back to bite us in the ass."

"Mm."

REGARDLESS OF THE late night, they only managed to stay in bed until 8. Kerry found herself a little after that on the porch in her bathrobe and slippers, enjoying the crisp air and bright sunlight of a calm Saturday morning. She stifled a yawn and watched a seagull soar overhead, trying to decide if there was anything in specific she wanted to accomplish.

She had several small projects going. Some planting in their small garden, sorting out her newly digitized photos into collections, and a barbecue brisket recipe she wanted to try. But right now, none of that seemed urgent, and she was content to listen to the rustle of palm trees in the winter wind and watch sail boaters heading out of the cut in the choppy waters.

Dar wandered out dressed in sweatpants and a sweatshirt, and sat down on the swing next to her. "I was thinking about what you said the other day," she said once the swing stopped moving.

Kerry regarded her. "That covers a lot of ground, hon."

"About me getting a new car," Dar said. "I think I want to."

"Yeah? Cool! What kind?"

Dar shrugged, and grinned. "I don't know. Let's go out and look at some. See if we can find one that fits me. Maybe I'll get a souped up sports car."

Kerry's brows twitched. "Hon, you're way too young for a mid life crisis. Aren't you?"

"Hey, you were the one with the Mustang, babe." Dar chuckled. "I don't really have anything specific in mind. Let's go see what's out there."

"All right by me." Kerry toasted her with her coffee cup. "Maybe we can look around for a place to put our new office while we're driving." She wiggled her feet in contentment. "I got an email from Jack. Everything's quiet at the datacenter this morning."

"He get any sleep?" Dar wondered. "Glad things are better. Doesn't make it any less aggravating though."

"We really need to turn this into a learning experience," Kerry said. "Not a good precedent."

"Well." Dar twiddled her thumbs. "Could be the sign of an independent, though wrong headed, mind."

Kerry chuckled wryly.

Dar sighed. "Maybe I should have woken up everyone else and had them fix it. Honestly, I just don't know what to do about this, Ker."

"We can talk about it at the office." Kerry got up and stretched. "Let's go find you a car, Dardar." She ruffled Dar's hair as she came past her and headed for the door. "And we can stop and look at cameras for me."

"That's my kind of shopping," Dar said. "Maybe I'll get a new laptop."

"Oh I can see this is going to be an expensive day." Kerry laughed. "Meet you in the shower?"

"Let's do it."

AN HOUR LATER they were dressed, and pulling off the ferry onto the causeway heading west. It was a beautiful day, cool and crisp and cloudless and Kerry almost felt like humming as she leaned back in the passenger seat of Dar's car, enjoying the splash of sunlight through the windows.

Chino was relaxing in the back seat, tail perpetually wagging, delighted to have been added to the excursion. "Growf!" She barked at a palm tree whizzing by.

"You tell 'em, Chi." Kerry reached back and tickled the dog's paw. "We're going to take you to get ice cream when we're done today. What do you think about that?"

"Growf!"

Dar had her sunglasses on and she was tapping the steering wheel with her thumbs, waiting for a light to turn green. "So where do we start?"

"Well." Kerry hitched one knee up. "Foreign or domestic?"

Dar thought about that for a minute. "Does it matter? I've had pretty good luck with both in terms of maintenance."

"It matters in terms of narrowing down our traveling, hon. Otherwise, just go find some random major street and start driving and we'll stop at the first dealership we find."

Dar made a little face. "Okay let's do that. Let's let a little random fate into it."

Fate, as it turned out, led them to an auto mall with six different manufacturers stretched across both sides of the street as far as the eye could see. Dar pulled into the first one and parked. "Here we are."

Kerry looked out the window. "Got enough choices here for you, hon?"

"Mm." Dar got out and opened the back door, attaching Chino's leash to her collar and standing back to let the dog hop out. They walked along the pavement to the first line of new cars, strolling between them and joining a number of other people doing the same.

"Now, what in the hell do I want?"

Kerry peered at the cars they were passing. "What I liked best when I got my buggy was sitting up higher. Do you like that?"

"Yes," Dar responded positively. "I like that, and a big engine. And leather seats."

Kerry chuckled. "Well that narrows it down a little. And honestly, I can't see you in a sedan, Dar. It's too boring."

"I'll take that as a compliment."

"It is," Kerry said. "So let's get past this Acura dealer and head for where the Jeeps are." She pointed. "Those are cute."

They went from one lot to the other, and now were roaming among taller, boxier looking vehicles. "Hm." Dar reviewed them. "Too squarish. They look too much like the one I have now."

"True."

They kept walking. Chino trotted alongside, head swinging from one side to the other, nose twitching.

"Ford. There's my Mustang," Kerry said. "It was a cute car."

Dar smiled. "Totally fit you. I remember thinking that when I saw it that night."

"It was fun to drive," Kerry said. "But not enough leg room for you."

"No." Dar spotted a profile. "But hm..." She diverted her steps. "What do we have here?"

Kerry regarded her target. "Ah," she mused. "An SUV married a pickup truck." She followed Dar over to the Ford Sport Trac row, where her companion started nosing around a dark red specimen.

"What do you think of this, Chi?" Kerry peered in a window. "Nice big crew cab back seat for you to ride in."

Chino hopped up on her back legs and Kerry just caught her in time to keep her claws off the paint job. "Ah ah ah." She cradled the dog as she sniffed at the open window "No claws."

Dar went around to the driver's side door and opened it, getting inside and looking around. "Leather seats," she remarked, with a grin.

"And a decent size engine," Kerry said, looking at the window sticker. She let Chino down and leaned on the door jamb, watching Dar adjust the seat to her long frame. It wasn't anything she would pick for herself. She glanced back at the bed of the truck. "We can put the bike in there, not to mention, camping stuff. Hey." She poked her head inside. "Could we pull this behind the RV?"

Dar had gotten things sorted out to her satisfaction, and reached forward to grip the steering wheel. Her motion attracted the attention of one of the roaming salesmen, and he came over to them.

"Good morning, ladies," the man greeted them with an amiable grin.

"Hi," Dar responded. "Can we take a ride?"

Kerry had enough experience with Dar's mentality to know when it was on a track and chugging. She opened the back door and slid into the crew cab, moving over so Chino could jump up and join her.

The seats smelled rich and pungent even above the new car smell, and she stretched out as the salesman hurried back with the keys and got into the front passenger seat. "Uh." He looked at Kerry. "We don't allow dogs in the cars...I mean, you know, for a test."

"Won't matter," Kerry said with a kind smile. "Just give her the keys." She patted Chino, who had curled up on the seat and put her head down on her lap. "Hi, I'm Kerry."

"Tom." The man handed over the keys. "Ah, you gals from around here?"

Dar started the engine and peered at the instruments. "Nice." She said. "Uncluttered."

"Ah, yeah," Tom said. "It's a nice truck. Got a eight-cylinder engine, yeah? This one's got the automatic package, but you can get manual too if you want."

"I don't," Dar said. "I usually need to use one hand for the wheel and one for a piece of technology." She put the truck in drive and pulled out. "I have an SUV now."

"Oh, yeah?" Tom looked at a page in his little book. "This truck's got a bunch of extras. The seats, the moon roof," he pointed up. "Wheels, rims, but we got base models too if you're interested."

"Four wheel drive?"

"Yeah," he said. "Some people like the two wheel better. I got a blue one in that."

Dar turned onto the main drag and gave the truck some gas. The engine made a low, growly noise and responded, putting a grin on its driver's face. She spotted a vacant lot on the next block and turned into it, going over the rocks and grass at a respectable speed.

"Uh, hey." Tom held on to the grab handle. "Take it a little easy, it's only got two miles on it."

Dar felt the suspension beneath her handling the uneven ground, and turned the truck in a tight circle. "Hang on, Ker."

"Hanging." Kerry had one arm around Chino and one on the handle." She glanced back through the window and saw gusts of dust churning up behind the truck, rocks bouncing out of the tire's path. "Got nice pickup, hon."

"It does." Dar got around to the entrance again and without hesitation she gunned the engine and bolted out across the six lane main street, turning left ahead of oncoming traffic and pulling into the flow going the other direction with smooth skill. The road was clear ahead and she accelerated, pleased with the power of the engine and the feel of the steering.

It wasn't a sports car. It wasn't an SUV. She'd always liked pickups. Dar glanced at the salesman who had his eyes closed, and his lips pursed and clenched. With a chuckle she aimed her direction back to the lot and turned into it, bumping over the retainer blocks and pulling into a spot in the front of the dealership. "We're back."

Tom opened his eyes and regarded her. "Okay. So...you want to see something else?"

Dar pulled her wallet out and removed a card from it. "I'll take it. Give us a minute and we'll bring the other one over to trade in."

Tom blinked. "You want to put a deposit with that?" he asked, taking the card.

"Nope. Put the whole thing on it," Dar said. "Whatever extras come with it, get them on, and have them shine it up. Okay?"

Tom eyed her with shocked respect. "Yes, ma'am!" He got out of the car and carefully put the card into his little folder. "I'll be right back!" He trotted off toward the low, beige building nearby.

Dar turned around and looked at Kerry. "This okay?"

Kerry chuckled. "Honey, it's very you and I like it. Actually, I like it better than the Lexus." She patted the seat. "It'll be great to travel with, and we can put all our camping stuff in the back. Let's go get your trade in and make this a done deal."

Dar got out of the front seat and closed it, bouncing a little on her heels. "My dad's gonna love it."

Kerry got out and waited for Chino to join her, and they started back to where they parked. "So far, so good today."

"Yep."

"Hope we get as lucky with my new camera."

IT WAS AN awesome enough day for her to mostly forget the previous evening. Kerry moved around to the front of Dar's new car and took another picture of it, pulling the camera back to regard her work in all its instantaneous, digital glory. "Huh."

The instant feedback was curiously charming and somewhat addictive. She focused on the front hood of the saucy truck and snapped another shot of it. "Y'know, Chi, I really like this thing"

Chino was seated nearby in the grass that ringed the parking lot they were parked in, watching her with intelligent interest.

"You like it?" Kerry knelt and took another picture. "Know what I think, Chi? I think we're going to end up driving this thing to Vegas instead of flying there. Would you like that? Drive across the country?"

Chino's tail wagged enthusiastically.

"We'll fix that crew cab up for you, right? Fold the seats down and put your bed in there." Kerry went on with her planning. "And put all our stuff and camping gear in the back. That's going to work out nice."

Chino got up and wandered over, snuffling at her knees.

"This is going to be cool." Kerry put her arm over the dog's back and hugged her. "Hey, where's mommy Dar?"

Chino's ears perked up, and she looked around, spotting a familiar figure approaching as her tail started whipping Kerry in the back.

"Ow."

Dar had emerged from the Dairy Queen, holding ice cream sundaes for the two of them, and a cup of vanilla for Chino. She ambled over to her family and beckoned them over to the back of the truck, where she let the tailgate down and perched on it. "Comes with a table."

"It does." Kerry opened the front door and put the camera down on the seat, capping the lens and closing the door. She joined Dar at the back and took her sundae, hopping up to sit on the tailgate and watch Dar give Chino her treat. "That's so cute."

Dar grinned, visibly in a good mood. "So. Think this was a good pick?" She indicated the truck. "For real, I mean, not just to save the salesman's mojo."

"I like it." Kerry swung her feet. "I mean, I really do. I think it's going to be perfect for our travels, and it's really cute and sporty."

"Mm." Dar gave a satisfied grunt. She let Chino finish licking out the cup, and then went on to her own sundae. "It was time for a change. I had that Lexus for years. I think I bought it two, or maybe three years before we met." She messed with the sundae for a minute. "It was all right."

"This fits your image better." Kerry nudged her with an elbow. "I have to check when my lease is up. Maybe I'll get something more exciting this time too. Do you always just buy your cars outright? I thought that guy was going to trip over his tongue."

Dar chuckled. "Yeah, I do. I mean, I got a good trade in for that old beast, and I can afford it. The truck wasn't that expensive. I guess if I wanted to buy a Mazarati maybe I would lease it or whatever."

"We always leased," Kerry mused. "But come to think of it, you don't actually have a credit card, do you? Just the Amex."

"Just the Amex," Dar said. "You actually have better credit than I do. Since I own that condo, and we own the cabin, I don't have any debts."

"So un-American." Kerry clucked her tongue.

"Yeah, well, credit was scarce when I was growing up." Dar crunched contentedly on her chocolate shell. "That's how I've managed to sock away most of my paycheck all these years. Not much to spend it on." She glanced at Kerry. "Until now, that is."

"Mutual spend."

Dar swallowed her mouthful. "Know what?"

"What?"

"I'm in the mood for a dive tomorrow. You up for it?"

"Absolutely. Can we stop back at the camera shop to see if they have an underwater housing for this little Canon beast?" Kerry finished her ice cream and tossed the container in a nearby garbage can. "Let's give it a real workout."

Dar closed the hatch and let Chino into the back seat of her new ride, then she slid into the driver's seat and looked around the cab with a sense of satisfaction.

Definitely a change. It was a more rugged interior than her previous car and like Kerry, she felt it really better reflected her. The Lexus was fine, and she hadn't minded driving it, but there was always a sense that it projected a tiny bit of status seeking she didn't think she possessed.

At least, she hoped she didn't. She remembered, vaguely, worrying if the car was equal to the ones her peers in the company were driving, but after a while other things had occupied her mind and she'd gotten used to the big beast.

She started the engine and shifted into drive, her peripheral vision catching Kerry fiddling with her new camera, unsurprised when she half turned in her seat and pointed the lens at her. "Run out of truck to shoot?"

"Heh heh." Kerry let the auto focus do its thing, and snapped the pix, getting a nice shot of Dar's profile.

They drove a few minutes down the road, then Dar pulled back into the photo shop's lot and parked. "Me and Chino will wait for ya."

Kerry hopped out and trotted over to the store, while Dar adjusted the seat back a little and relaxed, idly watching the late Saturday afternoon passersby.

Her cell phone rang. She picked it up and glanced at the caller ID, then opened it. "Hey, Alastair."

"Dar."

His vocal tone warned her. "Yeap. What's up?"

"Not going to dance around," Alastair said, in a very quiet voice. "The board has instructed me to terminate your employment and Kerry's. Right this moment."

Dar felt a flash through of several emotions, a blast of heat, and then of cold, and then oddly of relief. "Okay," she said after a moment of silence. "So that's it? They're not going to offer me a package, or hand over pension or anything?"

"No."

"Okay," Dar said again. "That's what I get for being honest?"

"Yes."

Dar heard more emotion in those short syllables than she ever had from Alastair. "Sorry, boss. I didn't really deserve that, and neither did you."

There was a very long moment of silence. "No," Alastair finally said, a clipped, rough word that Dar heard the tears in. "And that's the very last god damned thing I'm going to do for them because I just submitted my own termination at the same time. Fuck them all."

Dar looked up and saw Kerry coming at the truck at a run. The passenger side door jerked open. "What?" Kerry said. "What's wrong?"

Dar blinked, her mind operating on two separate levels. "Wow. That does work," she said, then exhaled. "It's Alastair. We've both just been fired."

Kerry slid across the seat and closed the door. "Done deal? Already?"

Dar nodded. "No benefits or anything. So we've got some planning to do, heath insurance and that stuff." She turned back to the phone. "Alastair, I'm sorry. I don't know what else to say to you."

He sighed. "They're sending some people to the Miami office, to take over your role. Might want to warn those folks there. I think they'll send an email out."

"Okay," Dar said. "I guess if they didn't give me a package, that means I also don't have a non-compete clause. After we go on vacation and come back, if you want a job, call me."

Alastair was silent for a moment, then he chuckled. "Know what? I just might. Dar, I'm damned sorry. I didn't want it to end like this."

Kerry moved closer. "Alastair?" She leaned her head against Dar's shoulder.

"Hm? Oh. Yes. Hello, Kerry," Alastair said. "I'm sorry about all this, especially after all that we went through."

"You know, maybe it had to end like this," she said. "There wasn't an easy way out."

He sighed.

"I feel bad about the good people we're leaving there," Kerry said in a more serious tone. "I'm going to call Mayte and Maria, Dar. I think you should call Mark. Let him know before they tell him."

Dar nodded. "I'll have our laptops couriered to the office, Alastair. Have them turned into security."

"Y'know? Me too," Alastair said. "I just texted the wife with that PDA thing. She's happy as a clam." He sounded surprised. "Maybe you were right, Kerry."

"Okay, Alastair. Give me a call later and we can make sure it's all wrapped up," Dar said. "I'm going to call Mari and Duks so they don't get surprised either."

"All right. Talk to you later," Alastair said, then hung up.

Dar put her phone down on her leg and looked at Kerry. "Know something?"

"I know I don't feel as bad as I probably should feel," Kerry said. "And, that we probably need to get that company up and going sooner rather than later." She sat back. "Wow."

"Yeah." Dar shook her head and opened her phone again. "Let me get Mari on the line so she can send out a note to the staff."

"Let me get her." Kerry took the phone. "Let's drive by that office complex we looked up and check it out. I get a feeling it's going to be a very busy week."

Dar leaned her elbows on the steering wheel and smiled wryly. "Sometimes, fate has a way of kicking you in the ass to make you start moving."

Kerry nodded as she listened to the phone. "Hey, Mari, this is Kerry. Yeah, something's wrong. Let me fill you in."

Dar focused her attention on driving, listening with half an ear as Kerry went through her speed dial list, thinking of all the things left undone at ILS that now she'd never get a chance to see happen.

At one level, it hurt. She knew she'd given as much as a human could be expected to give a job over the years, and the abrupt release burned.

But now that was in the past, and her mind was already moving ahead, looking forward to the new challenges and the next phase of their lives, since she'd already mentally accepted that change was coming.

Now, she was glad she'd spent all night fixing some dumbass problems in the datacenter. It was a completely acceptable way for her to end her tenure there, as she'd started it. No slacking, no compromise, just a job quietly well done. The company would go on. They'd find someone to take the spot, in fact maybe they already had, and everyone would settle down and accept it after a while.

A few people, notably Mayte and Maria, they'd take with them. They were family. But the rest would get over the shock, and maybe even take the opportunity for advancement. Maybe they would give Mark Kerry's job. Dar turned down the street where their possible office space was.

She nodded to herself. Might be good for everyone.

Kerry finally closed the phone. "Wow," she said. "She was kind of pissed."

"At us?"

"No."

"Oh. Well she's the VP of HR," Dar said, reasonably. "They really should have told her before they told us."

Kerry shook her head. "Anyway, she's going to send a note out. Duks was there. He didn't even want to talk to me." She frowned. "Guess we ruined their Saturday."

"We didn't do anything," Dar reminded her. "Okay, this is the place."

The phone in Kerry's hand rang, and she opened it. "Hello...oh, hi Mark." She glanced at Dar. "No, she's here. No...yeah, no it's true." She glanced at Dar. "Yeah, they just called us. What?" She listened for a long moment. "I was just about to call you. I just got off the phone with Mari. No, we're going to have the laptops couri—oh, well, okay sure, that would be nice if you did that."

"Going to come pick them up?" Dar mouthed.

Kerry nodded. "No we're not home right now. We were out shopping. Dar got a new car and...yeah, we're out near the Grove looking at some property." She paused. "No, not residential." She paused again, and glanced at Dar. "Uh...sure...sure, we could meet you for dinner out here."

Dar eyed her.

"Sure, Monty's on South Bayshore, in about an hour. See ya." Kerry shut the phone. "He sounded pretty upset. So I guess he wants to talk to us about it."

"Uh huh." Dar nodded. "I like Monty's. C'mon, let's look at this place."

"Yup, let's go." Kerry got out and let Chino out of the back. Then she turned as Dar came up next to her. "Hey."

"Hey." Dar had her sunglasses on, but she removed them as she rested her elbow on Kerry's shoulder.

"I'm sorry it had to end like that, sweetheart," Kerry said. "It really isn't fair to you, to what you've done there, or how you led us all to so many good results."

Dar studied her in silence for a moment, filtered sunlight catching the odd mahogany highlight in her hair. "No," she finally said. "It's not fair, but you know what? I'm glad."

Kerry blinked in surprise. "Huh?"

"The last two months of this would have been one long drawn out never ending frustration. I don't like that I was fired, or you for that matter, but it's done. Let's move on."

She draped her arm over Kerry's shoulders, looped Chino's leash over her hand, and they walked across the parking lot in thoughtful silence.

Chapter Seven

"I THINK WE'RE going to need to sit outside," Kerry said. "I'm not leaving Cheebles in the car." She took the dog's leash and waited as Dar addressed the seating person outside Monty's restaurant. The sun was setting, and a brisk, cool wind was blowing off the bay, making her glad she'd turned the collar up on her jacket.

"C'mon," Dar beckoned her, and they followed the host around the back to the deck, which was sparsely attended due to the weather. "They've got warmers back here."

Kerry was glad to take a seat in a relatively sheltered corner, as Chino sat down happily at her side, looking around with interest. "We're early."

"Yeah," Dar said. "Didn't take that long with the agent. That place had some definite plusses, but we'd need to do some reno to make it work for a tech company."

"Server room, for one thing," Kerry said. "But it was cute. I liked it. It seemed like a good size for us to start with."

Dar nodded and opened the menu. "Can I have a Jamaican coffee, please?"

"Sure," the waiting server agreed. "Good night for it. "

"Same here," Kerry said. "We're waiting for a third person. He should be here in a few minutes."

"Right, I'll get your drinks." The woman went off.

Dar leaned back. "Long day." She exhaled. "I think the whole thing's just hitting me."

Kerry reached over and put her hand over Dar's, squeezing the fingers. "It's...it's hard to accept," she said. "I keep thinking of stuff I have to do on Monday and then..." She paused. "I won't miss all the chaos, but I will miss the people."

Dar nodded.

"Hard to absorb that I won't be having coffee with the gang downstairs, or...oh crap. I've got to send a note to Colleen," Kerry said. "That's the hard part. You become used to stuff in your life, and then it's just gone."

Dar nodded again, sniffling a little. She looked down at the table, then out over the water.

Kerry squeezed her hand again. "Sorry. I'll stop that. We don't need to bring ourselves down."

The server came over with their drinks. "Can I get you some appetizers, ladies? How about a raw bar platter?"

"Sure," Kerry said. "That would be great."

The woman whisked off again.

Dar cleared her throat. "We don't need to bring ourselves down, that's for sure," she agreed. "I think it's just sort of starting to piss me off, when I think about it."

"We did resign," Kerry pointed out.

"We did. But it still pisses me off," Dar said. "I wanted to leave on my terms. Not theirs." She spotted Mark and waved him over. "Me and my ego. I'll get over it."

"Hey." Mark dropped down into the spare seat, his hair in violent disarray. "Should have took the truck," he said. "Dar, I'm sorry, I know you turned in your chit, but this sucks. I mean, shit, you know?"

"I know." Dar took a sip of her coffee, her composure restored. "So I went to DC yesterday, and first I get propositioned by the government, then Gerry Easton tells me they don't want to do business with ILS, just with me. So that's what I told Alastair, and that's what got me booted."

"Oh." Mark frowned. "Holy crap."

"Something like that, yeah," Dar said. "Wasn't something I looked for, but I can see that pissing them all off."

Mark sighed. "Sucks," he repeated. "Specially after last night. Thanks for hauling everyone's stones out of the fire. We're not even going to get to talk design with you about it I guess."

"Probably not."

The server came back and put down their platter. "Hi, there. Can I get you a drink?" she asked Mark. "Got two for one beer."

"Yeah, scotch and soda please," Mark said. "Double."

"Sure."

There was a little, almost uncomfortable silence, then Mark visibly steeled himself. "So. What are you guys going to do now?"

Kerry remained silent, waiting for Dar to answer. Dar was closer to Mark. She'd been his supervisor for almost as long as she'd been working there. The offer, which she sensed was coming, was Dar's call, just like her offer to Mayte was hers.

"Ker and I just got back from looking at some office space," Dar said. "We're going to open our own tech company. Wanna come work for us?"

Very straightforward. Kerry almost had to muffle a smile. No hinting, no feeling him out. So, Dar.

Mark blinked at her, then grinned. "You made that too easy, Big D."

"They didn't make me sign a non-compete, and there's nothing stopping me from moving forward with this," Dar said, briskly. "I can't take everyone. Company's too big and we're bootstrapping. But I'd welcome you as part of our new venture."

Hard to say who was more shocked when Mark lost his grip on his emotions and some tears escaped and ran down his cheeks. Kerry leaned forward at once and reached over to him, touching his arm. "Hey..."

"Sorry." He wiped his eyes with some annoyance. "I mean after last night and all the stuff you've done and..." He exhaled. "It just sucks."

"Yeah, that's true, it does suck. But you know what they say about lemons," Dar said, in a gentle tone. "We were on the way out anyway. This just lets us get started sooner, and without any restrictions. We're going to get the office lease settled, then go on vacation, then when we get back, we'll start lining up clients."

"We were thinking of doing our own datacenter," Kerry said. "And Dar wants to offer engineering services."

"It'll be different," Dar said. "Different scope, smaller, we don't have the resources ILS has."

Mark regarded them, sniffling a little. "Where'd you say the new place is?"

"We were looking at a place in the Grove," Kerry said.

"Fuckin A." Now a smile crossed Mark's face. "Can I start Monday? I don't want to have to face that place without you guys."

Dar smiled, visibly touched. "I think we need a day or two to actually create the company. Maybe give us 'til Wednesday."

Kerry leaned her elbow on the table. "You have four weeks vacation that just rolled over, Mark," she said. "Take it."

He nodded. "Barbara said the same thing. I told her I was coming out to meet you guys and she knew I was going to ask to go with you. She wants to try skiing."

"Do it," Kerry said. "But maybe if you're not leaving for Aspen for a few days you can come over to the new place and lay out a wiring plan. I think the last tenants were beanbag chair makers."

Mark's smile grew wider. "Absolutely."

"Know any place we can put a datacenter?"

"Absolutely!"

THEY ENDED UP with the moon high overhead, at a table that now had the three of them, plus Mayte, Maria, Maria's husband Tomas, and Colleen.

Dar had switched from Jamaican coffees to regular ones, and she was sitting back in her chair, one hand idly scratching Chino's ears.

"It's terrible," Maria said, for the nth time. "I simply cannot believe it, Dar, that they would treat you so." She shook her head, and her husband echoed the motion.

"No kidding," Mark agreed. "But, hey, you know? It could end up great for us, right?"

"I have told Maria, if she wishes, she should leave that place," Tomas said, one of the first things he'd said since he'd gotten there. "And Mayte also. I do not think it would be a good thing for them to be there now that you are gone."

Mayte looked expectantly at Kerry, who smiled and lifted her cup.

"We have something else in mind." Kerry said, "I've already talked to Mayte about it. I think it's just going to happen a little faster than I thought it would."

Maria beamed at her. "Mayte has told me," she said. "I was so happy."

Kerry looked over at Dar, one eyebrow quirking up.

"Yeah," Dar promptly said. "So here's the plan. We're going to get with a lawyer on Monday to set up the new company. We've just checked out some office space, but it's going to take us a few weeks to start all that stuff up."

Everyone nodded in agreement.

"I like the idea of taking my vacation," Mark said. "I don't think I could stand it there with someone else in charge. It would be a freaking horror show."

"Ai, yes," Maria agreed. "We just now got our vacations again for this year, no?" she said. "It would be nice to take a trip."

Kerry sighed. "Poor Mari."

"Who says she's not going on vacation too?" Colleen asked. "Here now I'm hoping you need an accountant one fine day."

Kerry chuckled. "I'm sure we're going to need a lot of things. We've got some pretty ambitious ideas, and some potential clients lined up already." She glanced at Dar. "Actually, Dar's got an offer to become the national technology czar. I don't think she's going to take it though."

"Really?" Colleen goggled at the tall, dark haired woman.

Dar half shrugged. "My reputation gets me in the worst trouble," she said. "But yeah, I think I'm going to wiggle out of that one. Way too much politics for me."

"Me too," Kerry agreed. "Anyway, it's getting late and we had a late night last night, so..." She looked around at them. "I guess if you're going to take vacation, send Mari a note. Mayte and Maria, I think if we're moving as fast as it looks, we might need you as early as a week from Monday. That be okay?"

Both women beamed at her.

"Can we get everything in place by then?" Kerry asked Dar. "I'd like to before we take off on vacation ourselves."

"I already sent a note to Richard Edgerton," Dar said. "We'll see. Everyone give Kerry your personal cell numbers, so we can keep in touch."

Hands reached for phones as Kerry took out her new gizmo, opening the contact program on it, and they gathered around her holding out back lit devices that outlined all their faces in a gray blue light.

Dar leaned back and watched, feeling the long day creeping up on her despite the coffee. It was good, though, to sense the energy of the people around her, and see the happiness in their faces as they made their plans. She looked over to find Maria sitting next to her, watching her face. "Maria."

"Dar," her former admin said. "Thank you so much for this."

Dar smiled briefly. "Let's see if I can run a company before you thank me. I could bust out, y'know."

"I do not think so for one moment," Maria said, confidently. "It will be a great success."

"With all the help, maybe so," Dar said. "I'm sorry, by the way. I was trying to get you an early out."

Maria reached over and touched her arm. "Mayte told me so," she said. "And thank you, Dar, but this is better. It is so exciting to be doing something new, you see?"

"I do."

"Okay, hon, I got everything." Kerry patted her knee. "Time to get home. My eyelids are sticking."

They all walked out to the lot in a group, through a Saturday evening crowd.

Mark eyed the Sport Trac as they paused by it. "Hey, is that a new ride?"

"Yeah, we started out this morning getting Dar a new car, and me a new camera," Kerry said. "And ended up being fired and having dinner with you all. Long day."

"Nice!" Mark circled the truck. "That's sweet, Dar. Cooler than that beige battle wagon."

"In fact," Kerry opened the passenger door and removed her new camera, "C'mon over and pose. It's an occasion."

They gathered in front of the truck and Kerry adjusted the settings, then pressed the shutter. "Got it." She straightened up. "I think a new future started tonight." She put the device away as everyone said goodbye, then she slid into the seat and closed the door.

Dar got in and closed hers. They looked at each other, then Dar laughed and shook her head. She started the truck as she watched their former and future colleagues part and go off to their own cars. "Y'know? This is going to be fun."

"Y'know? It is." Kerry half turned as Chino poked her head between the seats. "You can have a job too, Chi. We can bring her to the office every day, Dar."

Dar leaned over and gave the dog a kiss on the head. "We can. There's a nice big yard in the back of it too. You like that Chi? Not be cooped up in the condo all day?"

"Growf!"

"What's that old saying, Dar? An ill wind blows nobody good?" Kerry settled into her seat as they started home. "Or do I mean every dark cloud has a silver lining?"

"I think they mean the same thing." Dar stifled a yawn. "Remind me to send a note to my parents letting them know what's going on."

"They'll be pissed."

"Nah," Dar said."My mother thinks the company's a crock, and my dad thinks I work too hard."

"No, I mean they'll be pissed because you and I were fired," Kerry clarified. "As in, we were dissed."

Yeah, that was probably true. Dar got on the causeway and headed for the ferry terminal. It still stung. She was honest enough with herself to admit that. But things were going to be busy enough for her that she hoped that sting would fade, as she left ILS behind and entered this new adventure.

Would she be a good business owner? Dar had to wonder.

"Know what we forgot?" Kerry said, as they pulled into the resident's lane. "To transfer the sticker from your car."

The ferry guard came over to them uncertainly, until Dar rolled the window down and stuck her head out. "Oh, Ms. Roberts," he said. "New car?"

"New truck," Dar said. "I'll get a sticker for it tomorrow at the office."

"No problem." He leaned on the car and glanced inside. "I'd love one of these. My baby Sea-Doo would maybe fit crosswise in the bed there."

"Sea-Doo," Kerry mused. "Hm."

"Uh oh." The guard grinned. "You forget that for Christmas?"

"Apparently I did," Dar drawled. "Have a great night."

He backed off and she closed the window as they were directed onto the ferry. Dar glanced around and smiled a little. Most of the cars around her were Mercedes and BMWs, and one in the front, a Mazarati. Her Lexus SUV had been borderline. Her Sport Trac definitely was out of place.

"The Grove is cute," Kerry said. "Didn't you used to live down there?"

"I did. Probably ten minutes from Monty's. I liked it. You could walk to places and there are a lot of nice, old trees around."

Kerry eyed her speculatively. "There's a marina there. You want to look around maybe?"

Dar was silent for a moment. "You mean, move down there?" She pondered the dark waters going past them, as they crossed the channel and headed for the island side dock. "Huh."

"Just a thought," Kerry said. "Might as well get all our massive life changes over at one time."

"We'll be down there a lot. Maybe we'll see someplace we like," Dar said. "I don't mind the island."

"I don't either. It's gorgeous, and we have a beautiful home." Kerry crossed her ankles. "But some of those places we drove by were pretty cute."

"And they have unique architecture."

"Mm."

"Let's see what we find," Dar said. "But maybe let's wait to look until we've got the company set up and running, our staff hired, and our vacation accomplished."

Kerry chuckled, then she exhaled. "Oh crap."

"What?"

"We're going to have someone clean out our offices. I've got a bunch of personal stuff there," Kerry said. "And everyone I would have thought to ask to do that is either going to be on vacation or helping us start up our new company next week."

"Mari'll do it," Dar said. "I don't have much there."

"And we need to courier those laptops since Mark's excuse for meeting us had nothing to do with them." Kerry scratched Chino behind the ears. "They would probably let us go in there to drop them off and pick our stuff up."

"I don't want to do that," Dar answered in a definite tone.

Kerry looked at her.

"Go in there, with security around us? Everyone staring at us? No thanks."

"Okay, hon." Kerry touched her arm. "Just a suggestion."

"In fact let's get a courier to bring them tomorrow. I want them out of our house," Dar said. "Before something happens and the first place they point blame is at me, figuring I have some sort of half assed back door access." She drove off the ramp and headed around the perimeter road toward their condo.

"You mean you don't?" Kerry asked, after a brief pause.

"No," Dar said. "I don't."

"Good."

"Yeah."

"Do me a favor though?" Kerry asked. "Can you take those pictures of me off your laptop before you give it back?"

Dar paused then relaxed and started laughing.

Kerry slapped her lightly. "We'll get through this, Dardar. I know we will."

"Idiots." Dar let the chuckles wind down. "I'm not sure who's going to be bit in the ass by this the most."

"Well, nobody but me better be biting your ass."

"Growf!"

DAR STRETCHED HER body out and felt the light tickling scratch on her navel as Kerry stirred beside her. She looked up at the ceiling and for a moment considered a normal Sunday, then she remembered the prior day. "Buh."

"Felt good to sleep," Kerry muttered, almost incoherently.

"Uh huh."

Kerry snuggled up to her and she curled her arm around her back, her thumb tracing an idle pattern. "It's gonna be weird not going to work tomorrow."

"Mm." Dar sighed. "I keep thinking about stuff I was going to do. My brain keeps going in circles and then tripping."

"Aw, hon." Kerry gave her a sleepy hug. "Give it some time. You had a lot going on."

"Mm."

"I love you."

Dar smiled, unable to resist the power of that sentiment to lighten her heart. "Back atcha." Her body relaxed, and the buzz of thoughts evaporated. "Still up for a dive today?"

"Uh huh." Kerry nodded. "After we wake up."

Dar took the hint and settled down, watching the slits in the shutters take on just the bare hint of pre dawn. She turned her thoughts to the things they needed to get done and contentedly ran over the tasks at hand, letting the past fade out as she considered how to structure their new company.

Their new company. Dar nodded a little. Roberts Automation. It was a name, and a plan and a future, and to have it become so sudden and so present felt just a little startling to her.

Startling but good. Good, but a little scary, since she'd spent her whole life depending on a structure around her that now she had to provide for others.

Could she succeed?

"Hon?" Kerry burred softly. "What're you gonna do if Jose wants to come work for us?"

Dar pondered that. "Hire him," she said after a moment. "I was just trying to figure out how I was going to do the stuff I never liked doing — like sell things. You just reminded me why I don't have to."

Kerry patted her on the stomach. "Sleep."

"You made my brain wake up," Dar complained. "Now I have a picture of Jose in my head. That wasn't nice, Kerry."

"Sorry."

"Maybe I'll get up and make us pancakes."

Kerry was silent for a long moment. "Now you woke my brain up." She rolled over and sighed. "Oh well. We can sleep in whenever we want for a while, huh."

"Mm"

"Okay, let's get up."

They threw shirts and shorts on and wandered into the kitchen, accompanied by Chino. Kerry started pulling pans out of the cupboards while Dar busied herself with the coffee maker. Once the brew was going, Dar went over to the dining room table where their new PDAs were and picked up hers. "I have a message."

"It's kinda cool knowing I don't have to worry about what's in my work inbox." Kerry got out the pancake mix and some eggs.

"Mm...ah, Mark created a mailing list and sent a message to all of us," Dar said in an amused tone. "You can take the man out of the enterprise but not the reverse it seems." She thumbed through the other lines on the screen. "Ah, my folks." She opened it.

"Glad we tagged our personal mail to that, not the work mail," Kerry said. "Remind me to send out an e-dress change note later."

"My dad says, 'Dardar, that's some good news there. Them people look to you like the gov'mint looks to me. Ain't no win in it.'"

With Dar's deliberately added drawl, Kerry had no problem imagining Andrew's speech. "He's right."

"And my mother adds 'I thought that board was stupid. I didn't realize they were that stupid.'"

Kerry chuckled.

Dar continued to read a moment. "She's reminding us to schedule an sale of our stock options first thing tomorrow morning."

"Can we do that?" Kerry asked, pouring the pancake batter out into six roundels on her griddle. "Oh wait, we can with the vested ones, can't we?"

"Need to ask Richard," Dar said. "I think we can. There weren't any strings attached to those that required us to remain employed to sell them. Hm...I should check mine. I started getting them ten years ago. Have to see what the price was back then."

"Legitimate profit, Dar. Most of that increase you had a significant something to do with," Kerry said. "I remember us having a conversation about how important to the daily ops continuing to increase profit was."

"Yeah." Dar smiled. "I'm going to go into my office and start blueprinting." She took the device with her and settled behind her desk, letting her elbows press against the wood surface as she considered what she wanted to do next. "First things first."

She logged into the condo's router and checked it, clucking her tongue as she saw the encrypted tunnel to ILS's systems still up and passing traffic. She disconnected it and removed the configuration, pausing a moment and adjusting the access list on the device to prevent any attempt to bring it back up from the other side.

It was a bit of finality, and while she was in there, she remotely connected to the router in the cabin and did the same, feeling better once that was completed.

Then she went to her desktop and deleted the secured share folder she'd kept there that contained various diagrams and work notes she used from time to time.

Kerry appeared with a cup of coffee and a plate, and she set them down. "Whatcha doing?"

"Housekeeping," Dar said. "Getting rid of all the hooks and links to the company I had here." She pecked away with one hand and picked up the coffee cup with her other. "Thanks."

"Dar? How many things are in their systems that you kept track of in your head?" Kerry asked. "Wait, hold that thought, let me get my breakfast."

Dar pulled the plate over and cut a square of the pancakes off with her fork, spotting the embedded chocolate chips with a piratical chuckle. She had gotten the mouthful down by the time Kerry came back and she swallowed and took a sip of coffee to wash it down. "All the stuff in my head is in online documentation," she said. "I'm not that kind of asshole."

"Dar." Kerry settled on the couch in the office, balancing the plate on her knees. "You're not any kind of asshole. You just put on a very good asshole act sometimes."

Dar finished her configuration changes and cleared her desktop, pulling up a browser.

Kerry checked her own gizmo. "I have a message from that real estate agent. Dar, I like this thing. You think we can get more for the rest of the people we're going to be working with?"

"Sure."

"The agent says the management company approved us," Kerry said. "On a Sunday. They must really want tenants." She looked up. "They say they're willing to give us a move in first month discount if we sign papers today."

"Do we want to do that, or look around some more?"

Kerry pondered. "I like that place a lot. There was something about it that really clicked with me."

"Have them draw up the papers," Dar said. We'll take the boat over and sign them at that little marina, and then we'll head out and do a dive. We can pick up some lunch there and take it with us."

Kerry grinned. "Sounds like a plan. Can we have the courier meet us there, too? Get everything done at once?"

"Sounds like a plan."

"RICHARD'LL BE HERE tomorrow morning." Dar slowed the engines to almost idle as they approached the public marina. "He said he wanted to take care of all this stuff the right way for us before we got ourselves into a pickle."

"Awesome. I'm not real fond of pickles," Kerry said. "There's the guest slips. I think we'll fit in that end one, won't we?"

Dar angled for the berth, skillfully maneuvering the Yankee into place with gentle bumps against the rubber bumpers. "Tie us up?"

"Sure." Kerry was already heading for the stairs. She scaled down the ladder and crossed the back deck, climbing up on the transom and untying their stern rope.

Dar held them gently against the dock until Kerry finished then shut down the engines. She tugged down the sleeves on her hoodie and climbed down the ladder, making an idle check of the dive tanks valves before she hopped off onto the dock.

They walked along the dock to the marina office and spent a few minutes with the dock master, then continued on past the parking area and onto the main street beyond.

Their proposed new digs were a five minute walk, and they enjoyed the stroll, the mid morning sunlight peeking through the trees that lined the road.

"It's nice down here," Kerry said after a few quiet moments. "Did you move just because your aunt left you the condo?"

Dar thought about that for a minute, casting her mind back to that time. "Yeah, I guess." She half shrugged. "I remember thinking then what a gag it would be to change my address to the island in the office systems, and how it would sting so many of those assholes who used to look down on me."

"Down on you?"

Dar nodded. "For coming up from the ranks, being a redneck, all that. Even though I inherited the place, it was still a hoot telling people where I was moving."

"Mm. Even my parents had heard of the place." Kerry smiled in remembrance. "It's nice though."

"It is, but it's not really my style. I like the cabin better." Dar steered her across the parking lot to the office facilities, where she saw the agent and a tall man standing waiting for them. "Here we go."

"Here we go," Kerry agreed.

The agent, a woman, hurried forward. "Hello, I'm Sally Ramirez." She offered her hand. "Thanks for meeting up with me at such short notice."

"Dar Roberts." Dar took her hand and released it "This is my partner, Kerry."

The woman half turned. "This is Marcus Tisop, he's the owner of the building. He wanted to meet you."

The man stepped forward. He was tall, and had dark, short cut hair with an arrow shaved into his head on both sides pointing backwards. He looked to be in his thirties, and was wearing a short-waisted black corduroy jacket and jeans. "Hello, ladies."

"Hi," Kerry responded. "Nice to meet you."

"So," Marcus said. "Sally tells me you're up for signing a lease today? I know it seems like we're in a rush, but, actually, we're in a rush."

"I see," Dar said. "Want to sit down and talk about it?"

They went into the little garden area and sat down. Sally pulled a plastic folder with a rubber banded cover out of her briefcase and laid it on the table. "I had these drawn up," she said. "I know you said you wouldn't have your incorporation documents for a few days, but that's okay."

Dar and Kerry exchanged looks. "Okay." Kerry put her elbows on the table and folded her hands. "So what's the deal, Mr. Tisop? You about to declare bankruptcy on this place, or is it haunted, or..."

Marcus chuckled. "Seems like that, huh? Place has been vacant for a few months so you might be close on your first guess, and it's been around a while, so maybe you're close on your second," he added. "Last tenant only lasted three weeks. The ones before that were here a long time, but they lost their business after 9/11. Travel agents."

"Ah," Dar said.

"So I'm stuck at this job," Marcus said. "And I can't leave it until I get a tenant 'cause I won't be able to pay the mortgage. You know?"

"Got it," Kerry said.

"So when Sally told me she had someone interested, I'm all over it. You folks passed the checks, and seem like nice ladies, and I would love to have you as tenants."

"I'm guessing you'd love to have us as tenants even if we were Darth Vader and Yoda opening a nail salon," Dar said, dryly. "But let's talk about it for a minute." She folded her hands. "We talked yesterday to Sally about using the space, and how much liberty we'd have to do construction and changes."

Marcus chuckled. "Touché," he said to her former statement. "She told me you're doing something with computers?"

"That's right," Kerry said. "It's a technology consulting company. Or it will be when the papers are finished. So we'll need power and air conditioning, a place to put in servers, that sort of thing."

"Cabling upgrades," Dar interjected. "I liked the hardwood floors, but we'll need to put in work spaces for staff and conference facilities."

Marcus's eyes lit up and he looked at them in visible delight. "You've got carte blanche. Do whatever you want to the place. The travel agency had some computers, but I think they were older than I am." He tapped the folder. "I put that in there when Sally told me you were some high tech people. It's all to my advantage, right? If you do leave, that makes the property a lot more rentable."

Dar smiled. "Now that's a mercenary attitude I can respect," she said. "How did you get into the landlord business?"

"Ah." Marcus sighed. "My grandmother owned property all over the Grove. When she died it got split up between me and my five brothers and sisters. I'm not really into being a landlord, but I had to do something with it. Would have been different if it was houses...but she was into commercial property."

"What do you do?" Kerry asked.

"Marketing and sales, for Sedanos supermarkets," he said. "I'm tired of it. I want a change. You know what that's like?"

"Yes," Dar and Kerry answered at the same time.

"Right, so if you're really interested, let's do it," he said. "I'll even give you a signing bonus. We do a deal today, I'll hook you up with my brother's electrical company with a fifty percent discount on all the work."

Dar started laughing. "Nice."

Kerry regarded him with wry amusement. "We'll sign, but the final paperwork on it will need to wait until the ink's dry on our corporation, and we have a company bank account to pay you out of."

"And that'll be?" Marcus was already grinning, jiggling his knees.

"End of the week, most likely," Dar said. "My lawyer's due here tomorrow."

"Deal." He held out his hand. "Sally, get them papers out. Want a real tour after that?"

Why yes, they would like that. A half hour later they were being let into the front door of the space again, and now they took their time in looking around.

"The nail salon only used this front section," Marcus said. "What a mess that was. I had to have the floors resurfaced after they left."

The entrance was a relatively square, open space that had a staircase behind it going up to the second floor. To the right and left were large open rooms, and Kerry wandered into one, turning in a circle inside it.

"Conference room?" Dar asked, examining the door.

"Mm."

Behind the entrance past the stairwell was a large kitchen with windows that opened onto what might once have been a little garden but now was a roughly mowed and clipped space that had stone tables and benches along its perimeter.

The two-story building was in a square, with the open space in the middle and open walkways on the second level that linked the offices upstairs.

"We had jalousies," Marcus said. "I had them taken out, and hurricane proof glass put in for these inside windows."

Dar nodded. "Good idea. Outside ones have shutters?"

"Yup."

Kerry leaned toward Dar. "What's a jalousie?"

"Tell you later," Dar whispered back. "Old Florida thing."

They continued along the bottom floor, where besides the conference rooms on either side of the entrance there were long, open rooms with worktables down the middle of them, several storage closets, and custodial rooms. The short side on the other end of the building was a rear exit, and loading dock, along with another set of stairs.

They climbed up to the second level, which was mostly offices. On the front side above the main entrance there was a suite of them. Two decent size rooms that split the corner, a small utility space on the inner edge, and a large administrative area with a curved desk and a set of bathrooms.

Kerry eyed it, turning to look at Dar with a quirk of her blonde eyebrow.

"Yep," Dar answered the unasked question, patting the curved desk. "That one storage space on the left side downstairs I think I can convert to a server room. It's got a demarc."

"We'll need to have someone come in and check the power feeds," Kerry said. "And verify the AC tonnage."

Marcus regarded them. "You guys really are tech, huh?"

"Yes," Dar said, as she wandered into one of the two offices and went to the window, looking quietly out at the leafy street that fronted the building, catching a glimpse of the marina in the distance.

Definitely not the view she'd become used to, but as she glanced around at the room surrounding her, imagining a desk, a design workstation, and a big white board, she saw herself working in it, almost able to hear the hum of activity around her, and the muted ringing of phones. "This'll work."

"There's even an outlet in this corner for a refrigerator full of milk chugs, hon." Kerry had entered and was exploring the space. "And eventually a big monitor on that wall so you can see your net health metrics."

"Mm." Dar turned and leaned against the windowsill. "You happy here?"

"I am." Kerry indicated the door to the second office. "Much shorter walk," she said. "We're starting small, and spending our rent on real work space, not marble floors and a twelve story atrium."

"It feels right," Dar agreed. "Enough space to bootstrap, but not like I feel like I'm paying for image."

"And there's enough space out there for both Mayte and Maria," Kerry noted in satisfaction. "We're going to need systems, and software. Sheesh there's a lot to do."

"We already have some software," Dar said. "I kept a copy of my code repository at home. I'll have to recompile it for us, but it's got my sizing and engineering prototypes and the base of what, believe it or not, ILS uses for their accounting and HR systems."

"Really?"

"Yeah, and I worked on it enough off hours not to feel bad about using it." Dar pushed off the window and indicated the entrance. "Let's get going, I hear fish calling my name."

"Can we paint the walls something other than white?" Kerry asked, as they walked with Marcus outside. "Something like sea foam green or light blue?"

"Sure," he said. "You can paint it bright red if you want to. I had to have it painted after the travel agency left. They had murals of Europe all over the place."

They paused outside. "Let me walk you to your car," Marcus suggested, while Sally stood by with her signed papers, looking extraordinarily pleased with herself.

"We didn't drive," Kerry said. "If we get all our paperwork in place, I think we might want to get in here as early as Wednesday to start making some plans. That okay?"

"Sure." He held his hand out. "You live around here that you walked? I thought you had an address out on Fisher Island?"

"We do." Dar took his hand and released it. "We took our boat over here. We're going diving now. Have a good rest of your Sunday."

KERRY WAS SPRAWLED, dressed in her dive jacket, savoring the westering sun as they bobbed at anchor just off the reef. If she opened her eyes she could see Biscayne Bay, and when the wind shifted she fancied she heard snatches of music off the beach.

On the table at her left hand was what was left of a platter of fresh seafood, and she picked up her glass of white wine and sipped it.

Dar was lying on her back on one of the cushioned benches, her bare feet draped over the stern, white cotton sweatpants covering her long legs. "What a nice day," she drawled. "Great seeing those hammerhead sharks, huh?"

"Great getting you silhouetted against them," Kerry said. "I can also see us spending time at that raw bar near the new office. That platter was awesome."

"It was." Dar turned her head and regarded Kerry sleepily. "I have to call Bridges tomorrow. What the hell am I supposed to tell him?"

"No?"

"Agreed, but how do I say no to him and not piss him off to the point he blackballs our nice shiny new company?" Dar asked. "I'd like to pick up Gerry's new contracts. That'll be a pretty good bootstrap for us."

Kerry pondered the question. "Can you say no to his czar idea, but still do the programming for him?"

Dar half sat up. "Ker, that's the part I don't want any part of."

"Mm...yeah I know." Kerry got up and picked up a lonely looking oyster, bringing it over and offering it to Dar's lips. "But you know, I was thinking. He's going to get that program done no matter what you say. Could you do it so that it wouldn't be so scummy?"

Dar swallowed the oyster, and licked her lips.

"I mean..." Kerry sat down on the edge of the bench and leaned her arm across Dar's hips. "Think about it, hon. What he's talking about might have caught those guys before they blew up those planes, you know? Is there a way to do it that protects everyone but the bad guys?"

She saw the wheels turning behind those baby blues. "No one else he asks is going to give a crap."

"That's probably very true," Dar answered slowly. "I don't know. Depends on how much control he allows over it. Let me think about it."

Kerry leaned over and pulled up her sweatshirt, giving her a kiss on the navel. Then she put her cheek down on the spot and gazed quietly up at her partner, knowing a moment of surprising content, given everything going on. "I know there's a lot of unknown in our path right now, but I'm really excited about it."

Dar smiled gently at her, reaching over to push a bit of thick, blonde hair out of her eyes. "I'm kinda jazzed about it too," she admitted. "All this time, I had to deal with whatever it was ILS decided to do. Now...it's scary, but interesting to know we have to make our own decisions and live with what happens from them."

"Angie sent me a note after we came back up," Kerry said. "She said my mother's extremely pleased we got fired."

Dar's eyebrows both twitched and lifted.

"She said ILS got me into too much trouble." Kerry watched and felt Dar start to laugh. "Angie said after she heard about the board wanting to let Alastair fry, she decided they were horrible."

"Hm. Forgot she heard that when he was telling us," Dar said. "Your mother's growing on me, a little."

"Yeah, me too," Kerry admitted. "I remember seeing Alastair there, when we got up to the exchange, and he looked so pale, and so upset...I thought right then that whatever it was we had to go through was worth it just because it might help him out. I didn't care a squat about the stock exchange."

"Me either," Dar said. "I was so caught up in the fix, for about ten minutes there I didn't even think about what the hell it was I was doing. Just banging out those commands and then relief when it was over. My hands hurt." She flexed one. "But the coolest thing? It was those guys from NASA."

"Rocket scientists."

"Listening to them talk about how they got this thing done with high tech duct tape and brain cells..." Dar smiled. "Made me understand how the hell we managed to get to the moon."

Kerry blinked a few times. "Did you know there are people who think that was a scam?"

"Yeah. Some guy once said that to me when I was overseas at a conference." Dar shook her head. "I mean, I get it. There are people who think the government is hiding aliens from space too, and people who think Jesus rode dinosaurs. It's always tempting to recreate your most comfortable world view regardless of facts."

"So you don't think the moon landings were a government conspiracy?"

Dar eyed her. "Ker, based on your recent experience with the government, you think they could have spoofed those landings?"

Kerry started laughing.

"I mean, really?"

"Bwahahaha. No." Kerry continued chuckling. "Even my father, who let me tell you, was no fan of any Kennedy, used to pop a cork whenever someone suggested that. He said it was one of the prime examples of the ability of this country to define a goal and do it, regardless of how impossible it seemed at the time."

"I remember seeing the inside of the VAB for the first time," Dar said. "Seeing those rockets. Seeing the roomfuls of computers that they used, most of which had less power than my cell phone. We should take a drive up to Cocoa and tour the Cape."

"We should," Kerry said. "And now, we can. Maybe on our way up the state heading to Vegas?"

"After we finish setting up our new company in our new offices with your new name." Dar grinned. "Never figured retirement to be this exciting"

Kerry reluctantly got up and tickled Dar's navel. "How about some coffee? I think it's time we go in. Waves are coming up a little."

"Sure." Dar swung her legs over the edge of the boat and stood up, grabbing hold as the boat rolled from side to side. "Let me go retract the anchor, and get us moving. I don't want to lose those oysters."

"You never get seasick."

"There's always a first time." Dar climbed the ladder up to the flying bridge and took her seat behind it. She started up the engines and engaged them, moving the boat forward and disengaging the anchor before she started the chain retracting. The breeze was stiffening, and she was glad she had her sweatshirt on as she heard the anchor seat and she brought the bow around to head them back toward home.

Kerry came up to join her after a few minutes, with a thermos jug hung around her neck. She poured out some coffee into the mug in Dar's swinging holder and took the seat next to her, curling her legs around the bolted steel frame. She regarded the whitecaps. "Rough water."

"Yeap, think we have a storm coming in," Dar said, pointing to the northwest. "Cold front. I heard it on the radio earlier. Glad we got out when we did."

"Cold front? How cold?" Kerry asked. "Enough to call for our flannel PJs?"

Dar snickered.

"Speaking of PJs, can we have a casual dress code at our new office?" Kerry asked. "As in, nice jeans and khakis?" She leaned her elbow on Dar's shoulder. "And flex time?"

"Sure."

"This is going to be really cool."

Chapter Eight

KERRY LEANED BACK in her home office chair, answering yet another phone call. "Hello, Kerry Stuart." She paused, then removed the phone and looked at it before she put it back. "Uh. Yes, yes, that's me, thanks. I didn't expect you to...yes, no, that's fine." She scribbled a note. "Yes, I can be there. Thanks."

She hung up and shook her head. "Make time for a trip to the courthouse on Thursday. Got it. Like this week wasn't crazy enough as it is?"

She checked the clock on her desktop. Eleven a.m. and things had been, to put it mildly, jumping since about eight. Richard Edgerton had arrived and he and Dar were downstairs in her office, busy putting together the filing paperwork for their new corporation.

So that was in the works. She'd already signed her name to the papers, and retreated upstairs to work on the logistics of bringing their new company to life, glad she'd spent the past couple of years reconstructing new and acquired firms and setting up operations for them.

She already knew the steps to take, knew the contacts to call in, bringing in everything from temp workers to telephones, contacts that were surprised and in some cases dismayed to hear from her outside ILS, but interested and happy to work with her in this new venture.

Surprising, a little, since they were so rawly new, but also gratifying in that these big companies seemed to recognize a potential for a small startup to grow.

Her new PDA rattled softly, and she glanced at it.

She was glad she'd turned over hers and Dar's company cell phones to the courier, and she'd gotten a call from Mari saying that she'd received their equipment and locked them up for safekeeping.

The office, not surprisingly, was in chaos. Someone had spread around her personal email address, and her new little gadget was buzzing like a drunken beehive with notes from more people than she thought she actually knew there.

From security. From ops. From accounting. From the building custodial staff. Kerry thumbed through them with a sense of bemusement. People were angry, sad, outraged, disgusted. She picked out the one from Jack Bueno and read it again, almost able to hear the passion in his words.

A little surprising. A little humbling. Kerry imagined that Dar's inbox was quantum amounts fuller since she'd been at the company much longer and had a far deeper history there, and while certainly she'd made her share of enemies, she'd also made her share of devoted believers.

She sighed, and opened a few more messages.

Notes from other parts of the company, from small accounts in Wisconsin, New Hampshire, New York and Seattle. One from Nan in Herndon, expressing intense and straightforward upset at their leaving and including a picture of the ops group in Herndon, all with their thumbs pointing down. Kerry sighed. There were probably just as many who were glad to see them go, who saw room now for advancement, or who chafed under Dar's management style but they probably wouldn't send her notes relating that.

"Ker?"

She looked up to find Dar in her doorway. "Hey," she said, "my court date is Thursday."

Dar paused and cocked her head in puzzlement, then her expression cleared. "Oh, the name thing."

"The name thing," Kerry agreed, with a wry smile. "Crazy week, huh?"

"Mm." Dar walked over to her and handed her a paper. "Our option sales just went through," she said. "Richard wanted to get that done before ILS made a public announcement."

"You think they will?" Kerry took the page and glanced at it, then stopped and looked closer. She blinked, then looked up at Dar. "Holy crap."

"Yeah. Had more than I thought in that account." Dar shrugged somewhat sheepishly. "Richard thought maybe we could put it in to start up the business accounts for the new company. You think?"

"Sure," Kerry said. "That'll help with all those things we need to do for that office, and on-boarding people, and also maybe buying the Queen Elizabeth 2." She put the page down. "My inbox is blowing up."

"Mine too." Dar took a seat on the reading chair next to Kerry's desk. "I just got off the phone with Mari."

"And?"

"She's trying to get all the paperwork done to separate us. It's a mess," Dar said. "Because they'd been in the middle of creating our voluntary separation packages."

"Ah." Kerry leaned on her elbows. "Sorry, Dar. Don't feel bad for them, even for Mari. We didn't ask for this."

"No, I know. Me either, but PR's been on the line to her most of the morning trying to figure out what the hell they're going to release to the press."

"Ah. Yeah, bet that's a pickle for them," Kerry mused. "What are they going to say they fired us for? Because you were too popular with our customers? Because your competency was so overwhelmingly sterling that major institutions like the federal government wanted you all to themselves?"

Dar chuckled wryly. "I'm sure someone is working full time to come up with some story to explain it that makes them look good and intelligent, and makes us look bad."

"Well, from my side, they can't do much worse than my father's lawyers did on national television." Kerry said. "Good luck with that."

"Mari warned them not to play any games." Dar shook her head. "There's too much public press out there about me for them to say it was due to any issue with my performance. Or yours. Or the fact that we're married, because that's been a fact for a couple years."

Kerry frowned. "They're kind of idiots, Dar. They could have just asked us to resign early, couldn't they?"

"Not without saying why." Dar sat back and hiked one foot up on her opposite knee. "I think they had a knee jerk reaction to what Alastair told them about the contracts, and didn't think it through."

"Can they not say anything?"

"After having the CEO walk out and the CIO, and the VP of operations fired? Hon, they're a public company. I figure the word's already out and they're getting calls from stockholders."

"Ugh."

"Ugh," Dar repeated. "I'm guessing I'll get a call from someone at some point about it." She got up. "Back to the legal paperwork. Glad I have a lawyer doing it. I'd have just filled it all out in random crayon by now and submitted it." She pushed herself to her feet. "I'll tell Richard you're okay with using that to start up operations." She indicated the sheet, and winked, then sauntered out and back down the steps.

Kerry picked the paper back up and looked at it, then shook her head and put it away in a drawer. Then she went back to her list of things to do, picking up a pen and making another note.

"DAR, WE'RE ALMOST done here," Richard Edgerton said, sorting through the stack of papers. "Then I'll go right over and file these, and open up your accounts." He looked across the desk at her. "The irony of you using your options payout to start up your own biz isn't lost on me, by the way."

"Me either," Dar said. "I wasn't looking for this to happen this way, but..." She shrugged. "Might as well just take advantage of an early start and get things in motion."

"Okay," he replied. "So now, we talked about the differences between a general corporation, S Corp, and an LLC. All of them give you and Kerry protection in terms of personal finances, the difference otherwise depends on if you want to issue stock, and so on."

Dar nodded. "LLC seems to be the best choice for now, since I don't want to get involved in any stock, and we're self-financing. I want it to be as simple as possible at the start, because with my luck it's going to get a lot more complicated fast."

Richard chuckled. "Definitely keep it close to the vest for now. I don't know what those idiots at ILS are going to end up releasing, and the less public you are, the easier it's going to be to deal with whatever that is." He finished up the last paper. "Now, being as I'm a lawyer, I have to say, Dar...have you considered filing suit against ILS?"

"For?"

"Firing you? You didn't do anything to initiate that, you know. Based on what you told me, all you did was tell them the truth, which you really didn't have to do," Richard said. "You didn't solicit either of those offers. You've got a case, y'know."

Dar shook her head. "Don't want it. Kerry and I talked about it. It's not worth it, Richard. What would it get me? Is my retirement package worth what we'd spend in legal fees?"

"Oh, sure," Richard said. "Considering if they lose they pay them." He smiled. "Listen, Dar, I know money isn't on your priority list and given this stock windfall, it's not something you need to get this company started. I just wanted to ask the question because you know, it rankles me. As a longtime family friend, and as your lawyer."

"Let's get it going then. I want to get all this in motion before Ker and I take off for some R and R," Dar said. "I don't want the thought of lawsuits and attachments hanging over us. They lose far more than I do by firing me. I just lose cash."

"Well, being fired is not exactly good for your rep," Richard said.

Dar shrugged. "I'll let my rep stand for itself. There are enough people out there in the industry who know the truth. Enough customers whose asses I pulled out of the fire. It might throw people off at first, but in the long run, performance talks."

He smiled. "Take the high road?"

"Something like that." Dar returned the smile.

"Okey dokey." Richard got up. "I'll get the bank accounts open, your general account, and both payables and payroll. I've got your power of attorney, and I should be able to get all this filed by the end of the day."

"You'll be our corporate lawyer, won't you, Richard? I only know two of your kind and the other one works for ILS and is probably trying to find a way to screw me, if only to get ILS's ass out of the fire."

"Baird?"

"Yeah. He's sharp."

"He is," Richard agreed. "Matter of fact, I know him. Know the family."

"Hamilton and I had the perfect love-hate relationship. He loved my results and hated my personality and attitude"

"I'll keep an eye out for him, Dar, and absolutely I'll be your counsel. I haven't had this much fun in years."

Dar's cell phone rang and she opened it with a sigh. "Dar Roberts."

"Hello, Dar!"

"Hey, Alastair." She glanced at Richard and grinned briefly. "How's your first day of retirement?"

"Well you know, it's been good so far," Alastair said. "Been able to watch the circus and not have to be the ringmaster, as it were."

"Uh oh."

He chuckled wryly. "I've gotten a lot of phone calls, matter of fact, and I think there are some folks who are regretting some hasty action the other day."

"Little late for that."

"That's what I've been saying," Alastair agreed. "But there's some talk of cutting a deal, as it were, to prevent all that public messiness."

Richard sat back down and cocked his head to listen.

"You really think I'm going to go for that?" Dar asked, in a quizzical tone.

"Well, the board obviously hopes so, that's why they have me asking," Alastair answered dryly. "The deal would be, you and Kerry, and me for that matter, gets the package they were working for us, in return for saying you left early to concentrate on family life or raise goldfish or whatever canned BS it is they say for this sort of thing."

Dar tapped her thumb on her desk. "We'd have to abide by the non-compete, though. Right?"

"Sure."

"Really is too late, Alastair. We've already leased office space and my lawyer's on the way to file my incorporation papers. Sorry about that."

There was a moment of silence. "Wow," Alastair said. "You don't screw around, do you, lady?"

"Never have."

"All righty then, I'll pass that along," he said.

"If they're willing to drop the non-compete, I'll consider it," Dar countered. "Listen, Alastair, I gave almost twenty years of my life to ILS. I didn't deserve to be fired because of someone's jackass reaction."

"I know that, Dar," Alastair said. "Apparently the board's been getting angry phone calls ever since the news leaked out. Not to mention operations are pretty well disrupted across the board."

"Not my fault."

"Not your fault at all," Alastair said. "They told you to walk away, and that's exactly what you did, Dar. Cut the cord, broke all the ties, turned in your gear. Mariana said it was textbook. Board isn't stupid, really. They knew you were the brains of the outfit, but they figured they could find more brains. What they didn't know, and what apparently has become obvious, is that you also were the company's heart, and there's a lot of broken ones there today."

Dar stared at the phone in silence, caught off guard by the sentiment.

"Dar?"

"Yeah, I heard you," she muttered.

"Anyhow, I'll see if they'll bite on that." Alastair cleared his throat. "Call ya back."

Dar closed the phone and looked up as Kerry entered, her eyes flicking around the room. "Hey."

"Hey."

"Okay." Richard got up. "I'm heading out to file papers. Thanks for the pass for my car, ladies. I'll be back as soon as you're a company." He picked up his briefcase and ducked out the door, giving Chino a pat as he headed out.

"Something happen?" Kerry came over and sat on the desk. "You look weird."

Dar got up. "Let's get a drink." She led Kerry through the dining room and into the kitchen. "Alastair just called. The board wanted him to cut a deal with us."

"What?"

"Apparently someone realized they might have screwed up a little in firing us." Dar got herself a glass of milk. "So they wanted to give us our packages in return for us saying we left to go pursue other things."

"And...that's bad?" Kerry hazarded.

"Still have to have the non-compete."

"Ah. That is bad." Kerry nodded. "So I get it you told him no?"

"I told him no, unless they wanted to drop that." Dar turned and looked out the window. "But it wasn't that. Something he said just made my brain twitch."

Kerry stepped closer and put a hand on her back, rubbing it gently. "You okay?"

"Yeah." Dar took another swallow of milk. "You know I just got an email from the cleaning lady on fifteen. She sent me a blessing, through her son, who actually wrote the email. She said she'd miss me so much."

Kerry gave her a hug. "Well, I'll tell you, Dar. If we weren't partners, and I had come in this morning to find you gone, I'd have been a hysterical mess. So I know how those people feel."

Dar returned the hug and smiled. "I'm glad Maria and Mayte took time off. Wouldn't want to have them there having to deal with all the chaos."

"Me too. Colleen called me before from her cell. Duks had a department meeting and Col said you could tell he was pissed off."

"He was never into the politics," Dar said. "Never got the whole ego thing, just wanted everyone to come in and do their damn job."

"No wonder you two always got along." Kerry leaned against her and exhaled. "Okay. I'm going to go back and continue working on finding equipment vendors, setting up accounts with telecom providers, and deciding what color your desk is going to be." She gave Dar a kiss. "I've got a bunch of them already falling over themselves to work with us. Our favorite network vendor said she was glad we finally broke off on our own."

"Really? We won't be giving anyone multi-million dollar orders for a long time."

"True," Kerry said. "And they know that, but they also know if they put a new piece of technology in front of us, we'll find something profitable to do with it."

"Yeah, that's likely true." Dar walked Kerry back to the stairs and watched her trot up them. "You go, hon."

Then she returned to her desk and settled behind it, as Chino jumped on the couch and curled up in a ball. She picked up her new PDA and looked at it, scrolling through the page of new messages that had appeared since she'd gone to the kitchen.

"Wow," she muttered under her breath. "Who'd have guessed?" She opened one and read it.

> Dear Ms. Roberts.
> You probably don't remember me, but during the September attacks you showed up and defended me from a very angry customer and I have never forgotten that. All of the people in the New York office are up in arms, and in fact, they just walked out and I'm going with them soon as I send this. I hope the company knows what a bad thing it did.
> Charlene, the receptionist in the New York sales office.

"I do remember you, Charlene," Dar mused. "Glad you enjoyed that. Really was just my period cramps taking themselves out on some nitwad."

She opened another one.

> Dear Dar - it's Francois from the European office. I just want to say to you, we should be very ashamed. I am ashamed. There is no honor in this.

"Ah, Francois." She put down the gizmo and turned her attention to her computer, browsing the code archive she'd unearthed. "Glad I'm as disciplined as I am, Chi. Every time I did a compile and push to production, I iterated a copy here to my repository. You know what that means?"

"Growf?"

"It means we've got the latest versions of everything I wrote. Including Gopher Dar." She sorted through the files and checked the dates with a sense of satisfaction, stopping to take some notes on her pad of the programs she thought they would be able to use.

Then a thought occurred to her, and she hit the intercom key on the phone. "Ker?"

"Yeah?" Kerry's voice echoed softly.

"I just realized my desk and laptop are locked down with that new security program they made us start using," she said. "The one that requires my hash code and retinal display."

A soft snort of laughter came through the phone.

"And if they deactivate my network account, half the running systems in the company are probably going to stop working. Mark was going through a project to transition those to a regular service account before I left."

"Oh crap, Dar!" Kerry sputtered. "Is Mark in the office?"

"Oh, no. He's down in the keys again with Barbara. On a fishing charter." Dar scribbled another note on her pad. "Barbara sent me an email telling me she's going to name her firstborn child for me for getting him out of ILS."

"He stayed because of you."

Dar paused, and tapped the pen on the pad. "Yeah, I know," she said. "So anyway, you pick my desk yet?"

"How about clear glass?"

Dar's brow lifted. "I'll feel like a goldfish. What if I want to wear shorts to the office?"

"Clear glass top, hon. Wood and brass frame." Kerry started laughing. "Though I'm kinda thinking about that see through top and those shorts...hm."

"Kerrison."

"Okay, I've got AT&T on the other line. Got to go."

Dar released the intercom and chuckled, then the chuckle faded as her phone rang and she saw the caller ID. Ten seconds to make a choice. She took a breath, released it, then keyed the answer button. "Dar Roberts."

"Ms. Roberts, this is Dr. Bridges assistant. He would like to speak to you." The woman's voice was crisply professional. "Are you available for a call at this time?"

Might as well. "Sure," Dar said. "Put him on."

A buzz and a click, and a clearing throat "Roberts?"

"That's me," Dar said, putting her pen down and concentrating on the call. "Having a good Monday?"

"No idea yet. You thought about my offer?"

There was, Dar acknowledged, straightforwardness about the advisor that she appreciated. "I have," she said. "I don't think I'm either qualified or suited to be your czar."

"Huh," Bridges grunted. "Thought you would be interested in the power part of it.

"Not a talking head," Dar said.

"So it's no?" Bridges asked.

"To the job," she said. "The programming, on the other hand, that maybe we can discuss. I've got some experience doing that kind of system."

The smile in Bridges voice was very evident. "Well now, the day's getting better. Mind you, I don't want that organization of yours involved," he said. "You'll have to do this on the side or somesuch. I'm sure that's gonna be a legal nightmare, but it's too big an exposure for us. You got me?"

"I no longer work for that organization," Dar said. "So that's not an issue."

"Better and better," he responded. "You quit?"

Dar smiled. "Actually, they fired me. But I was going to resign in any case."

"Ah. Figured you were getting too big for their britches." Bridges chuckled softly. "So you don't want a government job, Roberts? Got good benefits."

"I'm opening up my own company. But thanks," Dar said. "If we can agree on the framework, we might be able to do business together."

"We might at that." Bridges now sounded dourly delighted. "Roberts, that's good news. Let me get together a paper from these idiots here and we can set up a meeting. For what it's worth, I agree on the czar thing. You'd be the biggest pain in the ass around here. Maybe this is a win, win."

"Maybe," Dar said. "I'll be looking for that meeting request."

He hung up.

Dar regarded the phone and sighed. "That's going to end up all right, or a complete disaster. Let's hope we get lucky."

THE BOARD ROOM was full of very agitated men, seated around a long, teak wood table dressed in business suits. They all looked up as the door opened, and then started to take seats as a man dressed in a faded flannel shirt entered, followed by a tall, urban figure in a well fitted suit.

"Hello there, boys." Alastair went to the end chair, which was obviously left free, and sat down. "I've got a rodeo my grandkid's riding in to go to, so let's make it short if we can, huh?"

"Try not to be so fucking smug, huh Al?" John Baker glared at him.

"Kiss my ass," Alastair answered, in the most congenial voice possible. "Boy have I been waiting years to say that." He turned his head and winked at the man who followed him in. "Right, Ham?"

Hamilton Baird, ILS's senior corporate council, gave him a wryly amused look, and sat down, having arranged some papers to his satisfaction. "No doubt, having heard it often enough, Al."

Baker ignored them. "Okay, so. We're not going to get any cooperation from Roberts, so what are our legal options?" He looked pointedly at Baird. "I hope you found something we can use for leverage."

Hamilton leaned back in his chair. "What would you fine gentlemen have liked me to find? You all did fire her." He lifted his hands. "You all want me to turn back time?"

"We have to have legal options. You're a lawyer," Baker said.

"I am, indeed, a lawyer," Hamilton agreed. "So as a lawyer, and as the senior legal hack here at ILS, I will tell you there is not much you can do about our ex-employee doing whatever it is she pleases, because you all, like wet noodle idiots, decided to fire her. It's a little late to be calling in Mr. Louisiana Lawyer now."

Alastair chuckled. "If you all had a single piece of sense, you'd just go with her offer. Let her go open a business. Take her package, and not end up being a thorn the size of a space shuttle in your ass."

"Well said, Al," Hamilton complimented him. "What he said." He pointed at Alastair. "That is also my legal recommendation."

"No way," Baker said. "I'm not giving her a fucking cent."

Hamilton lifted his hands and then let the drop. "All righty then, we could have done this over a text message. Al, you free for dinner?"

"Sure am."

"It's your job to find a way to nail her," Baker said. "Or did you sleep with her too?"

Baird's demeanor changed. He stood up and put his fingertips on the table, leaning on them. "Listen, you moron. It's my job to keep ILS out of trouble and make sure we do things in a legal way that keeps us out of the eyes of regulators. It is not my job to make up stuff and then have it crammed back down my throat in a court of law."

Baker stared at him in frustration.

"Dar Roberts and I have a long, long history of hen and cock fighting the likes of which God has not seen the end of. But." Hamilton held up his hand. "There is no person in this company, not you, not the rest of you morons, not even Al, who I respect more as a person, and as an employee who gave two hundred percent for this crack shack, than her."

Alastair smiled to himself, twiddling his fingers and regarding them as he nodded along with the words.

"So if you don't want to have my size elevens shoved so far up your ass you'd have to tie my shoelaces with your uvula, then do not repeat that statement." Hamilton sat down. "Now. I have given you my legal advice. You got any other idiotic thing to say?"

Jacques leaned forward. "You're serious, aren't you, Hamilton?"

"As a heart attack," Hamilton responded. "It's a damn disgrace what you people did. Not only was it stupid, not only was it knee jerk, shortsighted, and counter to the best interests of this damn company," his voice lifted to a yell, then paused to let the echo fade, "it's against the grace of God what you did to someone who gave so much to make ILS what it is. You all should be damned ashamed of yourselves."

"She was going to take those contracts!" Baker yelled.

"She earned them," Alastair spoke up. "Those contracts were ours because of her raw talent and ability." He folded his hands on the table. "But even in that, she didn't ask for them."

"Oh, bullshit."

Alastair shrugged. "Let's go get that beer, Ham. I've not got much more to say. I'll save what I do have for the press, and for the shareholders when they ask me."

Hamilton's eyes twinkled. "Nice being retired, ain't it?"

"You betcha!"

"Okay, hold on." Jacques held a hand up. "Yes, it is true. We overreacted."

"Now you, too?" Baker fumed. "None of you have balls!"

"That is not true," Jacques said. "I have a right to speak my mind, as you have, John, and has Pier, and Richard, and Toby, and also our two friends here. It takes a big person to admit fault. We did overreact."

Baker stared at him. "The shareholders are going to lynch us. Is that what you're bucking for?"

The Frenchman lifted his hands and then put them back on the table. "That is what comes with the responsibility. We have to stand behind our decisions. Perhaps this was a bad one."

Baker just sighed and shook his head, leaning it against a fist propped against the table. "Fuck."

Alastair spoke after a small silence. "Dar said to me that she'd go along with a package, and public silence, but she couldn't stop her business since it was already in place and going forward." He paused, and reflected. "Gentlemen, that's the best offer you're going to get."

"Sure she agreed. She gets money, and freedom and we just get shit," Baker said.

"John, you fired her," Alastair said, in a gentle tone. "She did not ask to be fired. She gave us six months notice she was going to retire from here."

Baker sighed again. "I just hate her," he said, bluntly. "If I had a gun, I'd have shot her the last time I saw her."

"Uh huh. Better hope you killed her on the first shot then, you weaseling jackass," Hamilton said. "Cause she'd break you in half otherwise, and if that didn't happen, then you'd get a knock on the door by her very Southern, very black and white, very Navy Seal father, and we would never find your body."

"Mm." Alastair nodded. "That's true. Y'know, the most relaxing time I had during that whole mess in New York was taking that train ride out to Long Island with Papa Roberts."

"Did I tell you I got cornered by those no neck lovelies from the Governor downstairs," Hamilton asked him. "They were doing a grand old Mafia family discussion with me up until Andy showed up and short sheeted them right on out of there. Gorgeous old salt."

"If you let her take this deal," Alastair said, "she will honor it, and not entertain the press with what will be hundreds if not thousands of stories about how we did business."

"You really believe that?" Baker asked.

"With all my heart," Alastair replied. "I've been in business all my life, John. I can count on my one hand's fingers how many people I would say that about across the length of my career." He pondered a moment. "And by the way, John?"

"Yeah?" Baker sighed again.

"Me personally? I won't ever forgive you for making my last act as an employee of this company firing those two," Alastair said placidly. "So do yourself a favor, and don't get in front of my truck when I'm driving on out of here."

"Alastair, the decision was all of ours," Jacques said, quietly. "It is not fair to let it stand on John's back."

Alastair merely smiled at him.

Toby Peterson cleared his throat. "Gents," he said. "It's hard to swallow. I was one of the first ones to agree with John on the firing, because it seemed to me that we were in danger of letting someone who was leaving take our customers with her."

"And that might be true," Hamilton remarked. "But firing her sure as hell wouldn't stop that."

Toby held a hand up. "We were mad. If we lose those armed forces contracts we'll have to go back and re-forecast the entire year. You think that's going to be fun?"

"If you treat Dar fairly, she might just tell them to leave those contracts with us and move forward with something else," Alastair said.

"Oh please." Baker rolled his eyes.

"He's right," Hamilton said. "If Al asked her to do that, she would."

Alastair glanced at him.

"She would," Hamilton insisted. "C'mon, Al. She could have sat in that hotel and watched you fry. You pulled that whole team off the job. Didn't have to do no crazy stunts, or nothing. No harm to her at all— you told her to do it."

"True," Alastair said.

"That was for you," Hamilton said. "Kerry risked arrest, and bodily harm to get that cable in place, with old Dar sitting on the floor with a pair of rocket scientists typing so fast you couldn't hear the keys. I saw it, sweat flying everywhere."

Alastair nodded, but didn't speak.

"Okay," Toby said. "I get it. You don't have to keep hammering me over the head, Hamilton."

"Don't I?"

"We should take the offer, the deal," Jacques said. "Really, we have no choice, if, as you say, there is nothing we can present to anyone as an excuse for what we did."

"You don't," Hamilton said. "The minute you all agreed to let those two women have a relationship and not say anything about it, you lost any ability to put that card on the table. That is, boys, the only thing on either of their dance cards that could possibly have given you leverage, and you let that go on for years, and gave them both bonuses and all that."

"That was your fault." Baker pointed at Alastair. "You told us to ignore it."

"I did," he agreed. "It was the best thing to do for the company at the time, and the yearly results that came after that validates the decision."

Jacques sighed. "You know what the worst of it is?" he said. "We will not have that...how do you call it? The magic to rely on anymore. We will have to do our jobs." He held his hand up. "I vote to accept the offer."

"Seconded," Toby said. The rest of the board grumbled but lifted their hands.

Baker looked at them. "I want it on the record I object," he said. "I will not vote for that."

"Unfortunately, you ass, we just need a majority," Hamilton said. "I will record that this board voted to accept the offer from old Dar, and I suggest that Al deliver the message, even though he doesn't actually work for us anymore."

Alastair nodded. "Sure," he said. "I'll do it."

Baker rolled his eyes. "So have we found anyone to go take charge of that nut house in Miami?" he asked. "The agency that's looking for us said they had one candidate, but they called and said they got another position."

Hamilton leaned over and whispered to Alastair. "Steak? I think our work here's done."

"Sounds good." Alastair stood up. "Folks, I'll deliver your message. If you keep your tempers and be nice, I might even agree to go over to Miami and hold the fort there until you can find a new CIO. Those people there trust me at least."

"That mean we have to pay you again?" Baker said, but his expression was mollified. "Least it'll give us some breathing room."

"Thank you, Alastair," Toby said, with a brief smile. "That would be nice."

"Right. Ham, let's go." Alastair dusted his hands off. "You ever see a rodeo?"

"Lord, I'm in deep cheese grits." Hamilton picked up his papers and followed as Alastair made his way toward the door.

KERRY BRUSHED A bit of dust off the sleeve of her sweater and took a breath, letting it out as she stood in line to go into the courtroom. She had a folder with papers clasped in her hand, and she glanced at the clock, as the doors opened to let them in.

There were about twenty people with her, and they all had sheets of paper like hers. She watched them all start shifting and moving as the clerk of the courts stepped back to let them go forward.

Thursday. Hard to believe it was already Thursday. They'd had two days of hurry up and wait, as things jerked into process from their standing start and now, finally, she was reasonably confident they could actually have Mayte and Maria come in on Monday and be able to do the things needed to make them employed.

Sort of. They still had a lot of stuff like medical benefits to work out and policies. Kerry rubbed the bridge of her nose and wondered if Dar would go for bringing an HR person on board yet.

She followed the line of people inside and found a seat, barely getting into it before a tall figure hopped over the row of chairs and joined her. "Oh. Hey!" A smile appeared as she recognized Dar. "Didn't expect to see you here, thought we were going to meet at the office?"

"Hey." Dar settled into the seat. "Didn't think I'd let you do this by yourself didja?" she asked. "C'mon, Ker."

"Well." Kerry ran a hand through her hair. "It's just a five minute thing, they said. I thought you were busy with Richard."

"All done." Dar leaned back and folded her hands on her lap. "We just got back from the bank picking up the checkbooks." She smiled briefly. "We better get that electronic fast. I can't remember the last time I actually signed a check."

Kerry smiled, feeling both more relaxed and happier now that Dar was at her side. She'd been halfway hoping Dar would show up for the court proceedings, but she didn't want to ask since Dar had been crazy busy for the last three days getting everything rolling.

And so had she, of course. "AT&T will be out this afternoon for a site survey," she said. "I told them I'd meet them when I was done here."

"Good." Dar regarded the courtroom with some bemusement. "Alastair said the board meeting was called for this afternoon. He thinks Hamilton might try to convince them to shut up and cut a deal."

"Hamilton?"

"Yes." Dar looked slightly embarrassed. "Apparently he came down on our side."

"Really?" Kerry had to smile. "I think you grew on him."

"I think he didn't want my father to show up at his townhouse with a baseball bat," Dar demurred. "There's going to be conditions I'm sure. Just remains to be seen if we'll agree to them."

Kerry pinched the bridge of her nose. "Hm. When's the meeting with Briggs supposed to be, tomorrow afternoon? Things are moving really fast, Dar. Sheesh."

Dar patted her back. "By the way, Gerry's due here tomorrow morning to talk about the contracts, and deliver our puppy. He just called me before I walked in."

Gerry. Puppy. "Bu...wh—"

"Kerrison Stuart?"

"I need a beer." Kerry stood up and edged past Dar's long legs. "Be right back, hon."

"You'll get one," Dar promised, watching Kerry make her way up the aisle and show her papers to the clerk, who stepped back and allowed her to go forward to face the judge.

Her PDA buzzed and she pulled it out to glance at it.

```
Hey, boss. Found a rad datacenter all the way
south near the cutoff to card sound. Empty. The guys
who were supposed to take it went bankrupt and it's
ours for a song. M
```

Ah. Dar grunted softly, putting the device away and returning her attention to her partner. Kerry was now standing up near the judge's bench, her hands clasped behind her, fluorescent lights reflecting slightly off her pale hair.

She had her blue sweater and her dark khakis on and in Dar's eyes, she looked adorable. Nervous, but adorable. Dar saw her square her shoulders and nod, and then reach up to take a piece of paper from the judge, who was regarding her with a mild and tolerant expression.

It's done. Dar got up and moved down the aisle to greet her as she came even with her, exchanging a grin as Kerry waved the paper at her. "That was fast."

"It was," Kerry agreed. "Let's go." She exhaled happily. "Kerry Roberts. You like how that sounds?"

Dar laughed. "What exactly are you expecting me to say to that?" She draped her arm over Kerry's shoulders as they exited the courtroom. "No?"

"Do you think it was weird of me to do this? Now that it's done?" Kerry asked after a pause.

Dar considered that as they walked down the steps and stepped out into the bright sunlight of a Florida winter's day. "I have to say I never really thought anyone would do that. I mean, want to change their name to mine," she said thoughtfully. "Back in the day, before I realized I wasn't going to get married, I think I'd decided I wasn't ever going to change mine."

"Really? No, never mind. Retract that. Of course you wouldn't," Kerry said. "You have every right in the world to be proud of that name."

"Well, my dad's family isn't exactly something he's proud of," Dar said. "But yeah, that never bothered me because he's my dad."

"Lucky you." Kerry paused, then smiled. "Lucky us."

"Let's walk over to the Thai place," Dar suggested. "They have beer."

"Now that I'm not in knots, they also have sushi," Kerry said. "I don't know why I was so nervous about that, all he asked me was something about was I changing my name to escape the law?"

"And you said?"

"I said no, just to escape the lousy taste of my upbringing."

"Nice," Dar said. "So let's get some sushi, then go to our new digs and see if I can beat the butt crack in punching down our circuits."

"Oh boy."

Chapter Nine

AT LAST THERE was some peace in her day. Kerry perched on an old wooden stool in what was becoming her office. She leaned a clipboard on her lap and wrote some notes on it. It was almost sunset and the light was glancing past the window, putting a golden glow on the leaves of the trees just outside.

There was a lot going on. She heard hammers and circular saws going in the offices to either side of her, and the distinctive jingle of the cable runners as they worked their way down the hall.

There were two sawhorses and a piece of plywood serving her as a desk, and she smelled the sea coming in the window, along with a spicy scent from some restaurant down the way.

She'd changed out of the sweater and khakis that she'd worn to the courthouse, into jeans and a sweatshirt, and she had the sleeves pushed up over her elbows as she worked.

"Ma'am?"

Correctly assuming she was being addressed, Kerry looked up. "Yes?" She motioned the figure at the door to enter. It was one of the maintenance people from the landlord's management company, who'd been detailed to assist them in moving in.

"There's a delivery for you downstairs," the man said apologetically, wiping a bit of sweat from his forehead. "Boy, this is a busy place all of a sudden."

Kerry slipped off her stool and put her clipboard down on the makeshift desk. "Lead on," she said, following him out and along the hallway. It was open to the outside, though there were shutters that could be slid down in bad weather. It over looked the inner square, and Kerry glanced down to see the newly contracted landscaping company busy at work.

"Nice to see the place being made up, though," the man said as he ambled along at her side. "Thought the kid was gonna have to sell it off for a bit. Pity. Been in that family a while."

"It's a nice building," Kerry said. "We liked it as soon as we saw it. Nice area, and the space worked for us."

He nodded. "Lot of history around here. It's nice. I live over there in that apartment building." He pointed. "You can walk to everything."

They went down the steps to the ground floor in the back of the building where a truck was waiting. "Hello," Kerry greeted him. "What do you have for us?"

The driver unlatched the back door of the truck and opened it. "That's yours." He pointed at the contents.

Kerry peered inside. "Ah, furniture. Cool."

"Sign?" The driver handed over the clipboard and a pen.

She scanned the packing list, mentally checking off the items, then nodded and started to sign the manifest, pausing after her first name. Then she smiled and continued to write, finishing with a slight flourish and handing it back. "There ya go."

The driver and his helper hopped inside and extended the rear gate, preparing to get a pallet jack into position to move the delivery.

"Okay, while we wait for the freight elevator to come down, I can separate what's first floor and what's second." Kerry stepped back to give room and folded her arms over her chest, regarding her first purchases for their new place.

Nothing very exotic. The nicest piece of furniture she'd reserved for Dar's desk, with a top that was adjustable to height, with a wraparound design that would be comfortable for Dar to sit at while she worked, and yet, would allow her to raise up part of it to stand if she wanted to.

Sometimes, she did. She got tired of sitting down like anyone else would and Kerry had found her more than once with her laptop on the drink credenza at the old office pecking away while she stood there.

There was also a smart board for Dar's office, and for the corner, a nice zero gravity chair and a reading light in case she wanted to chill out for a few minutes.

She'd spent a lot more time on Dar's office than her own. Her furniture was more or less the same, but she'd added a small work group table and chairs for the corner of her office rather than the relaxing chair.

For the rest of the offices she'd gotten modular desks and comfortable chairs. The floors had been covered and lined with rubber surfaces. "Okay, so, those two pallets go upstairs." She pointed. "Those three stay here, and the ones in the back, they go upstairs, too."

"All right," the driver said. "But y'know, we're just supposed to drop it at the dock." He eyed her. "Don't suppose you want to be hauling that all yourself, huh?"

Kerry smiled at him. "I sure don't," she responded. "But I'm open to a delivery fee. Interested?"

The driver grinned. "Now that's my kinda customer." He motioned to his helper. "C'mon, Jake. We're gonna get us some beer money. It's our last stop anyhow."

Kerry chuckled, taking a breath of the cool air and exhaling in contentment. There was a pallet jack and she thought she could figure out how to use it, but having two big strong men, who already knew how to do it made a lot more sense to her, especially since she had some cash in her pocket to reward them with.

Sometimes, it did not pay to play the butch card.

"Hey."

Kerry turned, to find Dar approaching. She was in jeans and a sleeveless sweatshirt, with a tool belt full of punch down paraphernalia strapped around her waist.

"Hey. Furniture's here." Kerry indicated the pallets.

"So I see," Dar said. "What do you want to do about telephones? I'd rather use the twisted pair for data, and not have to split off a pair for phones." She folded her arms over her chest, and regarded the pallet now making its way down to the floor. "Nice chair."

"Glad you like it." Kerry reached over and brushed a bit of pull string fuzz off Dar's bare shoulder. "Let's see what we can do about using an IP phone system. Let me call and see what revolutionary stuff is available we can prototype."

"Okay," Dar said. "Let me go back to installing that demarc. Looks like we can hook into the same pops for a ring that ILS did." She hitched her thumbs into her work belt and winked at Kerry, then sauntered back into the building.

"Scuse me, ma'am."

Kerry put her lustful stare on hold and backed up out of the way, looking down the service ally and spotting a small cafe on the corner opposite the end of it. "Be right back." She circled around the building super and strolled down the lane, which had the wall of their building on one side, and a thick leafy hedge on the other.

It was nice. Even the dumpsters she was walking by were relatively clean. She got to the corner and crossed the street, exchanging brief smiles with two women seated at a table outside before she entered the cafe.

It was mostly empty, but the staff was obviously getting ready for a busier evening. "Hello."

"Hey," the girl behind the bar greeted her. "Whatcha want?"

"Two lattes, extra shot of espresso, to go please." Kerry slid onto a stool to wait, as the woman busied herself with her order. The cafe had a coffee bar, with a case full of the usual pastry selections, and about ten small tables with menus stuck in table tents on them.

There were also tents on the bar, and Kerry removed a menu and studied it. After a moment she put it back, having found a couple items she could foresee herself ordering for lunch in the weeks to come. Next door to the cafe was a pizza shop, and next to that a Thai place.

Nice. At the old office, unless they wanted to take a car out, it was pretty much restricted to the cafeteria downstairs, or the executive lunchroom upstairs.

This ramble of choices seemed more fun.

The girl who had taken her order came back over to her and leaned on the other side of the counter. "You working around here? I saw you go by a few times the last couple days."

One of Kerry's very blonde eyebrows hiked a little. "Yeah," she said. "The next building that way." She pointed. "We just moved in."

"Oh! The old Supertravel place."

Kerry nodded.

"That's been empty a while," the girl commented. "The last people there, the nail people...they were cool. Had piercings and all that stuff."

"Ah."

"But no one wanted to go in there. Too much of a bummer, you know? Just them in that little space and everything else empty."

Kerry nodded again. "Yeah, I know what you mean. They would have been rattling around in there. It's a pretty big space for a small operation like that."

The girl waited for her to go on, but Kerry merely sat there with her hands folded. "So did your company rent part of it, or..." Now her eyebrow lifted in question.

"All of it," Kerry cheerfully supplied.

"So what do you guys do?"

Kerry cleared her throat. "It's high tech," she said. "Computer services, networks, that kind of thing." She observed the body language across from her and decided her interrogator was pleased with the information. "We're a new startup."

"Oh, that's very cool," the girl said immediately. "You hiring? When are you going to get that all going? Most of the companies that move in here already have all their staff." She reached behind her and secured a stack of paper to go menus. "Want to put these out? We love free advertising."

Kerry chuckled. "Sure." She took the menus. "We're probably going to start taking applications in a couple of weeks. We've got a lot of work we're doing on the building first, getting furniture and stuff in."

"Good to know. Is it all tech stuff?"

"Tech stuff, sure, but also regular office positions. Accounting, logistics, you know," Kerry said. "Spread the word? We don't mind free advertising either."

"You bet." The girl smiled. "I'm Janine." She offered a hand. "What's the company name?"

"Kerry, and it's Roberts Automation."

She took her coffees, paid for them, then retreated back toward their building with a sense of satisfaction. She heard snatches of music, and smelled something barbecuing somewhere nearby, and she smiled as she trotted up the back stairs and headed down the hall toward their new offices.

Yeah. This was good. She edged around the pallets in the hall and squeezed into her space, going to the interconnecting door when she heard Dar's voice drifting through it. "Hey, hon." She poked her head inside, then proceeded as she saw Dar by the window.

Dar turned, and spotted the coffee. "You rock." She took hers. "I was just thinking about who to call to have a coffee machine installed here."

The building super was standing there, having been the other half of that conversation. "Well, we used to have a service, you know, Continental or something," he said. "The last people, they just had a Mr. Coffee drip machine," he added. "Used to leave 'em on all the time. Smells bad, burnt coffee."

"It does," Dar agreed "I'd rather have a small local company in here. Anyone around who'd be up for stocking dorm refrigerators with drinks and maybe do single cup coffees?"

The man looked at her in surprise. "You mean like one of the shops around here?"

Dar nodded. "Nerds need caffeine, sugar, and protein," she said. "It keeps the brain cells spinning."

He put his hands on his hips. "Now that's an interesting question. Lemme ask around." He gave Dar a look of respectful appreciation. "I guess all them vending machine people and stuff will be asking to talk to you. They pulled all that stuff out after the travel people left."

"Not fond of them, especially the ones that take your money," Dar said.

"Well." Kerry took a sip of her coffee. "We really think we should set a better example than candy bars."

Dar just started laughing, shaking her head and wandering off back to where the drivers were unpacking her desk.

Kerry had to chuckle, acknowledging the irony. "We'll figure out something. We're going to have a few more people showing up on Monday to work."

The man nodded, then they both turned as a soft knock sounded on the door frame. "Hello, sir."

Their landlord came in, looking around with appreciation. "You folks don't waste any time."

"No we don't," Kerry said. "We've got our papers and our checkbook. Why not come over to my space and I'll square that away with you." She went back to her office followed by Marcus, putting down her coffee on her temporary desk and pulling over the leather case full of documents. "Sit."

He pulled over a stool and parked himself on it, hooking his leather booted heels on the rungs. Today he was dressed in an Ambercrombie and Fitch zipped hoodie and jeans, with a leather wristband to compliment the outfit.

Kerry wondered briefly if he was gay. Her gaydar was unreliable at best. "Okay so, here's a copy of our incorporation documents, and a check for the first month. You did say we'd get half off, right?" Her eyes twinkled a little as she handed it over. "I think we're making up for it in renovation."

"No argument." Marcus took the papers cheerfully. "I'm getting a lot more out of this deal than I thought I would. I looked you guys up on the Internet. You're sorta famous."

"Sorta," Kerry said with a brief grin. "In a notorious, fifteen minutes of fame kinda way."

"Why'd you decide to cut out on your own?" he asked in a curious voice. "Seemed to me like you all were doing great."

Kerry rested her elbows on her knees as she watched the drivers diligently delivering her desk across the room. "Yeah, back to the wall, facing the windows, guys." She paused, then returned her attention to their landlord.

"I'm just being nosy," he said. "You don't have to answer that."

"I don't mind," Kerry replied. "ILS fired us. So we walked down the street, and opened our own company." She felt a sense of curious satisfaction saying it. "Stuff happens, you know?"

"Sure do!" Marcus sighed. "More than you know. I just got fired from Sedanos. They said they wanted someone more Latino to be their marketing head." He eyed her. "You don't seem Latino. Want someone to do your marketing for you?"

Kerry was caught between sympathy and laughter. "Don't you think that's a conflict of interest?"

He shrugged. "It's Miami."

Yes, that was true. "Let me talk to Dar about it," Kerry said. "I'm not sure we're ready for a marketing department yet, but we will when we're up and going."

He grinned at her. "I like you guys. My mother would have liked you guys. You're family and you're not cheapskates."

Ah. "Guilty on both charges," Kerry answered easily. "From what I've seen around the Grove so far, we should be comfortable here."

He nodded. "No problem. Most of the businesses that move in here, they're looking for an audience, you know? But no one around here needs high tech. At least, the kinda stuff you were talking about. So you're not competition."

"That's true." Kerry hadn't thought about it that way, but now, the interest of their neighbors made more sense. "We'll be clients. Trust me. Nerds who work here will go and eat, and drink and buy stuff if it's walking distance. I know my kind."

"Exactly," Marcus said. "And you're not a pawn shop. But I was kinda curious...what kind of customer do you have? Who buys that stuff?"

"Today? Almost everyone," Kerry said. "High tech, meaning computers, and wireless, and high speed Internet, and web sites. Pretty much everyone needs it. At ILS, we had to deal with the biggest of companies to make the financial model work. Now, we can take small customers we'd never have looked at there."

Marcus nodded the whole time she talked. "You get it."

"I get it," Kerry said. "But..." her eyes twinkled again, "we could get some bigger clients that might surprise you."

"Ker?" Dar poked her head in the door. "If your desk is here, can we borrow your sawhorses to set them up in the conference room so our friends have somewhere to meet with us tomorrow?"

"Sure." Kerry got up and picked up her things off the plywood. "Does that mean we need to rent folding chairs for them?" She stood back as two of the building people entered and started taking away her table. She let them remove it, then she walked over to her now assembled desk, where the drivers were waiting patiently. "Thanks, guys."

"No problem," the lead driver said. "This stuff went together easy. Not like that cardboard stuff."

Kerry offered him a folded bill. "I really appreciate it."

The man glanced down, then up at her with a broad grin. "Lady, so do I." He motioned to his partner. "Let's go. We got beer to drink."

She waited for them to go, then she set her things down on the surface of her new desk and perched on a corner of it. "I think we're going to like it here."

Marcus grinned and bounced on the stool. "I think the feeling's mutual!"

"AHH." KERRY SPREAD her arms out on their jacuzzi, gazing up at the night sky full of stars. "What a day."

The doors to the condo slid open behind her, and the smell of chocolate emerged. She glanced to one side to find a steaming cup being set down by her, joined by a plate of freshly cut fruit. "That looks awesome."

"So do you." Dar joined her in the tub, settling into the hot bubbling water with a contented sigh. "So, how many goons you think Bridges is going to send to talk to us?" She picked up a slice of apple and munched on it.

"Hopefully not more than we have chairs for." Kerry closed her eyes and savored the rumble of the bubbles against her skin. "Can you believe it's been less than a week, Dar?"

"Crazy," Dar said, glancing at her new cell gizmo as it rang. She reached over and picked it up, then opened it as she saw the caller ID. "Evening, Alastair."

Kerry slid over to listen.

"Tell Hamilton I say hi," Dar said. "Yes, the sound you hear is the jacuzzi."

"Well, glad you're getting a chance to relax, Dar." Alastair's voice came through the speaker. "So are me and Ham, matter of fact. We're in that steakhouse near the big office. Just got out of the board meeting and I'm of the opinion, Maestro, that I'm owed a beer."

"He got it for us," Kerry whispered. "Or he wouldn't be calling you that."

Dar covered the mouthpiece and smiled, nodding at her. She then removed her hand. "So what can I do for you gentlemen this evening?"

"Here's the thing, Dar," Alastair said. "It took some convincing, but we got the board to agree to your terms. You can go on about your new business, and they'll finish out the retirement package, including paying you until your resignation date."

Dar's eyebrows shot up to her hairline. "And...I have to do what?"

"Stay clear of the press," Alastair said. "Don't solicit existing ILS customers, or employees," he added. "Except for the two customers who have already approached you, that is. Can't do anything about that, I suppose."

Dar and Kerry exchanged a long look. "Alastair, I'll see what I can do about Gerry and the existing contracts," she said. "Bridges, that I have limited control over."

"Understood."

"Three existing employees are already coming to work for us," Dar went on. "Two of them solicited us before we left, and I asked Mark Polenti to come with us the night you fired me."

"And the other two are?" Alastair didn't sound very surprised.

"Our admins."

Dar heard Hamilton laugh in the background. "I mean, c'mon, Alastair. I'm probably only going to hire fifty people. You've got a quarter million of them."

"Not me," Alastair protested. "I'm retired." He paused a moment. "Well, it is a right to work state, isn't it? If they come to you, as in, if they resign and decide to go elsewhere, not much we can do about it."

"True."

"But, Dar, please, don't solicit people," Hamilton's voice edged in. "Why would you have to? They all want to come work for you and live in your garage. We all know it. You even offered Al a job. I could get a complex."

"I don't think I can afford you, Hamilton." Dar started to smile again. "We'll be judicious, I promise. I mean, hell, Alastair, we don't even have benefits or anything set up. Those people aren't stupid. They have families."

"I would have come to work for you without benefits," Kerry commented. "Hell, you were the benefit I was interested in. I didn't even know what you were paying me until I got my first auto deposit."

Dar gave her a droll look.

"I heard that," Hamilton cackled. "And I totally do believe it's true."

Dar sighed. "Listen, we don't have the scope to handle most of ILS's customers. We're starting small, and see where it all goes. I'm not out to put them out of business. I just want to make a living."

"Maestro, do you not realize those men in that boardroom are scared to death of you all doing just that?" Hamilton said. "They're pissed off because they've become used to rolling in the dough based a good part on your work, and now they ain't got that."

Dar sighed again. "They'll find someone. I'm not a rocket scientist."

"Yes, you are," Kerry said, at the same time both Alastair and Hamilton did.

"People!"

Alastair chuckled. "All right, Dar. It's your own damn fault."

"Yeah, I know," Dar responded in a resigned tone. "But you know what, Alastair? That goes both ways. I hear them out there talking crap about me, all bets are off."

There was a momentary silence "I'll make sure they know," Alastair said. "We'll send the papers down for signature. In fact, I'll bring 'em myself. I told the board I'd go down there and try to smooth some feathers. Lot of still very upset people in that office."

"Nice of you."

Alastair sighed. "Well, I'll give them someone to yell at, anyway," he said. "Talk to you later, ladies."

"Night, Alastair. Night, Hamilton." Kerry had her chin resting on Dar's collarbone. "Enjoy the beer."

Dar closed the phone and put it down. "I should feel like that was a win. Why don't I?"

"Strings."

"Ugh."

THE ISLAND GYM was mostly empty, the early morning light pouring into the spinning area and casting long and still shadows across the floor.

Kerry finished her set of sit-ups and paused, wiping her face off with her towel.

Off to one corner, Dar was busy doing some punching bag work, her hands encased in blue leather gloves as she batted at the hanging ball with a steady rhythm.

Kerry watched her for a minute, then crossed her arms over her chest and started another set, twisting a little to each side as she pulled herself up, to give her trunk muscles a little workout as well. It felt good. Tiring, but good. She finished the set and unhooked her legs, swiveling around and putting her feet against the ground, stretching as she stood up.

"How's your ribs?"

Kerry turned to find Dar still boxing in place nearby, bouncing back and forth from one foot to the other. "Fine," she said. "Haven't had a twinge for weeks."

"Good." Dar tapped her gloves together. "If you were going to have one, it would be on that board."

"Uh huh." Kerry hung her towel around her neck. "Don't remind me."

Dar batted her playfully on the shoulder, then bounced back over to the boxing area, leaving the hanging bag behind and going for the big body bag instead, unleashing solid hits on it.

Kerry went to the shoulder press instead and seated herself, pausing to adjust her grip as the door opened and two other residents came in to join them, making the crowd in the gym now equal to four. This early it was usually like that. The place would get busier as the day went on, and was positively crowded just after work hours.

Dar really enjoyed the boxing stuff. Kerry had positioned herself to keep her in view, and she enjoyed watching her graceful rhythm as she worked around the bag, trading hits with kicks, the impacts loud enough to raise a small echo.

She, on the other hand, stuck with her shoulder presses, leaning forward to keep proper form as she shoved the handles up over her head, sucking in a breath as she lowered them back down and felt the ache.

Again, it felt good. She'd been stuck for a while with just some light swimming while her ribs healed, and though she'd gotten enough out of it to keep herself in trim, it wasn't the same as the exercise she got from the weight training she preferred.

Weird, since she'd taken so long to decide if she liked the exercise or not, but now that she'd gotten used to it, skipping it made her feel a distinct lack of energy. She was happy to get back to her regular routine.

She finished her presses, and went on to the line of leg machines, giving her upper body a rest as she hooked her feet under the quad bar and settled back to start flexing, folding her hands across her stomach. "Hey, Dar," she called over, now that she was much closer.

"Yes?" Dar paused in her assault on the bag and turned, putting her gloved hands on her hips and raising a brow in question. She was wearing a pair of threadbare sweatpants and a sports bra, and the effect was curiously sexy. "Did you need to ask me something?"

Did she? Kerry wrestled her thoughts back around. "What do we want to name the puppy?"

"Brownie?"

"Dar."

"Cupcake?"

"Dar!"

"How about Chocolate Chip."

"Didn't I feed you breakfast this morning?" Kerry said, in fond exasperation. "Seriously."

Dar sauntered over and rested her arm against the machine Kerry was seated on. "I was serious. It's a brown dog," she said, reasonably. "We named our cream colored dog Cappuccino, didn't we?"

Kerry finished her set and let the weights down. "We did," she said. "But Brownie?"

Dar deftly unlaced her gloves with her teeth, and pulled them off, flexing her hands. "How about Coffee?"

Kerry covered her eyes and mock sighed. "Paladar Katherine."

Dar chuckled, reaching over to ruffle Kerry's sweat drenched hair. "You name him. I'm going to go take a shower and finish puppy proofing the house."

"Oh, right behind you." Kerry got up off the machine, feeling the all over ache of muscles well used. "How about, Mocha?" she asked, as she tagged along toward the changing room. "Chocolate and coffee. Brown dog. That work?"

"Mocha," Dar burred. "I like it." She went to the teak door locker they shared and opened it. "I hope Chino doesn't decide to chew us in our sleep for this, though."

Kerry chuckled. "I was trying to remember how I felt about getting a baby sister," she said. "But I was too young. I don't even remember what it was like when Mike was born."

"Mm." Dar tossed her gloves and boots inside, then grabbed her towel and headed for the shower. "Sometimes I think about what having a sibling would have been like," she said. "But my parents, I think, were pretty sure one was enough."

"And I agree."

"I'm sure you do."

"C'MON, CHI." KERRY motioned for her to hop up into the truck. "We're going to the office, and you're going to meet a new friend."

"Growf." Chino settled on the big bench seat, her tail wagging, delighted to be included again in their travels.

"I think she likes coming with us." Kerry got into the passenger seat of the truck, while Dar was leaning over the front window, putting their new sticker on. She leaned back and hiked her leather booted foot up to rest on her opposite knee. "Feels good to not have to worry about what's going on in that old office, you know, Dar?"

"Yes, I know." Dar swung back into the truck and closed the door. "I never realized how it hung over me until it wasn't there." She started up the truck's engine. "I know we're going to be involved in our own stuff, but it's not the same thing."

"No." Kerry idly petted Chino's head as the Lab stood up on the back seat and shoved her muzzle between the front seats. "I always dreaded my cell phone ringing. I knew it was something down, something broken, some customer pissed off. You get tired of the—I'm really sorry and I'll try to get that fixed for you—type of conversations."

"Yeah." Dar pulled out and drove slowly around the golf course, going between trees and bushes, bright flashes of flowers, and a brief glimpse of a peacock before she reached the turnoff to the ferry terminal. "I feel like a weight's off my shoulders to tell you the truth."

Kerry smiled at her, turning in her seat to watch her profile.

"It's like it's all brand new." Dar parked, and leaned back in her seat, giving Chino a scratch under her jaw. "I didn't think it would be like this."

"Me either," Kerry admitted. "Oh crap, forgot to tell you. I got a call from Colleen while you were getting dressed. She's got all our stuff."

"Ah," Dar said. "Cool."

"Including your fish," Kerry said. "She told me she fed them some corned beef."

"Aw." Dar smiled a little. "I sort of missed them. They were nice to look at. Want to have her meet us at the new office with all of it?"

Kerry smiled back. "Already asked her, she's meeting us there. She said Duks told her to take the rest of the day off."

Dar watched the channel go by. "Gerry's going to meet us there at one? I think that's what he said."

"Yes," Kerry said. "Having Chino meet the puppy in a neutral space is probably a good idea." She regarded her pet. "Not that she's got an aggressive hair on her body, but you never know." She tickled Chino's ears with her fingertips. "We can watch them play together before we bring him home."

"Mocha," Dar drawled. "Mocha and Chino. It's trendy precious, but I don't care."

Kerry chuckled.

The ferry docked, and they rolled off, heading along the causeway in the bright noon sun.

FRIDAY, EVEN AT lunch time, already had a sense that it was a downhill slide into the weekend. There were more people on the streets, and the cafes seemed fuller. Kerry was in her office getting things sorted out, boxes of her knickknacks and office stuff sitting on her new desk.

"You know, I like this place," Colleen said. "Much less hooliganism going on."

"Well for now." Kerry studied the built in shelves between the windows and brought a box over to start populating them. "But yeah, it's quieter over here, and more relaxed." She glanced over her shoulder. "How's it going over at the other place?"

Colleen made a face. "Kind of a wreck, really." She perched on Kerry's desk. "Not so bad by us. You know we bean counters keep to ourselves, but it's a riot on ten and on fourteen."

Kerry nodded. "Yeah, I figured. There were a lot of things in flight there. I had about ten projects in motion when they cut us loose, and God only knows what Dar was into." She removed a stack of pictures from a box. "Thanks for getting all this stuff in case I haven't said it twice already."

"No worries, m'dear." Colleen waved the thanks away. "I was glad to do it. The two of your offices were like tombs, with the burritos gone and all that." She indicated the box. "I put in that brass name plate they gave you at that party. Dar's was glued to the door, but yours was in those holders and I could get it out."

Kerry lifted it out and studied it. "Well." She smiled. "I got promoted out of this firing, and got a better name. But it's a nice keepsake. Thanks."

"You got the name done?" Colleen asked. "Already?"

"Yesterday," Kerry said. "So when our new business cards get here, it'll be Kerrison Roberts." She grinned at Colleen. "You think it's weird?"

Colleen shook her head. "For you? No. You've been stuck like duct tape on Dar since you met her."

Kerry's face reddened a little.

"Oh, c'mon. You know you were."

"I was." Kerry reached up to pinch the bridge of her nose. "And damn, my family's been a pain in my ass the last couple of years. Feels good to leave that name behind."

"Ker? Gerry's here." Dar stuck her head in the office and gave Colleen a smile. "Stick around," she said. "We can grab a cup of something after we finish these meetings."

Colleen looked pleased. "Surely," she said. "And I want to meet this new puppy, since I get to your place so often."

"C'mon, Chi." Kerry scooted through the door and joined Dar, as they went to the window to watch the long, dark car drive up. "Ah. Formal."

"Well, he is a general."

"Yeah, I know."

It parked in front of the building, as close to the door as possible, and the front doors opened as two uniformed officers jumped out. They opened the door and Gerry Easton emerged, with his aide, who had a wriggling armful of Labrador puppy to wrangle.

"Let's go." Dar led the way down the stairs and they got to the door at the same time the military party did. She pulled it open and stepped back. "C'mon in."

"Ah, Dar! Excellent." Gerry hustled inside. "You boys look around, hm? Don't break anything."

The two officers disappeared.

"This way." Kerry indicated the left conference room. "It's not fancy, but we're trying to get things going here." She opened the door, displaying the newly painted and carpeted room, with its makeshift table and mismatched chairs inside.

"Growf!" Chino spotted the puppy and got up on her hind legs to investigate, nearly knocking the aide down. Her tail started wildly waving.

"Put that little man down," Gerry said, as they squashed into the conference room and he closed the door. "Quite a travel day," he said. "Pretty weather here though. Very nice."

The aide put the puppy down and he immediately raced over to Chino, touching noses and starting a tick tacky dancing paw wagging tail lick fest with her.

"Growf!" Chino crouched down on her front legs.

"Yap!" The puppy let out a squeaky bark.

"Oh my gosh, that's so cute." Kerry sat down on one of the chairs they'd scrabbled together for the room. "I think she likes him!"

Gerry took a seat across from her and watched with a look of beaming content. "Sure looks like it."

The puppy scampered over to where Kerry was sitting, attacking her boot with enthusiasm. Chino came after him, slamming into Kerry's knees as she got her nose between the puppy and Kerry's shoe.

"Ow. Easy." Kerry leaned over and picked the puppy up. "What do you think you're doing, huh, little man?"

The puppy scrabbled up her chest and tried to get to her chin, poking his tongue out.

Dar started laughing, as she sat down next to Gerry, watching the show. "I think that one's yours," she said to Kerry. "Chino, come over here before you knock her down."

Chino trotted under the table and came out next to Dar.

"Did you say hi to your grandpa?" Dar asked.

"Heh." Gerry folded his hands on the table, and motioned the aide to sit down. "So you're moving very fast here, eh? Been only a week?"

"Only a week," Dar agreed. "Been a little crazy."

Gerry nodded. "So, what happened? I thought you were going to run it out as it were."

"You happened," Dar said bluntly. "I told them about the Joint Chief's not wanting ILS in the mix due to our international setup. Between that, and the executive branch wanting me to work for them, board lost their minds and booted us. Figured to cut their losses, or something like that."

"Insane," Gerry said. "Like little boys."

Dar lifted her hands and let them drop. "Just got this started faster. Didn't think you would mind."

"Not in the least." He reached down to pat Chino, who had poked her nose into his elbow for attention. "Well, madam, didn't you grow up to be a pretty girl." He stroked her head. "Look just like your mother, how d'you like that?"

Chino's tail wagged at the attention, then she turned her head and spotted the puppy upside down in Kerry's arms, getting his tummy rubbed. She scooted under the table to investigate.

"So we finished the incorporation work yesterday," Dar said. "I just got my checkbooks, we rented this space, talked to a few people about coming on board — it's been nuts."

"I can appreciate that," Gerry said. "But it's a good move for us, if you know what I mean." He pulled out an envelope and put it on the table. "That's the specification they want. Had a bunch of the boys, couple from each service, sit down and powwow, and that's what they came up with."

Dar opened the envelope and pulled the clipped papers out, scanning them quickly.

"Dar, how about some coffee?" Kerry still had the puppy in her arms, and he'd calmed down and was blinking sleepily. "Gerry?"

"Sure," Dar murmured distractedly.

"Joe would do me good," Gerry said. "Jennifer, give a hand, eh? You know how I like it."

The aide got up. "I'll bring in the dog things too, sir." She went to the door and opened it, holding it while Kerry went through ahead of her. Chino followed them and after the door closed, it seemed overwhelmingly quiet inside.

Dar had unclipped the papers and she was reading them. Easton waited in silence, playing with his wedding band a little as he sat there, apparently content to simply wait for her to finish.

The writing was dense. Dar scanned it stolidly, reaching the point where she started thinking ahead of the words, the comprehension of the subject in place as her head started to shake back and forth a little.

"Problem?" Gerry hazarded.

"Ungh." Dar rested her head on her hand and continued reading, and Gerry leaned back in his chair, folding his arms over his uniformed chest as he regarded the blank wall.

"Okay," Dar finally said. "Done."

He started a little, and turned to look at her. "So? What do you think, Dar? Something you can do?"

Dar straightened the papers out and clasped her hands over them. "I can, but I won't."

"Eh?"

"I won't. It's the wrong idea. Wrong structure," she said. "The general idea is okay, but the structure isn't scalable."

He blinked at her. "Haven't got a clue what you just said, Dar. Good? Bad? Yes? No?"

Complicated question. "Can we set up a meeting for me to talk to them about it, maybe do a white board session?" she countered. "Present a different way to get the same results?"

"Ah, they came up with nonsense. I get it." He patted the papers. "Long as you commit to getting this rolling, do it how you want to. Right? I'll send these boys down here to talk to you. They'd love the break from the weather."

She put the papers back in the envelope. "Deal," she said. "Oh wait. We probably have to sign something now, since we don't have a preexisting contract."

Easton made a snorting sound.

Dar chuckled softly. "It's going to have to wait until I get home anyway. I don't have a typewriter, a computer, or a printer here yet."

"No problem." Gerry took a pen out of his pocket and turned the envelope over, scribbling on it for a long minute. "We know how to do things like this in the Army, don'tcha know. Can't tell you how big a weight this lifts off me, Dar. Was told to find someone else to do this, and hadn't clue one where to start looking."

"There are other companies who do what we do, Gerry," Dar said. "I could have given you names."

"Would have been second best though." He continued writing.

Dar twiddled her thumbs. "Wasn't like that the last time I did a job for you. I thought you were going to have me whipped on the yardarm, or whatever that saying is."

Gerry snorted again. "Navy," he said, finishing his writing and signing underneath. Then he turned and looked at Dar. "I know that ended up in the crapper," he said. "My fault."

Dar's brow lifted.

"My fault, because I should have stood fast on it." Gerry leaned on the table and regarded her. "We sorted it out, sure. People got punished. Press would have been bad. But we'd have survived it."

"And now it doesn't matter," Dar said, quietly. "Because of the attack."

He nodded. "Right."

"I'm sorry I was a part of that project. Wrecked a lot of old memories," Dar said. "No matter how big of a jackass Jeff turned out to be, I still remember growing up playing with his kid."

Gerry frowned. "You were too close," he said, after a brief pause.

"I was." Dar pulled the envelope over and took the pen from Gerry's hand. She spent a minute reading the hand written contract, then she smiled and signed it, her slanting script distinct from her old family friend's. "Water under the bridge though. Now it's a new day." She put the pen down. "So thanks for becoming our first customer."

Gerry looked relieved. "Glad you feel that way." He held his hand out, and she clasped it. "Listen, now. This thing, it's important." He watched her nod. "Fool us once, shame on you, fool us twice, shame on us. We let them get us. Failure in intelligence they said? Well it's true. I know it and you know it. Embarrassing all around. But it can't happen again."

"Got it," Dar said. "I'll do my best, Gerry. But I'll need a chance to get this company up and going. Don't expect me to deliver anything overnight."

"No worries." He waved a hand. "Now, about those other contracts. The ones from before."

"Leave them with ILS," Dar said, then after a brief pause, she smiled faintly. "For now."

He studied her face. "You sure, Dar? Got an opportunity to get the whole enchilada."

"I'm sure. We don't have structure for that. Yet. ILS does a good job of support. Let them keep it. They renew next year anyway."

He nodded. "All right."

The door opened and Kerry and the aide, followed by Chino and the puppy entered. "Coffee all around." Kerry put the tray down. "You all wrapped up?"

Dar handed her the envelope. "Our first contract," she said. "Stick around, Gerry, a team from Bridges is due here any minute."

"Hah. Fancy boys, most of 'em." He moved his chair to play with the dogs. "Probably run from these two." He picked up Mocha and let him chew his finger. "Look at that vicious little man."

Kerry leaned over and gave Dar a kiss on the head, and patted her shoulder. "Might have been nice to get the sign on the door first, hon." She whispered.

Dar chuckled, and shrugged.

Kerry chuckled with her. "And a couple of employees...maybe a PC or two. I know we'll make it work."

"We will," Dar said. "One way or another, we will."

Chapter Ten

WHEN THE NEXT car came there were secret service agents in it, and instead of a fancy boy it was Bridges himself. He swept past the reception area and glanced around, then took his sunglasses off. "You may think I used this as an excuse to take a few days off in Florida at the government's expense."

Kerry had just come down the stairs with a cup. "Well, glad we didn't open an office in Michigan then." She held the door to the conference center open. "C'mon in and join our little circus."

Bridges eyed her, then he motioned one of the agents forward. "No offense, Stuart."

"None taken. I've had secret service agents peek in my bedroom since I was six," Kerry responded mildly. "My sister had a crush on one of them I still tease her about."

The agent paused and looked at her, then grinned and moved past, glancing quickly around the room. "Just some Army people and a couple dogs, sir," he reported, with a twinkle in his eyes.

"About what I'd expect to find here." Bridges pushed the door open and entered. "Ah, Easton."

"Hello there." General Easton had his jacket off, and he was tossing a ball to the end of the room. "Didn't figure to see you here."

"Back at you." Bridges regarded him, then looked around. "Damn spook was right. Couple of Army people and some dogs. Where the hell is Roberts?"

"Dar'll be right back." Kerry sat down at the makeshift table.

"What in the hell is this?" Bridges took a seat and picked up the puppy. "This one of yours, Easton?"

"Both of them are, matter of fact," The general said. "Pups of my Alabaster."

Bridges held the puppy up and examined it. "Cute." He put the puppy down, and watched as Chino came over, snuffing at the creature and giving Bridges a doubtful look.

"Entertaining." Bridges dusted his hands off. "You just moving in to this place, I take it?"

"Signed the lease Monday," Kerry said, sipping her tea. "By next Monday, we might even have a few employees and toilet paper in the bathrooms."

He chuckled dryly. "A little too much chaos to suit you?"

Kerry pondered that question, her ears catching the rhythmic sound of Dar coming down the steps. "No, not really. I was looking to make a change, after September."

Bridges nodded, looking up as Dar came in the room. "There you are, Roberts."

"Hello." Dar came over and sat down across from him. "Sorry. Had to talk to the electrical inspector." She put her hands on the table. "I didn't expect you to be here. Thought you would send someone from your staff."

"And waste a trip to Miami in the winter?" he responded. "What kind of fool do you take me for?"

Dar lifted her hands in a faint shrug. "I live here."

Easton got up. "Well, I know you lot have things to discuss. We'll be getting on, back to the hotel and then a few days of R and R." He winked at Bridges. "No fools here either."

Dar stood back up. "Gerry, give us a call tomorrow. We'd love to have dinner with you." She extended her hand, which he gripped and released.

Easton gave her a genuine smile. "Absolutely, Dar, I will." He reached down to give the puppy one more pat. "Little man, you take care of these ladies, all right? Be a good boy."

"Yap."

"We'll take good care of him," Kerry said. "And I think he and Chino are going to get along just fine."

Then the general was gone and they were facing each other around the table. Bridges studied them in silence for a moment. "Well, here we are people."

"Here we are." Dar was carrying a portfolio and she now opened it. "I've had some time to study the requirements document you sent." She studied a page thoughtfully. "It's an ambitious project."

He lifted his hand and rotated his finger, brow lifted.

Dar folded her hands. "The technology, the algorithms that this would take don't exist."

"Yet," Bridges said, dryly. "Listen. Cut to the chase, Roberts. I know this thing is outlandish. I had ten people in my office yesterday telling me it was pie in the sky. Can it be done?"

"Did they say it couldn't be done?"

"Yes," Bridges said. "That's why I'm here. The last time everyone told me something couldn't be done, you ended up doing it."

Dar exhaled. "I don't know if it can be done."

"That's what you said the last time."

"Last time I was encouraged to find a way by the fact you were going to railroad a friend of mine and destroy the company who paid my paycheck," Dar replied bluntly.

He shrugged. "End justified the means. You can call me an asshole all you want, Roberts, but no matter — it was worth it." He indicated the portfolio. "You going to try it or not? I've got a pool and a scotch and soda calling my name."

"Two conditions."

He rolled his eyes.

"One, no one tells me how to write this," Dar said. "No one has a say in how it's done but me."

Bridges raised his eyebrows.

"Not going to have a committee instructing me how to design," she continued. "I didn't put up with that at ILS, and I won't with you."

Now he smiled. "As it happens, Roberts, I agree with you a hundred percent. Done. Go on."

"Two, you give me access to all the systems you want to parse the data, so I can write filters for them," Dar said. "Giving them raw access is useless. It's too much data. I need to narrow focus the intelligence to what they need to look at."

Now he looked serious. "Maybe they don't know what they're looking for," he said. "I don't want anything held back from them on some namby pamby privacy crap."

Dar shook her head. "If you don't focus this, it's a waste of your money and my time. Last thing you want is to have a system that does fracture all that privacy crap, but doesn't find a bad guy who blows up Penn Station."

Bridges grunted. He eyed Dar for a moment, then shifted his gaze over to Kerry, who was sipping her tea with a mild expression. "You're both undergoing a security profiling, you know."

"We already have top secret clearances," Kerry replied.

"This is more than that," Bridges said. "Everyone you bring into this thing is going under a microscope. You get it, I'm sure."

Kerry nodded.

Dar nodded.

Finally he sighed. "All right, Roberts. You get what you're asking for. Now here's my condition. I find out you're scamming me, or you go public with what you're doing, you both go to Guantanamo and you're never coming back." He looked quickly at both of them, but neither flinched. "Understood?"

"Understood," Dar responded quietly. "You get billed for my time and for any resources, at a cost plus twenty five percent for the development period. I'll hand over a set of milestones to you, and before it goes into production, you and anyone you want, comes here to get a demonstration and sign off. If it's what you want, we'll agree on a price for it. If it's not what you want, you don't owe anything more than that."

He relaxed visibly. "Now that's a deal I can shake on. Most companies would have asked for ten mil up front to squander. It's a deal, Roberts." He held out his hand and Dar took it and they shook. "For the record, the fact that everyone else told me this wasn't do-able is in inverse proportion to my confidence that somehow, you can."

Dar gave him a skeptical look.

"They told me what you did," he remarked in a conversational tone. "With the cables, the NASA guys, little miss butter wouldn't melt in my mouth breaking into the exchange." He looked amused. "Woulda made a decent movie. Pissed off a lot of politicians, and gave me a laugh for the day when that bell rang and all that crap started flashing."

"I didn't break into the exchange," Kerry said. "My mother got me in."

Bridges laughed. "Did she know why?"

"No."

He laughed again. "They would have arrested the lot of you if it hadn't worked. Had all the charges ready, sabotage, and the rest of it. You got lucky."

"And we're dealing with you again, why?" Kerry inquired.

"Wasn't me," Bridges said, surprisingly. "You can call it bullshit, but believe it or not, Stuart, I was on your side. Told them it was stupid, not to mention dangerous playing that game. You knew too much. Your company knew too much. That's why we need to back them off from the tricky stuff."

"From what Hamilton said, we'd never have gotten to testify so what was the danger?" Dar asked.

"You can only go so far with that. You can put Arab looking men and dirty turban heads in jail and no one much cares. But you two would have caused a lot of fuss," he said. "You look too good on TV."

Kerry rolled her eyes.

"Think about it," he said. "Roger Stuart's kid and the daughter of a well known artist and a war hero? Would have been easier just to have them shoot you."

"And we're dealing with you now, why?" Kerry asked again.

"Because you know it has to be done," he answered straightforwardly. "And you're both idealistic enough to think you can do it the right way." He eyed Dar. "Don't think I don't know that. You'll try to do all that left wing protect the individual crap and, with any luck, I'll be able to take what you give me and get enough out of it to justify the pain in the ass and the cost."

"Why us then?" Dar asked. "Hire some redneck right wing hot shot who'll do it without any conscience. Be cheaper, and you probably can blackmail whomever you want then."

He paused and looked at her. She looked right back at him. "I could get offended," he said.

"Go fuck yourself," Dar replied. "That help?"

Bridges paused, then chuckled. "Okay, we can stop the asshole Olympics. You give it a go, we'll see where it takes us." He stood up, glancing at the corner where Chino was curled up in the corner, her head on her paws. Mocha was curled up against her, his head resting on her elbow. "I have a deer hound," he said. "More temperamental than those things."

Kerry got up. "Interested in a cup of coffee?" she asked. "There's a nice little cafe down the road."

He gave her a dry look. "Not dressed for it, but thanks for the offer." He indicated his neatly pressed suit. "I'll gather up my spooks and leave you to enjoy your weekend." He stood up and then paused. "Do we need to sign anything?"

Dar shoved the portfolio over. "G'wan. That's what Gerry did. I won't have printed contracts, or pens, or even a printer for another week."

He chuckled and pulled the packet over, scribbling his name on the top of it. "Glad you decided to get out of ILS," he said. "If anyone asks, we'll say you preferred not to have your motives mixed." He winked at them and pocketed his pen. "Later, people."

Then the door was closed, and he was gone.

Kerry sat back down. "Holy crap, Dar. We just booked enough business today to catapult us into some Gartner quadrant."

Dar regarded the two packets of papers on the table and shook her head. "No kidding," she said. "Fortunately, both of these contracts can be handled by small teams, so we can get started before we really get things rolling. I'll need to hire a team of database analysts and a pile of lamp stack people and front end designers."

Kerry regarded her. "We probably need to hire someone for HR and accounting first so we can give them some kind of benefit package, and of course pay them."

Dar nodded meditatively. "Have you figured out how we're going to make an offer to Colleen without breaking our promise to Alastair?"

Kerry smiled.

"I probably can't manage approaching Mari," Dar continued, in a regretful tone. "Colleen's been there a relatively short time, and she wasn't management yet."

"She will be now."

"You know who I'd like to find a way to bring in?" Kerry said. "Your buddy in NYC."

"Scuzzy."

"Yeah."

"She'd never move to Miami," Dar said. "But we could find a way to ask." She got up and gathered the papers. "Let me go run a compile on the financial sys—oh, wait, I can't. I don't have a computer here yet."

"Let's go, hon." Kerry went over and picked up Mocha, who woke up with a sleepily startled look. "Hey there, little man. We're going to take you to your new home."

"Growf." Chino looked up at her.

"You too, madam." Kerry patted her thigh. "I'm not picking you up."

They moved into the hallway, and Colleen was there waiting for them, leaning against the wall with her car keys in her hand. "Is that the new pooch?"

"This is Mocha," Kerry said. "He's Chino's little brother." She handed over the pup to her cooing friend. "Isn't he cute?"

"He is, just like she was when she was a baby." Colleen cradled the puppy in her arms and tickled his belly. "So how did things go?"

"Really well." Kerry glanced at Dar. "Dar, do you—"

"Want to take the dogs and get the car? Sure." Dar took Mocha from Colleen and whistled for Chino. "Be right back." She left the office and headed for the parking area, feeling just a touch overwhelmed and a bit lightheaded after yet another whirlwind day. "Glad it's the damn weekend, Chi."

"Growf." Chino was trotting beside her, sticking at her heel like the well trained dog she was. They had never needed to leash her, she came when called, and stayed when told, one of the few things in Dar's life that had proven utterly reliable.

Once she'd stopped chewing shoes, that is.

It was good to have a minute to just think, as she walked to the truck. Things were happening at such a breakneck pace, it was a relief to be able to regroup while Kerry made her offer to Colleen. Hopefully it would end up with them having dinner together back on the island.

"Hey there."

Ah, crap. Dar looked up to find their landlord just about to open the door to his own car. "Hey. We're just leaving."

He paused. "Yeah...um." He leaned on the frame. "Did I see soldiers here before?"

Dar opened the back door to the truck and waited for Chino to jump up, then put Mocha down next to her. "You did." She closed the door. "Customers of ours."

"Ah."

"Don't worry. Just for IT services." Dar got in the driver's side of the truck. "They won't be here often." She rolled down the window as he came over.

"So you have customers already?"

"We do." Dar acknowledged a moment of relief. "But they were people we knew before. We still have to find new clients."

"Sure," he said. "I was just a little surprised. I guess you guys are going to go full out next week, huh? My brother said he was putting a whole bunch of stuff in for you."

Dar nodded. "More employees will be around. We're looking for someone for HR. You know anyone?" She turned as Mocha scrambled up into the front seat, clawing at her leg. She lifted him up and set him down. "With any experience?"

He leaned on the door. "I might." He reached over and gave Mocha a pat. "He's cute."

Mocha put his paws up on the inside of the window and made himself heard. "Yap!"

"Send them over on Monday if you do," Dar said, spotting Kerry and Colleen strolling out of the building, Kerry with a knapsack over one shoulder, Colleen with a big grin on her face. "We gotta go."

"I will." He stepped back, then waved at the other two. "Have a great weekend."

Dar tickled Mocha under the chin. "Are you gonna last 'til we get home or are you going to piddle on me, huh?" She leaned on the windowsill as the two other women came up. "We set?"

"We are," Kerry responded. "Coll, follow us home? Let's do the Italian place and we can fill you in on the two contracts we just signed."

Colleen crossed her arms and leaned against the truck. "That I will," she said. "After I call my mother and tell her about my new job, and a promotion to boot." She looked really happy. "And that I can get rid of those linen suits. My life just got so much better, I can't tell you."

"Okay, see you over there." Kerry went around and got into the truck, taking the puppy from Dar. "We'll celebrate."

Colleen went for her car, and Dar started up the truck. "What a damned day."

"Uh huh," Kerry said. "I've got those contracts. Let's hope like hell the PCs and printers get there Monday. Can I get the specs for the servers you need to run all that software?"

"Sure." Dar pulled out of the parking lot and headed for home. "We need to get that, plus all the network components for the office."

"Sheesh."

"Some retirement, huh?"

Kerry exhaled. "Are we getting in over our heads already?" she asked. "Dar, we've got two major contracts already and we don't even have employees yet."

"Not true," Dar said. "We have admins, and we have an operations director, and an accounting director, and us."

"Ho boy."

"Listen," Dar said. "Just call up a placement agency on Monday and give them our requirements for everything else. Let them do the investigations and the work, and bring in qualified candidates."

Kerry considered that, then grunted. "Ah."

"It'll be fine, Ker."

They were quiet for a while as they drove, Kerry letting the puppy chew on her finger as she cuddled with him. "Bridges creeped me out," she said as they were pulling onto the ferry. "That whole passive aggressive Guantanamo thing." She sighed. "I didn't mind the stuff for Gerry. That's all pretty straightforward."

"That's why I left us an out."

"You really think they'll let us take an out?" Kerry looked uncharacteristically pessimistic. "What if they decide to take the code and do what they want with it?"

"Won't happen." Dar relaxed, reaching out and circling Chino's head with her arm, giving her a friendly rub. "Besides, weren't you the one who asked me to think about doing it?"

"That was before we talked to that guy just now again."

"Relax." Dar wriggled into a more comfortable spot as the ferry took off for the island. "Look at it this way, Ker, at least he was an out in the open jackass. No pretending."

"Mm."

"I think if I can do it, it'll be fine."

"I hope so." Kerry sighed. "Next time though, I'll just keep my mouth shut—oh, crap."

"What?"

"Glad you got leather seats."

KERRY SIPPED HER coffee as she watched the sun rise outside the kitchen window, remembering standing exactly in this place, exactly at this time, a week ago before her entire life had radically changed.

She took another sip and then smiled.

Well, to be honest, not really. She felt the motion and the nearness and then the warmth as Dar came up behind her, circling her with both arms and just leaning against her in silent content.

Her external life might have changed, but the important part, this part, hadn't budged an inch. She lifted her cup and offered Dar a sip, hearing the slurp right in her ear as Dar sucked some from the cup.

"Mocha managed to follow Chi down the steps," Dar said after she swallowed. "Glad we took the pebbles out of that rock garden of yours." She hugged Kerry a little tighter, rocking back and forth slightly from one foot to the other."Keeerrryy...I lloooooovvveee you."

Kerry smiled. "I'm so glad you saved Gopher Dar. I'd have missed that little sucker, you know that?"

Dar chuckled. "I packed up that repository and I'll bring it in on Monday. I can throw a tower under that desk and compile it on that."

"Mm," Kerry agreed. "Looks like it's going to be a pretty day." She indicated the soft glow of dawn streaking across the sky. "Got anything in mind you want to do, Dardar?"

"Chill."

"I can go with that."

"It's been nuts all week," Dar said. "Let's enjoy our puppy and two days to do nothing. Time enough on Monday to rejoin the circus. We have six weeks to get everything up and running before we disappear for two months."

"You think we can still do that?" Kerry asked, after a moment's silence.

"We're going to do that," Dar stated firmly. "I can compose code in my head just as easily going down a river as I can sitting in that office."

"Really?"

Dar nodded. "Most of Gopher Dar was done while I was in staff meetings."

Kerry's blonde eyebrows lifted up.

"I want my vacation." Dar wrapped her arms more firmly, then lifted Kerry off her feet, making her squawk. "Want want want." She hopped up and down a bit, forcing Kerry to hastily put her cup down. "Want!"

"Okay!" Kerry reached behind her and gave Dar a pinch on the butt. "Stop that!"

Dar did, releasing her after biting her earlobe. "Milk." She eased around Kerry and got a glass, heading to the refrigerator as her chuckling companion picked her coffee cup back up. "Actually, we should go get those new laptops today. I want to have something current with me next week."

"And two big screen monitors?" Kerry asked. "I got used to the one in my old office."

"You bet." Dar took her milk and went to the back door, which was standing open. She peered outside. "Hey you guys!"

Chino and Mocha were playing in the garden, barking at each other, while the bigger Lab backed off and the puppy chased her.

"Yap! Yap!" Mocha pattered after the big cream colored tail heading for the steps. "Yap!"

Chino trotted up the steps and nosed Dar's bare knees, giving her an affectionate lick as Dar reached down to pet her head. "Growf!"

"Aw." Dar moved down the steps to where Mocha was gamely trying to climb up them, the stone a little too tall for him yet. "C'mere, rug rat." She picked him up and tucked him under her arm. "Enjoy it while you can." She looked down at his small, rounded head, and he looked back up at her, his tongue hanging out of his mouth.

The stone steps were cold, and she retreated inside, where Kerry was buttering some whole wheat toast. "Is that our concession to health today?" She brought the puppy over and let him sniff Kerry's shoulder.

"Hah hah." Kerry smiled. "Yeah, the whole wheat is going to overcome the quarter stick of butter and slice of Swiss cheese all right. No, they just sent the wrong kind this week and I didn't have a chance to go over and change it."

"I like it." Dar accepted her toast and cheese, pulling her head back when Mocha realized there was something edible nearby and scrambled against her hold, his dark nose twitching. "Hey, not for you, kiddo."

"Here." Kerry put some puppy kibble in a dish, and offered it to him.

"Let me put him down before he eats my fingers." Dar set him on the floor and he engulfed his kibble, scattering bits of it across the kitchen floor.

Chino watched him with a worried, Labrador frown, then she applied her tongue to the errant kibble, gathering up the spillage while Mocha fixed his attention on the dish.

"He's really cute," Kerry said, after a moment of silent observation. "He's feistier than Chino was when she was that size."

Mocha looked up at her. "Yap!"

Kerry put her hands on her hips. "Excuse me, sir?"

"Yap!" The puppy stood up on his back legs and pattered at her leg. "Yap! Yap!"

"Growf!" Chino came over and nosed him, tumbling him onto the floor. He rolled over and got back up, galumphing over to her and scooting between her legs, making her whirl around and bark in surprise.

"I can see we're going to be entertained." Dar was leaning against the refrigerator, munching her toast. "We should take them down to Lincoln Mall. Get our new lappies down there and have some sushi outside."

"Sounds great to me," Kerry agreed readily. "We've never done that before."

"First time for everything." Dar's eyes twinkled. "We'll be the center of attention, with a brand spanking new Lab puppy with us."

"I like it." Kerry finished her toast and picked up a strawberry, taking a bite and chewing it. "And I like not having to arrange for and pick up our dry cleaning."

Dar chuckled.

"So, shower, gym, shower, Lincoln Road?"

"Well." Dar took hold of her again. "We can start with the shower. Sure."

KERRY LOOPED CHINO'S leash around her wrist as they strolled along the road, enjoying the sunny day and the active area. On both sides of the walking mall were small cafes, and there were many others out taking advantage of the nice weather.

She was in jeans and a hoodie, and so was Dar, the puppy cradled in her arms as they wandered. Mocha seemed quite satisfied to get what was for him an eagle eye view of his surroundings, his pink tongue poking out as he looked around.

"I didn't realize the brown ones would have such light eyes," Kerry commented.

"Almost the same color as yours," Dar said. "I didn't know that either."

"You know what? I just realized there aren't any computer stores down here, Dar. Except the Apple one."

"Yuck," Dar said instantly. "I hate that operating system. It sucks camel wangs."

"Dar!"

"What?" Dar glanced down. "You think the puppy's gonna get corrupted?"

"No, camel wangs are gross."

Dar's brows hiked. "How would you know?"

"Punk."

"Takes one to know one."

"Just for that, let's go inside." Kerry steered her toward the store. "Maybe I'll like these kinds of computers."

"Bet you won't." Dar amiably followed her, and they entered the quiet, mostly white interior that had lots of screens and computers to peruse.

They drew attention immediately, or, at least Dar did as every female employee immediately gravitated to the puppy, making cooing noises that drew round eyed reaction from him.

"Chick magnet." Kerry gave her a poke as she guided Chino over to where the desktops and laptops were. There were a number of different kinds, one sort of roundish and weird looking, and another that was square and looked like a regular tower case, only in silver with pretty piping.

"What do you think of these, Chi?" Kerry touched the tower keyboard admiring the large screen. "It's kinda nice, huh?" She looked over at Dar, who was still surrounded by admiring girls. "Wish I had my camera."

"Growf." Chino stood up and put her paws on the table, peering at the screen.

One of the girls took Mocha from Dar, freeing her to inspect the laptops on the table she was standing near. She poked a key with one finger then glanced up and met Kerry's gaze, shrugging her shoulders, she walked around the table and came over to where Kerry was standing. "They're not bad looking." She grudgingly admitted. "I just hate how they work."

"Why?"

"Candy assed operating system," Dar replied promptly. "Hides everything from you like you were a two year old."

"Well." Kerry navigated the nearest mouse. "It doesn't seem that different from a regular one." She opened up an icon. "I mean, that shows you what's on it, right?"

Dar's brow was creased. She took over the mouse. "Wait a minute." She opened a black screen. "Is that a terminal window?"

"Is it?" Kerry stepped back out of her way as she edged in front of the tower. "More to the point, is that good or bad?"

"Hang on." Dar typed in a command, her eyes popping open a little at the response. "What the hell?"

"What?"

"Son of a bitch." Dar straightened abruptly. "That's Unix." She looked accusingly at a sales boy who had wandered over. "That thing is running Unix?"

He nodded. "It's a BSD variant. Darwin kernel," he said. "It's not an official fork, but it's pretty solid."

Dar put her hands on her hips. "When the hell did that happen?"

Kerry nudged her. "Does that mean you like them now? I like that laptop. It's sexy."

Dar eyed her.

"Like you are." Kerry completed the thought, with a smile.

"They switched to OS X last year," the salesman provided amiably. "We like it. It makes the screen a lot nicer. This model, it's got full length PCI slots. The laptops just got DVI out."

"So there's no more of that weird interface anymore?" Dar asked.

"You mean OS 9 and those things? You can run an interpreter and run those old programs if you have them," he said. "But I don't think it will do that forever. They're trying to get people to switch everything over to the Cocoa framework. I do some development work on the side. It's pretty cool."

"If it's called Cocoa, it must have your name on it," Kerry said from her peanut gallery position alongside Chino.

"Ha ha," Dar responded.

"Coders like them because they're true multitasking," the boy said. "And a lot of tools can run on Darwin."

Dar folded her arms. "All right. Get me one of the laptops with the most ram and hard drive space. I'll give it a try," she said. "You want one?" she asked Kerry. "If it's got a UNIX base, I can probably get my compilers to work on it."

Kerry considered the machines. Then she shrugged. "Let me try one of the smaller ones, those white ones there." She pointed. "Whatever the nicest one is, I'll take it."

The sales boy beamed at them. "That's cool," he said. "I like customers like you, who even bring puppies. It's like Christmas."

Dar started laughing.

"Let me go get them wrapped up for you." He trotted off.

"See?" Kerry bumped her hip against Dar's. "Not so bad, huh?"

"Remains to be seen," Dar said. "They still could be absolute crap, even with Unix on them." She played with the keyboard some more. "That's a pretty crisp screen though."

"Better for your eyes," Kerry kidded her gently.

"Since I have a lot of code to look forward to, probably not a bad thing," Dar surprisingly admitted. "Been a while since I spent more than a minute here and there with my head in a text editor."

She clicked a few more things, then abandoned the mouse and circled the table to go and rescue Mocha. "C'mere, critter, before they squish you to death." She took back the reluctantly given up puppy and curled him into the crook of her arm. "No laptop for you."

"Yap!" Mocha squeaked up at her.

Kerry spent a few more minutes playing with the desktop, admiring the screen and the acrylic surround. "Y'know, Chi, these are actually pretty cool."

Chino hopped up and looked at the screen, her tongue sticking out of the side of her mouth. Kerry spotted a camera and clicked on it, delighted to see a box open and display Chino's nose. She clicked the picture, and smiled, as it transferred to the box. "Look, Chi. You're there for posterity."

"Growf."

One of the girls wandered over. "Is that what the puppy is going to look like grown up? They're cute, even big."

"They are." Kerry put her arm around Chino, and got an affectionate lick on the arm. "They're gorgeous, funny dogs with a lot of personality."

The girl came closer and patted Chino. "They're not like pit bulls, right?"

"Right."

Chino's tail wagged at all the attention.

"I think they're about as far from pit bulls as you can get in a species. Except for maybe, cocker spaniels," Kerry said. "Just very sweet, gentle dogs."

The sales boy came back with two white bags and a swipe machine. Dar traded him her credit card for the bags, and handed one to Kerry. They had strings in them, and could be worn almost like backpacks and Dar got hers situated as one of the girls helpfully held Mocha for her.

Kerry came over and took the puppy as Dar signed the slip, waving goodbye to the gang as they left with their new toys. "That was painless." She held the door for Dar then followed her back out into the sunny weather.

"Yeah, and we'll get to try something new." Dar took back Mocha as they strolled along the street. "Let's find a likely spot for lunch."

They found a nice cafe with tables outside and settled into one of the corner ones. Kerry set her bag down on the table and relaxed, stretching her legs out and crossing them at the ankles.

Dar had put Mocha's little puppy harness on, and he was busy exploring under the table, sniffing everything. He came around and sat down on Dar's foot, watching the passersby with wide puppy eyes. "Yap!"

"Yap," Dar barked back at him. "Do you know how nice it is to just sit here, and not worry about anything going on at work?" she asked Kerry. "Two glasses of white, and the sushi boat," she added, to the Goth looking waitress who had sidled up.

"Yes, ma'am," the waitress responded. "Would you like a bowl of water for the dogs?"

Kerry smiled at her. "Sure. Thanks." She waited for the woman to disappear. "You're right. This is nice," she said. "I mean, we've got stuff to do next week, but right now, there's nothing going on, nothing we need to worry about."

Dar nodded.

"That's cool." She watched Mocha chew the laces on her hiking boots. "Kind of a shame the new business is taking off as fast as it is."

Dar chuckled. "Hon, you can't have it both ways."

Kerry sighed. "I know. I sound like a schizoid. I told you I was all hot to open our own business, I just thought we'd have a little time to chill out before we did it. I should have known better. Our lives just don't work that way."

"After we get things rolling, we can relax again," Dar said. "Once we bring in people to do the work."

Kerry gave her a droll look.

Dar returned it with a brief, wry grin.

The sushi arrived, distracting them from their people watching. Kerry smiled with pleasure and wielded her chopsticks with skill, selecting a bit of sashimi and adding some soy and sesame seeds to it. She put it in her mouth, then looked down to find Mocha on his hind legs with his front paws scrabbling at her knees, whines escaping from his mouth.

She swallowed. "Little man, you don't need to eat raw fish." She tapped him on the head with the ends of her chopsticks. "Get down."

"Yap!"

They both chuckled, then Dar glanced up. "Ah."

Kerry caught the word and looked to see what Dar was looking at. "Hey, Eleanor," she greeted their former co-worker and sometime antagonist. "Want some sushi?"

Eleanor pulled up a chair and seated herself. "I can't imagine bumping into you two like this, but you know, I'm glad I did," she said. "Let's talk."

Dar and Kerry exchanged looks.

"SO LOOK," ELEANOR said. "We've never been best friends."

"No." Kerry responded. "You were one of the more hateful people I met at ILS, matter of fact."

Eleanor stopped, and regarded her in some surprise.

"Be fair, Ker." Dar maneuvered another piece of sushi into her mouth. "I gave her good reason to be."

"Dar."

"It's true. I never hid for a minute when people pissed me off." Dar chewed thoughtfully. "Not even with you."

Eleanor chuckled dryly. "That's very true. You never had to wonder what you were thinking. It came right out your mouth." She paused. "But you know, I came to actually appreciate that."

Kerry grunted, and returned her attention to the sushi.

"Right around the time with Ankow," Eleanor said. "After Jose and I realized the potential of that new arrangement of yours. We were at a bar, having a drink, and he'd just sold some crazy amount of contracts on it and he said to me, "shit, the bitch was right.""

Dar chortled softly.

"I stopped caring that you made me nuts," Eleanor said. "So did he."

"Back at you," Dar said, taking a sip from her glass.

"You knew how to make the right decisions."

"I always knew that," Kerry said.

Eleanor gave her a droll look.

"Aside from our relationship," Kerry said. "I have total trust in Dar's choices." She wiped her lips with a napkin. "I don't always understand them, but they always prove out."

"Not always," Dar protested.

"Hon, they do." Kerry gave her a fond look. "Even if it takes a while to unravel the clusterfuck ball, they end up right."

"Exactly," Eleanor said. "So." She leaned forward. "I'm not one of the people who's going to come running to you for a job. I've worked all my career for ILS. I intend to retire gracefully from them and spending my elder days playing craps in Vegas."

Dar smiled. "I can picture that," she said. "Size of company we are isn't going to need your panache."

Eleanor regarded her. "That might be the only nice thing you ever said about me. So you're not going to build ILS V2?"

Both Dar and Kerry shook their heads in perfect unison. "We figure it'll maybe end up being forty or fifty people," Dar said. "I'm aiming at custom solutions, systems that make new things happen. I don't want to be ILS. I want to go home at the end of the day and not think about work for a change."

Eleanor looked profoundly relieved. "We, and I mean me and Jose, don't want you for a competitor. It's going to be hard enough to replace you where we are."

"That might be the only nice thing you ever said about me," Dar replied, with a faint twinkle in her eyes. "We're going to concentrate on systems design and software as a service. Maybe put up a datacenter down south."

"Maybe we'll end up subcontracting you," Eleanor said, after a pause. "No hard feelings, Dar. Everyone in that building misses the both of you. I've never seen so many—"

"Pissed off people?" Kerry suggested.

Eleanor shook her head. "Sad people. It's like someone in the family died around there."

Dar was caught off guard, and for a moment it showed. Then she drew in a breath and lifted both hands up, then let them drop in the table. "Wasn't my choice how it happened."

"You could have lied," Eleanor said. "But we all knew that wasn't your style."

"No."

Kerry studied Dar's face. "You know." She cleared her throat a little. "Maybe it wouldn't be a bad idea to just say..." she paused. "Maybe arrange a company get together...maybe down at Crandon Beach or something and we could stop by so folks can get some closure."

Eleanor smiled. "Thanks for not making me work for that, Kerry. I think we could arrange that. Maybe next weekend?"

"You can't say we're showing up officially," Dar said, though she looked a lot happier. "I agreed I wouldn't contact anyone. Part of the deal to not have to announce to the press we were fired."

Eleanor rolled her eyes. "Alastair told us yesterday. I think he was trying to be consoling. I'm pretty sure he wasn't expecting one of the security guards to ask why they did something so stupid in the first place then."

"Poor, Alastair. He's taking one for the team, I think."

"He's taking one for you," Eleanor said. "Or at least, that's what he said. Said he owed you one." She exhaled. "Anyway, thanks for agreeing to do a drive by the party. Unofficially. We'll put the word out through the usual channels, though I heard your admins were AWOL."

"Absent with leave. They're on vacation," Kerry said. "We were pretty close to them, and I think the whole thing affected them more than most people."

"And Polenti." Eleanor smiled briefly. "I was in the room when they asked him if he wanted to step up into Kerry's slot and he told them to fuck off. Nicely done. I don't blame him. You know they asked Michelle Graver, right?"

"Really?" Kerry's brows lifted.

Eleanor just laughed. "Five or six others from Fortune 100s, did the same. Some board member's nephew? The same. Had more sense than his uncle." Eleanor glanced up as the waitress hovered. "Can I get a glass of Chablis, please?"

The waitress glided off.

"Maybe they should bring in someone from another industry," Kerry said. "Someone who has no idea about ILS, or us."

Eleanor leaned back in her chair, crossing her pant suit covered legs. "That was Jose's idea too. Just bring in some egghead with no clue about what we do. Make it much easier for the two of us, you know?"

Dar chuckled dryly and picked Mocha up to sit him on her lap. "That infrastructure should hold you for a few years. Just get someone who can keep things even keeled, and who's service oriented," she said. "Who knows what'll be on the table in three or four years? Tech moves at light speed."

"True." Eleanor sipped at the wine the server had just delivered. "So. Haven't ever seen you two down here. What's up? Slumming?"

"Shopping." Kerry indicated the boxes. "And we wanted to show off our new puppy." She reached over and tickled Mocha on his chin, getting a lick on the hand for her pains. "Right, Mocha? Aren't you brand new?"

"Yap!"

Eleanor rolled her mascaraed eyes. "What are those, anyway?"

"Labrador Retrievers." Kerry leaned back as Chino hopped up and put her paws on her lap, sniffing interestedly at the sushi. "No raw fish for you, madam."

Dar picked up a small bit of rice ball between her chopsticks and offered it, watching with an indulgent grin as Chino delicately nibbled it off the end of the wooden implements. "They're really good dogs," she told Eleanor. "So long as you can survive them being chewing machines for two years." She let the wriggling puppy down to explore, but kept hold of his leash.

"I have cats," Eleanor replied. "They're declawed."

Of course. Kerry dodged past Chino's head and captured another piece of sushi, popping it into her mouth then almost burst into laughter as the dog investigated where the fish had gone, sniffing at Kerry's lips with an intense, worried look.

"Hey!" Eleanor let out a yell, jerking her feet off the ground. "That thing just pissed on me!"

Chapter Eleven

"I THINK THAT was a successful day." Dar wiped Mocha's feet off and set him down in the kitchen. "We got laptops, we got sushi, had a nice walk, and our puppy piddled all over Eleanor's Prada's."

Kerry was in the living room with her box and bag, busy unpacking her new laptop. "He's a good judge of character already," she called back. "Sorry, I know you said you were hell on wheels to her but she was still an ass, Dar."

Dar wandered in from the kitchen and sprawled on the love seat, pulling over her own box. "She was never that bad to you. I think you just hated her because she hated me."

Kerry considered that. "Well." She opened her box and studied the sleek machine inside. "That certainly pissed me off, hon, but even beside that, she's a viper."

"Mm." Dar had her new laptop out and on her lap. "These are nice." She opened the top and pressed the power button, her brows lifting at the piano like chord sound that resulted. "Huh."

Chino came over and jumped up next to her, turning around twice and then curling up in a ball. She exhaled with an almost human expression, her eyebrows twitching as Mocha came over and stood up, putting his nose against hers.

"Aw." Kerry looked up over her new screen. "They're so cute." She reached over and grabbed the camera on the table and lifted it up, switching it on and snapping a picture of the two dogs, and her beloved in her sweatpants and very white socks. "So are you."

Dar looked up at her. "Me?"

"You." Kerry smiled and set the camera back down. The laptop had booted and she ran her fingers over the touch pad. The screen was somewhat similar to what she was used to but the interface was sleeker. She connected the laptop to the condo's Wi-Fi and opened a browser.

Dar was busy pecking away at the keyboard. "Huh...there's a Darwin version of my compiler. Let me go grab that, and see if I can bring up my analytics on this thing." She settled with her back against the love seat arm, and one leg slung up over the back of it, with the other propping up the laptop.

Kerry was doing some browsing. "You going to write a mail server or are we going to go commercial?"

"Let's run an IMAP server. If the firewalls and all that get there next week I can work on that," Dar said. "Actually, Mark can work on that, and we need to get some Linux admins in because I'd rather use lamp stacks than IIS."

"I love it when you talk all sexy like that," Kerry said. "Want some cherries?"

"Already have yours. What more do I need?"

Kerry started laughing. "I got a call back from that employment service. They'd totally love to work with us, and can bring in a turnkey package."

"Good." Dar tapped away. "Hey, Ker? Thanks for getting that thing next weekend together. Be good to go and say hello to everyone, but in a neutral place."

Kerry smiled. "You should have seen your face when she said that stuff about someone in the family dying. I almost got up and hugged you."

Dar blushed, blinking a little as she typed.

"It would make me feel good to see you feel good about seeing all those people," Kerry went on. "I want to see them all hugging you. Promise me you won't wig out."

"No promises," Dar muttered, but a smile tugged at her lips.

"Okay, I have a bunch of software downloading." Kerry got up. "Let's go start dinner. Gerry's going to be here at six?"

"Uh huh. He's a steak and potato guy, by the way."

Kerry paused at the entry to the cobalt and white kitchen, and regarded her. "Oh my gosh, what I am going to do? I've never ever had to deal with one of those before." She parked her hand on her hip. "Guess I've got to throw away all those soy burgers and alfalfa sprouts."

Dar looked up and grinned, lifting both hands off her keyboard and turning them upward, and then letting them drop. "That was a dumbass thing to say, huh? Sorry about that. I didn't really think you'd feed him rabbit food."

Kerry chuckled and retreated into the kitchen, thinking a little about how their relationship seemed to have morphed these last couple months. She wasn't sure if it was the trials they'd been through, or just the process of their growing up and into each other, but she'd gotten the feeling that they had gained stability in each other that hadn't been so evident before.

She felt like she could say anything to Dar now.

Humming lightly under her breath, she opened the refrigerator and removed three T-bone steaks from the meat compartment, already dusted lightly with spices. She set them on the counter top and went back for the small, thin-skinned golden potatoes, dumping them into the little basket in the sink and running water over them.

"Yap!"

Kerry paused in scrubbing the taters as she got a visitor. "Yes?" She watched Mocha's tail wiggle furiously. "What can I do for you, little man?"

Mocha sat down and looked up at her. "Yap!"

"Oh my gosh, you're so cute." Kerry grinned at him. She got a little puppy kibble and put it in his dish, watching him inhale it, tail wagging almost continuously.

"Ah. He's got you trained already." Dar came in, sliding a little in her socks. "Good boy! I figured he might be hungry since he just tried to get milk out of Chino."

Kerry eyed her. "Really?"

"Well, she does look like Alabaster." Dar walked away with her mug of milk, giving Kerry a wink.

Kerry went back to her scrubbing, ending up with a bowlful of potatoes she set aside and covered with a paper towel. "Let's see. String beans will be pretty safe, huh?"

"Yap!"

"Not for you." Kerry shook a bean at him. "Has Chino taught you how to use the doggy door yet?"

Chino appeared in the doorway and looked at Kerry with a quizzical expression.

"Go on, show him how to go outside," Kerry instructed Chino, who had now attracted Mocha's attention. The puppy pattered over to her and walked between her legs, coming out from between her front ones and sitting down. Chino soberly licked the top of his head, then she walked over to the dog door and pushed her nose through it.

Mocha looked astonished. Then he bolted forward and tried to get through the door with her, ending up tumbling outside with a startled yelp.

Chino barked, pulling her head inside to give Kerry a look before she continued out the dog door in pursuit of the puppy. "Growf!"

Kerry chuckled. "Sorry, Cheebles." She went back to preparing her fresh string beans, cutting the ends off and enjoying the scent of the vegetables, one of the few Dar would eat willingly. She did manage to get her to try others in stir-fry, when they were either covered in sauce or wok fried and therefore not vegetable tasting.

Carrots were also successful, along with baby spinach, especially when she folded the latter into cheese omelets. Dar amiably tolerated this adjustment of her ingestibles, understanding that Kerry had her best interests in mind and she'd really gotten pretty good about trying new things.

But there was nothing new today. Kerry nibbled on a raw bean as she reviewed her ingredients, satisfied that she'd produce something completely acceptable, especially considering she had, hidden in the refrigerator, one of the Death by Chocolate cakes Dar was so fond of.

She heard barking outside and peered out the kitchen window that overlooked the garden, spotting Chino down on her front legs as Mocha charged her with puppy enthusiasm. They had a rope toy between them and they both grabbed it, tails wagging.

Too cute. Kerry leaned on the counter and idly watched. The sun had started to go down behind them, and it lit the oceanfront with a golden glow that was very different than the light they got in the summertime. Less moisture, she reasoned, letting her eyes track a circling gull.

She opened the window, letting in the rush of the surf and the distinctive scent of the winter air and tasted a hint of salt on the back of her tongue.

She heard the sound of the sliding glass door and then spotted Dar going to sit down on the swing with her new laptop, tucking one long leg under her as she concentrated on the screen. The breeze was tangling her hair, and as she watched, Dar pushed it behind her ear, displaying a brief flash of her blue eyes.

Then another flash, as if sensing the attention, Dar looked up and right into her eyes, a smile appearing along with a gentle twinkle.

Kerry leaned her chin on her hand and savored the moment. "What a lucky son of a bitch I am."

Dar crooked a finger at her, and Kerry abandoned her preparations, picking up a bottle of ice tea from the refrigerator as she made her way outside, feeling the breeze as it blew in through the open glass doors. "Yes?"

"C'mere." Dar patted the seat next to her. "Let's try the photo booth."

"The what?" Kerry sat down anyway, leaning an elbow on Dar's thigh.

"Photo booth." Dar clicked in something, then a moment later Kerry was looking at herself on the screen. "C'mere." She pulled Kerry closer and they were both in the frame, and a click later their slightly skeptical and bewildered looks were frozen in perpetuity. "Heh."

Kerry stared at it. "What's that for? Is it an application just to take pictures of people sitting in front of your laptop?"

"Yep." Dar looked fondly at it. The resolution wasn't great, but the picture made her smile, and she saved it. "I like this thing," she said. "I got my repository mounted to it, and I just compiled Gopher Dar." She sounded satisfied. "This keyboard's comfortable to type on, too."

"And it has crazy little apps that let you take pictures of yourself," Kerry mused. "I'm glad you like it, sweetie." She patted Dar's belly. "I'm going to start dinner. I'll cook the steaks medium rare."

DAR FELT THE swing move as Kerry got up and she paused to watch her head back inside the house, leaving the sliding glass doors open as she disappeared back into the kitchen.

Mocha scrambled through the dog door and raced around into the patio with Chino close behind him, a bit of cloth trailing from his teeth.

"Whatcha got there?" Dar grabbed him as he ran past, picking him up onto the swing and inspecting his prize. She rescued the fabric.

"Hey, Ker? We need to buy an underwear hamper."

"Yeah?" Kerry called from the kitchen.

"Yeah. With a top that locks."

Dar heard the footsteps and looked up to find Kerry with her hands on either side of the sliding glass door, leaning out to look at her. She held up the fabric and grinned.

"Good grief." Kerry rolled her eyes, and retreated again.

Dar balled up the underwear and stuffed it in her pocket, then put the puppy back down on the floor. "Now, where did you find that, huh? I hope you didn't find that out in the garden." She inspected one of Mocha's paws, already a healthy size and promised a lot of further growth. "C'mon, let's go see if there are any more out there."

She picked up the laptop and brought it back inside, dropping off the machine on the counter before she opened the back door and went down into the little garden. There was a flight of stairs down from the house, terracotta stone with a forty-five degree turn in the middle that ended up at ground level.

It was quiet there, the area surrounded by a stuccoed wall around a space of about thirty square feet, filled with grass, and little beds of flowers and herbs in raised crates and baskets that Kerry puttered with in her spare time.

The grass was trimmed and tended, and high tech. It was planted over a filtration and irrigation system that drained to the sewer and was sprayed down at night to rid the turf of both salt and dog piddle. There was a door in the middle back of the wall, a wrought iron gate that allowed the gardening staff to come inside, and tidy up on weekday mornings.

Dar pulled out one of the biodegradable bags and attached it to the neatly hanging scooper, roaming around the yard and cleaning up while she searched for more clothing. There were big river rocks outlining the flower beds and in one corner, a little fountain that Kerry had made from a slew of the stones piled up was sedately splashing water out that ended up in a bowl Chino headed right over and drank from.

Dar liked it. Before her relationship with Kerry, the place was very plastic and boring, with ficus hedges and sea grapes planted around a central area that had a stone table in it. Now, there were metal flat sculptures fastened to the walls, and two hanging chairs that were fastened to the underside of the kitchen, and dog toys in various states of shred scattered around.

There was even an installed speaker system so they could play tunes outside, and fans that they would turn on when it was muggy to stir the air around.

If they'd lived a little further north, she figured they could swing a fire pit. Dar sat down in one of the swing chairs and regarded the space, deciding maybe she would get one to surprise Kerry anyway. It would be nice to sit out here and have some hot cider in the couple of months they had of winter weather outside.

Birds fluttered overhead, and she heard a peacock off in the distance.

The phone rang inside, and she heard Kerry answer it, supposing it was the ferry terminal telling them of Gerry's arrival.

She watched the dogs play, and took a breath, and when she let it out, the sense of odd surrealism she'd felt since the prior weekend dissipated and this new reality took its place.

It didn't feel so weird anymore. She could think about being fired, and it no longer felt embarrassing, or made the pit of her stomach tense up.

Chino came over and nuzzled her knee and she stroked her head, watching Mocha attack a leaf that had the temerity to float into the garden and land near him.

She thought about the get-together next weekend and smiled.

Kerry trotted down the steps and joined her, wiping her hands off on one of her kitchen towels. "You'll never guess who that was." She dropped into the other chair and swiveled around in a circle. "My mother."

"She coming to dinner, too? At least she eats steak, unlike mine," Dar said.

"She was just coming out of an intelligence committee meeting. Apparently they were being briefed on this new Internet counter terrorism system the president's commissioning."

"Ahh."

"And apparently some of my father's old friends said they'd never support it if ILS were involved."

"Hoisted on their own petard, I'm guessing."

"Mom admitted she had a hard time keeping a straight face, especially when Bridges reluctantly agreed to remove them from any consideration," Kerry said. "It's going to be hilarious when they find out it's us doing it."

"Let's hope I can," Dar said. "Gerry on the way? I thought I heard a car outside."

"Yep." Kerry got up. "She said she liked being the only one in the room who had all the facts, for a change." She held out her hand to Dar, and they walked up the steps together, with the dogs rambling after them. "But she said the whole privacy thing was freaking them out."

"Points for them."

"They wanted to know if the system could identify people specifically who were going to sites like—"

"Like porn," Dar said. "All of them were imagining their next campaign having to explain why they were glued to www.poledancinggirls.com."

"Might make politics more popular then, huh? I can picture those debates on TV."

"OKAY." KERRY CAME into the conference room with a small box. "I've got us some communication until we get a phone system in here."

Mayte and Maria were going through papers with the employment agency, and Mark was opening some boxes on the other side of the table, sorting through cables and packing peanuts. All of them were visibly tanned, and equally visibly in a good mood, dancing a little to the music from the radio Kerry had plugged in.

They were all in jeans or cargo pants, and Maria was even wearing a pair of Ugg boots she would never have worn in the staid ILS offices.

She could almost sense the lightness in the room. "One for each of you." She handed out boxes. "It's this new thing from Handspring. Dar and I were testing it and we like them."

"Cool!" Mark broke off from his unpacking and opened the box. "Hey, I saw these on Tech TV the other day." He glanced up. "We going to set up personal mail on them?"

"Until Dar gets the mail server compiled," Kerry said. "She's been working on that today."

"Saw her. Got a Mac, huh?" Mark chuckled. "Freaked me out."

"She likes it." Kerry looked up as the door opened, and Dar stuck her head in. "We were just talking about you."

Dar grinned. "Mark, give me a hand will ya? They delivered the racks."

Mark put his hands on his hips. "So when heavy stuff has to be lifted, I'm the guy around here?"

Dar looked at him, then looked down at herself, then back at him, both eyebrows lifting. "What?"

"You don't count, boss." Mark nevertheless stuck his new gizmo in his cargo pants pocket and headed for the door. "You've got bigger biceps than I do."

Kerry snickered.

"Don't you start," Dar said to her. "I've got the accounting module running. Colleen's looking at the table structure." She winked at Maria, then disappeared after Mark and the door swung shut.

"Okay." Kerry finished handing out the gizmos. "How are we doing here?"

"I think we're set," the woman from the agency said. "My gosh you people know how to fast track!"

"Of course," Maria said. "Did I not say we were the bomb?"

Kerry sat down at the table, which was actually a table now, the furniture van having arrived about an hour ago. "Great. The personnel office is pretty much set up down the hall, and I think the office supply truck just showed up outside, so we'll have clipboards and pencils and all that stuff coming in."

"Does that mean our things are here too, Kerry?" Mayte asked, looking up from examining her new phone. "We can get all of our desks settled."

"Yep," Kerry said. "So we can abandon our little cave here and get rolling." She led the way out and down the hall to the room they'd set aside on the first floor for personnel, across from the suite of newly repainted offices that would be the accounting department.

Colleen, having heard them approach, popped out of her inside wall office that had huge windows opening into the garden space in the middle. "Ah, I've got me some neighbors do I? Hello there!"

"Colleen, this is Mary Jo Bensen, she's from the staffing company," Kerry said. "She'll be bringing in candidates for us, including your startup group."

"Comin' thru!" Mark interrupted them, pushing a cart in front of him that had computers and monitors. "Got your PCs here."

"Hey, flat screens!" Colleen looked approvingly at them. "Nice."

"Yup." Mark started to pick up the screen. "A lot less workman's comp with these things. They weigh like nothing." He entered Colleen's office and disappeared.

"Great. I'll leave you here to get settled." Kerry pointed at the office set aside for the staffing company. "Mark'll get you set up with a machine and a printer."

"Great." Mary Jo stuck her head inside. "Nice space." She shouldered her big case full of papers and went inside.

"Okay, now back up to our offices," Kerry said. "All the office supplies are there." She led the way up the steps. "Lot of progress today."

"Yes," Maria agreed. "And, Kerrisita, it's so much fun."

"A lot of fun," Mayte chimed in.

"Starting from scratch, you mean?" Kerry asked. "That's what's so cool for me. Everything we're doing we decide on. We don't have to put up with anyone else's ideas."

"Exactly, yes," Maria said, as they reached the top step and entered the big office suite on the corner. "I am so glad there is no gray, and no moron."

"Maroon, Mama." Mayte grinned. "Yes, it is nice." She looked around the outer office, which was bigger than her space was at ILS by far, and had steel and glass furniture that was sleek and modern looking. "Let me go unpack those boxes." She went over and picked up the first one, opening it and peering inside.

Maria smiled, and folded her hands, with a contented expression. "It is good," she said to Kerry. "We make the rules, yes?"

"Yes." Kerry half turned to face her. "You know, Maria, Dar and I were talking and we really thought that for this new office, we should have someone in the position of office manager, don't you think? To be in charge of all the arrangements and things."

Maria considered. "Yes, I think that is a good idea. Someone who everyone can call to get correct answers." She nodded, then looked up at Kerry, who was smiling at her. "Is that not correct, Kerrisita?"

"Will you be our office manager, Maria?" Kerry asked, after a slight pause. "We're only bringing people to work here as managers we really love and trust, and you were on the top of the list. We don't want you to be an admin, or Mayte either."

Maria put her hand on her chest, her eyes going wide. "Kerrisita!" she said, on an intake of breath. "You want me to do this?"

"Absolutely," Kerry said. "In fact, we thought that office right over there would be a nice spot for you." She indicated the corner space across from their suite, which had windows that let the sun in from both the central open space and the outside. "What do you think?"

Maria still had her hand on her chest. "Jesu." She glanced past Kerry at her daughter. "Mayte, did you know of this?"

"No, Mama." Mayte peeked over the box at her. "But I like it," she added with a grin.

"Let's go check it out." Kerry guided her across the hall to the new office, pushing the door open as she caught sight of a moving shadow inside. "Ah, look. A tech is here setting it up for you."

Dar straightened up, a handful of cables clutched in her fingers. "Almost done." She watched Maria's stunned face. "This okay for you?"

Kerry had picked a half round desk, in wood, chrome, and glass like Dar's was, and it had a big, executive size leather chair behind it.

Maria went over and touched it, then looked at them. "This is for me, truly? Dar, I did not expect this. Are you sure?"

"We're sure." Dar finished connecting the cables and adjusted the angle of the monitor. "I remember you once telling me that back in Cuba you'd had a managerial position, but here, no one respected that." She coiled up a cable with gentle, precise motions as she looked up at Maria. "Well I respect that."

"You and Mayte were ready to come to work for us without even asking what you'd be doing," Kerry said. "That's a lot of trust, Maria. We want to make sure we pay that back."

Maria sat down on the chair and put her hands on the desk. "I am thinking for sure it is you who are the bomb," she said. "Yes, I will do this. I will be in charge for you."

Dar grinned. "Sweet."

"We're going to make Mayte our operations manager," Kerry told her. "But don't tell her yet. I've got her nameplate being made up."

"Ee!" Maria clapped her hands together, then put them on her cheeks. "It is like Christmas, again."

Dar chuckled. "For us too. I didn't think owning a company would be this much fun, to be honest." She turned on the PC she'd just installed. "Now I'm gonna get back to building us a computer system. Mark's hooking up the routers and we've got a temporary Internet circuit in, just a DSL, but it'll be something."

"Dar." Maria got up and came around the desk, opening up her arms. "You are such an angel." She gave Dar a hug, which Dar returned.

"We will do a beautiful job for you."

"I know." Dar released her, smiling as Kerry stepped up and got a hug in turn. "We'll get both you and Mayte assistants to boss around. It's going to be a blast."

They all started laughing, though Maria's eyes were bright and wet with tears. "Dar picked this office for you," Kerry said. "She's really good at that. I remember finding out she picked mine."

Dar blushed a little. "Well, I didn't get assistants often," she muttered.

"Oh, yes." Maria said, immediately. "Jesu, we spent so many days making sure the furniture was just so, and getting a pretty leather desk pad, and so on to make sure you felt welcome, Kerrisita."

"And I did." Kerry took hold of Dar's hand, bringing it up to her lips and kissing the knuckles. "So we hope you and Mayte feel welcome here, because we want to have a lot of fun, and be successful together."

A knock at the door made them turn to find Mayte looking in. "Oh, Mama, it's so nice," she said. "You can put a plant over there in that corner in the sun."

Dar and Kerry eased out the door, leaving the two of them to plan the decoration of the space. They walked together hand in hand back to their own space, moving from the sunlit hallway into Kerry's office. "That was cool," Kerry said. "Dar, they never actually even asked me what we were going to pay them."

Dar chuckled. "You didn't ask me that either. Let 'em be surprised on payday."

"Like I was."

"Like you were. Hell, like I was. I never asked either when they made me VP." Dar wandered from Kerry's office to her own, sitting down in her chair and resting her forearms on the table. They weren't being crazy really as the salaries would be in line with industry standards, but they were already known quantities, and they knew what kind of work they could expect from them.

Same with the rest of the startup team. There were no unknowns there. Dar leaned back, feeling the leather warm to her skin. The outlines of this new office were already becoming familiar. The built in cabinets, freshly painted, already had some things from her old office and from home on them.

Stuff she'd never have had at ILS, Dar acknowledged, spotting a teddy bear on one shelf dressed in a cutoff shirt and wearing sunglasses she assumed was supposed to represent her.

She smiled at it, since it had attitude even for a stuffed animal.

Her fish were perched on the low shelving behind her under the window, seemingly pleased they had something to look at besides her inbox. Someone had extended their little tank, and now there were six cubes they could swim in and out of and not contact each other, and even some colorful gravel and a water plant for them to hide in.

Her desk had a big monitor on it and a mouse and keyboard, waiting for her to bring up a tower system to plug into them, all sitting on the glass top of her new desk, which was sleek, with an angled surface that let her rest her hands comfortably while typing.

The chair was nice, too. Dar settled back into it, feeling support along her spine. She swiveled the chair around and put her boots up on the low shelves, holding her hands over her thighs as though a laptop were there. "Good."

Mark poked his head in. "Hey, Dar? We're grabbing tacos for lunch. Want some?"

"Sure." Dar crossed her ankles and let her hands rest on her legs. "They get those racks in?" She watched him nod. "After lunch we can get the network up then."

He nodded again. "This is pretty cool," he admitted. "It's like...we always had to deal with stuff that was put in before our time. You know? Here, if it's fucked up, it's our fault."

Dar chortled softly. "Very true. Go grab lunch."

Mark disappeared, and she waited to hear his steps on the stairs before she got up and went into the admin area that Mayte had claimed. She saw evidence of the young woman's personalizing of the space, something that she noticed was absent in their old office.

Everyone seemed to be expanding to fit their new roles. Dar grinned, as she walked out and into the hallway, imagining it already full of people, working on their projects.

"Ma'am?" A delivery person dodged into her view. "I have a box here? Can you sign for it? No one's downstairs."

"Sure." Dar studied the clipboard. "Ah, the rush order." She took the box and handed back the signed form, then she carried the box over to a windowsill and perched on the edge of it. "Hope they spelled everything right."

She opened the box and sorted through the contents. Desk and wall plates. The desk ones carefully carved hardwood, and the wall ones chased steel backs with solid black fronts.

Down near the bottom, the company name. Dar let her eyes run over it a few times, a smile tugging at her lips. "Roberts Automation. Would you look at that." She touched the icon she and Kerry had decided on, a dark, solid blue ball bisected with four silver compass points, and the name in slanted serif font.

Above that, names and titles. She took the box and went back in her office, putting down her two on her desk, then going into Kerry's space to drop off hers.

Then she started making the rounds, taking advantage of everyone being out at lunch to put her little surprises on desk pads for her startup crew to find when they came back. She put Mayte's down, then went over to Maria's office, then she started down the hall to the big space that Mark had settled in.

He'd been surprised at the big, windowed space she'd assigned him, but after he read the plates, maybe he wouldn't be. Dar whistled melodically under her breath, enjoying the moment fully as she passed the empty offices, waiting for their new occupants, and trotted down the steps to get to Colleen's space.

She passed the new server room, sticking her head in to find the workmen finishing the walls, and one side of the raised floor already in and sporting ten brand new racks that had just been assembled.

"Hey." The nearest workman put his square in his tool belt and came over. "Electrical guy said for me to tell you all they brought in the new service. Those lines are hot." He pointed at the thick, black cable running up the sides of the racks, terminating in plugs for the new machines. "Thirty amps per leg he said."

"Good." Dar held her hand up to the air conditioning vents. "We'll see if this tonnage will hold us for now. Might need more."

He simply nodded. "Locksmith'll be in later. Said you wanted some special locks on the door there?"

"Yup," Dar said, sticking her head in the small room behind the server space, where an old telecom backboard rested, along with cables and pipes that came in from the outside. On one side, a single box was alive, blinking lights flickering sedately. Underneath it was a cardboard box full of gear, waiting to be installed. "That's for later." She took the last of the items out of the box she'd been carrying, and put the empty container down next to the gear. "For twist ties."

She waved at the workmen and left the room, pausing to drop off Colleen's new name plates and getting around to the back stairs just in time to meet the gang on their way back in, their hands full of paper bags.

Kerry brought up the rear, laughing with Colleen at something, and then after a second, she sensed Dar's presence and looked around until she found her. "Hey babe."

Something she definitely would not have done back at ILS, unless they were in private. "Hey cute stuff," Dar responded. "Find someplace good?"

"They got bacon on their tacos," Mark said. "Dude."

"Bacon?" Dar repeated. "Nice."

They took the bags through into the central open space, setting up camp on the plywood trestle table that had been moved out from the conference room. There were folding chairs scattered around and soon they were ensconced and munching.

Dar swallowed a bite of her taco. "Wow, that's good."

"Skirt steak, bacon, cheese, and hot sauce," Kerry said. "Had your name all over it, Dardar."

"Ay, yiyi," Maria said. "Kerrisita!"

"Look who's talking, Senora Carnitas with mojo." Kerry grinned when Maria stuck her tongue out at her. "Dar's been eating like a rock star on tour a lot longer than I've known her. She has lower blood pressure and cholesterol than I do."

Mayte giggled.

Dar merely licked some steak juice off her fingers and waggled her dark eyebrows.

"These are really good," Colleen said. "Real stuff, y'now? Not Taco Bell."

Mark pulled something out of his pocket and set it on the table. It was buzzing softly. "I should, like, mail this back to them, huh?" He said. "I gave 'em my two weeks today. I could have waited another week, but screw it."

"What did Mari say?" Kerry asked, wiping her lips.

"She wasn't surprised. She knew what was up," Mark said. "She told me about the meet up at the beach on the weekend. I said maybe me and Barb would stop by."

"Yes." Maria sipped on her ice tea. "I also have called and told them that Mayte and I will be leaving. Mari was very nice about it."

Mayte nodded. "Si, she was. She called me and wanted to ask what we would do for the health insurance."

Everyone glanced at Dar, then at Kerry.

"Well," Kerry said. "I'm waiting for a call back from two of the providers that we used at ILS. I know we can't get the rates they got, because they're so much bigger, but I think we can get a plan that makes sense. You all will keep your benefits until ILS terminates you."

"Righto," Colleen said. "My dad's construction company has a small business plan. Not bad. He's got some better benefits than I got either at the bank or ILS."

"I'm cool," Mark said around a mouthful of taco. "I'm on Barb's plan. I never used our stuff anyway."

"We bumped into Eleanor on the beach," Dar said. "She told us about the meet up. We said we'd swing by to say hi to folks."

"I heard." Mark's eyes twinkled a little. "I got texts from half the department."

Dar grinned, but kept munching.

"Well, back to work." Mark pushed his wrappers into a bag and stood up. "See ya inside." He got up and the others did likewise, straggling back toward the door to the inside while Dar and Kerry remained outside, finishing their lunch.

Dar took out her last taco, enjoying the taste. "Door plates came in."

"Yeah?" Kerry wiped her fingers on her napkin and washed down her last bite. "Did they come out nice?"

Dar nodded.

"They in the office?"

"I went around and put them on people's desks."

"Oh. Mark and Mayte are going to be surprised." Kerry laughed in delight. "This is so much fun."

A loud voice made them both turn around to locate it. Through the propped open door they could see the rear entrance, where a man was standing pointing in the opposite direction.

"Get outta here! I told you once, I ain't telling you again."

Kerry folded up her napkin. "Wonder what that's all about?"

"Shut the fuck up, you asshole," a voice yelled back. "I'm just checking for some boxes in the trash. Leave me the hell alone!"

They exchanged glances, then got up and headed for the door together, almost bumping as they went through the opening. "Let's find out," Dar said, as they crossed the hall and emerged on the loading dock to find one of the building maintenance men facing off against a scruffy, bearded man in a wheelchair.

The maintenance man turned. "Scuse me. Let me go call the cops for this jerk." He pushed past them and went into the small facilities office just off the dock.

That left Dar and Kerry regarding the man in the chair who stared back at them and scowled.

"What the fuck are you looking at?" he said. "Get your asses back to the beauty parlor fore I kick them."

Dar put her hands on her hips.

"I've got a bad feeling about this," Kerry said. "And it was such a nice day, too."

"You hear me?" the man shouted. "Get outta here!"

"Hey!" Dar responded after the echo faded. "Shut up." She dropped her hands and walked over to him. "Shut up, before I knock that chair over and you with it."

Kerry blinked a little in shock. Dar wasn't usually that blunt with people she didn't really know, and was sympathetic to the disabled as far as she'd ever seen.

"What?" The man stared at her, apparently as shocked as Kerry was.

"You heard me." Dar stopped within reach. "Who the fuck do you think you are making trouble for those guys? They're just working stiffs. They don't need you pulling crap out of the dumpster and making a mess for them. Take off."

He backed himself off from her. "You serious?" he asked. "I'm just looking for some fucking boxes, bitch. I'm homeless."

"And?" Dar blocked the way to the dumpster. "Try asking for them. People usually respond better to that."

"You ain't got no respect," he said. "Go to hell." He turned and started off, wheeling himself along with short, savage thrusts of his hands.

"Wow." Kerry came over and eyed her. "You were kind of tough on him."

"Being disabled, or being homeless for that matter, doesn't get you a free asshole pass," Dar said. "Besides, he'll just come back after we leave." Dar went over and inspected the dumpster, which, in fact, had plenty of flattened boxes in it. "I should have them come empty this."

Kerry bumped her shoulder against Dar's. "Chill, hon. They're just boxes."

"I know. I just don't like people being idiots for no reason." Dar turned as the maintenance man came back, with a second, much larger man. "Hey."

"Where'd he go?" The man asked. "I got the cops coming."

"Dar scared him off," Kerry said. "Who was that guy?"

"You scared him?" The bigger man said. "You should be careful, lady. That guy's a nutter," he said in an earnest tone. "Got him a gun, some kind of veteran or something. He rams cars and stuff in the lot, makes trouble around here, too, with the cafe and stuff."

"Yeah," the other maintenance man said. "You nice ladies should be careful. We don't want any trouble with this guy. Gonna have the cops go find him and chase him off. Don't worry about it."

"I'm not," Dar said, mildly. "I just don't like jerks." She put a hand on Kerry's shoulder. "C'mon. Let's go finish unpacking."

They walked inside and up the back staircase. "Let's ask Marcus about that guy," Kerry said. "Sounds like he's been around for a while."

"Mm."

"Remember we don't have a slew of security guards here, hon."

Dar eyed her. "You really think I ever depended on the security guards at ILS for anything?"

Kerry chuckled wryly. "I know, but we're not in a huge building surrounded by them anymore and I'd hate to see someone take a shot at you in the parking lot, you know?"

Dar considered that as they got to the top of the stairs. She took a breath, then visibly let it out. "Yeah, I get it," she said. "Sometimes I don't think before I talk."

"Especially when someone challenges you." Kerry tucked her hand inside Dar's elbow and bumped gently against her.

They walked along the upper hall and paused as Mark came out of his office. He had his nameplate in his hands and held it up, pointing a thumb at his own chest. "You're kidding right? Me, a director?"

"Expensive April Fool's joke." Dar smiled back at him. "Don't like the title? You can make up one if you want. You guys took a risk coming with us. I want to make it worth your while."

Mark grinned and gave his plaque a brief hug. "I never gave a shit about titles," he said. "But my family's gonna get a kick out of it. 'Specially my dad. He's said for years Barb wore the pants in the family cause I was just some grunt geek and she had the degree and fancy job title."

"Your dad's an ass," Dar responded. "You haven't been a grunt geek in a long, long time."

"No, I know," he said. "He's stuffed shirt that way. Banker."

"Enjoy it." Dar gave him a slap on the shoulder and she continued along the hall. Kerry gave Mark a wink before she followed. "Saw the DSL was in," Dar called back over her shoulder. "Let me know when you want to mount the WAPs."

"Speaking of grunt geeks," Kerry kidded her. "I think you secretly like power tools."

"Secretly?"

Kerry shook her head in mock despair as she parted from Dar and entered her own office. It smelled like new computer inside and she went to her desk, sidetracked when she spotted the wrapped items sitting on the surface. "Ah hah." She sat down and pulled them over, unwrapping the larger of the two and turning it around so she could see it.

For a moment, she studied it in silence, feeling a prickle of surprise, and a very slight shortness of breath. Just her new name over the logo, and the word owner, but seeing it there was almost a shock.

Almost.

She put it down on the smooth glass surface of her new desk, admiring the beautifully carved wooden letters.

A soft knock came at the door and she looked up to find one of the carpenters there. "Oh, hi."

He pointed at the other wrapped item. "Want me to put it on the wall for ya? Been doing that for the others."

"Sure." Kerry handed over the wall plaque. "Thanks."

"No problem." He retreated back into the antechamber, shutting the door as he worked on it.

She heard Mayte talking to him, but the words burred out as she returned her gaze to her desk plate, resting her chin on her fist and smiling.

"Like it?"

She looked up to find Dar in the doorway between their offices, leaning against the jamb. "Do you really have to ask? C'mon, Dar."

Dar strolled across the room. "You know one thing I don't like about these desks? I'm not sure I want to sit on them." She perched on the windowsill instead. "We should get them to make these sills a little wider, and put a cushion on them for when we visit each other."

"Anything you want, hon." Kerry turned in her chair. "I'll go buy a recliner for you if you want. Spend your whole day chilling out with that laptop next to me. I'd love it."

"So would I, but I'd probably spend most of my time messing with you instead of working. Or tweaking Gopher Dar."

Kerry chuckled gently, watching the sunlight outline Dar's tall form. "You need a haircut." She leaned back and parked her boots on the sill. "Though the shagginess is kinda sexy."

"There's a haircut place down the street next to that cafe. Maybe tomorrow I'll go," Dar said. "It's nice to have a lot of stuff around in walking distance." She got up off the sill. "Glad you like the paperweight. I'm going to go finish installing the mail server."

"Nerd."

Dar's eyes twinkled. "Takes one to know one." She gave Kerry's ankle a pat and sauntered back through the door into her own office.

Kerry's gizmo beeped and she looked down to see a text message waiting. She scrolled over and clicked on it. "Ah." She got up. "The replacement for the phone company. Let's go see what that's going to be like."

She took a moment to position her new desk plate on one end of her desk, making sure it was aligned with the edge of the glass surface. She backed up a step and regarded it with a happy grin and then went to the front door, opening it cautiously in case the carpenter was still working.

He was, but not on her plate. He was putting Mayte's plate up on the half wall that fronted her desk and he looked up as she entered. "You get these for everybody?"

Kerry paused. "Everyone will get a name plate, sure. But these are special since this is the startup group for the company, like a day one kind of thing."

The man nodded "Nice, he said. "What do you people do?"

Always a tough question. "Computer stuff." Kerry fell back on her usual description. "Programs and things like that."

He stood up and put his hammer into his work belt. "Yeah? You hiring? My kid loves computers, but he don't want to go work for no big company. He's a little different."

"Send him over," Kerry said. "We're hiring for a whole bunch of positions." She steadfastly refrained from asking him to quantify the difference, figuring if ILS could survive Scuzzy, there wasn't much she couldn't handle. "First floor, down the hall from the conference rooms, there's a recruiting group there with all the paperwork."

He smiled. "See if I can get him off his computer game to come down here." He sighed. "Kids." He eyed her. "Got any?"

"Dogs," Kerry responded. "Two of them. That's enough for me."

"Yeah, my wife says we shoulda stuck with cats." He dusted his hands off. "Thanks, ma'am, see you all later."

Kerry continued down the steps to the front door where two men were waiting, one in a polo shirt and cargo pants, the other in a suit. "Hello."

"Uh...Ms. Roberts?" the man in the suit asked. "I'm Juan Carlos Jimenez, and this is Alfredo Rojas. We're from Fortinet. You asked to see some information about an IP PBX?"

"Yep." Kerry barely remembered to answer to the name. "That's just what we need, and in the short term. Let's sit down in here, okay? I think we've got some coffee and drinks on the cart, too."

They followed her into the conference room, now tidied up and starting to resemble a business space. A projection system was piled against one wall waiting for installation, but a white board was already fastened to the opposite flat surface, and the small Rubbermaid cart did, in fact, have some coffee ready on it.

"Kerry?" Mayte poked her head in, eyes lit. "Oh, I am sorry. You have visitors," she said. "I had the cafe come in to do a service to see if you liked it, yes?" She pointed at the cart.

"Yes," Kerry said. "Looks great. C'mon in and sit in on this meeting, Mayte. I think I'll ask you to take charge of the phone system implementation."

Mayte gladly complied, closing the door and joining them at the table. She put her pad down and took a pen from her sleeve pocket, waiting for them to go on.

"Great," Juan Carlos said. "So let me make sure I got all the details in. This building, it's your only location?"

"For now." Kerry smiled.

He nodded. "Sure. You said maybe fifty people?"

"Yes. Right now we have about a half dozen. But we're hiring, and we'll eventually have around fifty people in this office."

Juan Carlos looked at his notepad. "So we figure a phone for every person, yeah? Plus ten public phones? You going to want them in the hall? What about in the conference space?"

"We should have some nice phones in here to make the teleconferences," Mayte said unexpectedly. "Many people will want to hear and speak clearly, and also, to put video."

Kerry could hardly manage to stifle a surprised grin. "Right," she said.

"Right," Juan Carlos agreed. "Now, you understand, this isn't an old style PBX, right? It's IP?"

The other man with him reached over and put his hand on Juan Carlos's wrist. "JC, don't embarrass us. These people know what IP is."

Kerry chuckled.

"Oh." Juan Carlos blinked. "Okay."

"You may not know who Dar Roberts is, but I do." Alfredo's eyes twinkled a little. "Though I don't think the industry's heard she's parted ways with ILS yet."

"They haven't," Kerry said. "Couple more weeks for that. We just hung up our own shingle, so to speak." She turned to Juan Carlos. "So, yes, we do understand this isn't a traditional PBX. What I really want to know is, how soon can you install it."

"Well, sure. So you want to place an order then?"

Kerry nodded. "We do."

"We have to do some paperwork." Juan Carlos seemed flustered. "We have to get the business side done, I mean, the contracts, and I guess they will want to do a profile, and get credit check done and all that. It could take a few weeks."

Kerry leaned her arms on the table. "If I pay cash up front, how much can I shorten that?"

Alfredo smiled. "Let me go make some phone calls. See what availability is," he said. "Can I assume you want whatever the top of the line is?"

"You can, but I don't need anything with mahogany inserts or gold trim. Put all the value in the hardware."

"JC, pack your stuff up. We don't need you." Alfredo patted his shoulder kindly. "Just go book the order. I'll take care of the delivery." He glanced up at Kerry. "You're going to need SIP circuits?"

"I have Metro E being dropped," Kerry said. "But if you can source yours, I'll take them. Coordinate with Mayte, she'll get you the node counts and she can sign off on the dial plan. Shouldn't be too hard with only fifty people."

"Shouldn't be."

"Got any cool new toys you want us to test out for you?"

Alfredo smiled. "Maybe."

"We're trying out these." Kerry pulled out her Handspring and showed it to him.

He took it and examined it.

"Could you make it so our phones at the desk go to these when we're not there?" Mayte asked. "And we would also like to find a way to take the faxes and put them in our emails. Can you do that?"

Alfredo nodded. Juan Carlos just sat there, his eyes going from one to the other. "Can I buy you all some cupcakes or something? Do an errand?" he finally asked with a slightly embarrassed laugh. "Hold the door? Maybe carry a box?"

"That's a good idea with the faxes," Kerry said. "Then we won't need analog lines."

"Okay we'll work up a deployment plan," Alfredo said. "I'll work with Mayte and we'll get it done." He handed the gizmo back to Kerry. "Any chance of getting to meet her?"

Kerry laughed. "Sure." She got up and went to the door, opening it and walking out into the front hall. She looked both ways, then spotted Dar on a ladder halfway down the long corridor. "Hey, hon?"

Dar's head turned. "Yes?"

"Come meet our VOIP providers. One of them's a fan of yours."

With a faintly exasperated snort Dar got down off the ladder and headed in her direction, seating a screwdriver into her tool belt as she walked.

Kerry watched her dust her hands off, and noted the contented expression on her face and understood this hands on work really was something she enjoyed and always had. When she thought of the times Dar seemed the happiest, it was when she was in the thick of things, cables wrapped around her neck, making things work.

Not when she was being an executive, having to deal with the politics of that. "C'mon, tiger." Kerry took her by the hand. "Want to see the specs for the new phones?"

"You bet," Dar said. "They got gig pass through? What class PoE?"

"Let's find out."

Chapter Twelve

DAR LOCKED THE door behind them as she zipped up her jacket, waiting for Kerry to move forward a little before she followed her down the path toward the parking area. "Good day," she said, as they walked between the thickly planted hedges. "Want to go swimming tonight?"

"Absolutely." Kerry shifted the strap on her briefcase. "They've got a slew of resumes for programmers they want you to look at tomorrow to make sure they're looking for the right people."

"Sure." Dar hit the door opener for the truck and opened the cab door, putting her own briefcase in and grabbing Kerry's to join it. "Who was the kid with the skateboard and the piercings I saw in the hall?"

"Ah. One of the construction guys sent his son over. I had Mark talk to him." Kerry settled herself, with a satisfied sigh. "He's a hacker."

"Really a hacker or a script kiddie?" Dar started the truck, glancing around her out of long habit. They were almost alone in the parking lot, the rest of the staff having gone about fifteen minutes prior.

"Really. Mark liked him," Kerry said. "Said he'd be good for security as long as you made sure he didn't turn the mainframe into a gaming server and put it out on the Internet. I think you should talk to him before we decide to take a chance."

"Takes one to know one, that what you were thinking?" Dar chuckled. She backed out and was about to pull out of the lot when something caught her peripheral vision. "Heh. There's our belligerent friend."

Kerry peered across the trunk and spotted the man in the wheelchair. "What's he doing?"

"Arguing with someone, again." Dar was about to pull out again when the argument suddenly escalated and the man the disabled man was arguing with grabbed him and pulled him out of the chair, dumping him on the ground and starting to kick him. "Whoa! Son of a bitch!"

Kerry released her seat belt at the same time she felt the truck shift into park. She had her door open a second after Dar dove out of hers, and she was on the ground and running only a step behind her.

"Hey!" Dar let out a bellow. "What the hell are you doing?"

The attacker paused and turned, visibly surprised to see two women charging at him. "Get the fuck out of here!" he yelled, taking a step away from the disabled man and bringing his fists up. "I'll kick your ass!"

"Not before I call the police you won't." Dar pulled up in front of him, both of her own hands balling into fists. Her knees bent a slight bit as her weight came over the balls of her feet. "Leave him the hell alone."

"Lady, this ain't none of your fucking business. So go back to your truck, and go the hell home," the man said. "Stay out of my face."

"Or?" Dar asked, after a brief pause. Her voice dropped and she tilted her head slightly to one side, watching him.

The man was caught flat-footed. "What?"

Kerry circled him and went to the disabled man's side. He was rolling over and trying to get to his chair, cursing under his breath. "Can I help you?"

He froze and looked up at her.

Dar edged to one side, drawing him away from Kerry. "You said, stay out of your face. I said, or, as in, or what? I enjoy pointing out to gutless jacktards their own lack of knowing what the hell they're saying."

"You calling me gutless? Bitch? I just got back from Afghanistan. You want to see guts? Let me cut you open so you can see yours." He pulled a knife from the small of his back.

"This is not Afghanistan." Dar held her ground, studying the angle of how she'd have to move if he did something stupid. "This is a public street, in the city of Miami, and you can't kick the shit out of people, or stab them, without getting your ass thrown in jail."

"He'll cut her," the disabled man said, suddenly. "He doesn't give a shit."

Kerry righted the wheelchair and swung it over. "She'll kick him in the head first. Can I help you get up?"

The man struggled upright and grabbed the edge of the chair. "Just hold it still, m'kay?"

Kerry did, moving around so she could keep Dar and the knife wielding man in sight. "Dar, I'm calling the cops," she said, in a loud tone. "I'm not putting up with this nonsense outside our office."

"Screw you all." The man with the knife glanced behind him, then he shoved the knife into hiding and took off, running down the street and disappearing around a sharp bend in the road.

Dar went over and helped Kerry hold the chair still, while the disabled man hauled himself up into it, showing significant strength in his upper body. "Thanks for fucking nothing," he told them. "Now I have to deal with that asshole calling me a pansy cause some girls came and helped me."

"He's the one who ran away," Dar said.

"You said you were calling the cops. Sure he ran. I would have, too, if I had legs anymore." The man adjusted himself. "Fucking cigar eaters. Don't need them patronizing my ass either."

"If you all weren't always fighting in the street they'd probably leave you alone," Dar said.

"Right." Kerry released the chair and stepped back. "But we really aren't going to put up with this outside our office, so the next time I will call the police."

"So keep your jackassery away from us," Dar added. "You and the rest of your buddies find someplace else to argue."

The disabled man looked from one to the other. "Who the fuck are you people? What the hell are you doing here?" he asked, rolling forward a foot or two.

Both women took a step back.

"My name is Kerry, and this is my partner, Dar." Kerry felt a sense of the ridiculous that almost made her lightheaded. "We own the company that rented that office building." She pointed at it. "That's what we're doing here."

"And we're not going to have our staff tripping over people fighting on the sidewalk," Dar said, glancing up as she caught sight of a patrol car slowly cruising toward them. "Better take off if you want to avoid the cops."

He stared at them for a minute more, then got his hands on the rails of his wheelchair and turned it around. "I need a drink anyway." He shoved himself away, shaking his head repeatedly until he disappeared into the distance.

Dar took a breath, then released it. "Let's go home and play with our new puppy," she said. "I've had about enough pointless idiocy for the day."

"You're such a crusader." Kerry felt the shaking in her knees relax as they walked back to the idling truck. "But you know, we really need to talk to Marcus tomorrow. Stuff like that's just not cool."

"Got that right."

The cop car cruised past, slowing to watch them get in the truck and close the doors before they sped up again and continued down the road, pausing at the corner, then turning right and heading the direction both the men had.

Dar regarded the disappearing taillights then turned and looked at Kerry. "Maybe we do need to think about having a few security guards around."

Kerry buckled her seat belt. "At least until your dad gets back in town."

"Mm."

THE WAS ENOUGH done, and enough installed by the following afternoon for Dar to settle in at her desk, her new laptop on one side, her desktop on the other, and an 11 x 18 size pad of graph paper in front of her ready for her to start considering structure for their two projects.

It felt exciting. She was relaxed and comfortable, glad to be in jeans and a sweatshirt with its sleeves pushed up above her elbows, looking forward to an afternoon of high level design.

They had extended offers to five people, the network was all patched and ready to go, the DSL link was active, the WAPs were installed and working, and she was starting to hear the faint rattle and buzz of activity echoing softly in the halls.

She had light coming in behind her, and she uncapped the dark blue pen and sat for a minute, hand holding up her head as she considered how she wanted to start building these new things.

On the shelf across the room, there was a new music player that Kerry had installed for her, with a little remote control she could use from her desk. It was playing some quiet new age music now and she felt her body moving gently to it as she started to sketch out her design.

Logic symbols and boxes, shapes and arrows in a mental shorthand that truly only meant something to her, as she put down how this system should talk to that system, at what level, with what language. It wasn't something she'd learned in school, rather, it was something she'd invented to be able to put down on paper her own way of getting things done.

Part diagram, part logic flow, part high level structure. It felt impossibly good to be sitting here in the quiet, with no screaming people or ringing telephones to interrupt her concentration.

Nice.

She started with Gerry's project, boxing in the services he commanded and scribbling in their names, along with the systems each used to collect their data in a veritable cornucopia of neatly formed shapes. Then she paused and regarded them before she put a bigger box in the top center, labeling it with neat, precise capital letters.

Then she drew lines between the services and their programs and the box, turning her head a little sideways to write in the data stream types and languages the systems would be speaking.

Another box went below that, and then she spent five minutes or so writing in the intent of the system, along with lines that ended in circles, with names applied to all of them.

Then she sat back and studied it.

Wasn't really that difficult a design. She drew in a makers box on the bottom and added the name of the system, her name, and systems architect after it, a smile appearing on her face as she filled in a few more details, glad she hadn't lost her touch during the years she's spent running things.

You could. She'd seen designers become project managers and lose the ability to go back to initiate things. But she'd done enough development and stuff on the side that she thought it wouldn't take all that long for her to get that edge back.

Kerry came in, sipping from a bottle of ice tea. "Whatcha doing, hon?"

"Making Gerry's plan," Dar replied. "C'mere and I'll show ya."

Needing no prompting, Kerry came over and perched on the windowsill. "You're writing it out longhand?"

"Sure," Dar said. "Despite what Visio would have you believe, it's actually easier to do this from scratch with a pen and a pad. So look."

"I'm looking."

"Six services. Each of them uses different databases. SQL, MySQL, Oracle, DB2, Sybase, and Informix."

Kerry regarded the pad. "Are you actually telling me that they couldn't decide on using the same database, any of them?" she asked in patent disbelief. "No way."

"Yes way," Dar said. "So, having them all talk to each other is pointless. We'd spend our entire time writing interfaces that stopped working as soon as they patched or upgraded."

Kerry studied the paper. "So they all talk to the big box."

"Mm. So we use this." She pointed at the first square. "We use an enterprise service bus. It's a universal translator. Takes input from all those systems, and rewrites it into a common structure."

"Hm. I remember learning about them in school. We didn't have one at ILS though," Kerry said. "I remember seeing a test system at the college that let them bring in data from fake fast food joints."

"No we didn't," Dar said. "I wouldn't allow systems to be installed that weren't a common interface. We used Oracle across the company because I told everyone if they tried using anything else they were going to pay for the enterprise support group out of their salaries."

Kerry nodded. "I can picture that meeting," she said. "There's a point to standardization."

"There is. You reduce your support matrix if you limit the needed skill sets," Dar said, then paused. "Boy do I sound like a talking head or what?"

"I love your talking head. Feel free to try out your lectures on me anytime."

Dar smiled. "Uh huh. So then, we put in a data warehouse." She pointed to the second box. "The genius of this is that we strip the data of source, so it's pure data. Then we can run analytics on it, and I'll write a natural language report generator so they can just ask it questions and it will make the connections for them."

Kerry studied the page, then looked at her. "You can do that?"

"I can do that. Listen, I know you're more used to seeing me in an operations role, but I started as a programmer."

"No, I know you did." Kerry sat back. "I mean, I realized, just going day-to-day in the company, that there was an awful lot of stuff there that you personally created. I was just going wow in my head about the natural language thing. That's hard."

"It's hard," Dar agreed. "But I've been thinking about it for a while. We have to make it so that it's not so hard for them to interact with these systems, so they feel comfortable with it. Otherwise they'll just ignore it and go back to writing everything down on library cards."

Kerry drew in a breath, appreciating this newly revealed facet of

Dar. It was like getting to know her way back when, before she went on a personal track that would get her kudos and prestige. "That's totally cool," she said.

Dar grinned. "Glad you think so. I'm going to scan this in and put it in an official structure, then send it over for Gerry to run by his ops team. I don't expect they'll give me any grief over it."

Kerry leaned over and gave her a kiss on the cheek. "Awesome. So how long would it take a normal person to figure this out?"

Dar chuckled. "I've been doing this a while. Give me some credit for experience. Feels good to be doing it again. I missed being an architect. I figured that out after I did that new network." She leaned back in her chair. "That's why this whole new thing's been so much fun."

Ah. It was like music. "Totally glad to hear that, my love." Kerry grinned. "I knew you weren't happy there. You were in a box you didn't much like, but you weren't sure how to get out of. You couldn't have gone back there."

Dar nodded. "Right. Crazy making. Only thing that kept me from going nuts was you."

Kerry ruffled her hair and then kissed the top of her head. "Love you." She meandered around the desk and headed back for her own office, where she heard her gizmo ringing from where she'd left it. "Be back in a minute."

Dar watched her until she disappeared, then returned her attention to her pad, adding a few more details before she got up and went to the scanner on the wall shelf. She triggered the scan and went back to her desk, watching the paper appear on her monitor.

It had come together fast, but then, she'd been thinking about it since the meeting, putting together ideas in her head she wanted to try and use to give Gerry the best result.

Because she really wanted to do that. The contract would have been hard to sell for ILS. They'd have had to build in far too much overhead to cover the contract costs. Here, it was much simpler, and she could work on building a support team after they got to a certain point.

She filtered the drawing into her diagramming program, a custom written set of code that did block and character analysis and produced a digital version of the drawing she'd done, complete with the writing, converted into a font that was a reasonable facsimile of her handwriting because she'd coded it that way.

She cleaned it up and removed the grid lines, then opened up the newly started mail program and connected it to the equally newly christened mail server.

Very raw and very basic. It wasn't the pretty mail they'd used at ILS, but it encrypted the mail, and gave them email addresses in their new company domain. She looked up Gerry's email address in her phone, and then she attached the plan and rattled off a few lines of basic explanation.

Then she sat back and studied the mail, unable to suppress a smile as she clicked send and watched the server obediently move it along its way.

Mark stuck his head in. "Hey, boss. I got the website set up. Figured we'd just go with NetSol and let them deal with the hassle until we've got a datacenter to house production stuff in."

Dar nodded.

"So, it's just basics." Mark came over and pointed at the PC. "Dub dub dub RobertsAutomation.com. Go on and hit it."

Obediently, Dar typed in their domain name, pleased when it came back with relatively snappy response. "Ah." She regarded the screen that now showed a page in what was becoming their corporate colors, with the company logo on it and contact information. "Short and sweet."

"We need a web guy to do stuff with it," Mark said. "I just wanted to get the page up and secure the domain."

"We'll get that going." Dar studied the generic page. "Give it some personality."

"Yup," he agreed. "You want anything added to that page? I still got my notepad open."

Dar considered. It really was just a splash page, with a contact number she recognized as Kerry's. That would change once their phone system was in. The address of the building was there, and under the About Us page was a listing of the startup crew with their titles.

Mark grinned. "Had to. I wanted it to be out in the world so I can tell my relatives to hit the page if they didn't believe me."

Dar chuckled. "Looks good for now. Custom application and system design. I like it." She pushed the pad over to him "I just sent our first spec out to Gerry Easton. Let's see if they like it."

Mark sat down on the chair across from her desk and studied the pad. "You know what the coolest thing is?" he asked her. "Not getting two a.m. phone calls yet."

"We'll set up support groups for the service groups," Dar said. "With some crossover, maybe contract a few overseas groups for follow the sun."

"Yeah, but it's gonna be freak-out city if they have an issue and we've got to call up ILS and bitch them out for network problems." Mark's eyes twinkled. "At least, for now."

Dar's eyes also twinkled. "For now," she conceded. "Though, I really don't want to be ILS. I want us to stay a little small so we can react to what's going on. Look at all the businesses that tanked after 9/11 — couldn't change."

"I was thinking that myself before," he admitted. "How cool it was just to have a little crew here and everyone tight."

"Nice to just be sitting here working on this stuff." Dar smiled quietly. "Really nice to know my phone's not going to ring and have some board jerk on the other end chewing my ass." She drew the pad back and flipped the page over, considering the new clean space waiting for her imprint. "I was getting really tired of that."

"Bet you were." Mark got up. "Let me go get the backups going. We just got the library hooked up." He circled the chairs and ambled out. "Later."

"Later." Dar tapped her pen against her pad, settling down with her chin on her hand again as she pondered the teal squares.

Bridges's project would be different. She'd have to be very careful how she structured it, and there would be the issue of access. It would also require a natural language interface, but instead of the regulated structure of the databases, this would need to be able to handle the free form fire hose of data that was the Internet.

Slowly she sketched in several squares. Then she drew a mesh between them, but after a minute, she pulled off the page and crumpled it up. No, it couldn't be modular. "Has to scale," she muttered, drawing a bunch of circles, as she bounced in the chair a little, making it squeak.

Another crumple. The Internet was a distributed system. There was no central point, no one place it all went through.

Dar got up and went out to the antechamber, where Mayte was busy assembling a set of files behind her desk. "Hey, Mayte."

She looked up and smiled. "Did you need something?"

"Just going to get a drink." Dar rambled down the stairs, emerging on the bottom floor and ducking into the conference room where the drink cart was set up. She observed her choices, then selected a cup and got some coffee, adding a little cup of flavored creamer and stirring.

"Uh, hey."

Dar turned to find the kid with the skateboard she'd seen the previous day standing in the doorway. "Hey."

The kid looked half embarrassed, half annoyed. "I came here yesterday?"

"Right." Dar focused on him. "Your father's one of the carpenters. He sent you here to get a job."

The kid looked relieved. "Yeah, right. So I was here yesterday, and they told me I had to come back today and talk to somebody about working here."

Dar took a seat and waved him in. "I'm the somebody. C'mon in."

He eyed her dubiously, but entered the room and put his skateboard down, sitting down in a chair across from her. "So I talked to this guy yesterday."

Dar nodded. "Mark."

"Yeah. So he talked to be about some security stuff."

Dar studied him. "You want to do security stuff?"

He shook his head. "No, not really. It's all cool, the hacker stuff and all that, and I guess it would be okay to look around for that stuff happening, but it's kinda boring." He paused. "If I want to do that I can just sit on the Internet at home or at the library."

Dar counted herself highly entertained. "So what do you want to do?" she asked. The kid was about Kerry's height, with sandy blonde hair, hazel eyes, and a smattering of freckles across his nose. His body under its cotton t-shirt and jeans was gawky and angular. "Or, what do you like to do?"

He considered her for a long minute. "I like to make stuff."

"Hm." Dar tilted her head a little. "Stuff like what? Like programs?"

He shrugged.

"Got some code with you?"

He held up a thumb drive.

"C'mon." Dar got up and motioned him to follow her up the steps and back across the hall into her office. The antechamber was empty now, but she heard Mayte's voice coming from Maria's new office.

She circled her desk and held her hand out, taking the drive and inserting it into the USB port in her laptop.

"They won't run on that," the kid said.

"Don't want to run anything." Dar sat down and pulled up her editing system. "I want to see the code." She scanned the drive and selected a file, bringing it up in the editor and studying it.

The kid gave her a more interested look. "You program?"

Dar glanced up at him and nodded, then went back to the screen. She bumped the desk slightly with the chair, and her desktop screen came to life, but she ignored it while she concentrated on the text.

A soft chitter distracted her though, and she looked up to see Gopher Dar appear, doing a little dance across the screen. She chuckled softly and went back to the laptop.

"What's that?" The kid asked, after a minute of silence.

Dar looked up. "What's what?"

"That." He pointed at Gopher Dar. "Is it a game?"

Dar leaned away from the laptop screen. "That's a program. Doesn't really have a purpose. Just a recreational thing."

The kid got up and came over, peering at the screen. "Wow." He watched Gopher Dar sashay across the desktop, waggling a finger at the two of them while it rambled around in a circle.

Dar moved her desktop mouse and clicked on him, and he jumped, turning and scowling at her.

"That's some killer graphics." The kid moved his nose almost up to the screen. "Look at the fingers! No jags or pixilation at all."

"No, it's all mathematic. Vector based," Dar said. "Sees the screen as a grid, and interacts with everything it finds."

Gopher Dar sat down and folded his arms over his chest, sticking his tongue out at them. Dar captured his tongue with the mouse and he grabbed at the pointer with both hands.

"Holy shit." The kid almost crawled on top of the desk. "So this isn't a game or anything?"

"No." Dar regarded the little beast. "Just entertainment."

"You could make a rad game with that," the kid said. "Is it a wrapper? Could it work with like, a swordsman or something?"

"Probably. I'm not sure why I picked a gopher. Just because it was goofy looking probably."

The kid slowly turned his head to stare at her. "That's your stuff?"

"Yeah."

"No way."

Dar leaned back. "No way what?" she asked. "No way I wrote that because I'm female, or too old, or...?"

The kid blushed. "Sorry, didn't mean to dis you." He sat back in his seat. "That's the kind of stuff I like to do. Making characters and games and stuff. I've got this idea." His voice grew animated. "It's this game console idea where the characters interact with you and you can make them do stuff."

"That what this is?" Dar pointed to the laptop. "I can see the decision tree metrics."

The kid grinned. "It's a simple version of it. The whole thing's too big, and I didn't want to drag my external hard drive with me here."

Dar turned and switched to her keyboard, calling up the program that was running in a background window. She typed out a dozen lines and cut and pasted a few places, then recompiled the program and restarted it.

Gopher Dar blinked out, then reappeared, this time with a sword in his paw and a Robin Hood outfit on. He looked around and waved the sword, chittering loudly at them from behind the glass.

"Sweet," the kid said. "Can you show me how to do that?"

"Depends." Dar rested her elbows on her desk and laced her fingers together. "That's decent code." She indicated the screen. "You want to develop it for us? Get paid to write on it?"

He stared at her for a silent moment. "For real?"

Dar nodded.

His reaction was unexpected. He sat back in his chair, looking stunned, an unfocused look to his eyes.

Dar waited.

"My dad thinks this is all kid stuff," he finally said. "He wanted me to get a job at a bank."

"What's your name?" she asked, quietly.

He made a face. "Don't laugh. It's Arthur."

"I never laugh at anyone's name, given that mine's Dar." Her eyes twinkled a little.

"That's not a girl's name."

Dar half shrugged. "Okay, Paladar Katherine."

"Really?"

"Really. So you want to come work for us, Arthur? I'll hire you as a programmer and that can be your first project. If you get it how you like it, I'll write some hardware code to make it run on a platform and maybe we can both make a few bucks." Dar folded her hands, watching his jaw drop a little. "Yes? No?"

He paused then he grinned like a Cheshire cat. "Fuck, yeah." Then he clapped his hand over his mouth. "Sorry."

Dar pulled the thumb drive out and stood up. "No problem. Let's go down to the HR office and get your paperwork done. Can you start on Monday?" She handed him the drive.

"Not tomorrow?"

"Sure, why not?" Dar waved him ahead of her. "Let's go surprise your dad."

KERRY AND MAYTE strolled along the street together, heading for the coffee shop. It was another bright and sunny day, and the sidewalks were full of people. "I think having them do the drink service is going to work out," Kerry said, as they neared the cafe.

"Yes. They are close to us and also, they agreed to charge us just for what was used," Mayte said. "So it is not just spending money and wasting things."

"And they have relatively healthy snacks," Kerry noted. "I like that idea better than a vending machine with chocolate bars in it."

Mayte looked confused. "You do not like chocolate now?"

Kerry chuckled. "You know I do. It gets delivered to my office on a regular basis. But if someone's missed lunch, I'd rather they have something that's actually nutritious instead of pure junk food."

"Not so much the chips and pretzels."

They entered the cafe, and Cheryl, the girl behind the bar, looked up and waved, already used to seeing them. "Hey, girls!"

"Hey." Kerry took over one of the stools and sat down. "Latte, for me."

Mayte perched on the seat next to her. "Some chai tea for me."

"No problem. Hey, Gary wanted to talk to you if you get a chance," Cheryl said. "And there's a guy, Robier? He carves really cool wooden business signs. Wanted to know if you wanted one for that big old barn over there."

Kerry's ears perked. "Handmade?"

"Sure."

"Absolutely." She handed over one of her brand new, just off the press business cards. "Tell him to give me a call."

Cheryl grinned. "You betcha." She tucked the card away. "Did you guys have a problem with that old scrounger yesterday? We heard something like that. He and some buddies of his were around here trying to get Gary to give them our day old bread."

"You mean the guy in the wheelchair?" Kerry asked.

Cheryl expertly frothed milk for Kerry's latte. "Yeah. I don't even know what his name is. But he's around here a lot, trying to snitch stuff. We've got to watch the condiment trays outside if he's around."

"He was looking into our garbage," Mayte said. "For some boxes."

Cheryl put down Kerry's coffee and started fixing Mayte's chai. "He gets stuff out of all the dumpsters around here. I used to feel bad for him, and for some of the other homeless guys, but if you don't give them what they want they get all asshole on you."

"That's pretty much what happened," Kerry said. "The maintenance men chased him off and he was rude and angry with them. Is he actually a veteran?"

Cheryl shrugged. "Gary thinks he is. I mean, it sucks a little that they went to war on our behalf and now they're living in the streets, you know?"

Kerry nodded soberly. "My father-in-law's retired Navy."

"Bet he doesn't live in the street." Cheryl eyed Kerry.

"No, he lives on a big yacht that his kid bought him," Kerry said, with a smile. "But he did live in the streets for a little while I think, when he got back from the Middle East, before he and Dar hooked back up."

"Dar's papa is a very nice man," Mayte said. "Not rude like those others were."

Cheryl nodded. "So anyway. This guy, Wheels, or whatever his name is, he got back about six months ago. There's a shelter thing nearby here, and they hang around that place."

"The building men told us he was dangerous." Mayte accepted her cup of chai and offered up several bills for it. "Is that true, do you think?"

Cheryl shrugged again. "People can be creepy. He stares at me sometimes. It makes me uncomfortable," she admitted. "I try to make sure someone's around when we close at night, to walk me to my car."

"I get that." Kerry sipped her latte. "They were outside when we left the other day and they started fighting. Normal people would have hit the gas and left, but of course we stopped and tried to help."

"Kerry!" Mayte sounded dismayed.

"Yes?" Kerry gave her a wry look.

"You should be careful."

She shrugged. "Anyway, I get that they can be rough. I told them I was going to call the cops if they messed around outside our building again. I hope they took me seriously."

"They call the cops on them all the time," Cheryl said. "Sometimes they chase them off, but they're kinda sympathetic to them, you know?"

Kerry did know. She could see the police officers feeling bad for the veterans. "If they start taking stuff, it's not about being sympathetic."

Just then, the kitchen door swung open and Gary, the owner of the cafe entered. He was a short stocky man with grizzled red hair and an explosion of freckles all over his head. "Hey!" He came over. "There ya are. I just got back from your place looking for you."

He leaned on the counter. "So you liked the setup, right?"

"We did," Kerry said.

"So when you get going there, can we talk about doing catering for you, for meetings?" Gary asked. "Like when you get clients in, that kinda thing. My cousin runs a shop down on South Beach and he does that for some of the biz down there. Better than bringing in pizza, yeah?"

Kerry considered that. "Okay, we can make a deal for that, and try it out. I like the drink service, and the tray your guys brought over today was perfect."

Gary beamed at her.

"Only thing is, we can't make it an exclusive because you don't have stuff like pizza and cheeseburgers," Kerry said. "So if we make it that you're our first call for catering, but you're okay if I bring stuff in from fast food joints sometimes, I'm okay with it."

Mayte looked a little confused, but she stayed quiet.

"Sure," Gary readily agreed. "Not sure why you'd want to bring in McDonald's, but heck no accounting for tastes."

"I know my audience," Kerry said, with a rueful smile. "In that case it's a deal." She held out a hand and he took it. "So now that's decided, can I get a large mocha to go please? And two of those chocolate chip muffins."

Kerry clasped her paper bag and her to go cup as she walked alongside Mayte back toward their office. "I really like this area."

"Me too. But there is no McDonald's," Mayte said.

"No, I know. But two things," Kerry said. "One, you never want to give any vendor an exclusive unless you have to. They stop wanting to compete if they know they don't need to."

Mayte nodded "I see."

"Two, sometimes you just need a cheeseburger. Even a vegetarian one," Kerry said. "Other cultures have their comfort foods. I guess yours might be black beans and rice, or yucca, right?"

"Si, yes. It is what we have many times, with limes, and also roast pork. Though not too much. It makes you very heavy."

"For those of us with a long line of American ancestors, it's pizza, cheeseburgers, BBQ ribs, or fried chicken. None of them are particularly healthy, but they sure taste good. "Or, for instance I make Dar grits all the time with her breakfast."

"Grits?"

"Yeah. Ground hominy. I'd never heard of it before I started living with Dar. Never even had it in a restaurant down here, but it's something she grew up with and loves. It's like a cereal," Kerry explained. "But you have it with biscuits and gravy, and maybe eggs for breakfast."

Mayte pondered that. "I cannot even think about what that might be like. Is it good?"

They entered the office building and climbed the steps, hearing voices on the second floor. "I've acquired a taste for them," Kerry said. "By themselves they're kinda tasteless, but if you put enough stuff on them they're pretty good."

"You must be talking about my favorite breakfast item," Dar said. She was standing on the second level with a gangly young man with a skateboard. "Meet Arthur. He's going to be doing some programming for us."

Arthur was carrying a folder along with his skateboard, and he shifted it to under his arm and extended a hand to both women. "Hi."

"Hi." Kerry returned the clasp. "So he's the first programmer? He gets to pick his space then. You done that yet, Dardar?"

"Nope. Just finished with HR," Dar said. "Want to do that? Mayte can you get desk stuff ordered for him, and a desktop and monitor? He'll run Linux."

"Sure," Kerry motioned him forward. "Let's get you a home away from home, Arthur."

Mayte scribbled a note and trotted off to her desk, and Kerry led their new acquisition off down the hallway toward the office space they'd laid out for the programmers. She remembered the conversation yesterday about the kid, and wondered about the change in his job assignment. "You do some programming now?"

"Yeah," he said. "Games and stuff. I showed some of that to that other lady, and she was okay with it."

Kerry chuckled. "If Dar was okay with your stuff, everyone else will be okay, too." She pushed the door open to the programmer's area and casually kicked a doorstop to hold it there, making mental note to ask her beloved partner what her thought processes had been on this one.

She wasn't nearly so hypocritical to wonder about the hiring choice. Dar made those by instinct, and she'd been a prime example of it.

"Yeah, she's got skills," Arthur said, looking around the room. "This is cool."

Dar had designed the space, having the best insight into the psychology of its inhabitants. The room was on the inside wall, overlooking the garden and each cube space had window real estate and walls high enough and enclosing enough to allow for a blocking out of the surroundings.

The desks were wide and had adjustable levels for monitors and keyboards, and there was task lighting built into the overheads to allow the overhead fluorescents to be turned off. There was enough space in each cube to permit a worktable, or a beanbag chair, or a small refrigerator, all of which Kerry explained to Arthur as they toured all the spaces.

"That's rad." Arthur became steadily more cheerful as they talked. "My brother does system design and his place is like a three-by-three desk and potted plant."

"No, we know from experience that you can't get creative work out of people if they're in a box they can't personalize," Kerry said. "We're going to be a small company. Everyone's going to be important."

They had stopped at the last cube in the corner where a little angle in the room had given this workspace an angularity the others didn't have. Arthur peered around it then he put his folder down on the desk and leaned his skateboard against the wall. "This is okay."

Kerry pulled out her gizmo and tapped out a message to Mayte, glancing at the cube number. "Sounds good."

"What's that?" Arthur eyed her phone. "That a Handspring?"

Kerry nodded. "We're testing them." She pocketed it. "Did HR tell you about the security check?"

"They said something about the government," he responded. "I didn't really get all that."

She perched on the edge of the desk. "Not a big deal. Everyone we hire gets a background check. We do work for the government, sometimes."

"Yeah?" He looked interested. "Cool. What do they look for? I got busted for tagging once."

Kerry smiled. "That'll probably pass. Just tell your family and friends if they get a call don't freak out," she said. "You might want to reread the page in there about confidentiality when you get home. Did Dar say when she wanted you to start?"

"Tomorrow," Arthur said. "I was doing some work with my dad, but I suck at it and he'll be glad if I stop. I power stapled him in the leg the other day."

Kerry laughed out loud. "Yeah, I really suck at what my dad did too," she said. "Then sure, we'll see you tomorrow. Give us a chance to get you some gear in here."

Arthur gave her thumbs up.

Kerry pulled one of her new cards out and handed it to him. "Give me a call if you have any questions."

He glanced at the card. "You and that other lady sisters?" he asked. "You don't look alike."

Kerry casually stuck her hands into her front jeans pockets. "We should probably get this out of the way now since you asked. No, Dar and I aren't sisters. We're domestic partners. We live together."

She paused and waited, watching his facial expression carefully.

He looked up after a second. "Oh, you mean you're gay?"

Kerry nodded. "Sometimes people find that uncomfortable."

"I don't care," he said. "Maybe I would if you were my girlfriend. You guys aren't all political about that? I don't like all that stuff."

"We try not to be political at all." Kerry smiled gently. "I had enough of politics growing up. My father was a senator. So if you're expecting rainbow flags and all that, probably not going to happen."

"Okay, that's cool," Arthur said. "The guys I game with would give me shit if I was a part of that, and I don't want to deal with it."

Really, refreshing honesty. "Then we're good," Kerry said. "We will have dogs here though. That okay by you?"

Arthur grinned wholeheartedly for the first time. "I like dogs. What kind?"

"Labrador Retrievers." Kerry motioned him ahead of her.

"Saw that other lady has fish. Can I bring in my iguana?"

"He live in a tank or on your shoulder?"

Chapter Thirteen

DAR SHUT HER systems down, leaning back as the silence took over the room, allowing her to enjoy the spears of golden sunset peeking through her window.

She heard Kerry in her office talking, and the soft, easy chuckle that drifted through the open door.

She was looking forward to going home, and having a light dinner with her, then spending a little time in the island gym together.

They were the last to leave, and that, too, felt a little funny since she was used to knowing that though they were gone, somewhere in the building there were night operators and off shift workers, keeping their eyes on things throughout the night.

Here, when they left, they locked the door, and that was it. Dar got up and slid her laptop into her backpack, zipping it up and slinging it over her shoulder as she heard Kerry finishing up her conversation. She turned off the little desk lamp and walked over to the interconnecting door, leaning on the sill.

Kerry grinned at her, and held up one finger.

Perfectly content to wait, Dar went over to the window and sat down on the wide sill with its fabric covered padding. She leaned against the window and watched the foot traffic outside, seeing some groups of young men and women strolling down the road heading for the waterside.

She halfway wished they had the boat docked. She felt like putting the bow to the wind and wanted the crisp breeze in her face. She wondered briefly if Kerry would be up for a night dive.

"Okay, so let's plan on that tomorrow," Kerry was saying. "I need to wrap this up. I've got an appointment I'm late for."

The appointment smiled, watching her reflection in the glass. She pulled out her Handspring and reviewed it, then accessed a little program she'd downloaded earlier that day. The hourglass spun for a while, then delivered her up the marine forecast. She had to regretfully forget her idea of a dive when she noted the ten-foot seas offshore.

Ah well. Maybe they'd end up swimming.

"Bye." Kerry finished her call and came over to the window, putting her knee on the padded bench and leaning against Dar's back. "Hey, love of my life."

"Hey." Dar turned around and circled Kerry's knee with one arm. "I was going to suggest going out for a float tonight, but the water's too choppy."

Kerry peered out the window, then at her. "And you know this how?"

Dar held up her device.

"Ah." Kerry smiled. "Want to stop by the sporting goods store to see what we're going to need for our trip instead? I know we could look it all up on the interwebs, but I'd like to see what it all looks like up close."

"Sure."

"Then let's go." Kerry leaned over and gave her a kiss on the lips. "That was our phone provider on the line. They'll have a shipment for us in by Friday. I'm letting Mayte run with it."

Dar returned the kiss, standing up and pulling Kerry upright with her. "I got a note from Gerry," she said when they parted a little. "I think his guys like the plan, but I need to go up there next week for a day and talk to them."

"Good. By then we should have a little gang of programmers for you to get to work with." Kerry kept herself pressed against Dar's body, content to absorb the warmth and affection soaking into her.

"Yup." Dar rocked them both back and forth a little. "This is so cool." She exhaled happily, then squeezed Kerry one more time before she released her and draped an arm over her shoulders as they headed for the door together.

This time there were no fights going on outside and they were able to get to Kerry's car and settle themselves without incident. Dar peered both directions, but the road was clear. No sign of anyone loitering, and she leaned back in satisfaction as Kerry got the car started and they pulled out of the lot.

They headed west, crossing through the city and out to the western suburbs, pulling off the highway into one of the big malls on the edge of the county. "We can grab dinner here too," Kerry said. "They've got a lot of restaurants and a Dave and Busters."

Dar snickered. "You just want to try and beat me at skee-ball again."

Kerry gave her a look, one blonde eyebrow arching up. "Try? I beat you like egg whites the last time, Dixiecup."

"I got you back at the basketball."

"And I had no handicap at that, huh?"

They parked and walked inside the mall, bypassing various stands and kiosks as they steered their steps into the big Bass Pro Shop that took up a large percentage of one side of the complex.

"Oh wow." Kerry paused, as they studied the inside of the store. "There's a lot of stuff here."

Dar's eyes were already twinkling. "This is going to be an expensive trip." She eyed the boating section. "You think we should actually put together a real hurricane kit?"

"You're not looking at that bucket of MREs are you?"

KERRY REVIEWED THE notes on her desk with a sense of bemusement. She selected one and dialed the contact number, pausing to wait for it to connect. "Hello, I'm looking for John Chavez." She paused and considered a brief second. "I'm returning his call. From Roberts Automation."

She listened to the hold music then detected the sound of a receiver being picked up in haste. "Hello?"

"Hello? Is this... Kerry, is that you?"

"Sure is," she said. "What can I do for you, John? I assume by your note you know I'm not with ILS anymore, so I'm not sure I—"

"No, no, I know. I know." He broke in hastily. "I guess word's getting out and I saw your new website. I wanted to call and see what you guys were up to."

"Well," Kerry said. "I guess we're up to opening up our own business. Dar and I just incorporated two weeks ago or so. Got an office going and all that."

"Great."

"Great?"

"Great, as in can we meet? I'd like to talk about some projects."

Kerry pulled her phone away from her ear and stared at it, then returned it to the side of her head. "Okay, John, but you don't even know what we're doing so I'm not sure—"

"You're not going into the cleaning business are you?"

"No," Kerry said. "It's technology, naturally, but—"

"Great," Chavez broke in again. "That's what I figured. We've got a bunch of projects, blue sky stuff. I'd love to have you look at them and let me know if we can contract you guys." He paused. "I wanted to make sure I get on the list first."

Kerry blinked. She opened her mouth, then closed it. Then she shook her head a little. "Sure, John, I'd love to talk to you. Want us to come down there or you want to visit our new offices? They're in the Grove." She checked her watch. "What day's good for you?"

"You free today?" he asked. "I'll bring lunch in."

"How's two p.m. for you? I can't do lunch, Dar's already picking mine up."

"You got it! Me and Manuel will be there at two. Looking forward to it. Later!"

Kerry released the line and studied her phone with a quizzical expression. Then she turned over that note and picked up the next one. "Cherise Montez. *All Dade Paper*." She tapped the note against her chin. "That's another one I had in my contact list." She dialed the number. "Hello, I'm looking for—oh, hi Cherise. Yes, it's Kerry. I got your note and I—" She listened and hurriedly called up her calendar. "Well, sure I can do Monday. What's this ab—ah, yeah, I guess it's going around." She listened again. "*Infoworld* email alert. I see."

"Anyway, glad I got in touch with you, Kerry," Cherise said, echoing slightly through the phone. "My senior management called me the minute they saw that, and wanted me to just sit down and talk with you about some things."

"Sure. Looking forward to it," Kerry said. "See you on Monday."

She disconnected the line, then looked up as she heard a sound and found Dar's lanky frame in her doorway. "Honey, I think word's gotten out about our leaving."

Dar came over and put a piece of paper down on the desk. "It has. Glad that website had your phone number on it and not mine."

Kerry picked up the paper and examined it. "Oh, that email alert. Cherise, from *All Dade Paper* just called me." She read through the article. "It's pretty noncommittal on why we left," she said, noting the almost complete lack of details, but the addition of a link to their new web site.

"Hamilton keeps his word," Dar said. "And so will we."

"Wonder how long it will take for the *Herald* to call us." Kerry put the paper down. "We said we wouldn't go after their customers, Dar, but what are we supposed to do when their customers come after us?"

Dar waggled her eyebrows. "I'm sure they're not going to ask us for the same things they asked ILS for. Maybe we'll catch those little projects that ILS wouldn't even quote."

"Uh huh. Kind of how that whole thing with Gerry and the president worked out," Kerry said. "I don't want us to have to worry about delivering all this stuff when we're just only barely open."

Dar ruffled her hair. "Then we say no. Not even ILS bid on everything, remember?"

That was true. Kerry had even made that decision a time or two when the numbers hadn't made sense, or when the requirements were very specialized and they would require incurring unreasonable startup costs for it.

"Okay, well let's see what all this chatter gets us," Kerry finally said. "Who knows? Might turn out to be nothing." She picked up the next note, and examined it. "City of Miami. Do we want to talk to them?"

Dar evaded the question and meandered off. "I'm going to go program something."

"Chicken."

"Speaking of, come get your lunch." Dar winked at her, as she disappeared.

Kerry put the note down and selected a different one, putting it next to her phone before she got up to go retrieve her share of what smelled like chicken curry. Dar had discovered a tiny Thai place down the road, and if the scent was any indication, it was a winner.

She didn't resent Dar for assuming she'd handle the calls. They'd agreed from the outset she'd be in charge of the customer contact side of the house, with the exception of those two little special deals with the government that were pointed directly at Dar.

Dar trusted her to keep them from getting into contracts that were outside the scope they'd defined for themselves, and to keep them going in the right direction where she herself might go off into unprofitable tangents just because a project interested her.

Kerry chuckled as she crossed the floor and ducked into the adjoining office.

Dar had put the bags and boxes on the small table across from her desk, and Kerry opened the containers and set out two plates to fill, since Dar had gotten tied up in a conversation with the maintenance chief. She sorted out the brown rice and the fragrant red curry, and brought one of the plates over to the desk with a tall cup of Thai coffee.

"Thanks, gorgeous." Dar came back in the office and went to her desk. "Lock company'll be here Monday to do the install. I got them to agree to let us put biometrics on the offices, but they need access to the outer hallways and the maintenance rooms."

"We can do scan cards," Kerry said. "But we should put cameras in." She took her own plate and perched on the window ledge with it. "Especially if we're going to have to pass the government's security standards."

Dar nodded, her mouth full of chicken and rice.

"You want to try those eyeball scanners again?"

Dar shook her head.

"Palm locks, then?"

Dar shrugged and swallowed. "Better than thumb prints. That never did work for me." She examined her thumb. "I think all that typing wore the ridges down."

Kerry got up and came over, putting her plate down and peering at the digit. Then she leaned over and kissed it. "If the darn thing can't read it, too bad."

Dar grinned in response. She reached up and chucked Kerry under the chin then she went back to her plate, while Kerry settled back on the window bench to chew in silence.

"Y'know," Dar said, after a little while. "Maybe we should have shared an office." She studied Kerry's relaxed form, legs extended on the bench, sun splashing across her chest. "We spend more time in each other's anyway."

Kerry tilted her head and smiled. "We're such kooks. What are we going to do for Valentine's Day, by the way? It's coming up."

Dar tilted her seat back and put her feet up on her desk. "Let me think about that," she said. "Is it my turn this year to come up with a surprise?"

"Yes."

A soft knock came at the door. "C'mon in." Dar remained where she was, waving a fork at Maria when she came inside. "Hey, Maria."

"Si, hello," Maria said, bringing over a set of folders. "There are many things to take care of, but before this all gets in the box I would like to ask a favor."

"Sure," Dar said. "Whatever you want, yes."

"Dar."

Kerry chuckled. "My god you're in a good mood," she told Dar.

"I am," Dar said. "Seriously, Maria, what do you think you could ask me for that I wouldn't say yes to? You want to paint that office black or something?"

"Tcha." Maria clucked her tongue. "No it is this, my neighbor has a young daughter, and she is looking for a first job. Could she work with us to make things in order?"

"Sure," Dar said. "The last person you recommended was Mayte. You're batting a thousand." She chewed a mouthful of curry chicken and rice and swallowed. "Bring her in."

Maria smiled at her. "Thank you, Dar. This girl, she is very nice, but also, very shy. It would be good for her to work with some nice people." She put the folders down and then trotted out, closing the door behind her as she started to talk to Mayte in Spanish.

Kerry let her plate rest against her knee for a moment, as she glanced outside. "Ah."

"What?"

"Our friend is back." Kerry watched the man in the wheelchair come along the road, glancing either way before he turned in and started to make his way through the parking lot.

"Yeah?" Dar's voice was suddenly much closer, and then she was leaning over Kerry to look out the window. "Yep, there he is all right. Not with anyone this time." She watched him move between the cars and end up popping up onto the sidewalk, pausing before he started along the edge of the building. "Heading for the dumpster I guess."

"Do we really have such interesting garbage?" Kerry asked. "Hey, we just had those big servers come in. Can we give him those boxes?"

"Mm."

"I mean, it's not like we get those kind of things all the time, and they're pretty solid," Kerry said. "If he could use it, why not?"

Dar scratched her nose. "Yeah, I guess. Seems weird though. Wouldn't it make more sense if we're going to give him anything, that we find out if there's something more permanent than a cardboard box we could do?"

Kerry turned her head to regard her in some bemusement. "You want to help him?"

Dar shrugged a little. "Not really," she answered honestly. "I just think I'd feel like a jackass just saying 'hey buddy, you want a box?'"

Kerry scooped up the last of her chicken and chewed it in thoughtful silence for a minute. "Yeah maybe you have a point there. I think I just feel bad, mostly because I know your father."

Dar leaned on her knee, bumping against Kerry's shoulder lightly. "I feel bad about feeling bad about that. Because the guy was a jackass."

Kerry wound her arm around Dar's thigh and squeezed it. "Our consciences can be a bitch sometimes."

"Sometimes," Dar agreed, pushing off the sill and stepping back. "Anyway, I guess it's okay to get him those crates, but we should put them in there when he's not around, and let him think he's snitching them from us."

She went back over and dropped into her chair, pulling her laptop over and getting it arranged on her knees as she tilted back and put her feet back on the desktop.

Kerry got up and put her plate in the garbage, adding Dar's to it before she gave her a kiss on the top of her head and headed out the other door.

The outer office was empty, and she crossed through it and walked along the hallway around to the back and down the back stairs. She crossed the hall and went out the back door, pausing to look around from the top step of the loading dock.

The area was empty, the dumpsters undisturbed. She waited a moment, then walked down the concrete steps and circled the big green disposals, seeing nothing but fallen leaves around them, the token South Florida acknowledgment of winter.

She walked along the edge of the service area, and looked down the long path between the back section and the front sidewalk, each side bounded with Chinese cherry hedges that were thick, and almost head high on her.

On one side, the hedges went flat to the building edge. On the other, they were a barrier to a slim open space between the property the building sat on and a wall to the next structure.

Kerry cocked her head to one side, and listened, then she slowly strolled along the path, glad for the warmth of the sunlight drenching her as she walked.

It was quiet. She saw butterflies hovering over the hedge tops. In the trees that overlooked the wall of the next yard she heard birds singing.

Midway down the path she paused, and regarded the hedge on the wall side. It had thick leaves, but she saw several broken branches, and there seemed to be a not quite natural gap in the otherwise lush foliage.

She strolled on, kicking the few loose leaves from the path with her boots, until she got to the front of the building and came around again to the entrance. Here she paused, and regarded the little front porch, overhung with iron lattice that held baskets of sturdy winter flowers.

"Interesting," she commented to the empty space. Then she went in the front door and paused, surprising Mayte and a slim, red haired woman who was behind the reception desk. "Ah, hi there."

"Kerry, hello." Mayte turned. "This is Angelina, who has come today to start with the reception area. She is from the staffing group."

"Hi there, Angelina." Kerry extended a hand.

"It's good to meet you," Angelina said courteously. "You're the owner, right?"

"One of them, yes," Kerry said. "Welcome to the gang. I think by Monday you'll actually have a phone to answer."

Angelina smiled, showing cute dimples. "They said you were just starting. They weren't kidding I guess. I just came in to fill out my paperwork today, they said I could start Monday."

"Great." Kerry waved, and moved past, trotting up the steps to her office.

She found Dar talking to a tall, tattooed man with a ponytail, dressed in jeans and a leather shirt, and she made bets with herself regarding his reason for being there. "Hey."

"Hey," Dar said. "This is John Robier. He makes custom signs." She paused. "He's looking for you."

Kerry held out a hand. "Yes, the folks at the cafe down the road told me about you." She regretfully lost her bet, and studied the man, who had a rugged, powerful looking face with a beard and mustache in a mix of gray and brown.

He nodded. "Said you wanted a sign?"

"We need a sign," Dar acknowledged.

He put a much thumbed through portfolio down on Dar's desk and opened it. "This is the stuff I do. See if you like it."

Dar went around the back of the desk and settled into her chair, pulling over the portfolio as Kerry came around to join her. There were pictures in the notebook of signs of varying vintage and size. "I like that one." Dar pointed at a shot of a relatively square one, with the background carved back and stained and the letters prominent, almost three dimensional. "Can you do a logo like this?" She indicated desk plate.

He picked it up and examined it. "Sure. How big you want it?"

"Good question." Dar got up "Let's go look at the front door, and you tell us what size it should be."

The carver gave her a quick, appreciative look. "That's different." He followed her out the door and Kerry followed him. "Usually customers want me to shut up and carve."

"If we wanted that we'd just mail order it from *Signs R Us*," Kerry said.

They walked outside and down the sidewalk a little, then turned and regarded the front of the building.

"Could put it above the door," Kerry said.

"Mm." Dar folded her arms.

"I think it would look better on the second level there, like a four-by-three, or a five-by-three feet," Robier suggested. "See it better from the road." He looked at her. "You're the only tenant, right?"

"Right." Dar closed her eyes and pictured that in her head. "Over the door it would be too narrow. And by the side there, the iron lattice would block it."

Robier nodded.

"I like the idea of it up on the second floor, Dar. That's right under our window," Kerry said.

"Okay, we like it." Dar turned to him. "Make it as big as you think would look good."

"I need the logo," he said. "And I'll get working on it."

They turned as they heard footsteps, and Kerry recognized her afternoon meeting. "Hey, John, hey Manuel." She extended a hand. "See? We're so new we're still arranging for our company sign."

"Great! We're the first ones then." John smiled at her. "Hi there, Dar. How's it going?"

"Busier than I thought it would be," Dar said, with a wry look.

"Hope we can add to that." John didn't miss a beat. "Can we talk?"

Dar and Kerry exchanged glances. "Sure, c'mon in." Kerry escorted them past and into the office. "Conference room's first door on your left."

Dar waited for the door to close then she laughed and shook her head. "Okay, so you need a deposit from me?" She turned back to the carver.

"You didn't ask how much it is," Robier countered.

"When I have to file my first corporate financial results I might care," Dar said. "Right now I don't. I've never started up a company before, so I want things done right, and getting a local artist to do a sign seems right."

Robier studied her, then he smiled, his face shifting from wary and slightly skeptical, to warm and friendly in a heartbeat. "Seems like you're doing all right already." He jerked his head in the direction of the door. "Gary said you guys do high tech?"

"We do high tech," Dar said. "I know it's kind of a weird location to put high tech, but I spent the last fifteen years in an office on Brickell and I was over it."

He nodded. They walked over to the little patio in the front and sat down on the iron chairs. "I did high tech for a while after I got out of the service," he said. "Telecom install, you know?"

Dar chuckled. "Oh yes I know."

"Worked out of a central office near Doral. Just day after day of same old, same old, until Andrew hit. I think I worked two months straight, no time off, almost twenty hours a day."

"Sucks," Dar said. "You can only do so much of that."

"Right. I got to where I was having flashbacks. Felt like I was back in the service with all that stress. So I just stopped. Quit one day, and went to work on construction the next." He sniffed reflectively. "Got to learn how to use band saws, and something about the smell of sawdust got into me so I started carving."

Dar studied him for a long moment. "That's a good story."

He nodded again. "Could have ended up like some other people, sweeping the street or on meds, or gone crazy, but that was an anchor. Then when I got good at it, it became something a lot more, because then, you create things."

"Computer programming is like that," Dar said, briefly. "You start with nothing but an empty page and end up with something that does things." She leaned her elbows on her knees. "I wanted to get back to that, and that's what ended up with this." She indicated the building.

He regarded her. "You been in the military?"

Dar shook her head.

"Funny. You kinda have the look," he said. "No offense or anything intended."

Dar's lips twitched. "I grew up on a Navy base. My dad's retired Navy."

It seemed odd to be this forthcoming to a stranger, she suddenly realized. Odd, but not really wrong. There was something about him she instinctively liked, or at least, that's what she told herself.

Robier grinned. "Okay, that's probably it. My dad's retired Marines. Never lets me forget it, since I went Army." He cleared his throat. "One thing I learned doing my own thing, is how sweet it is to be your own boss."

Dar nodded emphatically. "That's what I've been learning the last couple weeks. I never really expected it to be as different as it is." She leaned back in the chair and hiked one boot up onto her opposite knee. "Been a revelation."

"Sure was," he said. "Well, I don't need no deposit. The materials hardly cost me anything, it's all in the work. So I'll go get started on it, and let you know when you can expect it." He stood up and waited for her to stand as well. "Good to have you in the neighborhood."

He held out his hand and Dar clasped it. "Glad your neighbors recommended you. Thanks."

He lifted his hand and waved, then made his way down the sidewalk, turning left at the end of the path and starting back down the road in the direction of the cafe.

Dar stuck her hands in her front pockets and watched him go, leaning back against the wrought iron and enjoying the afternoon breeze.

A soft knock on the glass nearby made her look up to find Kerry looking back at her from inside the conference room. She crooked a finger at her and smiled.

Dar pushed away from the lattice. "Getting fired was the best thing that ever happened to me." She opened the door, catching a hint of freshly baked chocolate chip cookies in the air.

KERRY FINISHED HER laps and stretched her arms out along the edge of the heated pool, glad to keep most of herself submerged and not exposed to the chilly air. "Damn that feels good."

"It does." Dar had just surfaced after doing a few underwater somersaults and turned over onto her back, stretching her body out with luxurious thoroughness. "Hey."

"Hey." Kerry extended her legs and crossed them, sinking down in the water and feeling the pull against her shoulders.

"What do you think about taking the boat up to Crandon Marina tomorrow for the party?" Dar asked. "We could take some people for a ride maybe."

"You know what I think?" Kerry asked. "I think you're really getting into driving that boat."

Dar grinned, taking up a position and stretching her own arms out along the coral stone verge. "Me wanting to take the boat out twice this week make you think that?"

"Mm." Kerry tilted her head and gave Dar a kiss on the shoulder. "Sure I'd love to take the boat, hon, long as we stay near the Intracoastal if things get rocky. I've had a chancy stomach with that thing since we got back from the islands."

"We can take Chino and Mocha," Dar said. "I bet they'd like to meet everyone."

"I bet everyone would like to meet them," Kerry countered. "We should have taken them to work today. You might not have lost that laptop case."

Dar chortled softly. "Little terror."

"I don't know how he got out of that laundry room," Kerry said, with a sigh. "And left the gate intact. That's what I don't get."

"Opposable paws," Dar said. "He opened the gate, then closed it behind him."

"Dar."

"Okay, Chino closed it."

"Dar!"

Dar lifted her hands up and put them down. "What do you want me to say? They have psychic powers?"

"Urgh." Kerry let her head rest against the stone. "Want to go down to the cabin after the party?" she asked, after a moment's quiet.

"Yes."

"Was that part of the plan, too?"

"Maybe. Depended on what you said to it." Dar eyed her. "We have to introduce Mocha to the cabin anyway. Don't we? There's not that much for him to chew down there I don't think."

Kerry smiled, her mind already moving ahead to waking up on Sunday to a run on the beach, maybe a ride on the bike. "I'm so up for that." She exhaled happily. "Before we get attacked by another dozen customers next week. Sheesh, Dar."

Dar chuckled. "That was pretty out of the box," she admitted. "I like the idea of some of those initiatives, though. Most of them are in our scope."

"Most of them are in ILS's scope too." Kerry grew serious. "Are we going to be in trouble with this? I know we didn't solicit them, but if someone looked at it from the outside, it looks pretty bad, doesn't it?"

Dar detached herself from the edge of the pool and started a slow backstroke across the surface. "No." She said as she crossed back over toward Kerry. "I really don't think so, Ker. It's not existing business, and they approached us. I'm not going to turn down legitimate work because they happened to get introduced to us at ILS."

"They could say we were stealing work from them," Kerry said, launching from the wall and swimming alongside her. "Should they have the right of first refusal?"

Dar stroked cleanly through the water, pondering the thought. Overhead, the stars were crisp and bright, the sky completely clear as it almost never was. "Should they? I don't know, Ker. Let me ask Richard on Monday. See what he thinks."

"Not that I mind getting business." Kerry turned over on to her back and blinked the warm water out of her eyes. "I just want us to be clean in this. I don't want a confrontation with them."

"Yeah, I get that. Problem is, we're in the same industry. They could make the case any work we do they had prior art on," Dar said. "So if that's going to be an issue, I'd rather put the work ahead of it and deal with the fallout."

Well, that was true. Kerry had to admit privately. After all Dar had really only worked for ILS, so by definition, anyone approaching her would have known her in that role, with the exception of the military contracts. Those she'd earned the hard way, very young, coming sideways into the industry.

But these guys? And the ones visiting her on Monday, and Tuesday, and then the City of Miami?

"Relax, Ker." Dar caught up to her, swimming with that sinuous grace Kerry always envied. She wrapped her arms around Kerry and kept flexing her legs, driving them both through the water. "Truth is, we brought a lot of value to them. People recognized that, and want to exploit it."

"Mm." Kerry let her legs drift down to the bottom now that they were in the shallow end. "I just think we should be careful. We want to be successful, but in a legitimate way." She poked Dar in the belly. "As much fun as it would be for us to toss them head over heels in the marketplace."

Dar grinned. "You know what their biggest problem is? It's not that we're competing with them." She rested her forearms on Kerry's shoulders. "Their biggest problem is the gap we left. How much of their current service offering was my intellectual property?"

Kerry studied her face. "What do you mean?" she said. "Your programs?"

Dar shook her head. "The way we did business. The way we structured accounts. The way a new service was laid out, how we sized things. That whole matrix."

Kerry blinked.

"That was all mine," Dar said, in a mild tone. "Not sure I ever mentioned that."

"Not sure I ever thought about where that came from," Kerry muttered, after a minute. "I mean, I knew the analytic schemas were yours, but..."

Dar smiled. "So. Like I said, let's see what Richard says. I think if it ever came down to going into court, if they lost business to us, they would have to admit why they were successful all those years."

"Ah." Kerry exhaled. "I see what you mean."

"But it might not come to that. They might compete and win. Some clients might not want to risk a startup. Lot of deeply conservative people in the client list."

And that, Kerry thought, was true to a point. "Maybe they'll go after all those really conservative ones that wouldn't have anything to do with them with you in charge. Use it as a selling point."

"Maybe they will." Dar suddenly grabbed her and lunged off to the side taking them both underwater. She pinched Kerry on the butt then let her go, whirling in mid water and kicking off in the other direction.

Kerry let out a squawk underwater and chased her. They splashed across the pool until they reached the other side, when Dar got her hands on the side of the pool and pressed herself up and out of the water just a whisker ahead of Kerry's grabbing fingers. "You punk!"

Dar chuckled, going over to the table they'd left their towels on and quickly wrapping herself in one of them, handing Kerry hers when she climbed out after her. "Here, polar bear."

Caught in the act of shivering, Kerry mock glared at her as she got the soft terrycloth around her. "No one in Michigan would even think about standing around at night in a wet bathing suit in winter."

"Frostbite," Dar remarked simply. "You have to put up with a lot in Florida, but this is one of the upsides. It's just a little chilly."

They strolled up from the pool area onto the path where they'd left their golf cart and got in. "Now if we were in Michigan, this would need to have heated seats." Kerry turned the cart and sped it along the cart path, winding around the side of the old Vanderberg Mansion and then along the beach front to where their condo was perched overlooking the sea.

As they pulled up to the outside gate, a chorus of barks and yaps marked their approach, and then the sound of the dog door bursting open and the patter of toenails was heard.

"Ah, the family is coming to greet us." Kerry tapped in the code to unlock the back gate and squeezed inside as Chino and Mocha reached them. "Hey, guys!"

"Yap!" Mocha's tiny nails scrabbled at her knee, and she picked him up and cradled him in her arms. "Enjoy this while you can, little guy. I won't be able to do this for long."

Mocha licked her chin with great enthusiasm, then nibbled on it.

Dar pulled the gate shut behind them. The lights were on in their little garden and the wall cut off the brisk breeze, making it more comfortable to walk. She smelled the scent of mesquite wood, and the little grilling area near the wall bore evidence of use. "Did you leave something on?"

"I did," Kerry said, giving Mocha a hug before putting him back down on the ground. "We have some fish fillets in those little packets and sweet potatoes and wax beans."

"Yum."

"And a bottle of white wine chilling. So let's go change and come enjoy it." Kerry herded the dogs up the steps and opened the door, following them inside.

DAR ADJUSTED THE throttles as she piloted the boat through the narrow entrance to Crandon Marina. It was busy, and she could already hear the sounds of the beach front across the road from the basin they were going to park in. "Did you get us a slip on the far eastern side, Ker?"

"Yep." Kerry was on the back deck of the boat, Mocha's little harness leash clamped firmly in one hand. The puppy was almost beside himself with excitement, standing up on his hind legs and staring out over the transom with wide amazed eyes. "On the pontoons there, to the right."

"Cool." Dar eased through the clustered vessels and headed for the spot indicated, which only had a few boats moored to it. It was the furthest from the marina, but easier to maneuver. "Glad we decided to map the place out. That would have been a long ass walk on the west side."

It would still be a walk, but there was a path Dar saw up through the trees that would lead them to the main road, where they could cross over and enter the beachfront park area the shindig was being held in.

Twenty-twenty hindsight would probably have indicated driving, but they'd decided to manage the hike as a trade off on taking the sea route out after the party was over.

Dar spotted the slip number Kerry had given her, and she put the engines into idle as the light current took them toward the pier. There were bumpers over the pontoons, and as they approached, a young man in light sweatpants and a short sleeved shirt trotted over and waited expectantly for them.

She skillfully played the throttles to counter the current, slowing their forward motion to almost nothing before nudging the bow into the slip as the dockside helper reached over and grabbed the forward tie line and got it around a well used cleat. "Thanks," she called out to the man, who waved, as he moved aft and took the other line Kerry was holding out to him.

She kept the boat against the dock until he tied them off, then cut the engines and secured them.

"Hold on there, you guys!" Kerry called out. "Just hang on!"

Dar moved quickly to the ladder and slid down it, in time to grab Chino's leash as the Labrador started to try and jump off the boat onto the dock. "Got her."

Kerry picked up Mocha and stepped onto the dock, waiting for Dar and Chino to do likewise. "Whew." She put the puppy down as Dar got Chino's leash straightened out. "Next time, let's think this through a little more."

"Live and learn," Dar said. "C'mon guys."

They walked down the floating dock and onto the path, then headed up through the trees toward the road. It was another pretty winter day, but the high seventies temperatures made their short sleeved shirts comfortable, and Kerry exhaled in contentment as they made their way through the trees. "What are these, Dar?"

"Sea grapes," Dar responded. "This entire area used to be full of those Australian pines, but Andrew cleared them off over in Boggs Park at the tip of the island and they replanted a lot of grapes and sawgrass in its place."

They emerged on the road and went to the nearest crossing, waiting for the traffic to clear before trotting across. On the other side was another path, and this one led east toward the ocean and the picnic area just beyond the first fringe of trees.

They had just barely entered the area when yells started going up. Dar looked ahead of them to find people running and waving. "Here we go."

Mocha stopped in the path and barked at the oncoming crowd. "Yap! Yap! Yap!"

"C'mon, little man." Kerry patted her leg. "Let's go meet people."

"Growf." Chino chimed in, her tail wagging gently back and forth, as the crowd swirled around them and they moved forward into it.

"GLAD YOU STOPPED by, Dar." Alastair was sitting on a piece of the seawall, dressed in khaki shorts and a golf shirt. "Nice shindig."

Dar was sitting next to him, with Chino curled in a ball at her feet, damp and exhausted. "It is nice," she said. "We should have done this more."

"Yes, we should have," Alastair agreed. "So how's it going?" He glanced sideways at her. "Hear you've got the new office space up and going."

She folded her bare arms over her chest, her skin absorbing the sunlight and drying the seawater from her bathing suit. "Full speed ahead," she said. "Aside from Gerry and the government, I've had some nibbles for some new projects from six or seven potential clients."

Alastair chuckled. "I figured you would after that piece ran. Board's a little uncomfortable with the idea that reporter put forward about innovation."

"There are plenty of innovative people left there, Alastair. I only took myself, my wife, and four people with me. And that's all. I gave my word on it."

He scratched his nose. "I think it's you they're uncomfortable about. As in, was that guy right, and were you the driver behind a percentage of the success we've had in the last decade?"

Dar rolled her eyes.

Mari approached them and took a seat next to Dar, giving her a pat on the leg. "Had a lot of people come up and tell me they were really glad you came," she said. "Not that it should be a surprise to you, or to Kerry."

They both looked over at a nearby cluster of picnic tables, where Kerry was surrounded by her former staffers, a smile on her face. She had a t-shirt on over her suit, and some board shorts on against the chill, and she was more than a little windblown.

"It's a nice party," Dar said. "I was just telling Alastair we should have done this more often."

She nodded. "Hard to get budget for it but you're probably right."

"How much could this cost, Mari?" Dar asked. "It's all burgers and dogs, and condiments from the local warehouse store. You don't rent the space, do you?"

"No, I know," she said. "You just get tired of fighting when you want to do employee recognition stuff. No offense, Alastair, but I kind of had it up to here listening to you all in budget meetings telling us we had to tighten up when we know the whole board had golf memberships and tickets to ball parks."

Alastair regarded her soberly. "Executive perks," he said. "But that comes with hiring executive talent."

Mari looked at him, then looked at Dar, then got up and walked off, shaking her head.

"Now what did I say?" He sighed. "Can't make anyone happy down here it seems."

"I think her point was, you never offered me any of the perks," Dar said, hiking a knee up and resting her elbow on it. "I was never one of the good old boys."

"You never wanted any of that," he said. "Don't tell me now you did."

"No, I didn't. But the discrimination was pretty evident. If you have a VP of HR, that matters to them, and Mari and I go back a ways.

Maybe she thinks one less golf membership should be translated to a couple more beach parties for the rank and file."

"You came from the rank and file," Alastair said

"And I would way rather have had beach parties. Maybe I should have initiated that," Dar said. "I realized lately that my support in the company always came from the ranks. Not you all."

"And that's why the board wants to make sure your replacement is one of them, not one of the gang," Alastair said. "Tried to talk them down off that ledge, but they weren't having any of it. So they're bringing in some guy who worked as CIO for one of our competitors for three or four years. I hear he's a hard ass."

"Brook Higgs?"

He nodded.

"Alastair, he's an idiot," she said, bluntly. "He got the job with those other guys because his daughter was screwing around with the CEO's son."

Alastair regarded her in surprise. "Didn't know you followed gossip, Dar."

"I don't. He told everyone in that think tank high level tech exec meeting last August," she said. "The one you made me go and speak at."

"He said that in a panel?"

"He said that at dinner, with eight of us at the table," Dar said. "Too much free booze in play. But he must have put in a decent team because they're not doing all that bad."

Alastair sighed. "Well, he starts in two weeks. The board likes him, he's on the membership committee of two of the big clubs in Houston. Think they're going to base him there, not here."

"Uh huh."

"He's got a hot young guy he's bringing in to take Kerry's place," Alastair went on, after a moment. "He'll be in Miami. No one's really looking forward to it. Except for me, since I told the board I'd hang around here until the new guys were in, and then I'm back to my ranch."

Dar exhaled. "Well, sorry about that." She looked over as the crowd around Kerry burst into laughter. "Uh oh. That's probably an embarrassing story about me getting told."

Two of the building security guards came over, waiting hesitantly until Dar noticed them and waved them forward. "Hello, Ms. Roberts," the taller of the two said. "We just wanted to come over and tell you how much we missed you."

Dar smiled at them. "Given that the best thing about me you could say is I know your names, why?"

"Because you know our names," the man said immediately. "Hardly anyone else does." He glanced at Alastair. "Excuse us, sir."

"No problem, people," Alastair said. "I never had any illusion as to who exactly ran the company up until last month. I'm glad Dar got the personal respect she did, and that so many of you spoke up about that to me. Loudly."

The two guards returned the smile. "Ms. Roberts, I know you said you can't take a lot people with you, but if you ever need security people at that new place of yours, please let us know," he said, firmly. "Because I'd leave ILS in a heartbeat."

"Me too," the woman with him agreed. "I still remember the night we had that guy in the lobby yelling at us in some language, and everyone we called just told us to call the police." She looked at Alastair. "Then Maria called you and you came down and took care of him and it turned out all he wanted was to get hold of his wife because his daughter was giving birth before her time."

Dar blinked. "That was a long time ago," she said.

The woman nodded. "It was my first week at work," she explained. "And I was so scared because he was so upset, but then people told me, no matter what the problem was, you would solve it."

"Poor guy," Dar said. "He had just moved here, he and his wife relocated from Europe. He had no idea what to do and neither did his wife." She glanced at Alastair. "I ended up driving them to Jackson and interpreting for them. No one in the emergency room spoke German."

"When was this?" Alastair asked.

"Ninety-five or ninety-six," Dar guessed. "I remember telling the desk not to tell anyone I'd done it."

The woman nodded. "That's right."

"Why?" Alastair asked, in a curious tone.

"Wasn't what you paid me for?" Dar felt more than a little embarrassed, and she was pretty sure she was blushing. "But anyway, you two, you're right. I can't ask you to come work for us. But if you happened to find yourselves unemployed, come see me. Can't guarantee there's a place, but we can always talk about it."

The man grinned. "Thank you," he said. "And thanks for coming over today. We all..." He looked vaguely behind him and gestured with one arm. "We wanted to get to say goodbye."

Unexpectedly, Dar felt a lump rise in her throat, and she paused a minute for it to ease. "Me too. Sorry it went down like that. Wasn't really fair to anyone."

"No, ma'am, it wasn't," he said. "But we're glad you're doing okay."

They waved, and turned to leave, scuffing through the sand heading back over to where an ever larger crowed was gathering around the picnic tables.

"Y'know, Dar? You're right. Wasn't really fair to anyone," Alastair said, after a long pause. "Wish I had a chance to go back and do it all over again."

Dar paused thoughtfully, then shook her head. "Water under the bridge." She stood up. "C'mon, let's go get some of those marshmallows and enjoy the party." She towed Alastair over to the crowd, with Chino trotting behind them. "Let's have fun."

OTHER MELISSA GOOD TITLES

Tropical Storm

From bestselling author Melissa Good comes a tale of heartache, longing, family strife, lust for love, and redemption. *Tropical Storm* took the lesbian reading world by storm when it was first written...now read this exciting revised "author's cut" edition.

Dar Roberts, corporate raider for a multi-national tech company is cold, practical, and merciless. She does her job with a razor-sharp accuracy. Friends are a luxury she cannot allow herself, and love is something she knows she'll never attain.

Kerry Stuart left Michigan for Florida in an attempt to get away from her domineering politician father and the constraints of the overly conservative life her family forced upon her. After college she worked her way into supervision at a small tech company, only to have it taken over by Dar Roberts' organization. Her association with Dar begins in disbelief, hatred, and disappointment, but when Dar unexpectedly hires Kerry as her work assistant, the dynamics of their relationship change. Over time, a bond begins to form.

But can Dar overcome years of habit and conditioning to open herself up to the uncertainty of love? And will Kerry escape from the clutches of her powerful father in order to live a better life?

ISBN 978-1-932300-60-4
eISBN 978-1-935053-75-0

Hurricane Watch

In this sequel to *Tropical Storm*, Dar and Kerry are back and making their relationship permanent. But an ambitious new colleague threatens to divide them—and out them. He wants Dar's head and her job, and he's willing to use Kerry to do it. Can their home life survive the office power play?

Dar and Kerry are redefining themselves and their priorities to build a life and a family together. But with the scheming colleagues and old flames trying to drive them apart and bring them down, the two women must overcome fear, prejudice, and their own pasts to protect the company and each other. Does their relationship have enough trust to survive the storm?

ISBN 978-1-935053-00
eISBN 978-1-935053-76-7

Eye of the Storm

Eye of the Storm picks up the story of Dar Roberts and Kerry Stuart a few months after *Hurricane Watch* ends. At first it looks like they are settling into their lives together but, as readers of this series have learned, life is never simple around Dar and Kerry. Surrounded by endless corporate intrigue, Dar experiences personal discoveries that force her to deal with issues that she had buried long ago and Kerry finally faces the consequences of her own actions. As always, they help each other through these personal challenges that, in the end, strengthen them as individuals and as a couple.

ISBN 978-1-932300-13-0
eISBN 978-1-935053-77-4

Red Sky At Morning

A connection others don't understand...
A love that won't be denied...
Danger they can sense but cannot see...

Dar Roberts was always ruthless and single-minded...until she met Kerry Stuart.

Kerry was oppressed by her family's wealth and politics. But Dar saved her from that.

Now new dangers confront them from all sides. While traveling to Chicago, Kerry's plane is struck by lightning. Dar, in New York for a stockholders' meeting, senses Kerry is in trouble. They simultaneously experience feelings that are new, sensations that both are reluctant to admit when they are finally back together. Back in Miami, a cover-up of the worst kind, problems with the military, and unexpected betrayals will cause more danger. Can Kerry help as Dar has to examine her life and loyalties and call into question all she's believed in since childhood? Will their relationship deepen through it all? Or will it be destroyed?

ISBN 978-1-932300-80-2
eISBN 978-1-935053-71-2

Thicker Than Water

This fifth entry in the continuing saga of Dar Roberts and Kerry Stuart starts off with Kerry involved in mentoring a church group of girls. Kerry is forced to acknowledge her own feelings toward and experiences with her parents as she and Dar assist a teenager from the group who gets jailed because her parents tossed her out onto the streets when they found out she is gay. While trying to help the teenagers adjust to real world situations, Kerry gets a call concerning her father's health. Kerry flies to her family's side as her father dies, putting the family in crisis. Caught up in an international problem, Dar abandons the issue to go to Michigan, determined to support Kerry in the face of grief and hatred. Dar and Kerry face down Kerry's extended family with a little help from their own, and return home, where they decide to leave work and the world behind for a while for some time to themselves.

ISBN 978-1-932300-24-6
eISBN 978-1-935053-72-9

Terrors of the High Seas

After the stress of a long Navy project and Kerry's father's death, Dar and Kerry decide to take their first long vacation together. A cruise in the eastern Caribbean is just the nice, peaceful time they need — until they get involved in a family feud, an old murder, and come face to face with pirates as their vacation turns into a race to find the key to a decades old puzzle.

ISBN 978-1-932300-45-1
eISBN 978-1-935053-73-6

Tropical Convergence

There's trouble on the horizon for ILS when a rival challenges them head on, and their best weapons, Dar and Kerry, are distracted by life instead of focusing on the business. Add to that an old flame, and an aggressive entrepreneur throwing down the gauntlet and Dar at least is ready to throw in the towel. Is Kerry ready to follow suit, or will she decide to step out from behind Dar's shadow and step up to the challenges they both face?

ISBN 978-1-935053-18-7
eISBN 978-1-935053-74-3

Stormy Waters

As Kerry begins work on the cruise ship project, Dar is attempting to produce a program to stop the hackers she has been chasing through cyberspace. When it appears that one of their cruise ship project rivals is behind the attempts to gain access to their system, things get more stressful than ever. Add in an unrelenting reporter who stalks them for her own agenda, an employee who is being paid to steal data for a competitor, and Army intelligence becoming involved and Dar and Kerry feel more off balance than ever. As the situation heats up, they consider again whether they want to stay with ILS or strike out on their own, but they know they must first finish the ship project.

ISBN 978-1-61929-082-2
eISBN 978-1-61929-083-9

Moving Target

Dar and Kerry both feel the cruise ship project seems off somehow, but they can't quite grasp what is wrong with the whole scenario. Things continue to go wrong and their competitors still look to be the culprits behind the problems. Then new information leads them to discover a plot that everyone finds difficult to believe. Out of her comfort zone yet again, Dar refuses to lose and launches a new plan that will be a win-win, only to find another major twist thrown in her path. With everyone believing Dar can somehow win the day, can Dar and Kerry pull off another miracle finish? Do they want to?

ISBN 978-1-61929-150-8
eISBN 978-1-61929-151-5

Storm Surge

It's fall. Dar and Kerry are traveling — Dar overseas to clinch a deal with their new ship owner partners in England, and Kerry on a reluctant visit home for her high school reunion. In the midst of corporate deals and personal conflict, their world goes unexpectedly out of control when an early morning spurt of unusual alarms turns out to be the beginning of a shocking nightmare neither expected. Can they win the race against time to save their company and themselves?

Book One: ISBN 978-1-935053-28-6
eISBN 978-1-61929-000-6

Book Two: ISBN 978-1-935053-39-2
eISBN 978-1-61929-000-6

Partners

After a massive volcanic eruption puts earth into nuclear winter, the planet is cloaked in clouds and no sun penetrates. Seas cover most of the land areas except high elevations which exist as islands where the remaining humans have learned to make do with much less. People survive on what they can take from the sea and with foodstuffs supplemented from an orbiting set of space stations.

Jess Drake is an agent for Interforce, a small and exclusive special forces organization that still possesses access to technology. Her job is to protect and serve the citizens of the American continent who are in conflict with those left on the European continent. The struggle for resources is brutal, and when a rogue agent nearly destroys everything, Interforce decides to trust no one. They send Jess a biologically-created agent who has been artificially devised and given knowledge using specialized brain programming techniques.

Instead of the mindless automaton one might expect, Biological Alternative NM-Dev-1 proves to be human and attractive. Against all odds, Jess and the new agent are swept into a relationship neither expected. Can they survive in these strange circumstances? And will they even be able to stay alive in this bleak new world?

Book One: ISBN 978-1-61929-118-8
eISBN 978-1-61929-119-5

Book Two: ISBN 978-1-61929-190-4
eISBN 978-1-61929-189-8

Other Yellow Rose books you may enjoy:

Struck! A Titanic Love Story
by Tonie Chacon

Their hearts were struck long before the ship hit the iceberg.

Megan Mahoney, the apprentice ticket agent who stumbles across an unused ticket and takes a leap of faith to create a chance for a new life and love in America.

Emily and Ethan Westbrooke, American shipping magnates, twins who were sent away from their home and family in order to hide the shame of their sexual desires.

Frances Cheswick, the spoiled darling of the Cheswick family. She's too young for love, but she knows what she wants. And, Frances always gets what she wants.

Alice Pearce, goddaughter to Frances's mother. Her ticket for a second-class berth makes her question her place in the family and in society at large, but what she finds there makes a permanent place in her heart.

It was the adventure of a lifetime on the maiden voyage of the luxurious *Titanic*. Their hearts, like the ship, were on a collision course with destiny.

ISBN 978-1-61929-226-0
eISBN 978-1-61929-225-3

199 Steps to Love
by Pauline George

At 61, Lucy finds herself divorced and decides to go on holiday to Whitby. There she meets the gallery owner, a woman named Jamie, who she is drawn to in ways she can't yet understand.

Jamie is also drawn to Lucy, despite the advice of her best friend against lusting after a straight woman.

But just as they come together, Lucy leaves without explanation, not only putting a physical distance between them, but an emotional one as well.

Can they overcome the distances and find each other? Or is it more than just the miles that's keeping them apart?

ISBN 978-1-61929-214-7
eISBN 978-1-61929-213-0

In the Midnight Hour
by Brenda Adcock

What happens when you wake up to find the woman of your dreams in your bed? All-night radio hostess Desdemona, Queen of the Night draws her listening audience with her sultry, seductive voice, the only thing of value she possesses. During the day she becomes an insecure, unattractive woman named Marsha Barrett, living in a world with too many mirrors. She is comfortable with her obscurity until she meets Colleen Walters, a tall, attractive woman hired to expand her listening audience by selling Desdemona to new markets. When she wakes up in bed with Colleen after a night at a club, Marsha is terrified. A woman like Colleen would never go to bed with a woman like Marsha. She might dream about such a thing, but in the harsh reality of daylight, it would never happen. Beauty is only drawn to beauty and Marsha refuses to believe beauty could ever be drawn to anyone who looks like her. Just as she begins to believe happiness may be possible, the past returns determined to destroy them.

ISBN 978-1-61929-188-1
eISBN 978-1-61929-187-4

It's Elementary, Too
by Jennifer Jackson

What happens when personal and spiritual confusion lead to intimacy apathy?

It's Elementary, Too, follows Jessica and Victoria through the emotional and psychological aftermath of a recent school shooting.

As an elementary school teacher, Jessica was held hostage, her life threatened, and she witnessed the assailant assassinated before her. Initially suffering from Post Traumatic Stress and survivor's guilt, her denial of emotional struggles eventually spawns even greater issues.

Victoria tries to maintain the act as stoic protector, but it weighs heavy on her emotional stability. After numerous rejections, she turns her back on teaching and her life in Austin and finds a separate path full of inviting promises.

Studies show most primary relationships falter after traumatic life events. This story examines the gradual emotional and intimacy decline and the possible resurrection of Jessica and Victoria's relationship. The ultimate question: is love really enough?

ISBN 978-1-61929-218-5
eISBN 978-1-61929-217-8

OTHER YELLOW ROSE PUBLICATIONS

Brenda Adcock	Soiled Dove	978-1-935053-35-4
Brenda Adcock	The Sea Hawk	978-1-935053-10-1
Brenda Adcock	The Other Mrs. Champion	978-1-935053-46-0
Brenda Adcock	Picking Up the Pieces	978-1-61929-120-1
Brenda Adcock	The Game of Denial	978-1-61929-130-0
Brenda Adcock	In the Midnight Hour	978-1-61929-188-1
Janet Albert	Twenty-four Days	978-1-935053-16-3
Janet Albert	A Table for Two	978-1-935053-27-9
Janet Albert	Casa Parisi	978-1-61929-015-0
Georgia Beers	Thy Neighbor's Wife	1-932300-15-5
Georgia Beers	Turning the Page	978-1-932300-71-0
Rrrose Carbinela	Romance:Mild to Wild	978-1-61929-200-0
Rrrose Carbinela	Time For Love	978-1-61929-216-9
Carrie Carr	Destiny's Bridge	1-932300-11-2
Carrie Carr	Faith's Crossing	1-932300-12-0
Carrie Carr	Hope's Path	1-932300-40-6
Carrie Carr	Love's Journey	978-1-932300-65-9
Carrie Carr	Strength of the Heart	978-1-932300-81-9
Carrie Carr	The Way Things Should Be	978-1-932300-39-0
Carrie Carr	To Hold Forever	978-1-932300-21-5
Carrie Carr	Trust Our Tomorrows	978-1-61929-011-2
Carrie Carr	Piperton	978-1-935053-20-0
Carrie Carr	Something to Be Thankful For	1-932300-04-X
Carrie Carr	Diving Into the Turn	978-1-932300-54-3
Carrie Carr	Heart's Resolve	978-1-61929-051-8
Carrie Carr	Beyond Always	978-1-61929-160-7
J M Carr	Hard Lessons	978-1-61929-162-1
Sharon G. Clark	A Majestic Affair	978-1-61929-178-2
Tonie Chacon	Struck! A Titanic Love Story	978-1-61929-226-0
Sky Croft	Amazonia	978-1-61929-066-2
Sky Croft	Amazonia: An Impossible Choice	978-1-61929-180-5
Sky Croft	Mountain Rescue: The Ascent	978-1-61929-098-3
Sky Croft	Mountain Rescue: On the Edge	978-1-61929-206-2
Cronin and Foster	Blue Collar Lesbian Erotica	978-1-935053-01-9
Cronin and Foster	Women in Uniform	978-1-935053-31-6
Pat Cronin	Souls' Rescue	978-1-935053-30-9
A. L. Duncan	The Gardener of Aria Manor	978-1-61929-158-4
A.L. Duncan	Secrets of Angels	978-1-61929-228-4
Verda Foster	The Gift	978-1-61929-029-7
Verda Foster	The Chosen	978-1-61929-027-3
Verda Foster	These Dreams	978-1-61929-025-9
Anna Furtado	The Heart's Desire	1-932300-32-5
Anna Furtado	The Heart's Strength	978-1-932300-93-2
Anna Furtado	The Heart's Longing	978-1-935053-26-2
Pauline George	Jess	978-1-61929-138-6
Pauline George	199 Steps To Love	978-1-61929-214-7

Melissa Good	Eye of the Storm	1-932300-13-9
Melissa Good	Hurricane Watch	978-1-935053-00-2
Melissa Good	Moving Target	978-1-61929-150-8
Melissa Good	Red Sky At Morning	978-1-932300-80-2
Melissa Good	Storm Surge: Book One	978-1-935053-28-6
Melissa Good	Storm Surge: Book Two	978-1-935053-39-2
Melissa Good	Stormy Waters	978-1-61929-082-2
Melissa Good	Thicker Than Water	1-932300-24-4
Melissa Good	Terrors of the High Seas	1-932300-45-7
Melissa Good	Tropical Storm	978-1-932300-60-4
Melissa Good	Tropical Convergence	978-1-935053-18-7
Melissa Good	Winds of Change Pt 1	978-1-61929-194-2
Regina A. Hanel	Love Another Day	978-1-935053-44-6
Regina A. Hanel	WhiteDragon	978-1-61929-142-3
Jeanine Hoffman	Lights & Sirens	978-1-61929-114-0
Jeanine Hoffman	Strength in Numbers	978-1-61929-108-9
Maya Indigal	Until Soon	978-1-932300-31-4
Jennifer Jackson	It's Elementary	978-1-61929-084-6
Jennifer Jackson	It's Elementary, Too	978-1-61929-218-5
K. E. Lane	And, Playing the Role of Herself	978-1-932300-72-7
Helen Macpherson	Love's Redemption	978-1-935053-04-0
Kate McLachlan	Christmas Crush	978-1-61929-195-9
J. Y Morgan	Learning To Trust	978-1-932300-59-8
J. Y. Morgan	Download	978-1-932300-88-8
A. K. Naten	Turning Tides	978-1-932300-47-5
Lynne Norris	One Promise	978-1-932300-92-5
Paula Offutt	Butch Girls Can Fix Anything	978-1-932300-74-1
Surtees and Dunne	True Colours	978-1-932300-52-9
Surtees and Dunne	Many Roads to Travel	978-1-932300-55-0
Vicki Stevenson	Family Affairs	978-1-932300-97-0
Vicki Stevenson	Family Values	978-1-932300-89-5
Vicki Stevenson	Family Ties	978-1-935053-03-3
Vicki Stevenson	Certain Personal Matters	978-1-935053-06-4
Vicki Stevenson	Callie's Dilemma	978-1-61929-003-7

Be sure to check out our other imprints,
Mystic Books, Quest Books, Silver Dragon Books,
Troubadour Books, Young Adult Books, and Blue Beacon Books.

About the author

Melissa Good is an IT professional and network engineer who works and lives in South Florida with a skillion lizards and Mocha the dog.

CPSIA information can be obtained
at www.ICGtesting.com
Printed in the USA
LVHW112026050919
629630LV00022B/103/P